QUEEN OF CHAOS

Fourth Element Book #3

KAT ROSS

D0964899

Queen of Chaos

First Edition

Copyright © 2016 Kat Ross

No part of this book may be reproduced in any form or by any electronic or
mechanical means, including information storage and retrieval systems, without
written permission from the author, except for the use of brief quotations in a
book review.

This story is a work of fiction. References to real people, events, establishments,
organizations, or locales are intended only to provide a sense of authenticity and
are used fictitiously. All other characters, and all incidents and dialogue are drawn
from the author's imagination and are not to be construed as real.

Cover design by Damonza

Map design by Robert Altbauer at fantasy-map.net

ISBN: 978-0-9972362-7-9

FOREWORD

Imagined worlds are intricate, alluring and often demanding places. The usual rules no longer apply. As readers, we are confronted with new geographies and new creatures, with magic systems that operate under their own set of rules. So if you need a quick refresher on people, places and things in the Fourth Element universe, I've included a glossary at the end of this book.

I also thought it made sense to tell you that *now*, because there's nothing more annoying than finding it *after* you finish and thinking, oh, that would have been nice to know when I was struggling to remember what a *satrap* is!

Anyway, thank you, dear reader. Without you, none of it would matter.

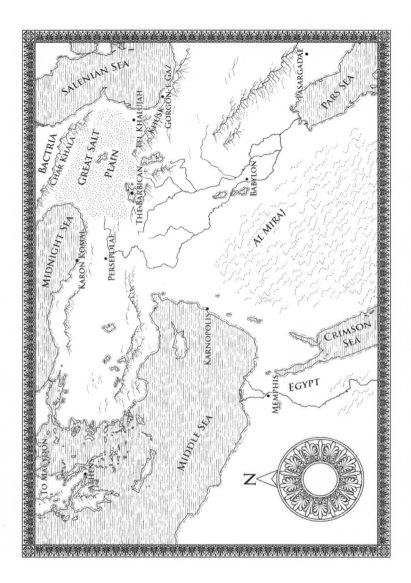

PART ONE

The wound is the place where the Light enters you.
—Jalaluddin Rumi, The Masnavi

❧ I ❧

TIJAH

She stretched out flat on her belly in a fold of earth, the late afternoon sun beating down on her bare neck. Goddess, she missed having long hair. Myrri used to braid it each night before bed. Her gentle smoothing and tugging always made Tijah sleepy.

The memory would have brought angry tears to her eyes if she had any left to shed. But after the things she'd seen, and the nights weeping silently so she wouldn't wake the children, Tijah's heart was cold and heavy as a stone.

Oh, sister. I'd give anything to have you at my side again.

Anything at all.

Myrri didn't answer, but that was because she'd never spoken a single word aloud in her life. Also because she was dead.

The silence managed to be more accusing than any imagined response. If Tijah had gone down into those tunnels with her, Myrri would still be alive. She could have saved her with the bond, the way Nazafareen had saved Darius. Or they could have died together, as they were always meant to. She'd never for a moment considered that she might be left behind. Alone and consumed with regret. It was the cruelest fate imaginable.

Tijah squinted through the waves of heat rising from the white, cracked earth. Beads of sweat carved a slow path down the side of her nose. She hadn't moved a muscle in an hour. Hardly so much as blinked. She was watching the village below for any signs of life. There were none.

It looked like the other villages they'd passed in the last four days crossing the Great Salt Plain—a dusty collection of mudbrick houses with rounded roofs and narrow slits for windows to keep out the desert heat. Except this one wasn't a charred slaughterhouse.

Why?

Tijah knew what the necromancers and their Druj did when they swept through a village. She had seen the aftermath a dozen times so far. The first one she'd known was coming because they could all smell it from leagues away. When little Abid saw what had been done to the sheep in their pens, he'd gotten sick to his stomach, vomiting right on Parvane's bare feet. At that point Tijah had ordered Achaemenes to take the five children and give the village a wide berth, cursing herself for not doing it earlier. She was the only one to enter. She'd hoped to find survivors.

Tijah heard the buzzing of flies in her dreams now, on those same nights when she woke with a scream trapped in her throat and the image of faceless men standing over her with knives. So many horrors, all congealing together. So many bad men in the world.

She'd made herself count the dead at each village. At first to honor them, to remember the lost. But that's how she came to suspect the Druj weren't killing them all. Oh, there was no lack of burned and tortured corpses. But Tijah could see it wasn't enough. That meant the necromancers were taking fresh slaves at each stop. Maybe the wights too.

Afterwards, when the culling was finished, they would put the place to the torch and carve up every last living creature that remained. From what she could tell, the Undead didn't eat the animals. They killed for the pleasure of it.

But either this particular village had been spared—highly unlikely—or overlooked. Well, it was a stroke of much-needed luck. They'd run out of food and water a day ago. Since the succession of ghost towns, Tijah's priorities had radically shifted. She no longer expected to buy horses or provisions. Her only goal at this point was keeping everyone alive.

She'd thought about turning back. Not herself, but Achaemenes and the kids. She should have tried harder, the moment they came to that first village.

"Do you care so little for them?" Tijah had demanded. "This plain is a battlefield. Not even that! A charnel house."

"We can handle a few Druj," Achaemenes replied.

"Can you?" She stared at him until he looked away. "Did you know the necromancers use fire? They're not stupid. They know how to deal with daēvas. And they're hard to kill, much harder than the Undead."

She could see from his face that in fact, he had not known about the fire. Very few did. Tijah only knew because she'd fought them once before, but the so-called Antimagi had not crossed the mountains in generations. Until now.

Still Achaemenes dug his heels in. "We're going to Gorgon-e Gaz," he said, iron in his voice. "And we're going to find our parents and let them out." He glanced at the children, sitting blank-eyed in the dirt, waiting to be told what to do. "They need to know who they are. They need to know they're not Druj. You've no idea of the things that have been done to them. The lies they've been told."

Tijah had nothing to say. If Myrri were here, she'd agree. So on they went.

And Tijah found herself warming to the stark, forbidding landscape. The perfect emptiness of it, the silence. She didn't think she could have stood being in a city, with its teeming multitudes and staring faces. That made her remember Karnopolis and what had happened there. But the Great Salt Plain had an austere beauty Myrri would have appreciated. Scorching during the day and cold at night, but oh, the stars! More than she had seen since leaving the golden, shifting dunes of Al Miraj all those years ago.

They had walked and walked, and seen many strange and wondrous things that eased the other horrors: spires of pure white crystals thrusting up from the earth like half-buried palaces, and rivers of salt driven by the wind to look like hair, and a dry lake pitted by some ancient hailstorm that turned out to a morass of sticky mud. They had almost gotten stuck in that one. After-wards, Tijah was careful to avoid anyplace that didn't have a thick crust of salt.

Most of the villages had an oasis nearby, so Tijah managed to refill their water skins until the last one, where she'd found corpses stuffed into the well. That was yesterday.

Now it was far too late to turn around. And Tijah wanted to go to Gorgon-e Gaz too. Needed to go. It was the only way she could think of to avenge Myrri's death and if it cost Tijah her own, she could accept that.

In fact, she was counting on it.

But the kids.... She still planned to leave them somewhere safe. Tel Khalujah, maybe. There were Water Dogs there and a high wall. Garrisons of soldiers.

So why haven't they been sent here? Why haven't you seen a single red or blue tunic among the dead?

Tijah shifted the tiniest bit to avoid a pebble digging into her right hip. This wasn't the first time that little voice had asked unanswerable questions. The people of the Dasht-e Kavir were helpless as goats staked out for a pack of hyenas, abandoned by both their old King and new. And if none of the eastern satrapies had sent aid either, when news had surely reached them of the massacres by now, that meant....

Tijah didn't want to think about what that meant.

She watched the village until the sun hovered just above the peaks of distant mountains. The one good thing about the Great Salt Plain was that no one could sneak up on you. It stretched flat and featureless in all directions, with nowhere for an army to hide itself. Wherever the Druj had gone, she felt reasonably certain it wasn't here. Besides the lack of bodies and flies and stench, the ground around the village wasn't churned up the way the others had been. The necromancers and their minions were foul, unearthly things, but they left hoof- and footprints just like men did.

Tijah crawled back to the clump of scraggly brown bushes where Achaemenes waited with the children. Like a crucible, the desert had both reduced and hardened him, boiling away any spare flesh along with the last shreds of innocence. His eyes were haunted, but then so were her own.

"Nothing moving down there," she said.

"Someone must have warned them," Achaemenes said, the kids clustered tight around him like ducklings. "They got lucky and ran."

"Probably. Or they're hunkered down. Hiding."

Tijah did not mention Ash Shiyda, the village she'd been called out to with the Water Dogs several years before. A merchant caravan had reported possible trouble in the area. When her company arrived, Ash Shiyda appeared to be deserted. In fact, the Druj had been waiting for them, holed up in the empty houses. That's when she'd killed her first revenant. She remembered the eyes like mirrors, the terrible wounds on its body, squirming with maggots. It held its longsword with cracked, raw hands. The weapon had been nearly as tall as she was. If Myrri hadn't distracted it while Tijah snuck around behind....

"Listen up." Tijah braced her hands on her hips and gave the kids a hard stare. "What do you know about the Undead? About Druj?"

They shuffled their feet. Pegah glanced at Achaemenes for his consent to answer and Tijah wanted to shake her until her perfect white teeth rattled.

"Come on," Achaemenes said, scrubbing a hand across his jaw. His beard was coming in and he had an unconscious habit of stroking the wispy hair when his authority was invoked. "Remember your lessons with the magus. Let's start with liches."

"Like shadows," Parvane said promptly. "If they touch you, you're dead." She poked Abid, who giggled, stuck his tongue out and pretended to sag to the ground.

"And how do you stop them?"

Most of the kids chimed in with the answer, all except Anu, who, when she wasn't bickering with the others, usually refused to speak at all. "With air!"

"What about wights?" Achaemenes asked.

"Cut their heads off!" Pegah said, eyes shining. She was only four years younger than Achaemenes and worshipped the ground he walked on.

"And revenants?" Tijah said.

"Undead soldiers, returned from the grave," Parvane chanted. Words she'd memorized by rote. "You have to behead those too. When they're born, they come out of the ground."

"Stinky old Druj!" Abid jeered, collapsing in laughter. It had been two days since he saw the eviscerated sheep in their pen, entrails draped across torn bodies, eyes staring glassily into the sun. Only two days. But with the resilience of children, he'd managed to erase the scene from his mind.

Ordinarily, Tijah would envy him for it. Sometimes she wished she had the same amnesia. But not today. Not when all their lives depended on staying alert and *afraid*.

"You think it's funny because you've never seen one," Tijah said quietly, but with a touch of menace. "Never felt the air whistle past your face as you try to keep them from chopping you to pieces with their iron swords."

Abid's grin slid away. Small and scrawny for his age to begin

with, he suddenly looked a lot younger than six. Tijah felt a little
bad for scaring him but it had to be done. The Druj were no fairytale ogres. Maybe it had been a mistake to keep the children away
from the villages. Maybe they needed to see.

"You listen to me," Tijah said. "If we come across any liches,
feel free to unknit them with air. That's what daēvas do best. Did
the magi teach you how?"

The older kids nodded firmly, the two younger ones a bit more
uncertainly. Achaemenes just watched, his face unreadable.

"Now wights are fast, really fast," Tijah continued. "A good
friend of mine lost her sister to a wight. I've seen them. They
look like a person, except for the eyes, which are all black." Tijah
touched the corner of her eyelid. "Once they take you, it's over.
There's no coming back. So if you see something like that, don't
hesitate for a second. It's not a human, not a daēva, and it will kill
you in a heartbeat. You run, understand? Same for revenants.
They're even worse. We see any of those, you let me take care
of them."

The kids stared at Tijah, at the hilt of the curved sword she
wore across her back. Pegah looked on the verge of rolling her
eyes, but Tijah's expression made her sigh and brush an invisible
mote of dust from her tunic instead.

"Abid can make a crack in the earth," Bijan whispered. He was
almost as quiet as Anu, and always had a worried crease across his
forehead. At seven, he was the closest in age to Abid, and the
boys were friends.

"Want me to show you?" Abid asked, bouncing on his toes.

"Not right now," Achaemenes said firmly. "And not without
permission. You all know earth can break bones. It's easy to draw
too much."

"We don't need anyone's *permission* to use the power," Anu
muttered under her breath.

Achaemenes ignored her. Nothing seemed to ruffle his calm.
Tijah almost snapped back at her—it wouldn't do to have a

mutiny on their hands—but thought better of it. She'd talk to the girl later. They only had a few hours of daylight left, and she wanted to get in and out of the village quickly. They'd yet to see any actual Druj, only the aftermath of their passage across the plain, but she knew they were out there. A whole army of them. Tijah climbed to the top of the low rise where they had stopped to rest. A series of arid foothills hemmed the village from the west. Otherwise, the Great Salt Plain stretched in an uninterrupted sheet of parched earth as far as the eye could see. Tijah figured they were two or three days from the Khusk Range. Gorgon-e Gaz lay on the other side.

She shaded her eyes with one hand, sweeping her gaze along the flat line of the horizon, where the sky grew soft and fuzzy, as though someone had smudged their thumb along it. It was a trick of the heat, she knew. Just like the shimmering quicksilver pools that looked like water. In the Sayhad, travelers died chasing those pools, which always floated just out of reach.

"So the village is safe?" Achaemenes asked.

"I didn't say that. I said it *looks* safe. See the difference?"

"I only meant—"

"I know what you meant. Too bad daēvas can't sense Druj. That would make it simple. But we have no choice. I doubt there's another water source for fifty leagues. So in we go."

The sun touched the tops of the hills, painting them reddish gold. A flock of birds winged past in ragged formation overhead. They must be migrating. No place was worth stopping at for long in this wasteland. Tijah imagined them going somewhere green and wild, an island in the middle of the ocean surrounded by wave-beaten cliffs echoing with the roar of the sea. The thought made her wistful. How pleasant to be able to simply fly away....

"Everyone stay close," she said, taking the bridle of their mare. The animal barely responded to her touch. Its head drooped, dark eyes fixed on the dirt. The horse had been intended for Myrri.

Tijah stroked its muzzle. "There's water down there, old girl," she murmured. "Half a league more. If I can do it, you can do it."

They all needed fresh water, desperately. Tijah herself came from the Sayhad and had a high tolerance for dry heat—more than for cold, that was certain—but even she couldn't go forever on a gulp of piss-warm water.

They picked their way down the hillside, Tijah in front with the horse and Achaemenes and the kids trailing behind, to the rutted road leading to the village. Parvane held her brother Bijan's hand. She was tall for an eleven-year-old, almost as tall as Tijah, who could look most men in the eye. Pegah had taken charge of Abid. As usual, Anu held herself apart from the others, although Tijah noticed she didn't stray far from Achaemenes.

As they neared the village, she saw the tops of walled gardens inside. The people who lived there would have to be self-sufficient to survive out here. They would have wells, and some kind of irrigation system. Tijah scanned a stone pen with a crude thatched shelter that offered protection from the elements. It smelled faintly of manure but the animals were also gone, which Tijah took as a good sign. No bloated bodies rotting in the sun.

The wind whistled across the plain, whipping a fine grit into her eyes. Tijah wished she still had her Water Dog *qarha*, which was easily the most useful item of clothing she'd ever owned. A long scarf that wrapped around the head, it served in rain and snow, dust and wind. But she'd left her old life behind. Now Tijah wore a plain tunic and trousers, once white but scoured to a dingy grey from their journey across the plain. The children still wore the blue of daēva slaves. That color alone would mark them out, if there were anyone within five hundred leagues to see it.

Tijah felt Achaemenes' eyes on her but kept her own straight ahead. He'd finally lost the limp in his right leg, she noticed. His infirmity had vanished the moment Nazafareen freed him from the bond but his mind hadn't accepted it for days.

How we cling to our old ways even when they no longer serve us.

When they reached the opening in the low wall where the road passed into the village, Tijah turned and gave the kids a stern look. Most of them hadn't a clue. They knew, but they didn't really believe. They wouldn't, until they faced their first Undead. But she wouldn't tolerate foolishness.

"Food and water," she said. "Don't touch anything else."

Tijah went into the first house alone while the others waited in the street. The bottom level had served as a stable, with bales of hay stacked against the walls and extra tack. Good news for the horse. She unsheathed her scimitar and slowly scanned the shadows until she felt certain the room was empty. A dark, steep flight of stairs led to the second floor, the stone worn smooth from the long passage of feet. Tijah peered up it, then began to climb, pausing on each step to listen for any sign of movement.

The gods only knew how long this village had been here. A thousand years, maybe. The people of the Dasht-e Kavir were descendants of the pastoralists who had once roamed free with their flocks. She remembered the magus at Tel Khalujah explaining about it in their history lessons while she listened with half an ear, daydreaming about one of the handsome young soldiers in the satrap's personal guard. What had his name been? Farhad? Or was it Farbod?

When Tijah reached the top of the stairs, she waited for a full minute. Just the wind, and the faint voices of the kids outside.

She cautiously began to explore the second floor. As soon as she saw the bedroom, her shoulders relaxed. She rolled her neck and was rewarded with a satisfying crunch. It was not like Ash Shiyda, everything perfectly intact except for the people. No, this had been a planned exodus. Clothing spilled from cedar chests as though a few favorite items had been hastily grabbed. She could see the dust-free spots on dressers and tables where sentimental keepsakes had been taken. Likewise, only the smallest, cheapest rugs remained. Most of the food was gone too, although she found half a loaf of hard bread and some shriveled onions.

Tijah gathered up the food and returned to the street.

"I think it's okay," she said. "Let's check the other houses."

"I'm thirsty," Abid whined, pushing the offered bread away.

"There's an aquifer beneath the hill," Achaemenes said. "They use it for irrigation." He tilted his head back and closed his eyes. Finding the nexus. Letting it guide him to water. "The well is in the middle of town."

Tijah hesitated. Goddess, she was thirsty. "All right. Lead the way."

They followed Achaemenes through the cramped, dusty streets. Some of the houses had been carved straight out of the slabs of sandstone that erupted from the plain. They looked like giant termite mounds, with irregular windows and pointy roofs.

The sun sank behind the hills. Deep shadows cloaked the alleys between the buildings. The dark, cave-like doorways and perfect absence of sound, except for their own footfalls in the dust, had a subduing effect on the children. No one spoke until they reached a central courtyard. Sure enough, it had a deep stone well, with a bucket on a rope.

The water was good and cold. Most of all, it was wet. When they'd all drunk their fills and Tijah had tended to the horse, she explored the houses fronting the courtyard. Most of the food was gone, but she had better luck in the rear gardens. A small orchard yielded a walnut tree and a few hard green pears. Tijah squatted in the shade and ate one. It tasted bitter and chalky. She'd probably have a stomachache later, but she was too hungry to care.

"You never told me what happened to your face," Achaemenes said, dropping down beside her.

Tijah looked up at him. The pain was better than it had been a few days ago, although her jaw still ached where one of the Al Miraji mercenaries had punched her. She wiggled a tooth with her tongue. It felt loose.

"Someone asked me too many questions," she said, chucking the core over a stone wall. "You should see *him*."

Achaemenes raised an eyebrow but let it go. "I'm going to look around," he said.

"Make yourself useful then. We'll need provisions. Warm clothing, blankets. This might be the last village standing before the Khusk mountains." She glanced at Abid, scuffing around in the dirt with his big toe. "They need shoes."

Achaemenes nodded.

"Don't go far."

"I won't."

After the kids devoured some scraps of dried meat and part of an old wheel of cheese Tijah had discovered in a cupboard, their spirits picked up. Parvane pretended to be a lich and chased Abid and Bijan around. Anyone who got touched was declared to be out of the game. They moved so fast Tijah could barely follow. Pegah, who was thirteen, obviously considered herself too old for such silliness, so she sat against the well and watched the others with an indulgent air.

Tijah almost put a stop to it, but it was the first fun the children had had in days and it seemed clear the village was long deserted. So she left them with Parvane and went inside one of the houses looking for anything useful. A few minutes later, Tijah heard raised voices outside. Not in alarm, but in anger. When she reached the courtyard, she found Anu and Parvane going at it. Anu gave Parvane a hard shove, knocking her on her bottom. After a moment of shocked silence, Parvane leaped to her feet. She was lunging at Anu when Tijah stepped between them.

"Knock it off," she said.

Anu spit in the dirt at Tijah's feet. Unlike Parvane, who kept her hair neatly combed, Anu's was wild and knotted. She had the Bactrian look, with pale skin peeling from the sun and light green eyes that now settled on Tijah with open defiance.

"I warned her not to touch me," Anu growled. "I warned her."

Tijah turned to the other girl, who crossed her arms defensively. "Why, Parvane? You know how she is."

"It was an accident!" Parvane protested. "Bijan pushed me. I didn't bump her hard!"

"What's going on?" Achaemenes emerged from the mouth of a dark alley. He carried a cracked water jug in one hand and a stack of blankets in the other.

Parvane cast him an appealing look. "Anu's like a wild animal, she always has been, you know that," she said, all batting eyelashes and reasonable tone. "There's something wrong with her. She *likes* to fight. No one can talk to her without getting their head snapped off. She never wants to play. She just sits there with that mean look on her face." And then Parvane did an uncannily accurate imitation of Anu, clutching herself and rocking back and forth with a sour, blank-eyed stare.

"That's enough," Achaemenes said wearily. "I don't care who started it. You're the older one, and this isn't the place for childish squabbles."

Anu kept her eyes on the ground, refusing to defend herself. Tijah had seen it before. The kid just shut down.

"But—"

"I said, enough." He turned to Anu. "You okay?"

No response. Achaemenes sighed, addressing Bijan and Abid, who had stopped playing to watch the outcome of the fight. "Tijah says the mountains we have to cross are very cold. Pegah, take your brother and check out the houses on the left side. Look for food and clothing mainly, but also weapons, needles and thread, anything useful. Parvane and Bijan, you're with me." Achaemenes stepped up to Anu, careful not to get too close. "Why don't you go with Tijah?" he said gently.

Tijah suppressed a scowl but held her tongue. She could see the wisdom of keeping Anu and Parvane apart for now, but she didn't relish the strange daēva girl's company. She didn't relish any of their company.

When the two of them were alone, she looked Anu up and down. The girl was still staring at her own feet like they contained the secret of life. "Don't want to talk, huh? Well, you're in luck because neither do I." Tijah turned her back and started toward a crooked house at the end of the square. A moment later, she heard the whisper of bare feet behind her.

The place was little more than a mud-brick hovel, with a narrow doorway leading to three rooms on the ground floor. The owners had packed in a hurry, leaving little behind. A crude wooden doll with no arms. A comb with half the teeth missing.

"You want this?" Tijah held it up. "Your hair looks pretty ratty. You might want to give it a comb sometime. No?" She tossed it aside, glancing at Anu out of the corner of her eye. "I could teach you some hand signs. That way we can communicate without talking." Tijah hooked her middle and ring fingers together, palms up. "That means go fuck a herd of camels. You can use it on Parvane anytime you want. I don't care."

Anu's lips bunched together as she tried not to smile. It made the girl look more like an actual person.

"I don't know about you," Tijah announced, "but I feel weird and kind of sad invading people's privacy like this, even if they're never coming back, so let's just get it over with, shall we?"

Anu didn't reply but she snapped out of her trance, helping Tijah search the place and piling whatever seemed worthwhile on the living room rug. Along the way, Tijah taught her a few of the more useful signs she and Myrri had devised when they were kids together.

"This one means stop talking so loud, I'm just mute, not fucking deaf," Tijah said, rapidly touching mouth and ear with a gleeful flourish. "This is yes"—a closed fist—"and no"—first two fingers of right hand tapping left palm.

Anu tried the last two out, her face intensely focused.

"Very good." Tijah grinned. "And this one means you're going bald from ringworm, you flaming son of a pimp."

An hour or so later, they all reunited in the square and made a pile of everything they'd found. Some of it was desperately needed—woolen jackets, a few pairs of sturdy leather boots, pickled vegetables in clay jars and salted mutton—while other items had simply caught the younger children's eyes. A toy chariot complete with horses that you could pull behind you on a string. A carved wooden cat.

Pegah took charge of sorting through it all, directing the younger children to pack the most practical items in a little cart they could hitch to the horse. She and Parvane chattered away, admiring this or that treasure, as Bijan and Abid dutifully followed instructions. The only one who did nothing was Anu. She'd gone off in her own world again, sitting in the dirt near the well and picking at her bare feet.

Tijah took Achaemenes aside, pitching her voice so low she doubted even a daēva could hear it.

"What's the story?" she whispered, flicking her eyes at Anu. "Was her amah a monster?"

Achaemenes shrugged. "No worse than the others. She's always been like this. Different. Awkward with children and adults both."

"Is she slow?" Tijah asked, doubting it. The kid had clever eyes when she bothered to look at you, and she'd picked up the hand signs quick enough.

"The opposite. Anu has a brilliant mind when she wants to use it. She was top of the class in lessons."

"Did the other kids resent her for that?"

Achaemenes shrugged. "Some did."

"So she got it on both sides then. That can't have been easy."

Achaemenes gave her an appraising look. "She could use a friend. I don't know if Anu has ever had one."

Tijah didn't like the way he looked at her, with pity in his eyes. Like he could see inside her. Like he thought maybe Tijah was the one who needed a friend. It made her angry. He couldn't possibly know what she felt.

"Well, she can look elsewhere," Tijah said, and her voice had a nastier edge than she'd intended. "That's not what I signed up for."

Achaemenes's mouth thinned. Tijah felt a surge of petty triumph that she'd finally gotten to him when a prickling sensation made her look across the square, through the thickening shadows, to where Anu crouched by the well. The girl was staring at them. She'd probably heard that last bit since in her irritation, Tijah had forgotten to lower her voice. Goddess-cursed daēvas.

"Shit," Tijah muttered.

"Do we stay here for the night?" Achaemenes asked. She could tell he was disappointed in her.

"Might as well. We'll move on at first light."

He grinned. "You mean I actually get to sleep in a bed?"

"I didn't say that." She pointed down the street. "There's a building over there that should do nicely."

It was the tallest in the village, four stories and solid stone mortared with lime. Tijah had seen it while she was searching a cluster of nearby houses, and had immediately marked it out as an excellent vantage point. The circular style was different from the other buildings, and the stones were much more pitted and weathered, as though the structure predated the village itself. Who had built it was a mystery, but Tijah guessed the settlement had eventually grown up around it. She thought perhaps the tower had been a lookout, dating back to the days when raiders from the hill tribes of Bactria would harry the herders of the Salt Plain.

Whatever it had once been, the villagers now used the tower to store grain. A ladder led to a windowless loft with bales of hay, and then a timbered roof that commanded a clear view in all directions. Tijah tied the horse to a post and gave her a handful of feed. The last faint glow of daylight was fading at the rim of the western horizon as Tijah and Achaemenes reached the top of the rickety ladder. Tijah sat on the edge of the roof and let her feet dangle down. She had never been afraid of heights, although Myrri hated them.

She pushed her sleeve up and touched the gold cuff that still circled her right wrist. If only Myrri had been afraid of enclosed places too. Then she might have stayed with Tijah and the horses by the bridge. The mercenaries wouldn't have snuck up on her and Myrri wouldn't be a greasy scorch mark in the tunnels under Karnopolis.

The soft voices of the children drifted up from the loft below. To Tijah's eyes, it was pitch black inside, but daēvas could see like cats in the darkness and the kids had no trouble scrambling up the ladder and making themselves little nests in the hay.

"How much farther to Gorgon-e Gaz?" Achaemenes asked, settling in beside her.

Tijah let her sleeve fall back down, concealing the cuff. "Two more days to the mountains, another two to cross."

"Do you think we'll make it?"

Tijah looked at him. "We'll make it."

He nodded, but not like he believed her. Just because it was the polite thing to do. "Why don't you get some rest? I'll wake you in a few hours," he said.

Tijah slipped down the ladder and curled up in the straw. The kids were already asleep. She listened to their soft breathing for a few minutes. All her icons—Mami Natu, the fertility goddess with her pendulous breasts; Innunu, Tijah's fierce patron, half woman, half falcon; and Kavi, the nine-headed, nine-armed deliverer of justice—had been lost in Karnopolis. But they lived in her heart.

Bring us safely across the Plain, she prayed. That's all I ask. What happens on the other side is for you to decide.

She felt as though she'd just closed her eyes when Achaemenes was saying her name in the darkness, softly so as not to wake the others. He didn't touch her, which she appreciated.

"You sure you're up for this?" he asked, as she blinked owlishly

17

and let out a jaw-cracking yawn. A pale trickle of moonlight from above let her make out the sleeping mounds of the children. "I can take the next watch too, easy. I'm not tired."

"It's my turn," Tijah replied, stumbling for the ladder.

She sat with her chin on her knees, eyes fixed stubbornly on the eastern horizon. Not even a hint of sunrise yet. She probably had a couple of hours to go at least. That was okay. She could handle it. She'd gone without sleep plenty of times.

The plain stretched ahead of her like a black ocean.

We'll make it. Achaemenes doesn't believe it, but we will.

She sat for a while, then paced the perimeter of the tower. Sixteen steps. It grew cold, the moon set, and she sat back down to huddle for warmth. Whenever her chin would nod toward her chest, she'd pinch herself and get up. Pace some more. In the hour just before dawn, a vision stole over her, clear as if she were seeing it.

Myrri. In the stern of a small boat on that black ocean. Beckoning. Too far off to see her face, but Tijah would bet she's wearing that wry smile, the one that only came out when they were alone together. Tijah is standing on the shore and she understands, even without signs, what Myrri wants.

I'm coming, sister. One way or another, I'm coming....

TIJAH WOKE TO THE FIRST LUKEWARM RAYS OF DAWN HITTING her face. She stirred, realized what had happened, and cursed fluently and with great feeling. It was the first time she'd ever fallen asleep on watch.

She jumped to her feet, shading one hand against the low angle of the sun. A moment of blindness as she squinted past the village to the desolate plateau beyond and Tijah came fully awake, heart pounding like she'd just run a footrace through the Sayhad at noon.

"Achaemenes!" she yelled, trying to keep the panic from her voice. "Get up here. Now!"

Moments later, a tousled head of brown hair popped out of the hatch. Achaemenes pulled himself up and then he was at her side.

"Holy Father," he breathed.

A huge cloud of dust obscured the plain not a league from the village, and it was moving fast, from west to east. The same way they were headed.

Along the road that passed right through the village.

"That's not a sandstorm," Tijah said, feeling sick and scared and guilty all at the same time. "There's no wind."

"That's an army," Achaemenes finished.

They looked at each other. Then they were running to the ladder. He said nothing about her falling asleep, neglecting her duty, and she didn't either.

Tijah dropped the last few feet from the ladder to the loft, Achaemenes behind her.

"Wake up," she barked.

Sleepy faces, blinking eyes. Pegah shot her an accusing look, like she was being a bitch just for fun.

"There's Druj coming," Tijah snapped. "A lot of them."

That got everyone moving. Bijan let out a whimper, clinging to Pegah's leg. Achaemenes snatched up their blankets and wadded them into a ball that he tossed through the hole in the floor.

"I'll get the wagon hitched," he said.

"We still have time to get out, but just barely," Tijah said, herding them toward the ladder as she did a quick head count: Anu, Parvane, Bijan, Pegah...

"Where's Abid?" Tijah demanded. "Where the *hell* is Abid?"

They gawked at her like a bunch of chickens watching a
fire juggler.

"He was here last night," Parvane said finally.
"When we fell asleep. He was next to Bijan."

Bijan crumpled under all the stares. "I didn't see him go,
I swear!"

"No one's saying you did," his sister said, pulling him closer
and glaring at Tijah.

Tijah turned to Achaemenes. "Get them out of here. Just go!
Head east. I'll find Abid."

"But—"

Tijah set her shoulders, cocked her head back. She knew how
to threaten. Even Nazafareen used to back down when Tijah put
on her mean face. "Just go! There's no time."

"We're not leaving Abid." Achaemenes's hair crackled with
static electricity as he gathered the power around him.

Idiot.

Tijah thought she could hear them coming now. Feel it too, a
subtle vibration in the bones of the old tower. The thud of
hundreds of boots hitting the ground in unison.

"Then help me find him," she said, knowing if they argued any longer, no one would get out of the village alive. "I'll take Anu. The rest of you stay together. He can't have gone far."

"We'll check the well. Maybe he got thirsty," Achaemenes said, face tight. "When I find him, he's going to be in serious trouble."

Tijah didn't comment on the ridiculousness of this statement. She was too terrified. Not as much for herself as for the kids. They would fight, but they were hopelessly outnumbered, and she knew exactly how it would end.

They raced down the ladder and fanned out into the empty streets, calling Abid's name. It was a beautiful morning, clear and crisp with a hint of autumn in the chill dew. On any other day, Tijah might have felt glad to be alive. To be rested and fed.

But she didn't notice the way the dawn brought out the seashell-pink of the sandstone or the deep blue of the sky. All she could see was the bodies from the other villages, what had been done to them before they died. And she was glad then she hadn't let the children see it too.

"Abid!" she called, spinning in a circle. Panic bubbled up inside her, urging her to *run, run, run*. Tijah swallowed it down. "Come on out, honey! No one's mad at you, I promise."

At least Anu kept her head. She stuck close but made sure to check any hiding spot that might attract the curiosity of a small boy. The problem was there were too many. The village seemed small from a distance, but when you had only minutes to find a single kid, it suddenly got a whole lot bigger.

"Something's happened to him," Tijah muttered, leaning on the doorframe of yet another empty house. "Why else wouldn't he come out? He must be able to hear us. It's enough to wake the.... Oh, no."

The breeze shifted, tugging on Anu's snarled hair, and that's when Tijah smelled it. The dusty stench of old corpses and rotting leather. Of urine and feces and other body fluids. It drifted through the village like an invisible fog, making Tijah's eyes water.

A flash of movement across the street, next to the wagon they'd loaded the night before. Abid, looking shamefaced as he climbed out of the cellar of a weaver's shop, something mewling in his hand. Anu ran over with her own mean face on, wagging a finger and scolding him.

Didn't she smell it?

But no, she was focused on the little ball of striped grey fur now. A kitten. They were petting it, cooing over it the way people do with kittens. Even ill-tempered Anu helpless to resist. Tijah took a half-step forward and froze, her feet going heavy and cold.

A shadow, darker than midnight, drifted along the adjacent alley. She had about ten seconds before it rounded the corner. If Tijah crossed the street, the cursed thing would see her. It had no eyes or ears, but it would know her and they would all die.

Look at me, kid. Look over at me, please Mami Natu, make her look...

Anu looked. Her smile of triumph at finding Abid slipped when Tijah emphatically signed *no* and pointed at the mouth of the alley. More frantic signing. *Please understand, Anu. Be a smart girl.*

Stop talking so loud, I'm just mute, not fucking deaf.

Anu slapped a hand over Abid's mouth and dragged him behind the wagon wheel just as the lich swept into the street between them, trailing fingers of raven-wing smoke. The sight of it was paralyzing. Tijah's head spun like she was staring through a trap-door into a bottomless abyss.

Oh no. You're not fainting here. No, you're not.

She tore her eyes from the lich and eased back inside, pressing her back against the wall until the wave of dizziness passed. Then she crept to the window and peeked out. Anu's pale face peered between two of the spokes. Part of Abid's blue tunic. He must be mushed against her. It was pathetic cover. Tijah would have given anything to trade places with them.

Please goddess, let Achaemenes and the others find a good place to hide. And don't let Anu panic and reach for the power.

Tijah bit her lip until she tasted blood, her breath shallow in her throat. How the hell could she have fallen asleep on watch?

Boots drummed on stone. The first line of revenants appeared, nine feet tall, broadswords as long as pikes. Tijah wanted to close her eyes but she couldn't be such a coward. So she watched as they marched past, Anu and Abid frozen behind the wagon wheel a few paces away, Tijah praying hard to her patron to help those kids hide, don't let them move or sneeze or anything at all, don't don't just don't...

Strings of dry, brittle hair hung cobwebby across faces that didn't bear looking at too long, especially not the eyes. Stains on leather armor, some of them still wet.

Tijah jerked her head back just before a wight turned its onyx gaze on the window she'd been spying through. Revered Mother, they were worse than the revenants somehow, weren't they? A travesty of the humans they'd once been. Scuttling along disjointed and graceless but with a startling rapidity, like beetles.

The wights grinned mindlessly as they passed. Men and women, a few children, even an old grandmother, sun-wrinkled and covered in clotted blood to the elbows. Their heads swung from side to side, scanning the empty windows for any sign of life. A few were gnawing on hunks of flesh, making Tijah revise her opinion on whether or not they ate. She knew the bodies were still alive, even if their original occupants had been forced out. Figures they had to feed on something.

Bile crept up her throat and she turned away to swallow, wincing at the acid in the back of her bone-dry throat. Then Tijah made herself look again.

Keep watching. Keep an eye on those kids...

Tattered shreds of darkness drifted here and there among the wights and revenants. The liches. They had no real form, not that you could stab or behead. But if one got close enough to touch you, you'd be dead within half a minute. She'd seen it happen before, right on this very plain.

Tijah didn't know what the liches truly were. Maybe what a wight looked like when it wasn't inhabiting a human body. Or maybe liches were something else entirely. She wasn't sure it even mattered. The only thing that mattered was that hundreds of the things were now passing three paces away from Anu and Abid.

Not to mention all the others.

Mami Natu, protect them too. Hide them from the sight of these creatures.

Tijah had never seen so many in one place before, but she knew the histories. Before the daēvas were bonded to the cuffs, the Druj had overrun the land in a red tide. One by one, the city-states fell. And then the Undead army reached the walls of Karnopolis. The ancient stronghold of the magi. The final stand of humanity against the Druj.

And the daēvas had turned them back. Sent them howling into the sea.

Human soldiers had fought and died too, but Tijah knew without the daēvas, they wouldn't have stood a chance.

Now the Undead armies marched again. Except this time, there was no one to fight them except a young king with a tenuous hold on his new empire and a handful of free daēvas who'd decided not to hold a grudge.

We are well and truly screwed.

Tijah wanted to sign something to Anu, to give her courage, but then she heard voices—human voices—and was glad she hadn't taken the chance.

"...search it house by house?"

Two necromancers appeared astride enormous black stallions, their blank-faced captives lolling behind. Neither looked particularly frightening if you'd seen them in passing on the street. Their faces glowed with good health and vigor—all of it stolen by the chains running from the necromancers' wrists to cruel iron collars around their victims' throats.

"Why bother? It's a waste of time. The people are gone. Their herds are gone." The speaker had long brown hair, neatly combed, and the build and eyes of a ferret.

"But our orders—"

"Are clear: to scour the plain. And so we shall. But if we don't make haste, all we'll find are the leavings of the other legions." He smiled horribly. "Don't you want to see a little action, Baradin?"

The second necromancer gave his chains an idle yank, knocking a woman from the saddle. She grasped the collar, toes hammering in the dust, as the huge warhorse dragged her along. The lack of reaction from the other captives as she choked and flailed chilled Tijah's soul.

"We do need fresh meat. This lot is almost worn out," he said musingly. "So be it. I say we ride straight for Tel Khalujah."

They both spurred their mounts to a gallop. Tijah methodically squeezed and released her fists.

If you'd tried to help that woman, even just to put her out of her misery, you'd be writing a death warrant for all of us.

The truth, but it didn't make her feel any better.

For a moment, she thought about what would happen if she just went out there and started hacking at them with her scimitar. Tijah figured she could kill a decent number before they got to her. If the kids weren't around, that's exactly what she'd do. Then she could join Myrri, where she belonged, and this whole sorry mess would be over.

But if the necromancers caught her instead of killing her.... If they made her talk....

Well, then they *would* tear the village apart, stone by stone, until they found the others. She couldn't risk it. And there would be plenty of time for justice later. Plenty of chances to die killing Druj. Her mouth twisted in a bitter, silent laugh. It sounded like they were all going the same way.

The last of the revenants lumbered past. All the dust they'd raised drifted through the street like brownish-red smoke. The rumble of boots grew distant. She caught Anu's eye through the haze and nodded once, her hands shaking with relief.

Tijah waited another few minutes, then stepped into the street just as a necromancer rounded the corner. He had no captives but he wore their grisly attire, a tunic and breeches of human skin. His face looked hardly older than Achaemenes. His eyes were another matter. Old and reptilian. They widened slightly when they saw her, not with fear or surprise but with anticipation, and she understood this was why he'd hung back from the main force. Looking for stragglers.

One smooth motion and his chains dangled from a pale hand.

Tijah staggered back, reaching for her sword. Too slow. He closed the space between them in a single stride and seized her by the throat.

"Pretty boy," he murmured. "Pretty, stupid boy. You're mine now. I won't share you with the others." He laughed. "Not unless they ask nicely."

Her fingers curled around the hilt. She snarled in defiance. And her arm went numb, as if it had been plunged into an ice bath. Pain exploded behind her eyes. A starburst of white agony so bad she thought it would kill her.

Metal clinking and clanking next to her ear.

Still alive then.

That terrified her worse than anything.

Run.

Tijah tried to form the word, tried to crack her teeth open wide enough to let it out.

Run, kids, run away before this one gets tired of playing with me. Before the others hear and come back.

And then she was facedown eating dirt as the necromancer started to give a howl that cut off abruptly. She rolled away. Head still ringing from the pain, even though it ebbed as she lay there panting like a dog in the sun.

Abid, face clenched in a rictus of fear and fury, Anu behind him. Red dust swirled into thick clods that stuffed themselves into the necromancer's gaping mouth. His back arched as he tore at his face, snuffling and making grotesque humming noises. Goddess, she could see the dirt working its way down his throat like a rabbit through a snake.

His form began to shimmer, to split in half, and she knew what was about to happen, she'd seen *that* before too. Tijah lunged, her scimitar raised high, and Anu seemed to instinctively understand because she yanked a big-ass knife from under her tunic and together they plunged them home before the bastards could finish replicating.

As the blades pierced their hearts, the necromancers shuddered and bucked. Their flesh was still fused at hips and shoulders like the strings of cloth dolls Tijah and her sister used to cut out. Both she and Anu took a step back. Finally, the twin monstrosities stopped moving, staring up at the morning sky with bulging eyes and trickles of dirt running from their mouths.

"We have to go," Anu said. "They'll know this one is missing. They'll come back for him." She turned to Abid. "My old amah said necromancers are important. They're like the generals. The others are the foot soldiers."

Tijah looked at her, at her ratty hair and determined chin. Abid's pants were soaked at the crotch. She didn't know if he'd peed himself when the Druj army walked right by him, or after. He still clutched the grey kitten in his grimy hands, stroking it in a mechanical way.

"What you did was smart," Tijah told him. "If you'd gone for a quake, it would have been too big. The rest of those bastards would have caught on. That was smart. Kept him from yelling."

He nodded, still looking stunned. Tijah kicked the bodies under the wagon, rolling them like logs.

"We have to go," Anu repeated anxiously, bouncing on her toes.

Tijah jumped up to the wagon bed and quickly found a couple of jackets and pairs of shoes that looked like they might fit. "Take this," she said, tossing a set to Anu. "You're going to need it in the mountains."

Tijah stuffed some extra clothes for herself and Abid in a sack she slung over one shoulder, along with half the food and water. She didn't want to take it all in case Achaemenes and the others came back for it later.

Goddess, just hide us for a few minutes more.

They crept through the village, more careful this time. Tijah kept thinking of the lich that had drifted so silently out of the mouth of the alley. How many more were away from the main force, scouting? When they reached the tower, she found the horse gone. The rope they'd used to tie it to a post was snapped clean through. It must have smelled the Druj and galloped in the other direction.

Tijah crushed her disappointment. "Okay. Let's get a quick look from the top. We need to see if there's a way out."

She sent Abid and Anu up the ladder first, then followed. They belly-crawled to the edge and looked down.

"Sweet Mother," Tijah muttered.

The village perimeter teemed with Druj. They had not followed the road through to the other side, as she'd hoped. They must have realized one of the necromancers was missing. Or they'd found Achaemenes and the other kids. Tijah didn't want to consider that possibility, but she had to.

"What are we going to do?" Anu whispered. The girl sounded calm, but Abid looked like he might throw up again.

Tijah thought hard for a moment. They couldn't hide. The Druj would tear the place apart. They had to get out somehow. Tijah figured if they could just get to the foothills, they could make their way to the Khusk Range. It was their only shot.

She was starting to realize what a miracle it was they'd gotten as far as they did on the open plain. Because from the vantage point of the tower, she could see other dust clouds on the horizon. Not just one company of Druj out there, but many.

She turned to the kids. "Do you think you can work together?"

They looked at each other.

"Yes," Anu said. She took Abid's grubby hand.

"Good." Tijah addressed the little boy. "Bijan said you're strong in the power. Is that true?"

He gave a solemn nod, the kitten pressed to his chest.

"I'm not asking you to break anything, or hurt yourself, nothing like that. I just want to whip up a strong wind. Get all that dust out there flying so we can hide in it." She glanced over the edge. Six revenants were headed for the tower, longswords drawn, lank hair hanging in front of their faces. "And you'd better do it right now."

"Close your eyes, Abid," Anu instructed. "Find the Nexus."

Serenity stole across his tired features as he reached for the place of nothing and everything. Myrri had tried to describe it to Tijah countless times, but she had a feeling it was one of those things you had to experience first-hand to truly understand. The children took deep breaths, chests swelling. Anu exhaled sharply. Within moments, both were panting hard. A faint breeze brushed Tijah's cheek. She smiled.

"Good job," she whispered. "Just a little more. I think we'd better get going."

The children were even stronger than she'd hoped. By the time they'd reached the bottom of the ladder, the breeze had become a gale. Anu heaved a final shuddering gasp, then began to slow her breathing down. Abid's cheeks were flushed red. He pressed his forehead to the ladder for a moment.

"Feel dizzy," he mumbled.

Tijah dipped a hand into the trough of water they'd given the horse and dampened his face.

"Can you walk?" she asked, crouching before him. "Just for a little bit?"

Abid nodded. Fear shadowed his eyes. "The Druj are coming for us, aren't they?"

She wanted to reassure him, but now wasn't the time for lies. "Yes." Tijah stepped out the door and was met with a stinging slap of grit that tasted like dirty salt. "Hold Abid's hand and don't let go!" she cried to Anu.

She grabbed the girl's other hand and raised an arm in front of her eyes, staggering forward into the wind. She could see vague shapes and shadows around them, but the dust was too thick to make out details. Tijah avoided anything that looked like it was moving. They hurried through the maze of streets. She hoped some chance of fate might bring them face to face with Achaemenes, but this didn't happen.

At one point she heard distant screams. Her feet started to move in that direction, but then she felt the sticky weight of Anu's hand in her own and forced herself to keep heading for the edge of town.

The salt stung her eyes, tightened her throat.

I'm sorry. I really am. But I have to save what I can.

And then they were at the low stone wall that sheltered the last houses to the east, clambering over it and running across the plain to the foothills. They stopped to look back only once, after they'd put a league or so between them and the village.

Fire and smoke and dust. The dark shapes of horses and their riders, galloping up and down just outside the gates. The sun a burning ball in the cloudless sky.

Both Abid and Anu looked exhausted. The wind they'd summoned had already begun to die off. And on the horizon, those lines of dust she'd seen from the tower were getting closer.

"Can we rest for a minute?" Abid panted. "She's tired." He

held up the kitten. It was covered in dust and mewling pathetically.

"No." Tijah dropped to her haunches. "But you can get on my back. I'll carry you."

"I'm okay," Anu assured her, scrubbing a hand across her eyes. "I'm fine."

Tijah forced a smile. Abid curled an arm around her neck and she started running again.

3

Tijah was glad she'd taken a few extra seconds to grab coats and shoes from the wagon because as they neared the jagged teeth of the Khusk Range, the days grew chillier and the nights became downright freezing. The three of them slept huddled together under a thin blanket, a million stars blazing like icicles above.

Her stomach felt hollow. Their meager supplies had dwindled to almost nothing. Tijah didn't dare approach any of the distant villages they glimpsed across the plain, even those without a smudge of smoke hanging above their roofs. But at least Anu had found them water, a tiny spring hidden in the rocks.

The trickle was enough to refill their skins, but not much else. None of them had bathed in more than a week. Anu's hair looked like a vermin-infested haystack. They were cold and they were hungry and they stank. The only ray of light, Tijah reflected, was that she couldn't smell much anymore.

"You'll be safe enough in Tel Khalujah," she told Anu and Abid as they carefully counted out a handful of nuts into three pathetic piles. The kitten gave a weak cry and Abid slipped it a scrap of cheese from his pocket.

32

"They have Water Dogs. I know them all well." Tijah knitted her hands together. They were chapped raw from sun and wind, the skin across her knuckles cracking painfully. She chose her next words with care. Let her own ghosts lie. "I used to live there, a long time ago. Anyway, the Water Dogs are very good at killing Druj. The best. It's what they train for. And Satrap Jaagos has regular soldiers too, hundreds of them. The city will hold. You'll be safe at Tel Khalujah."

Abid nodded, happy to believe, but she saw the skeptical glimmer in Anu's light green eyes. There was a world of difference between six and nine.

"Maybe Achaemenes will find us," Abid said hopefully.

Anu's lip trembled. "He's dead," she snapped. "They're all dead. So just stop pretending."

Abid's face flushed an angry red. "Don't you say that!"

"Anu—" Tijah began.

"It's just the truth," the girl muttered. She jumped to her feet and stalked a short way into the darkness, but not before Tijah saw the tears staining her cheeks.

"She didn't mean it," Tijah lied, pulling Abid close. "She's just scared."

Let the poor kid hope. It's all he has.

The food ran out and still they walked. Sometimes the wind whipped up salt devils that spun and danced across the waste. Whenever Tijah saw one, she thought it was the Druj. That they'd been hunted down at last. But the sheer immensity of the Great Salt Plain helped hide them. They were like fleas crawling across the face of the moon.

When she wasn't watching for dust clouds or frowning at the distant fires licking the horizon, Tijah kept her eyes on the mountains, grey-blue and capped with snow. Distances were deceptive out here. The Khusk Range had loomed ahead for days but no matter how far they walked, it hardly seemed to get any closer. That's how high the mountains were.

She was feeling lightheaded from hunger when she caught the familiar stench of death. They'd finally reached the foothills, and Tijah knew the area from her patrols with Myrri and the other Water Dogs. There were no villages nearby. Tel Khalujah lay at least a day's journey away.

"Stay here," she told the children. They'd stopped in the shadow of the mountains, on a sparsely wooded slope where the tree line ended. Whatever waited was over the ridge.

"No," Anu said, sticking her chin out. "You won't leave us behind."

"I don't know what's on the other side," Tijah said. "But it won't be good. Do you really want to see that?"

Anu just held her gaze, as Abid looked between them anxiously.

"Fine." Tijah hefted the almost empty sack. "Let's go. But you don't use the power unless I tell you, understand?

She scrambled up the steep, rocky slope, loose scree tumbling down with every step. Halfway up she crawled on all fours to keep from sliding down again. The only sound was the ever-present wind, but she slowed when she reached the knife blade of the ridge, worming the last few paces and motioning to the kids to stay back.

The scene in the narrow gorge below made her gut twist. They'd stumbled over the aftermath of a battle, and it was clear which side had lost. Everywhere lay soldiers in the livery of the former King, literally torn to pieces. Bright spots of blue and red in the piles of bodies signified the Immortals, what was left of them. Tijah thought the villages had prepared her for anything. But even though these men were not her allies, she felt sickened, especially for the daēvas who had been given no choice.

"Shut your eyes, Abid," she said.

Of course, the kids had ignored orders and wiggled their way up beside her to peek over the edge.

"It's too late," Anu said. No emotion showed on her face as she surveyed the carnage. "He looked already."

"Be quiet," Tijah said absently. "I need to think."

"The Druj came," Abid said. He clutched the scrawny kitten tighter and it gave a little yowl. "They killed everybody. Will they kill us too?"

"I said be quiet!" Tijah snapped. His face crumpled.

"You should listen," Anu said. "It's not *her* fault."

"Shut up, both of you." Tijah chewed her lip. A shallow river snaked through the center of the canyon, so clogged with bodies it had overflowed its banks. The grotesquely large ones had to be revenants. All seemed to be missing their heads. "I'm going down there."

"Why?" Abid's voice took on a whiny edge.

"Because I need to know what happened. Because there's water. If we follow it upstream far enough, it should be drinkable. And because they may have food." She turned to the children, too tired to argue or cajole or do anything but ask. "Coming or staying?"

"Coming," Anu said immediately.

"Stick close then."

The slope going down seemed even steeper than the slope going up, and they slid on their bottoms for most of the way. Nothing moved below, not even carrion birds or scavenging animals, which Tijah found distinctly ominous. She guessed the fight had occurred a day or two ago, although it was only a guess. The blood splashing the rocks—and there was a lot of it—had dried to a dark maroon.

Tijah began following the stream, circling around the mauled hunks of flesh and bone that used to be human beings. She tried not to look too closely, to focus on looking for packs and saddle-bags that might contain food, but everything was so defiled with gore, she started to give up. The kids trailed along behind her, pale and silent. Goddess, they were getting harder. Abid, who'd lost his breakfast seeing the dead sheep a week ago, stepped right over a limbless torso without comment. He gripped Anu's hand tightly, though, and this time she let him.

It had been a mistake coming through here. They should have just kept going. It was only another day to the gates of Tel Khalujah. Tijah knew she'd never get this awful tableaux—a severed arm still clutching a sword, a single hazel eye slowly bobbing past in the current—out of her head. And if *she* wouldn't, the kids would definitely be scarred for life.

Now this was interesting.

Tijah slowed as she passed a man curled on his side in the red-hemmed robes of a Numerator, one leg splayed out at an odd angle. He had wavy silver hair and a distinguished, kind face. The sort of face you'd expect to see on a benevolent old king. And he wasn't just any Numerator, she noticed. His tunic bore the sigil of the eye with a flame for the pupil. A Hand of the Father. The King's assassins.

What were they doing here?

Tijah spat at the man's feet just as his eyes shot open and fixed on her.

"Shit!" She scooted backwards, veins thrumming with a jolt of adrenaline.

Abid let out a squeak as Anu yanked him away. "Wight!" he screamed. "Wight!"

"It's not a bloody wight," Tijah said, recovering her composure. She stared narrowly at the Numerator. "Look at his eyes."

The old man gave a dry croak as Tijah approached. Blood soaked the front of his snowy white tunic, giving the sigil an even more sinister cast. *Must be a gut wound.* Chest and he'd be dead already. But people could live for a long time with a gut wound. She'd heard they were agony.

"Help me, child," he moaned.

Tijah crouched down just out of reach. "What happened

here?" she asked, trying to conceal the contempt she felt for this man. *Find out what he knows.*

"The Holy Father turned his face away from us," he said through cracked lips. "There were so many of them...."

"But why were you here in the first place? They need you on the plain, not in the mountains!"

His eyes rolled toward the stream just a few paces away. She could see his broken leg now, splinters of white bone poking through in several places. It smelled infected. What torture that must be, lying just out of reach.

"Water, please. Do you have any water?"

Tijah leaned forward, the last thread of her patience snapping. "After you tell me what the fuck you were doing here. Immortals mean you came from Persepolae. Why were you going to Tel Khalujah?"

He recoiled. A slug-like tongue slithered out and swiped his lips. "Not Tel Khalujah. By orders of Patar Araxa and King Artaxeros the Second, the Father bless his name, these brave men were tasked with arresting the kin of the traitor Nazafareen of the Four-Legs Clan."

Tijah glared at him. "They're all related, asshole. You're talking about hundreds of people."

The Hand said nothing. This, clearly, was not news to him.

"You're the one who was in her cell, aren't you? She told me about you."

"Please. Water."

"You wanted her to torture Darius. With the cuff."

Pale blue eyes flashed and she caught a glimpse of the man behind the bland, kindly mask. A rabid zealot. "I offered the demon a chance to confess his sins. To save his own miserable life."

Tijah studied the Numerator, her face growing icier by the moment. "You say you came here to arrest her kin. But you had no way to bring all those people back to Persepolae. So you were

just going to execute them, weren't you? Women and children
too." Tijah shook her head in disgust. "Your summer capital was
sacked by Alexander, by the way. The King is dead. Stabbed by his
own daēva." She laughed, a loud, giddy bray, and it felt so good she
wondered if she'd ever manage to stop, but then she remembered
the Four-Legs Clan. Nazafareen's mother and father. Her older
brother. What was his name? Kian.

"Tell me one more thing and I'll give you some water." She
pulled out the almost empty skin and shook it so he could hear
the sloshing. "Did your army get slaughtered before or after
completing its mission?"

The Numerator seemed to drift away for a moment. He
winced and curled deeper into himself, like something inside was
retracting. A snail pulling into its shell.

"Before," Tijah repeated, emphasizing each syllable.
"Or after."

"After," he whispered.

Her eyes blurred as she pushed up to her feet. "Let's go," she
said to the kids, who'd watched the exchange in silence.

"Wait! You promised me water!"

"I lied, fuckshit," she said over her shoulder, pouring the water
skin out on the ground inches from his grasping fingers. "Just
like you."

"I didn't lie!" He growled like a dog. "We found them and
flayed them, just as the Holy Father will flay you and that demon
spawn! I recognize those creatures walking beside you, wearing
the blue. Daēvas!" His voice broke, hovering on the edge of
madness. "Please. If you won't give me water, just...kill me. Put
me out of my misery. It's been three days." He sobbed. "Three
days. I pretended to be dead so the Druj would spare me, but I
cannot even crawl. I see you carry a sword on your back.
Show mercy!"

Abid's eyes widened. "Maybe—"

"No," Tijah said flatly. Her gaze fell on a young man, facedown in the current ten paces away. Not a soldier. He wore loose trousers over leather boots. One had come off, and she couldn't stop staring at the bare white foot covered in river mud. Just a boy. "There will be no mercy from us."

She walked away and after a couple of seconds, Abid followed, although he kept looking back.

"Heathen bitch!" the Numerator shrieked.

"I hope he takes a long time to die," Anu remarked matter-of-factly.

Tijah shook her head. The girl had a ruthless streak as wide as her own.

I've run from it all these years, but in the end, I'm a trueborn child of Al Miraj. I know the code of the eyeless gods. And there's no place for pity in the white-hot forge of the Sayhad. A twisted smile flitted across her lips.

Father would be proud.

HER WORST FEARS WERE CONFIRMED LATE THE NEXT DAY WHEN they reached Tel Khalujah. The gates to the city had been wrenched off their hinges and ashes still drifted through the air like snow, although the fires had grown cold.

"We're not going in, are we?" It wasn't Abid asking this time but Anu, who never showed fear at anything. Apparently, even she was wary of entering a large city that had been overrun by Druj.

"No, we're not going in," Tijah replied softly.

She stood there, staring at the twisted gates, feet frozen to the sooty ground. She hadn't cried for the Four-Legs Clan, nor even for Achaemenes and the other children who must surely be dead too. She thought she'd lost the ability to feel anything anymore. But seeing Tel Khalujah, with its beautiful spires and bustling markets, reduced to a mass grave, a scrapheap of blackened stone and splintered wood, almost made her lose her will to go on.

This is what the world will look like someday. All of it.

"Come." Abid took her hand and pulled. "Let's go. I don't like it here."

Tijah didn't move. She remembered the lush gardens, the humming of bees in summer. The two sets of barracks, one for humans, one for daēvas. How she used to sneak down to visit Myrri at night and they'd sit on her tiny, hard bed signing to each other, Myrri laughing her silent laugh, while Darius and Tommas took turns watching for Ilyas....

The weight of memory pressed down like a thousand tons of rubble.

Come, sister! Let's go to the stables and ask Tommas for a horse. We'll ride down to the river and tickle the fish on their bellies like Rasam taught me. Myrri's hands mimed tickling.

But they're all slimy, Tijah had objected. She'd never liked fish. They were bizarre creatures. She'd never even seen one before coming to Tel Khalujah.

Don't be a priss! Myrri pursed her lips and stuck her nose in the air. They both fell over giggling.

Tijah stared at the broken gates, unseeing, as Abid gave her hand another tentative tug. He cast a worried glance at Anu.

"I'll help you kill the Druj that did this," Anu said, stepping up. The top of her head barely reached Tijah's elbow, but her voice carried a surprising degree of conviction. "We'll make them pay. After we free the daēvas at Gorgon-e Gaz."

Do not linger here, sister, Myrri signed, and this time she was not a memory, but a silent voice in Tijah's head. *The dead are gone and the living need you.*

Tijah was quiet for a moment. Then she blinked like a woman waking from a dream.

"I used to play chaugan over there," she said, pointing to a grassy field half a league distant. "Do you know chaugan?"

They didn't, so she explained the rules as they put the dead city behind them, how it was played on horseback and you had to hit a little wooden ball with a mallet, which was even harder than it sounded. They followed the road away from Tel Khalujah and its ghosts, past the river to the woods beyond.

"Someone's behind us," Anu said after a while.

Tijah gave her a sharp look. "Human or Druj?"

"I don't know. But I keep hearing twigs cracking."

Tijah, of course, heard nothing, but she didn't doubt the girl's keen daēva senses for an instant.

"We'll circle back. Catch them at their own game. Do you think it's more than one?"

"Could be two. But it's not an army, if that's what you're asking."

"Good. One or two we can handle." Hope bloomed for a brief instant. "Could it be Achaemenes?"

Anu shook her head. "He'd never make so much noise."

"Okay. Well, I want both of you to be as quiet as Achaemenes. We'll cut around through the trees. Maybe there were survivors. They could have seen us." Tijah didn't think so—who would stay in those ruins for a single minute if they were capable of walking? —but she didn't know who else would be out here. The Druj had been sent to scour the land clean and that's precisely what they'd done.

Tijah retraced their steps through a well-tended forest of birch and aspen. It had been Satrap Jaagos's private park, where he'd hunt bear and boar. They startled a gazelle drinking at a stream and Tijah wished she had a bow and arrow, but then it leapt away with such grace she was glad it lived in the world even if her belly was empty.

Anu touched her arm and a few moments later a man strode into sight. At first she thought it was the Hand of the Father, pursuing them even though she'd seen his broken leg with her own eyes. Or maybe his ghost seeking revenge. As the man came closer, though, Tijah saw that while he also had silver hair, his face was much more deeply lined. Sorrowful.

She squinted through the dappled forest light. He looked almost familiar....

"Goddess," she breathed. "It's the magus."

"What magus?"

"Quiet, Abid," Anu hissed, reaching for him. Abid danced away.

Tijah remembered sitting in his study while he droned on about the Holy Father and the way of the flame. He knew she had her own gods, but still he persisted in trying to convert her. There'd always been something off about the man. As though he carried a dark, ugly secret inside him.

She held a finger to her mouth, just watching as he walked through the woods. He'd aged since the last time she saw him, and not well. The corners of his mouth bowed down in a permanent frown. His shoulders were stooped. He had a furtive air, eyes darting from side to side as though he expected an ambush at any moment.

Tijah slowly drew her scimitar and crept up behind him, padding silently on her toes. He turned just as she brought the hilt back, but by then it was too late.

✺ 4 ✺

NAZAFAREEN

I'd asked Lysandros where the dead were.

And he flashed that wintry smile of his and replied, "They're all around us, Nazafareen."

A gust of wind ruffled his raven hair. It smelled of the sea. Salty and cold and vast. It smelled like it had traveled a long way to get here, carrying traces of pine and ancient granite. I caught a whiff of barren ice-clad peaks in that wind, but beneath it all, like the lowest notes of a dirge, was the sea.

I couldn't see the dead, not a hint of them, but a millipede of fear scampered up my spine. Lysandros didn't think they could hurt us, but how could he know? This was only his second time in the Dominion. The place between worlds, where the leagues folded in on themselves and a journey of three weeks would take us only three days.

"Can *you* see them?" I'd asked.

"No. But I don't need to. I can feel them." He shook a lock of hair from his eyes. Fingered the scarred wooden handle of his axe. "The Watchers."

The Watchers. Yes, I knew exactly what he was talking about.

The reason the hair on the back of my neck refused to lie flat. The prickling sensation just beneath my skin. It made me think of slithering things that dwelt in the darkness of rotten stumps. Of empty houses where murder had been done. Of all the bad, secret places in the world where the sun's rays never touched.

Sometimes Lysandros called it the *shadowlands* or the *gloaming*, which seemed more appropriate since the quality of the light never changed. It was eternally balanced at that knife-edge moment right before the mantle of full dark fell, bathing everything in shades of silver and grey and deepest blue. The daēvas, of course, could see just fine. I, on the other hand, found myself squinting into the murk like my half-blind great-grandmother. Like her, I refused to admit I couldn't see, although Darius suspected.

The other constant was the sound of running water. Streams and rivers criss-crossed the land like a web of quicksilver, all flowing in the same direction toward that nameless sea. The only movement was the leap and splash of water, punctuated by the soft sighs of the horses and occasional creak of a harness. I thought we'd been riding for nine or ten hours, although I had no way to mark the passage of time so it was mostly an educated guess based on how much my ass hurt. If there was indeed a shore somewhere, it lay too far off to see. Rolling hills unfurled in all directions, some with trees I recognized. Juniper and spruce, oak and aspen. Despite the coolness of the air, the foliage seemed frozen in a perpetual summer.

There was nothing overtly alien about the place, except for two things.

First, the complete absence of sound other than rushing water. No birdsong or scurrying of small animals in the undergrowth. No chirping of insects. The four or us seemed like the only living things in a thousand leagues.

The second: my bond with Darius had vanished.

That was by far the worst. For the last two years, I'd carried a spark of him inside me. When he allowed it, I could read his every fleeting emotion and physical sensation as though they were my own. In the beginning, our bond had been a curse. But then he'd grown to be a part of me, one I would die before giving up. I'd known exactly where he was at all times. And when he touched me, the spark became a bonfire.

All of that was gone.

Through my own aching loss, I knew this was what Tijah must be feeling too: utterly alone, heart ripped in half. At least I still had Darius at my side and the solace of knowing the bond would be restored if we ever left the Dominion. Lysandros said neither elemental nor talismanic magic worked here. For now, the cuff joining us was just a piece of gold jewelry. I could hardly stand to look at it, clamped to the stump of my right arm like a dead thing. The roaring griffin, worked in such lifelike detail, seemed to mock my unhappiness.

You're no good for him anyway, Breaker. We both know which one of you has the true darkness inside. The poison. You destroy everything you touch....

I yanked my sleeve down and bit the inside of my cheek until the voice shut up. As usual, Darius handled the situation better. He sat straight-backed in the saddle, hard blue eyes scanning the trees to either side. His elemental magic might be useless here, but he was still daēva. Faster. Stronger. More attuned to danger. More attuned to everything.

He wore a grey-blue coat that faded into the rocks and loose trousers tucked into scuffed leather boots. Slightly wavy brown hair curled up at the ends where it met his collar. The reins dangled from his right hand. His left curled into a grey claw at his side. It hadn't healed despite the suppression of the cuff's magic, so I knew a part of him was still in there.

Delilah rode just ahead, spine even more rigid than her son. She carried herself like a warrior-priestess from one of Darius's stories, aloof and intimidating. Like Lysandros, she had adopted the uniform of the Macydonian cavalry, with a breastplate over boiled leather cuirass. Tangled black hair pooled across her shoulders, half-covering the long wooden staff strapped across her back.

She turned in the saddle to glance back at Darius and I was struck by the gauntness of her profile. The predatory beak of a nose, so like her son. The way the bones of her face cut too close to the surface, giving her the hungry look of a she-wolf after a long winter in the mountains.

Delilah had been thin when I first met her in the dungeons of Persepolae. Now she was a wraith. Her eyes, the same blazing blue as Darius, sank into shadowed hollows that looked like bruises against her pale skin. If she suddenly appeared out of the gloom, I might think she was one of the dead.

Her cool gaze turned back to Lysandros, who rode in the lead. Tall and slender with an olive complexion, the daēva looked like a man in his early thirties. In fact, he was at least as old as Victor, which meant *old*. A life measured in centuries, not years or even decades. He gripped the talisman of Traveling in one gloved fist, a spiral shell that hurt the eyes if one stared at it too long. I quickly looked away before the negatory magic inside me tried to break loose and shatter it. That would be bad. Very bad.

"There's a sheltered place to camp just ahead," he called over his shoulder. "We'll rest the horses for a few hours, then move on."

I muttered thanks to whatever god or goddess cared to listen. Then we topped a rise and I caught a glimpse of mountains far in the distance. They looked like thunderheads mounded on the horizon, although I hadn't seen a single cloud all day. Did weather even exist here? The wind came from that direction—although what point of the compass it was, I had no idea—and I thought perhaps the sea lay somewhere on the other side of the range.

I tightened my grip on the pommel, swaying in the saddle as the horses emerged into a clearing. A stream meandered through the far side, its waters grey and lifeless in the perpetual twilight. I'd been feeling out of sorts since we'd first passed through the gate into the Dominion, fighting waves of nausea even worse than the seasickness that had confined me to my cabin when we crossed the Midnight Sea weeks before. The only upside of losing my bond with Darius was that I'd managed to hide my illness from him. If Darius suspected, he might try to stop me from continuing, but I was determined to reach Bactria.

Part of me had always known we would have to face Neblis someday, and I'd rather die trying to save Victor than at the point of a revenant's sword when her Undead army overran the empire. Alexander's empire now, not that it mattered. If we didn't stop her, there would be nothing to rule but a blood-soaked wasteland.

"Are you all right?" Darius's gaze swept over me, missing nothing. I knew the curtness in his voice wasn't intentional. He hated having to ask. Hated the loss of our bond as much as I did. At least it made lying to him easier.

"Fine." I hoisted a leg over the saddle and the world lurched into a lazy spin, like when I was little and my father would take my hands and twirl me around until I screamed with dizzy laughter. I felt myself falling gracelessly to the ground, one foot still caught in the stirrup, when Darius's arm caught me.

"Nazafareen," he said sternly. "You're unwell. Why didn't you tell me?"

"Just tired," I muttered.

Darius gave me his *spare me the crap* look. Across the clearing, Delilah bustled about, pretending she didn't see me almost crack my head, but Lysandros stared at us for a long moment. He led his horse to the stream and unbuckled the saddlebags. Then he strolled over, lithe as a young leopard. He wore the garb of Alexander's elite cavalry, the Companions, which consisted of a loose grey cloak over a hardened linen breastplate and short leather skirt. Lysandros disdained both shield and helmet. He didn't even carry a sword, preferring a small double-edged axe from Qin called a *fu.*

"What's wrong with her?" he asked Darius, not even glancing at me. In the velvety darkness beneath the trees, his eyes were the color of nightshade, a violet so deep it was almost ebony.

"Nothing's wrong with her," I snapped before Darius had a chance to reply. "And she's right in front of you. I may be clumsy, but I'm not mute. A full day riding's worn me out, that's all." I disengaged myself from Darius and willed my knees to hold up. "I'm a weak little human, remember? We actually need to sleep sometimes."

"Are you?" Lysandros peeled his gloves off, flexing long, elegant fingers. "Not quite what I heard at Persepolae."

I flushed and forced myself to meet his eyes. The truth was I felt awful, but I wouldn't let Lysandros know that. He was too arrogant by half—even for one of the old daēvas. Lysandros gave me an appraising look, raising one hand as though to lift my chin. Darius's eyes narrowed.

"She says she's fine," he said curtly.

Lysandros let the arm fall back by his side. "Eat something, kid," he said, flashing that chilly smile. A lopsided twist of the lips that conveyed private amusement you weren't invited to share. "You look like a strong breeze might whisk you away."

I sat against a fallen log while Darius dug through the saddle-bags. Food held no appeal but I nibbled the piece of bread he offered, knowing he'd be relentless if I didn't. It tasted strange. Not stale exactly, but flavorless, like a mouthful of dust. Whether this was due to the weirdness of the Dominion or my own illness, I had no idea. Darius watched me eat as intently as a mother hen, and seemed satisfied when I swallowed the last bite and drank a few sips of water.

"I feel like we're being followed. Stalked," I confessed, wrapping my arms across my chest. In the gloom, I could scarcely see twenty paces beyond the edge of the clearing. "Do you feel it too?"

His eyes scanned the tree line over my shoulder, never resting. He hadn't touched any food himself. Darius's good arm lay relaxed across one knee, but he could whip his sword free in half a heartbeat if needed.

"We don't belong," he agreed. "The Dominion knows it."

"You speak as though it's alive."

Darius stayed silent for a long minute. When he spoke, it was with something close to reverence. "There's magic here. Magic in the trees and rocks and earth. It's nothing I can touch. Nothing familiar." He let out a breath. "But it's powerful, Nazafareen. And ancient. I'm almost glad elemental magic doesn't work here. I'm afraid it would be a twisted thing. Hard to control."

"Lysandros said the dead walk among us." I lowered my voice to a near-whisper. "Only we can't see them. Do you think it's true?"

A small muscle rippled in his jaw as Darius gripped the gold faravahar that hung on a chain around his neck. An eagle with spread wings, it represented the Prophet Zarathustra. The faith that had enslaved his kind and used them as soldiers to fight the Undead Druj. Most people would have thrown it away but Darius had kept it—treasured it even. He was a complicated man. I think it symbolized all he believed was good in himself, even though the magi had done their best to convince him otherwise.

"He told you that?"

I nodded.

"When?"

"Just after we came through the gate. Do you remember the place where the murk began to clear? When we forded that shallow river?"

"I remember."

"That's when I asked him. I was curious." In truth, I'd been thinking of my sister, taken from me at the age of seven by a wight. But the thought of speaking her name in this place filled me with superstitious dread.

"Whatever the Dominion is, I don't think it's heaven or hell. Something in between, perhaps." Darius drew me gently to his chest. I leaned into the warmth of him as he stroked my short hair. It was so good to touch him, to feel that connection between us even without the bond. Especially without the bond. Holy Father, I had missed him, though he'd been riding next to me. I laced the fingers of my left hand with his right and he rested his chin on top of my head.

"How can you know?" I asked.

"Look at this place, Nazafareen. The Dominion is a mirror reflection of ours, but with none of the color and life. It's not the Pit, but it's hardly much of a reward either."

I smiled. "Quite true, Darius. Lysandros thinks it's like *hamistagan*. That the dead await judgment here."

"Well, they seem to have left us alone so far." He kissed my temple, then unrolled two blankets and spread them out on the carpet of pine needles. Adding, almost too softly to hear, "And the dead are not what I fear the most."

I knew what he meant. I felt like a puppet on a string and only Neblis knew which way she would try to make me dance.

I was just stretching out on the blanket when two figures materialized from the dense shadows beneath the evergreens. Lysandros, with Delilah at his side. "Before you rest, there are some things we should discuss," he said.

Darius gave a single nod. Delilah took the log, crossing her ankles with a scowl, while Lysandros squatted on his haunches across from us. "In two days, maybe less, we'll reach the lake." He stared at me. Through me. Feral daēva eyes, unblinking. "So I have to ask. Is something wrong?"

I kept my face calm, gaze steady. *Piss off, Lysandros.* "Like I told you before, I'm fine."

"Good. Because once we get to the House-Behind-the-Veil,

we'll pass through a set of wards shielding it from the magic of the Dominion." His gaze rested on my right arm, and the second cuff linking me to Victor. "Both your bonds will come back to life." He glanced at Darius. "Our elemental magic will return as well. I hear you're as strong in earth as Victor is?"

Darius stifled a yawn. "Stronger."

"Really?" Lysandros's white teeth flashed in the gloom. "Well that *is* impressive. Too bad you can't give me a demonstration."

"You'll have your demonstration," Darius growled. "As soon as we get there."

"I'm sure. Personally, I prefer working with air. Fewer broken bones." Lysandros's grin widened. "You must be terribly brave. Or perhaps you *enjoy* pain? Some do, it's nothing to be ashamed of."

"The first priority is Victor," Delilah interrupted, casting an annoyed look at Lysandros. "When the bond returns, Nazafareen can lead us straight to him. I'll go with her while you two keep Neblis occupied."

"What about necromancers and Druj?" Darius asked. "How many can we expect to find?"

Lysandros shrugged. "I saw none when I was there, save for one necromancer. Judging by the refugees at Persepolae, Neblis has sent her main force across the mountains to ravage the Great Salt Plain and outlying satrapies."

"And the creatures that guarded you?" Darius said. "You said the power didn't touch them."

"I was alone," Lysandros replied. "There were too many to fight. But the four of us together...."

Darius nodded thoughtfully. "And once we're linked by the cuffs again, we should be able to work much greater amounts of the power, just as we did at Karon Komai when we fought the daēva Immortals. We'll pull Neblis's house down and bury her in the rubble."

"What of your fire magic?" Lysandros asked me. "Can you still feel it?"

He had asked me this before, of course, the moment we entered the Dominion. It was the key to our plan.

"Yes." *And it's eating me up from the inside out.*

"Tell me of this power," Delilah demanded. "I saw her use it at Persepolae, but what is it?"

Lysandros waited for me to answer. When I didn't, he said, "The short version? Magic that repels other magic."

"But what is its source?" Delilah frowned, which made her face even longer and horsier. "Not the Nexus?"

The Nexus. The place where all things in heaven and earth were connected. When daēvas worked the three elements, they reached *through* the Nexus to touch them.

"If it drew from the Nexus, it would be gone," Lysandros said with more than a hint of impatience. "Clearly, she carries the power within herself. It seems to be an inborn trait. Little is known about fire magic, but it's always humans who have the ability, never daēvas."

Delilah looked at me directly for the first time. "Can it be used to kill?"

I sighed. "I don't know. It's not like elemental magic. I can work that too, a little bit. Not as well as any of you. This is harder to control. When I let it go, I'm not sure what will happen."

"But you could break the necromancers' chains?"

"Yes, I imagine so."

"You didn't when the one called Balthazar stole the Prophet from you."

"No." My cheeks burned at the memory. "It was the first time I'd ever used it. I didn't know what was happening, only that he was trying to take the cuff and bond Darius himself. It was more instinct than anything else when I lashed out. It was enough to drive him off, but no more. If only I'd focused the power on his chains."

Delilah surprised me by nodding sympathetically. "Well, you couldn't have known. But it means you can use the fire magic to disarm any necromancers we find. Without their chains, they are only men and easily disposed of. The same holds true for Neblis herself. If she can be held at bay, even for an instant, one of us can finish her with a blade to the heart." Her tone left little doubt as to who that would be.

"You make it all sound so simple," Lysandros said languidly.

"That's because it is. Neblis may have forged a fearsome reputation for herself, but she is still just a daēva. No more."

"Victor believed she was more," I said quietly.

"And my husband was wrong." The edge in her voice could have chipped granite.

A brittle silence descended. The wind sighed in the pines.

"What about revenants?" Darius asked. "Wights?"

"I saw none inside Neblis's house," Lysandros replied. "I suspect she finds them distasteful." His tone grew wry. "Like a vicious dog you keep tied in the yard. Perfect for scaring the neighbors but not something you want sniffing around your bedroom."

"Other defenses?"

"She relies on the things living in the lake to alert her to trespassers. And there's no other way to get into the House. It's warded against the magic of the Dominion."

"So sneaking inside is out of the question?"

"I'm afraid so."

Darius digested this information. A lock of hair fell across his forehead and he brushed it absently aside. It made my chest ache. He looked confident and unafraid. I had a sudden vision of his face, masked in blood, blue eyes staring at nothing.

Neblis will use you, the griffin smirked. *Use you in ways you can't possibly foresee. If you had half a brain, you'd go find a deep, dark crevice and crawl to the bottom of it. She'd still hunt you down but it might buy a little time. How considerate of you to come running when she calls, like a faithful hound. But I suppose that's your nature, eh, Water Dog?*

"What exactly are these things that live in the lake?" Darius asked.

Lysandros shrugged. "Ugly. Hard to see—until they move."

"How much of a problem will they be?"

"Are you good with that sword?"

"Adequate." In fact, Darius was very, very good. A lethal blur too fast for human eyes to track.

"Not too much of a problem then."

"They managed to catch you and Victor," Darius pointed out.

Lysandros scowled. "We were surprised."

"All right. Let's say we get past them. Let's say we find Victor and Nazafareen counters Neblis's magic. What about Zarathustra? And what do we do with the holy fire? Try to destroy it? Or bring it back to Alexander?"

"It can be used to free other daēvas," Lysandros pointed out.

"True, but it's still dangerous," Delilah said. "The fire can also be used to forge new cuffs."

I listened to them debate without joining in. I felt more alone than I had since the day I'd first arrived at the magus's study in Tel Khalujah all those years ago, not even knowing what a daēva was, only that I would be chained to one for the rest of my life. I'd thought they were all demons then, Undead like the Druj. Repellent and treacherous, but a necessary evil to protect the empire.

How young I was. A girl of thirteen summers who thought she understood the world and the way things were. It turned out I was wrong about almost everything.

"What do you think, Nazafareen?" Darius asked. Fine lines crinkled the corners of his eyes the way they did when he was troubled about something. I hoped he'd written my silence off to exhaustion.

I think I don't want you to die. Like Tommas. Like Myrri. Because if you do, I'll die too.

I think if I had the courage, I'd slip away. Go finish this on my own. But I doubt I could escape from you three anyhow.

"I'll do whatever you tell me," I said.

He stared at me. "That's it?"

"That's it."

"No questions?" Lysandros asked airily. "Concerns?"

I suppressed a bleak laugh. "Concerns? Yes, all right. Here's one. Neblis knows what I am but she's not afraid. The opposite in fact. She wants me to come to her. So how does that fit into our plans?"

No one spoke for a moment. They'd thought of it, of course. They just didn't want to face what it meant.

"Maybe she doesn't understand what the fire magic can do?" Darius ventured.

I pried a chunk of dense, spongy moss from the earth and began methodically picking it to shreds. "Neblis has outwitted us at every turn. The Father only knows how old she is. I can promise you she understands it better than I do."

"So she wants to use your power to break a talisman. Or, more likely, to repel the daēvas fighting for Alexander." Darius reached for my hand. I slid it away, pretending I didn't notice. Hurt flashed across his face, and then his guard slammed down again. "I won't let anything happen to you, Nazafareen."

"You can't make that promise," I said, and Darius's eyes grew even cooler.

"It's obviously a trap," Delilah snapped. "And not a subtle one. Yes, she commanded you to come. But that doesn't mean we can't turn the tables on her."

I leaned forward. "And just how do you propose to do that?" Quiet despair gave way to anger, like a boot cracking through rotten ice. It never went away, the anger. Just simmered beneath the surface, waiting for a chance to erupt.

"Didn't we already discuss all this?" Lysandros asked no one in particular. "Or was she too busy sulking to pay attention?"

"Neblis will have something waiting." My palm itched to slap that smug look right off his pretty face. "You can be sure of it."

"Yes, she will," he agreed. "And if it's magic, you'll break it. If it's not magic, we'll kill it. See how that works?"

"You don't understand," I snarled. "Since I turned thirteen, I've been someone's weapon. First, I belonged to the empire. The King's dog, hunting down daēvas. Hunting Victor. I did what I was told and believed the lies they filled me with and Darius nearly burned for it."

"That's not fair—" Darius began, but I wasn't about to be stopped now.

"In Karnopolis, we played our part perfectly for the Numerators. How did that turn out? Myrri dead, the Prophet abducted and half the city burned."

Delilah watched me, saying nothing, her black eyes unreadable. Lysandros gave me a mocking salute. "On second thought, maybe you have a point."

I ignored him. "Neblis wants me in her arsenal and she must have a good reason. Some way to counter the fire magic, or worse, control it. There has to be something...something we're missing. I have no clue how to stop her and neither do any of you!"

"What are you suggesting?" Delilah asked coldly. "That we turn back? Leave Victor to die?"

"No. Of course not." I jumped to my feet, eyes blurring. "You wanted my opinion. Now you have it. Like I said, I'll follow whatever orders you give me."

"Nazafareen." Darius stood. The expression on his face—love mingled with pity—made my chest ache even more.

"I would have a word with you," Delilah said to Darius. "Alone."

This earned a look of incredulity that made me feel bad for yelling at him. "Now's not the best—" he began.

"It's fine," I said wearily. "Go."

He gave me a skeptical *are you sure* look and I nodded, forcing a grim smile. I didn't want to talk about any of it anymore, and I wouldn't get between him and his mother, even if she was a horrible woman with a lump of frozen iron for a heart.

Delilah's lips tightened. She didn't approve of the bond, or that Darius had chosen me over being whole again.

And maybe she was right.

5

I watched them walk off into the woods, dark heads bowed toward each other. Darius had accepted her much more easily than he had Victor. Delilah adored him, probably because he reminded her of the man she loved. It wasn't that Darius and Victor looked much alike, although they had the same generous, stubborn mouth. But they were both survivors. The empire had tried to break them, and been broken itself.

I lay down, staring at the blank slate of sky through the fir trees. The stream rushed along to my left, spilling over stones worn slick as ice, and I was glad for it because otherwise the silence would be maddening. A sudden breath of air made the branches creak and sway. This time, I smelled the sea very strongly. It filled me with a strange, wordless longing.

"So fire magic *does* come with a temper."

The soft voice in the darkness made me jump. I'd forgotten Lysandros was still there.

"Is that what they say?" I muttered.

"For what it's worth, you're right. About all of it."

I rolled on my side to look at him. He leaned against Delilah's log, legs stretched out, head thrown back. Where Delilah's profile was all harsh angles, Lysandros looked more human somehow. I had to concede he was handsome, although not in the oblivious way of Tommas. No, Lysandros was well aware of his charms, dubious as they might be.

"I know." I rolled to my back again. "We're screwed."

He laughed then, for once not mocking me but in genuine mirth. I suppose if I had lived hundreds of years, I might have been able to laugh at the prospect of my own death too.

"I'm afraid I have no answers for you. So I propose we talk of pleasanter things," he said.

"Such as?"

"I could tell you more about Qin."

I glanced at the tree line. Darius and Delilah were nowhere in sight. "All right...no, wait. Would you tell me how you met Alexander?"

Lysandros tilted his head and gave me a wicked grin. "Certainly, if you wish it, Nazafareen. Let's see. This was several years ago now. I'd just returned to the Free Cities, which had been neatly scooped up by Alexander's father, Philip. After some wandering, I ended up in Corinth. Have you heard of Diogenes of Sinope?"

I shook my head.

"He's a philosopher, one of the crankier ones. Philip had been assassinated and Alexander was the new King. Only twenty years old and eager to prove himself worthy of the crown. When Diogenes failed to come offer his warm wishes to the new hegemon, Alexander decided to go find him."

"And what were you doing there?"

"I had heard of Diogenes myself, and his eccentric habits." Lysandros's eyes shone with glee. "He liked to walk around the marketplace with a lighted lamp in the daytime and tell people he was looking for an honest man. His squabbles with Plato were legendary. I was curious about him and his exhortations one must lead a life of simplicity. Diogenes himself slept curled up in an empty wine cask and depended entirely on the charity of others."

"Sounds like a character."

"Oh, he was that. When Alexander arrived with his full retinue, Diogenes was sunning himself on the ground." Lysandros barked a laugh. "Alexander is so polite, he straightaway asked if there was anything he could do for Diogenes. Any special gift he could grant the famed Cynic."

"I suppose he wanted nothing."

"No, he had one request. Diogenes asked the new King if he would be kind enough to move to the side, as he was blocking the sunlight."

I laughed. "He didn't!"

"He did. I was there, begging for coins not ten feet away."

"What did Alexander say? Was he angry?"

"Not in the least. In fact, he was more taken with Diogenes than ever."

I smiled in the twilight. "That's a good story."

"It is, isn't it? And perfectly true. I must admit, I'd grown a bit weary of Diogenes's company by that point. He didn't lack a sense of humor but he was relentless in his pursuit of poverty. After fifty years at Duke Xiao's palace, the simple life seemed so... simple, if you know what I mean."

"You were spoiled rotten."

"Precisely. I watched Alexander walking away for perhaps three seconds before I tossed my wooden cup into the dust—my only possession—and went running after him." Lysandros slid a nasty-looking triangular dagger from a sheath in his boot and began to hone the edge with a whetstone. "He didn't believe me at first when I said I was a daēva. He had never seen one before. Not unbonded."

"So you showed him," I guessed.

"I did indeed. Perhaps my time with Diogenes had made me

contemptuous of authority, but I lifted Alexander with air and twirled him about."

I giggled. "That's a mad thing to do."

"Yes, he didn't take it well. Being insulted by an elderly, half-naked philosopher is one thing, but to be manhandled before all your officers and friends.... Well, we got off on the wrong foot." Lysandros smiled to himself. "But it was all sorted in the end."

"He cares for you, doesn't he?"

A faint flush crept into his cheeks and I suppressed my own grin. "I suppose we are close." He eyed me. "And now I have a question for you."

"Ask away."

"The huǒ mofa..."

"Yes?" When we were alone, Lysandros called it by the Qin name: *huǒ mofa*. He said it was very rare. One in a thousand could wear the daēva cuffs, and one in a thousand of those could safely wield all four elements.

His eyes grew serious. "Is that what's making you ill?"

"I'm not—"

"Yes, you are. I'm not a complete fool." He stared into the forest, blade and whetstone forgotten in his hands. "None of us are welcome here, you most of all. I'm only asking you to be cautious. We can't do this without you, Nazafareen."

I scowled at him. "What else do you know? Out with it."

Lysandros hesitated. "I've told you most of it. I didn't wish to frighten you. But there is one thing. Have a care how often you use the power. I've heard it can corrupt over time. Even those pure of heart can find themselves hungry to use the power for their own ambitions."

I fell silent. "It feels like a beast sometimes. Like a live thing."

He tested the edge of the dagger against his thumb and started sharpening it again. "So put a leash on it."

"The truth?" I felt reckless. "Sometimes I like it. Like the rage it feeds on. It feels close to...ecstasy."

Lysandros's head turned at a noise too low for me to hear. Then he stood in one smooth motion.

"It was a pleasure conversing with you," he said, giving me a half bow. An instant later he was on the other side of the clearing, tending to his horse, just as Darius and Delilah emerged from the forest. Darius threw himself on the ground next to me with that brooding, bleak look I remembered well from our days in Tel Khalujah.

"So," I said. "What did she want?"

"She grilled me again about our bond," he admitted. "She can't understand why I would want to keep it. Why I'd give you that kind of control over me." His eyes flicked to the griffin cuff around his own wrist, a mirror image of mine, then flicked away again. "Not to make excuses, but her bond with the King.... It brought nothing but shame and humiliation. For years."

The thought made me sick. I said nothing.

Darius sighed. "I'm sorry, Nazafareen. It's not you personally. And she is grateful for what you did."

"Breaking her cuff with that bastard? It was the least I could do." I looked at him closely. "But that's not what's bothering you."

Darius hesitated. "I'd hoped Delilah could tell me more about where the daēvas come from. We must have a true home somewhere. A history from before the war. Before the bonding. But she claims not to know. She says her parents never spoke of it. Delilah was only seventeen when she married Victor."

"He told me the same," I said quietly. "Before he left for Bactria."

Darius's knuckles whitened around the faravahar. "What if the magi are right? What if we *are* Druj, Nazafareen?"

"What, Undead?" I said, laughing uneasily.

Darius didn't smile back. "Not Undead. I mean impure. Evil."

I frowned. "Now you're being ridiculous."

"How do you know? Maybe the bond does temper our true nature."

My heart raced. "How can you say that, after everything—"

"Look at Neblis. Look at what the Immortals did to Persepolae. The slaughter."

"They had a good reason!"

"Revenge."

"Yes! Revenge. They were *slaves*. Considering the barbarity of their treatment, I'd say it was well-earned." I stared at him. "What about Lysandros? He was never bonded and yet he chooses to risk his life to save Victor, whom he doesn't even like. Does that sound evil to you?"

Darius's lilting western accent always grew stronger when he was upset. "There are exceptions to every rule."

I couldn't believe what I was hearing. "Have they poisoned you so? You're the best man I've ever known! No matter what they did to you, no matter how they twisted their knives, you've always walked in the light. I knew it in my heart from the moment I met you. My only regret is that I didn't see through the lies sooner. That it took me so many years. How can you even for one instant *consider that shit again?*"

My voice was steadily rising. Lysandros pretended not to hear, but Delilah turned to watch, a look of grim satisfaction on her face. It made me even angrier. "The truth is *I'm* the one with the darkness inside. You speak of our bond? Our bond is the only thing tempering it! And since you've been gone, I feel capable of anything." My hands shook with rage. "Do you understand now?"

Darius stared at me. He reached out a hand but I jerked back before he could touch me.

"Just get away from me," I growled through clenched teeth.

"You're bleeding," he said.

I scrubbed a hand across my mouth. I could feel the hot, wet rush of it. A nosebleed. But that wasn't the worst part. The blood staining my fingers was jet black and it smoked where it struck the earth, like droplets of molten metal.

Darius reached for me again but I staggered to my feet and

ran to the stream. Delilah gave me a wide berth as I splashed water on my face, rubbing until every last trace of that blood was gone. The water hissed faintly when it touched my skin. My left hand shook as I pressed my fingers into my eyes until I saw dancing motes of light. What was happening to me?

I wanted to lay waste to something. To everything.

Without speaking, I returned to the blankets and rolled up with my back to Darius. I listened to the steady rush of the water, hoping it would soothe me into oblivion, but sleep took a long time and it seemed only moments later that Darius's hand was gently shaking me awake.

Once, he would have shut me out. Gone cold and remote. But that wasn't his way anymore. If anything, he treated me with particular kindness. It made me sad to know he still doubted himself. Darius needed the truth. Needed to know his place in the world. And it occurred to me there was one person who might be able to tell him.

The Prophet Zarathustra. The man who'd invented the cuffs. Victor's friend and, according to Darius, a sorcerer too. He knew about Breakers. About the fourth element. About me.

The Alchemist must be wary of the price, lest it lead him to evil...

I ate a cold breakfast of bread and some withered apples, and we all climbed back on the horses. My aching legs protested but at least I managed to keep the food down. I felt better for having rested, the cloud of despair that seemed so heavy the night before dissipating as we left the clearing behind. The route Lysandros took followed the foothills, keeping the mountain range to our right. The land grew open and treeless and our horses devoured the leagues at a steady pace.

But then we entered another dense deciduous forest and even the grey light of the gloaming faded to little more than you might get from a sliver of moon. A light mist rose, obscuring all but the nearest objects. We'd fallen back into our usual pecking order, with Lysandros in the lead and Darius taking up the rear. I kept my eyes on the twitchy tail of Delilah's mount, only a few feet ahead. We instinctively drew together and I was glad to have Darius at my back, close enough that I could hear the soft exhalations of his horse.

"There's something up ahead," Lysandros called in a low voice. "A light."

Through the leafy tangle of oak, beech and chestnut, a faint glimmering appeared. It had a greenish-blue cast unlike anything I had ever seen before. We cautiously drew closer. The trees thinned, then vanished altogether. My horse's hooves made a faint squelching sound, as though she walked through mud.

"A trick of Neblis?" Delilah muttered. "Or something else?"

The strange glow intensified, bathing her gaunt face in dappled light that shimmered and pulsed in waves. My hackles rose as I recognized something constructed from the power. Not a talisman exactly, but akin to one.

"What is it?" Darius nudged his mount forward so he rode next to me. Tendrils of mist twined about his shoulders like a fairy cloak.

We shared a look of mingled wonder and dread. Iron rasped against leather as Darius eased his sword from the scabbard. Lysandros reined up a short distance away and we joined him, the four of us lined up before a wall of water roughly the same size as the enormous doorways in the palace at Persepolae, before the daēvas reduced it to rubble. The surface rippled, as if a gentle breeze swept across it. I couldn't see what lay beyond, the water was too murky, but I had the impression of shadows moving within and behind it.

Darius broke away and rode in a slow circle, disappearing behind the frozen wave and reappearing a minute later on the other side.

"I think it might be a gate," he said, re-sheathing his sword.

"But this one is different," I said. "The way we entered the Dominion through the river...that didn't look like a doorway at all. It was quicksand." I remembered the moment my head went under. The conviction I was about to die a slow, painful death. Squeezing my eyes shut against the inevitable, and finally discovering I could see and hear and breathe in the murk, as if it was all a grand illusion. "Lysandros had the talisman of Traveling so he *made* a way in."

"And it disappeared once we were through," Delilah pointed out.

Lysandros stared at the gate, a puzzled expression on his face. The way you'd look at a person who reminds you of someone else, but you can't figure out who. "The talisman Neblis gave me makes temporary gates," he said at last. "They only last a few minutes."

"So maybe it's another kind of gate," Darius suggested.

I rode closer until I could see my own warped reflection in the surface. The magic tried to lunge free, to burn and break, and I stuffed it ruthlessly back into its cage. Before anyone could stop me, I thrust my hand into the water. It was cold and strangely dry, and I immediately hit some kind of unyielding barrier. I hastily withdrew my arm.

"Nazafareen!" Darius looked at me like I'd gone mad.

"It's locked, whatever it is," I muttered.

"Then we go on," Lysandros said.

We rode away from the wall of water, following a stream that Lysandros swore he recognized from his last passage through the shadowlands when he was traveling the other way. The thick gloom dissipated and the ground grew firm again. We encountered nothing else of interest for the next several hours. I was nodding off in my saddle when Delilah stopped abruptly in front of me. I opened my eyes and saw the glow again.

"It must be another one," Lysandros said.

Darius scanned the ground and his brows drew together in consternation. "No," he said. "It's the same. Look, our own hoof prints are clearly visible." He pointed at the ground, where clods of wet earth had been disturbed. "That's where Nazafareen rode up to it."

Lysandros cursed under his breath. "We've gone in a circle."

"But we've been following the stream!" Delilah said.

"Perhaps it loops around."

"So you're saying we've lost hours." Her voice was clipped with fury.

"We'll make it up," Darius said soothingly.

He consulted with Lysandros and we struck out in a different direction. An hour later, I saw the green glow again. Delilah leapt from her horse. She looked ready to murder someone. Before Lysandros could say anything, she marched up to his stirrup.

"Just admit it," she growled. "We're bloody lost."

❧ 6 ❧

Lysandros ground his teeth in frustration. He stood a short distance from the gate, looking like a cornered animal, while his horse cropped at a delicate fan-like growth on the banks of the creek.

"It's not my fault," he snapped. "I followed the exact same landmarks as before. Ford the river, cross the hills, follow the stream. But they've moved!"

Delilah shook her head in disgust and Lysandros threw his hands up. "I swear it!"

"You make a poor guide, Lysandros," she said. "But I didn't expect much more from a man who has spent his life running away from duty."

"Spare me the lecture," Lysandros sneered. "Where was Victor's duty when he sold out his cousins for you? He allowed himself to be used as a hunting hound, running the daēvas to ground and leashing them all to spare your life, and where did it get either of you? Slaves for the last two hundred years, while the empire grew fat from their sweat."

"Don't you dare—" Delilah began, but he cut her off.

"I'm only here because I promised Victor I would oppose

Neblis's will in all things. Otherwise I would let him rot! Yes, I ran. There was no choice. But the moment I saw an opportunity to break the daēvas' chains, I returned and allied myself with Alexander of Macydon. What have *you* done, Delilah? Besides servicing the King?" He laughed. "Personally, I think I would have preferred the deepest, darkest cell in Gorgon-e Gaz to that—"

Delilah had grown deathly pale as he spoke. For the first time, I was grateful her power was blocked because she probably would have tried to kill Lysandros right there. Instead, she slapped him across the face.

"You go too far," she hissed.

Lysandros touched a hand to his reddening cheek and looked on the verge of slapping her back when Darius strode forward and placed himself between them.

"Enough," he said mildly. "This is not the place to settle old grudges. You'll have time enough for that after we find Victor."

Lysandros narrowed his eyes and stared at a distant point over Darius's shoulder. Delilah opened her mouth, then closed it again. She nodded curtly.

"It's clear we've gone in a circle, but that's easily remedied," Darius continued. "Wait here and I'll scout ahead. Lysandros, tell me what I'm looking for. You described a valley. How do I find it?"

"Where the stream emerges from the forest you should see two sharp peaks like fangs. The way between them is the pass over the mountains. Neblis's lake lies on the other side."

Darius nodded. "I'll find high ground and have a look." His lips quirked. "Try not to kill each other while I'm gone."

Delilah stalked off into the trees. Lysandros began whistling a tuneless melody as he returned to sharpening his knife.

"Keep your wits sharp," he said softly. "Don't let this land lull you into thinking it's empty."

The skin between my shoulder blades prickled and I could

have sworn the invisible watchers perked up at his words. Darius turned to leave and I slipped into step beside him.

"Take me along," I begged. "Please. Don't leave me here with those two. They're like cats in a sack." I lowered my voice. "And I'm sorry about last night. I shouldn't have snapped at you like that."

He scrubbed a hand across the stubble of beard darkening his jaw. "Apology accepted." And that was that. "We'll go on foot." He grinned. "How good are you at climbing trees?"

I grinned back, relief flooding me. Not only did I dread the thought of staying with Delilah and Lysandros, who were perfectly capable of murdering each other with knives or anything else that came to hand if their powers weren't available, but I hated to think Darius was angry with me. It wasn't his fault I had darkness inside me. He deserved better.

Darius took off at a jog, scanning the ground ahead for signs only his eyes could make out. The thin light trickling down from above cast everything in shades of grey and silver. He made barely a sound as he moved through the towering trees. By contrast, I sounded like an aurochs stampeding through a pottery shop, my feet managing to find every single dry twig and crackling leaf on the forest floor.

I stayed close to Darius though my legs ached with the effort of keeping up. The land began to rise and the sound of the stream fell away behind us. Finally, he stopped at the base of an enormous spruce tree, whose branches spread as wide and tall as one of the famed towers guarding the walls of Karnopolis. The thought of climbing it one-handed made my knees weak, but I wouldn't tell *him* that and for once I could conceal my feelings.

"I'll need a boost," I said, eyeing the lowest branches, which were still over my head.

"You're sure you're up to it?"

I nodded. "I feel a lot better since resting. Honest."

Darius slipped his good arm around my waist, but he didn't lift me up.

"You're wrong, you know," he said.

"About what?" There were so many possibilities.

"About yourself. You have goodness in you, Nazafareen. You're not this...whatever Lysandros calls it. This fire magic."

"But I am. That's the problem."

"Did you mean what you said? You don't trust your own judgment?"

I sighed. "I'm sorry, Darius, but yes, it's the truth. I'm so afraid of hurting the people I care for. It's like there are two of me, the protector and the destroyer. And it's getting harder to tell them apart." I paused. "I think your mother senses it. That's why she doesn't like me."

He made a noise of dissent. "My mother doesn't like you because she's jealous. She doesn't like you being bonded to Victor but she won't ask you to break the cuff because she thinks she might need your help when we're fighting our way out of Neblis's lair. You magnify elemental power, Nazafareen."

He tugged a hand through his hair. "Delilah has been through some terrible things. She has little reason to like humans, but none of that is your fault. She'll come to see it someday. And to accept that I'll never give you up, not for anything in the world."

My eyes got a little misty at this. Darius smiled. "Now, let's find out what we can see from the top of this tree. I for one don't want to spend any more time than necessary wandering around the Dominion."

He cupped his hand and gave me a boost to the lowest branch. I grabbed hold of it and swung myself up, then used the stump of my right arm to steady myself against the trunk as I reached for the next one. Darius had chosen well. The spruce's branches weren't thick, but they looked strong enough to hold my weight and best of all, they grew close together so it was almost as easy as climbing a ladder. Within a few minutes, we'd scrambled to the top and the Dominion spread out beneath us. Thick forest stretched for leagues in every direction. Through the fringe of needles, I saw the mountain range in the distance.

"There." Darius pointed. "The pass Lysandros spoke of."

I followed his finger to a place where two sheer peaks thrust up to the sky. The dull silver of the river led straight towards them through the foothills where the forest ended. Far to the west—if the noonday sun had been overhead—lay a swath of yellow prairie.

"We got turned around," I said. "Lysandros must have lost his bearings somewhere."

"It happens," Darius said, in a tone that implied, *but not to me.*

"Well, now we've got that sorted." I trailed off. "This might be the last time we're alone—"

Darius braced himself against the trunk and pressed his mouth against mine, soft at first and then more insistently. His good arm wound around my waist, pulling me tight against him. Mine stroked the short, silky hair at the nape of his neck. Neither of us was holding on to anything but each other anymore and a faint wave of vertigo crashed over me but it wasn't because of the void around us. For one brief, sweet moment, all that existed in the world was him. No Neblis. No huǒ mofa. Just the taste of his tongue, the heat of his hand as it slid beneath the edge of my tunic. He made a sound low in his throat and I'm not sure what we might have tried to attempt balanced precariously at the top of that tree, but then an eerie cry made us both stiffen. Harsh and high-pitched, it was the first sound I'd heard that wasn't running water or made by the wind.

"What was that?" I whispered against his cheek.

Darius shook his head, laying a hand across my lips. His eyes had gone distant again. I scanned the sea of tall firs but saw nothing.

"Keep still, Nazafareen," he whispered. "Find the quiet place inside yourself."

The urgency in his voice kept me from asking why. My heart pounded as I took a deep breath and tried to let my worry bleed away. The Nexus was blocked here. That's why Darius couldn't touch his elemental magic. But that didn't mean it was truly gone. I'd found it for the first time when the Immortals were hunting us in the King's forest. We had hidden ourselves in a tree not unlike this one.

I closed my eyes, measuring my breaths as evenly as the baker at Tel Khalujah used to measure flour for the bread. After a minute, my pulse slowed.

"Look," Darius said, so softly the word barely stirred the air.

I opened my eyes.

In the distance, six dark shapes circled above the river. They were too far to be more than a blur, but I had the sense of long tails and powerful wings.

"Holy Father," I breathed.

We watched for a moment as they wheeled in spirals low over the treetops.

"Move slowly," Darius whispered. "We don't know how sharp their eyes are."

"Do you think they're searching for us?"

"I don't know, but it seems likely. Look at how they fly in a pattern. We must warn the others."

I inched my way down the trunk, moving more quickly once I reached the thick lower branches.

"What in the Pit *are* those things?" I asked, dropping the last few feet to the ground.

Darius's face was grim. "Let's ask Lysandros."

We hurried back to camp. Delilah stood staring morosely into the gate, as far from Lysandros as she could get. She jumped to her feet when she saw Darius. Lysandros merely looked up from the axe he was sharpening with a raised eyebrow. "Well?"

"We found the pass," Darius replied. "And something else. Winged creatures, larger than anything I've ever seen before.

They looked like they were searching the forest where it touches the foothills."

Lysandros grimaced. "Abbadax."

"Abbadax?"

"That's what Neblis called them. They're her pets."

"Then we must elude them," Delilah said. "What's the terrain like? Is there cover from above?"

"Once the river leaves the forest, there's a rocky stretch to the pass," Darius said. "The foothills are wide open." He turned to Lysandros. "Is there no other way across the mountains?"

"Not that I know of," Lysandros said. "You saw them yourself. Those peaks are deadly. I suppose we could try to go around them..."

"If we're delayed, Victor will pay the price," Delilah said. "We cannot risk it."

"Which means we have to take the pass," Darius finished. "At least we'll be hidden until we reach the foothills. We can decide what to do then."

"How far is it?" Lysandros asked.

"Half a day, perhaps less."

"Then we rest here for one more hour and move on."

"We should go now," Delilah said, black eyes flashing.

"And risk killing the horses? Not to mention Nazafareen?"

They all stared at me.

"I'm—"

"Fine. Yes, I know. You keep saying that. But you look like death warmed over. And we can't afford to have you too exhausted to fight when the time comes." Lysandros cut off my objections with a slash of his hand. "It's the truth, and Darius agrees with me."

I scowled. "So we sit here and wait for those things to find us?"

"I thought you swore to do what you were told," Darius said mildly.

"Fine!" I threw my arms up. I was utterly exhausted. Climbing the spruce had used up my last reserves. "One hour."

"One hour," Lysandros agreed. "And I'm sure Delilah wouldn't mind watching the sky from that big tree over there."

Delilah's lip curled but she strode over to the trunk and scampered up it like a squirrel.

"Come on." Darius took my hand and led me over to the blankets he'd laid out.

"Stay with me," I said.

"Always," he replied with a smile.

And so I fell asleep with my head resting on his shoulder. The only sounds were the wind whispering in the pines and the rasp of Lysandros sharpening one of his weapons.

If he keeps it up, he'll file them all down to nothing, I thought, yawning.

❦

A HAND STROKED MY HAIR. I SAT UP, GROGGY AND DAZED, AND saw Delilah and Lysandros already mounted and ready to leave.

"Did you see them?" I croaked at Delilah.

She nodded. "Six. They flew off a few minutes ago." She sniffed. "Perhaps their mistress summoned them."

"Are you sure they didn't see us?"

"We were well hidden, and they never came directly overhead."

"I have no doubt they'll return, but it does offer us an opportunity," Lysandros said. "We ride hard for the pass."

Darius held out a hand but I ignored it and got to my feet. They thought I was weak. Perhaps I had nothing to prove, but perhaps I did. The brief nap had helped some. At least I didn't think I'd fall off my horse.

We rode away from the gate. This time Darius took the lead and Lysandros carried the rear. The older daēva didn't look happy about it and I wondered if they'd argued while I slept. Delilah wore a small smile on her face that said they had and Darius had won. I found it intriguing his sense of direction was still sharp despite the loss of his magic. It was something else. Some inborn sense, like a migratory bird.

I kept listening for that eerie cry, a cross between the screech of an owl and the crazed laugh of a hyena, but it never came. Darius guided us through the woods, across rushing streams and steep valleys where the trees grew so thick and gloomy I could scarcely see my hand in front of my face.

We found no more gates, nor anything else save for rocks and dirt and trees. I ate a cold supper in the saddle, and all of it had that same strange, flat taste, like eating the reflection of food instead of actual food. Darius had an apple, but I didn't see Lysandros or Delilah touch the rations in their saddlebags and it occurred to me that I hadn't actually seen either of them eat a thing since we'd entered the Dominion. Maybe the old daēvas hardly needed food anymore.

After many hours, the trees began to thin. It made riding easier, but we all watched the sky as the path grew more exposed. Had Darius been at his full powers, he could have sensed anything that approached, but I knew he was blind. My own negatory power didn't seem attuned to whatever lived in the Dominion. I'd felt not even a tingle of danger up in the tree before that distant screech.

The light grew a little brighter and the land began to rise. I heard a high, rushing noise, like water but subtly different. Darius reined up, frowning.

A vast grassland rolled out before us. The tasseled stalks soared over my head, and it was the wind passing through them that accounted for the hissing sound.

"Where did you come from?" he murmured.

The mountain pass still lay dead ahead, but the rocky plain we'd seen from the tree was simply gone.

"Better than open ground," Delilah observed.

"In some ways. Worse in others." Darius scanned the empty white sky. Then his gaze dropped to the rippling grasses, bronze in the half-light. "Anything could be hiding out there."

"This wasn't here when I came the other way," Lysandros said, his voice troubled. "I'd hardly forget such a thing." He turned to Darius. "You saw it yourself."

"Are you claiming the land simply moves about?" Delilah demanded. "Like squares on a game board?"

"Call it what you will," he replied coldly. "This wasn't here."

"I think I saw it before," I said, earning a flat look from Delilah. "Although it was much farther that way." I pointed to the left.

"Either way, we have to cross it to reach the pass," Darius observed.

We looked up at the icy pinnacles of rock that thrust from the ridge line of the mountains. Just as Lysandros described them, they were sharp as teeth and framed a narrow saddle. Neblis waited for us on the other side, a spider at the center of her web.

A sudden harsh cry startled my horse. It tossed its head and whinnied as I fought to stay seated. An instant later, Darius held the bridle, stroking the animal's muzzle and whispering calming words. I hadn't even seen him dismount. My horse pawed the ground once or twice, but she quieted under his touch.

"There!" Lysandros leaned from his saddle, pointing to the right. Three dark specks sped across the grasslands in the direction of the pass. They flew low, occasionally sweeping their great wings to adjust for a gust of wind. We watched them dwindle against the granite massifs of the mountain.

"The same hunting party, or another?" Lysandros wondered aloud.

No one replied for a long moment.

"I'd say let's wait for night to fall, but there is no night," he said finally. "So we'll dismount and walk. The grasses should conceal us from the air."

Delilah nodded and then looked startled that she had actually agreed with Lysandros about something.

Darius dropped the bridle of my horse and reached inside his tunic.

"I want you to take this, Nazafareen," he said, pressing a small object into my hand.

I looked down. His gold faravahar lay curled in my palm, the chain dangling between my fingers. "Darius, I can't..."

"Because you hate the Prophet?" he asked, and although his tone sounded light, there was something in his eyes more serious. I realized he was afraid I would refuse him.

"No, because it's a symbol of your faith. Your most prized possession," I said.

Darius did laugh then. "My faith? Is that what you think?"

I didn't know what to say. He still had the ability to confound me.

"My bonded magus gave this to me. It was a reward for having memorized the first three volumes of the Prophet's writings." His gaze fell on the outstretched eagle wings, the man standing in profile between them, his hands clasped in prayer. "It was a reminder that I was Druj and would always be Druj. The only hope of salvation lay in the bond, and in constant purification. The water blessing." He looked up, holding my eyes in that blazing, intense way he had that always made me think of a cornered animal. One that might just rip your throat out if you came any closer. "I used to believe that. But you've shown me another way, Nazafareen. I still revere the Prophet. He was a wise man, no matter how his teachings were distorted." He paused. "But I wear this because he's the reason we were joined by the cuffs. And I would gladly suffer every moment of torment they gave me over again if it meant I was finally brought to you."

My breath caught as he closed his hand on mine. Then he

took the faravahar and hung it around my neck. "Keep this safe for me, will you?"

I tucked the chain inside my tunic, where I could feel it against my heart.

Darius turned without another word and strode to his horse, leaping into the saddle with the grace of an acrobat. That faravahar had been a major bone of contention between Darius and Victor, who blamed the magi for corrupting his son. I'd always thought he wore it partly to annoy Victor. It had never crossed my mind that he wore it for me.

Once we were certain the abbadax had crossed the mountains, we led our horses into the swaying grasses. The tassels leaned close on both sides, tickling my bare arms and making a susurration like a million insects rubbing their legs together. Every now and then, a distant cry would shatter the silence and we'd all freeze like mice beneath the passing shadow of a hawk. But then the cries would move on and we would hurry along again. Dust wrinkled my nose and made my eyes water. I had several sneezing fits, earning dark glances from Delilah.

After an hour or so, Darius risked a quick view standing in his stirrups to make sure we still had our bearings on the pass.

"About halfway there," he reported.

"Anything moving?" Lysandros asked.

Darius shook his head. "The sky's clear."

A breeze swept the grasses. I could still smell the sea, but something else too, like sour milk. It ruffled my hair and brought relief from the still air in our little straw-colored tunnel. I was just reaching for my water skin when I noticed something odd. A wide swath of grass behind us was rippling the wrong way. Against the wind.

"Darius," I said warningly, and then I saw them.

Not flying but crawling through the grasses, which parted like water for their scaly underbellies. Ridges of feathers grew along their backs, stiff and gleaming like some kind of reddish metal.

They kept their leathery wings folded tight against their bodies, walking on powerful legs tipped with sharp talons.

I quickly counted six...no, nine.

"Abbadax!" I screamed.

Darius twisted in the saddle just as the first one unfurled its wings and struck. I barely had time to draw my sword before it was on me, hooked beak snapping. I stabbed at the serpentine neck but my horse bucked wildly and I overbalanced, tumbling to the ground. The impact froze the breath in my lungs. I dimly saw the blur of Delilah's staff as the abbadax loomed over me, reptilian eyes vicious and cunning. And then Darius was dragging me out of the way as it fell to the ground, blue ichor streaming from its nostrils.

The daēvas fought like demons while I desperately tried to suck in air. Lysandros's axes flew, finding their targets with deadly accuracy. Darius and Delilah pressed their backs together, blade and staff darting like lightning. The abbadax shrieked in rage as their numbers diminished. But those ridges along their backs and wingtips were razor-sharp. I saw Delilah take a deep cut to the arm as one slashed at her in its death throes.

Only three of the beasts remained in the time it took me to gain my feet again. They seemed to fear the iron in Darius's sword and I scrabbled for mine where it had fallen, shaking fingers closing around the hilt as one of the abbadax hissed and reared up. My whole arm shuddered as the blade plunged into the side of its neck. It shook its massive head, gurgling. And suddenly the eyes didn't look reptilian at all. They looked almost sorrowful. Almost *human*. I yanked my sword free and stepped back.

Darius swayed on his feet next to me. The last two had retreated a short distance. Their necks bobbed up and down as they chittered to each other. Lysandros strode to one of the corpses and pulled his axes free. He bled from a dozen small wounds, but none looked life-threatening.

"Neblis will have to do better if she thinks to slaughter us like sheep in a pen," he snarled, hefting the axes. "At least we know her intentions—"

And then the grasses bent. A rush of wings and a shadow from above. Talons hooked into the back of Darius's tunic, yanking him into the air. The last two abbadax bent their hind legs and leapt upward. Lysandros threw his weapons aside. He rushed forward and seized a clawed foot, dangling like the tail of a kite. Within seconds, all three had dwindled to specks in the grey sky.

🎇 7 🎇

BALTHAZAR

At the bottom of a nameless Bactrian lake, in a stone chamber deep inside the House-Behind-the-Veil, the daēva named Victor was dying.

It was not a swift thing, but rather a death measured in inches. Victor possessed great reserves of strength. He'd lasted more than a week now, and would last longer still, although how much was anyone's guess.

The Antimagus Balthazar could see the strain written across his chiseled features. Sweat plastered Victor's dark hair to his forehead. He kept his eyes fixed on a distant corner of the chamber, as far from the burning brazier as possible. The chains binding him to the pillar cut cruelly into wrists and ankles, but the flesh constantly regenerated itself so his wounds remained always on the verge of healing.

The daēva had been stripped of his clothes, the better to humiliate him. Queen Neblis had done it herself, slicing the tunic and trousers from Victor's body with an onyx knife. Dried blood the color of newly-turned earth streaked his muscular arms, one of which was circled by a golden cuff. Victor gave off the desperate scent of an animal caught in a trap.

"Ever seen one of 'em burn?" Molon asked, an eager pitch to his voice.

Balthazar glanced at his companion with disgust. They stood in one of the three doorways leading into the stark, vaulted chamber, which sat empty save for the prisoner.

"Yes."

"Is it as good a show as they say?"

Molon was even taller than Balthazar, but whip-thin with stringy blonde hair and lips that twisted in a sneer no matter what the rest of his face was up to. He wore a close-fitting tunic that hung on his bones like a second skin. In fact, it had *been* someone else's skin six weeks before—a slave who'd outlived his usefulness. Molon enjoyed such grotesque displays because he was an uncivilized beast. But Neblis had seen fit to give him the chains and make him an Antimagus, so Balthazar had no choice but to tolerate his company. There were few enough of them left these days.

"Come! Tell me. Didn't you see one die in the tunnels beneath Karnopolis?" Molon persisted, when Balthazar failed to respond. "Burn like a pyre of dry straw doused in pig fat?"

Victor blinked, his muscles twitching beneath the iron links. So he *was* listening.

"Leave us," Balthazar told Molon curtly.

Molon's scowl deepened but he inclined his head in assent. Balthazar was the most favored of the necromancers. Everyone knew he shared Neblis's bed. And for the first time in memory, they were the only two Antimagi in the House-Behind-the-Veil. The others had all crossed the mountains, leading her army of Undead to ravage the satrapies surrounding the Great Salt Plain.

"As you say, *Balthazar*," Molon replied, heaping as much scorn on the name as he dared. "Perhaps I shall pay a visit to the Prophet instead."

"Queen Neblis placed him in my custody," Balthazar snapped. "Touch him and I'll have your fingers."

"Have you grown soft?" Molon whispered. "Give us a few hours alone and he'll tell me all you wish to know. Or does wet work turn your stomach now?"

Balthazar couldn't help himself. He laughed. "Run along, Molon. Go play fetch with the Shepherds. Perhaps you can coax them to do some tricks."

The Antimagus simply stared at him. The emptiness in his gaze reminded Balthazar of a revenant, those Undead soldiers Neblis conjured to do her own *wet work*. Molon had always been strange, perhaps not surprising given the circumstances of his childhood. Finally, he spun on his heel and walked away. Balthazar watched him move down the corridor, arms hanging at his sides like dead things.

Balthazar himself wore Egyptian linen of the finest quality, embroidered with red serpents writhing along the sleeves and hems. The silky material stretched across his thighs as he squatted before the prisoner, studying his face. Victor had been bound on his knees, his back against the square pillar. The daēva's expression didn't change under the scrutiny, but a new wariness entered his black eyes.

"Do you want water?" Balthazar asked softly.

The barest nod. Balthazar stood and filled a bowl at a tinkling fountain in the next chamber. When he returned, he set the bowl down on the floor. Then he nudged the brazier with his foot until it was ten paces from Victor rather than two. The effect was immediate. Victor heaved a sigh of relief and sagged against his chains, head tipped back.

"Better?" Balthazar asked. "It must be exhausting to fight the flames every moment of the day. How do you manage to get any sleep? Or perhaps you don't sleep at all. A human would have gone mad by now."

Victor didn't reply for a long moment. Then he said in a dry croak: "Water."

Balthazar lifted the bowl to his lips, cupping the back of

Victor's head to help him drink. The daēva drained the bowl and licked his lips. He had a thick, bullish neck and dark beard stubble roughened his jaw. A strong, generous mouth and hawk nose completed the picture. Although it brought a brief stab of jealousy, Balthazar could see why Neblis might desire the daēva. He exuded a raw, undeniable masculinity.

Balthazar let Victor's head drop and stepped back.

"Who died in the tunnels?" Victor asked in a low voice. "Was it...was it my son?"

"I'll tell you if you answer my questions first," Balthazar replied. "What is a Breaker?"

Victor shifted, wincing as the chains cut into bruised flesh. "I don't know what you mean."

"Negatory magic. What does it do?"

"Again, I don't know. I've never heard of such a thing. Why don't you ask Neblis?" He grinned evilly. "Or does she not wish to tell you? Is she keeping you in the dark?"

Balthazar had no idea if the daēva was telling the truth. He decided to switch tacks. "Why does Neblis hate you so? Why has she gone to all this trouble to punish you, when she could have just had you executed?"

Victor drew himself up as far as his chains would allow and sneered. "How is that your business, *necromancer*?"

Balthazar smiled. "Did you know she plans to bond you herself? We're designing a special cuff, the Prophet and I. One that will link two daēvas—though not in an equal partnership, I'm afraid."

"Zarathustra is here?" For the first time, Victor sounded truly shaken. "You lie, Antimagus."

"I brought him back myself. The magi had him hidden away in the tunnels beneath Karnopolis."

Victor relaxed against the pillar, his eyes distant. "All this time..."

"His mind is warped but not ruined. He's being most cooperative."

Victor didn't reply. He seemed lost in reverie. Finally, he blinked and turned to Balthazar. "Keep your promise, Antimagus. Is my son alive?"

Balthazar shrugged. He nudged the brazier back into position, perhaps an inch or so closer than it had been before. Victor cursed him and pressed his cheek to the pillar. A low growl came from his throat.

"You didn't answer any of my questions," Balthazar chided. "So think on it some more, daēva. What is negatory magic? Can it be learned? You're even older than I am. I'm sure if you search your memory, you can come up with something useful."

৩⁂৩

BALTHAZAR STRODE DOWN EMPTY CORRIDORS HUNG WITH faded tapestries depicting kings long vanquished and forgotten. Moss grew on their stern faces like greenish beards. Moisture condensed on the stone ceiling, coursing down the walls and pooling on the floor. All in all, the slippery dankness made walking these halls more than a little treacherous.

The lake pressing in on the House-Behind-the-Veil was not actual water but it mimicked the feel of it, as every gate did. Balthazar sometimes thought he was living deep inside a cave. The pale death-cap mushrooms sprouting from dark crevices did nothing to dispel this impression.

Neblis didn't permit torches in her home for obvious reasons. The only sources of fire were the brazier holding Victor in check and the urn Balthazar had brought back from the Barbican. Instead, crystals occupied sconces at regular intervals along the wall, bathing the halls in glacial blue light.

Every few steps, he passed rooms filled with jumbles of priceless items: carved chairs and tables inlaid with precious gems, cedar chests overflowing with jewelry, carpets of exquisite craftsmanship, with borders of animals and intricate repeating patterns. Figurines of gold and ivory nestled amid colored Samarkand glass and whisper-thin porcelain from Qin. One room contained only a pedestal upon which teetered the shell of an enormous turtle the size of an aurochs. The next contained sacks of amber, coral and furs. A thick layer of dust cloaked all of these treasures. The point was not in the having, Balthazar understood, but in the taking.

He followed the corridors down and down. The air grew chillier. The ceiling lowered and the walls lost their glossy polish. Beads of moisture leaked from every rough stone surface, as though the lake were trying to force its way inside. Balthazar gave his arms a brisk rub. He disliked coming down here. If only the old man would give him something, he might be able to move him to a higher level of the keep.

Balthazar reached a final turning at the end of the corridor and unlocked the door of a small, dark cell.

"Have you brought me any ink?" A reedy voice inquired from the darkness.

"As a matter of fact, I have," Balthazar replied, producing a small pot from his robes. "It's my own recipe. I brought you brushes and vellum, as well."

The Prophet Zarathustra's deeply lined face creased in a boyish grin. "Truly?"

"Truly. I thought we could chat a little while you draw."

"It's rather hard to see in here."

"Yes, I apologize for that. But I'm afraid I can't request a move to better quarters until you tell me some things about the holy fire. Queen Neblis would certainly agree to it then."

The Prophet studied him. "You are Balthazar, the necromancer who brought me to this place."

"I prefer Antimagus, but yes, that is correct."

"My memory has grown hazy." He passed a hand across his eyes. "We are not in Karnopolis anymore?"

"No. The city burned. I saved your life." That much was true, if only in a literal way. "You are in Bactria now."

A shadow crossed the Prophet's face. "We traveled through the Dominion. The land of the dead. Things pursued us. Hounds..."

"They are called Shepherds, but you are safe enough now." Balthazar flinched away from the old man's steady gaze. *Safe* was a relative term in the House-Behind-the-Veil, but he would keep Molon at bay. He could do that much. "Tell me about the holy fire. What you call the fourth element."

"Do you have anything to eat? I'll tell you, but I'm very hungry."

Balthazar sighed. "Wait here."

He backtracked out of the dungeons until he found a servant scurrying through the keep. A handsome young man with curling brown hair whose eyes were even emptier than Molon's. Neblis's pets did not stay sane for long.

"Bring some decent food to the dungeons," Balthazar ordered. "And make sure the prisoner is fed thrice a day from now on. Wine and water too."

The man bowed low and darted off. Neblis chose her servants based on their grace and beauty. They were part of the scenery, like the perfumed flowers in the night garden and perfectly raked gravel pathways. Like the pretty figurines gathering dust, so easily broken if handled carelessly.

When Balthazar returned to the cell, he found the Prophet sketching a goat. The old man seemed to be fond of the creatures.

"The fourth element is a simple talisman, nothing more," Zarathustra said without looking up from his parchment. "A weaving of fire, air, earth and water, predominantly the first. It forges and breaks the daēva cuffs."

"I thought fire was too unstable to work," Balthazar said.

"Hmm, yes. There are ways," the Prophet replied cryptically.

"And what of the gold alloy? I need the exact proportions."

"Why?"

Balthazar hesitated. "To forge new cuffs."

Zarathustra shook his head, long white hair swaying like a tattered curtain. "They are an evil thing. I regret ever making them in the first place. King Xeros abused the cuffs to enslave the daēvas, and I will not give anyone else that power, especially not your Queen."

Balthazar's eyes narrowed. "You have no choice."

The old man smiled gently. "There is always a choice."

"A nice platitude but not true for all of us, I'm afraid." Balthazar thought of the things he had done for his mistress over the last two centuries. Murder and worse. There were no choices for him anymore.

"You don't believe in free will?" Zarathustra started on a second goat, this one a ram with a forked beard and long, curling horns. "How sad. It is one of the Holy Father's greatest gifts to humanity. The ability to discern the right path and to walk it despite the hardships that might entail."

Balthazar rubbed his forehead. This interrogation was wandering far afield. "I don't care to debate philosophy with you, old man. You have to tell me precisely how to make the cuffs or Queen Neblis will give you to Molon. I won't be able to stop it."

"The fellow with yellow hair?"

"He is the worst of us."

"I do not fear him," the Prophet said serenely.

"You should." Balthazar leaned against the cell door. "Seventy-odd years ago, Queen Neblis set me a task. To find children to raise as Antimagi. She had lost so many in the war, you see. I came into her service late and missed most of the fighting, but as you well know, her armies were shattered by the Immortals. Only a handful of us remained."

Zarathustra glanced at up at him. "We magi thought it was the last battle. The end of the world, when the sun would stand still in the sky and the seas would boil. And after the battle of Karnopolis, we believed the forces of the righteous had won. That a new age of enlightenment would begin." He sighed. "We were wrong. The real battle was yet to come."

Balthazar crossed his arms. "*These* are the last days, old man. And you will not catch us unaware this time." He stopped before revealing too much. "Returning to my story. The Druj were easily replaced but the Antimagi who controlled them.... That was a more difficult matter. Humans with the spark are rare and Water Dog scouts find most of them. I imagine you know this, but the same talent is required to wear the chains and daēva cuffs alike.

"I spent many years roaming the lands beyond Bactria, searching for suitable candidates. I brought Molon here when he was a boy of five. Queen Neblis raised him at the House-Behind-the-Veil, but she has no great love of children, nor is she an especially patient woman."

In fact, Neblis despised humans of all ages. Balthazar knew she blamed them for the sins of their race as a whole. Her necromancers were the sole exception to this rule, and only once they became useful weapons.

"Neblis placed discipline above all else. She wanted generals hard enough to command an army of Undead without wetting themselves." He paused. "So it became her practice to allow the older ones to train the younger ones with the collars and chains."

"You mean punish," Zarathustra said softly, a note of horror in his voice. He had finally laid his brush aside and sat with bony knees drawn up to his chest on the bed of filthy straw. "Deranged children raising other deranged children."

Balthazar said nothing. He still considered it the worst of his many crimes, what had happened to those boys after they were spirited away from their homes. Balthazar himself had been gentle with them (less so with their parents, if they raised objections). Molon had even smiled at him as he handed the child over to Neblis. It was the last occasion Molon did so for a very long time.

But despite what the Prophet claimed, Balthazar knew he'd had no choice. None at all. He'd watched his own family die grotesquely from the plague within a fortnight. Only he and his sister had survived, and she'd been forced to sell her body so they could eat. He'd vowed then never to be weak again. The world was an inherently vile place. And magic was the key to survival.

"I'm telling you this so you understand what sort of person you'll be dealing with if Queen Neblis gives you to Molon," Balthazar continued. "He will not be gentle. He...enjoys inflicting pain. It is his only pleasure."

The Prophet looked at Balthazar and his grey eyes were clear as a mountain stream.

"But you won't let her do this."

"If you tell me—"

"No." He shook his grey head. "You are not fully claimed by the darkness yet, Balthazar. I can see it. There is good in you, even if you deny it."

"You have no idea what stains I carry on my soul," Balthazar spat, shaken by a sudden burst of anger. "But it scarcely matters because I don't seek forgiveness, not from you or your Holy Father. I care nothing for redemption. When I die—*if I die*—I'll walk happily to the Pit to claim my eternal reward. I know exactly what I am."

He yanked open the cell door, overcome with the need to be quit of this pious old fool. Before it slammed shut again, he turned back to the Prophet. "Just because I give you a few scraps of food, do not make the mistake of thinking we are friends. I have no friends. Only masters and enemies."

Balthazar turned the key with a savage twist and swept down the corridor. Perhaps he *was* growing soft. First Victor and now Zarathustra. He shouldn't have lost his temper, but the Prophet made him uneasy. Guilty even, although that was ludicrous.

In the end, he knew both prisoners would die and there was nothing, *nothing* Balthazar could do to change that fact. Two more stains on a soul so foul and black it could pass for a lich.

You do what you must, as you always have. There is no choice.

And yet this time, the words rang hollow.

❧ 8 ❧

S leep eluded Balthazar that night. He lay in his spacious chamber atop one of the corkscrew towers, amid sheets of embroidered silk and feather-stuffed pillows, thinking about his sister, Artunis.

Before he went back to Karnopolis, she had not crossed his mind in years. Artunis was a ghost from his old life and the boy he'd been was centuries dead. Yet when he closed his eyes, he could picture her face with eerie clarity. She had been very beautiful. Dark hair and eyes, like Balthazar, with the same wolfish smile. Artunis had been fifteen when she died. With only three years between them, they'd always been close. At the end, she was more like a mother to him than a sister. He would have starved without her.

Balthazar ran a hand through his short hair. He used to comb hers every night after the men had gone. That was the best time of the day. When they were alone together and she would tell him stories about the fox and the fortune-teller, or Fatima and the King's treasure. He missed her voice, and a heavy, bittersweet feeling stole over him. It took him a moment to recognize it. Regret.

Balthazar laughed bleakly in the half-light. *Too late for that. Far too late*. He had chosen his fate two hundred years ago, when the magi cast him out for witchcraft.

And he loved his Queen. Loved her with a terrible, devouring passion that left no room for anything—or anyone—else. Not his dead sister and certainly not the Prophet Zarathustra.

Balthazar threw the covers back and padded to the tall, arched windows. The permanent twilight of the Dominion cast the gardens outside in shades of black and silver. He judged it to be the middle of the night, although with no moon or stars, he had no objective way of telling the hour.

At the far edge of the gardens, he could see the place where the creature Farrumohr dwelt. Sometimes it looked like an ancient stone well, other times a circular pool of liquid darkness. That was the nature of the House-Behind-the-Veil, and the Dominion itself. Appearances deceived. Turn one's back for a moment and the landscape might change—not dramatically but in small ways that made Balthazar feel his mind was slipping.

At this moment it appeared as a placid pool. Nothing stirred there. Perhaps Farrumohr was off carrying a message to Neblis's twin brother, Culach, in the Moon Lands. Balthazar hoped so. He distrusted the creature, in large part because he had no idea what it truly was. Not human, not daēva, not even restless dead like the things in the lake. Something else.

Something worse.

The night air brushed clammy fingers against Balthazar's cheek. He knew he wouldn't sleep again and decided to go for a walk in the gardens. He had much to think on. The Prophet, for one, and how to coax the old man into revealing his secrets. Balthazar had never balked at physical torture when it was necessary, but he found himself reluctant to harm Zarathustra. Was it some buried remnant of his former faith? Balthazar could hardly credit that. He despised the priests to his marrow, and the Prophet had once been the High Magus of Karnopolis.

He threw on a loose tunic and trousers, and splashed his face with water from a basin. A bronze mirror on the wall threw back a blurry reflection of a tall, well-built man in his early thirties, with straight black brows and a slightly crooked nose. What would Artunis think of him now? She used to call him *beautiful boy*...

Balthazar abruptly turned away from the mirror and strode from his chambers. It was no time for idle fancies. They were at war with Alexander, the young Macydonian King. He marched on Bactria and would cross the mountains any day now. And he had daēvas fighting for him, what was left of the Immortals who mutinied at Persepolae. Neblis said her brother commanded his own army, but Balthazar knew they were still trapped behind the wards of the Moon Lands. Time was slipping away.

His steps slowed as he heard the echo of voices ahead. One belonged to Neblis, harsh with barely repressed anger. The second deeper voice must be Victor. Balthazar crept forward, well aware daēvas could detect the sound of a single leaf falling to earth. He hoped the argument was too heated for them to notice him. Neblis had always refused to speak of Victor except in the most general terms, but it was obvious her hatred was personal. Balthazar wanted to know why.

When he reached the archway to the stone chamber, he took a slow breath and peered around the edge of a dusty tapestry.

Neblis paced back and forth before her naked captive. She wore a high-necked gown of silver and gold thread that trailed across the stone floor in a shimmering river. Her feet were bare. A high crown with dagger-like points sat atop fiery red curls. She looked beautiful and terrible.

Nearly twice her size but rendered helpless as a kitten, Victor said something too low for Balthazar to hear. The firelight reflected on his chains, making them writhe.

"I expected more of you," Neblis said disdainfully, "despite your many shortcomings. But you fell for the Prophet's tricks like a witless fool. All in all, you deserved what you got, Victor. Two centuries in that tomb they call Gorgon-e Gaz. You should have accepted my generous offer of an alliance when you had the chance."

Neblis had moved the brazier back some distance but not far enough. Victor's eyes kept flicking toward it and then away. He felt the lure of the flames, Balthazar understood that much. Fire was the daēvas' one weakness. The fourth, forbidden element. And the moment Victor reached for it, it would boil the blood in his veins.

"You can't trust mortals, any of them," Neblis continued, raking his body with her hungry gaze. "When will you accept that? What further abuses must they heap upon you? Their envy poisons them. They've always hated and feared our magic. That's why I took Bactria. They deserved it."

Victor shut his eyes. "Neblis, please..."

"Please what?" She stopped pacing. "Please *what*, Victor?"

"Move it away. I cannot speak to you like this."

She signaled to the shadows and a girl stepped forward. Fourteen or fifteen, just beginning to blossom into womanhood. She wasn't as pretty as most of Neblis's servants, but her eyes had a light not yet snuffed out. Something in her face, the curve of her mouth, reminded Balthazar of his long-dead sister.

The girl carefully lifted the brazier and carried it to the corner of the room. Neblis glided over to Victor. She smoothed the damp hair back from his forehead. Balthazar felt a knife twist in his heart.

"I have shown you mercy, Victor, even though I know you'll reach for the power at the first chance you get," she said softly. "But if you do that, you will fail. And I will find Delilah and give her to the Antimagi to play with. Do you understand?"

For a long moment, Balthazar thought Victor might try anyway. Emotions warred on his face. The chains creaked. "You have me at a disadvantage, Neblis," he said finally. "I would crack this pillar in half, but I have not eaten or slept in a week."

Neblis cocked her head. "Do you wish to now?"

"Just some wine, if you would."

Another signal and the girl scurried off, returning with a gold flagon set with jewels fit for a king. Neblis held it to Victor's lips and he took a long draught. He swallowed painfully.

"What have you done to Lysandros?"

"Not a thing. He carried a message for me back to Alexander." She smiled. "You should have company soon."

Victor's eyes narrowed. "What do you mean?"

"I mean your son and his bonded are on their way to rescue you. So they think."

Victor shrugged carelessly. "Do what you wish to them. The boy means nothing to me. He was a Water Dog, thoroughly corrupted by the magi."

Neblis stepped back. "Do you think me stupid? He's your own flesh and blood. I know you, Victor. You'd fight to the death for him even if you despised him personally. But it's not your son I care about. It's the girl. Farrumohr has found an excellent use for her."

"Farrumohr?'

"My trusted counselor."

Balthazar's lips thinned at this. *Trust* and *Farrumohr* were not words that should be uttered in the same breath, but Neblis was blind where the demon was concerned.

"I wandered in the Dominion for a long time, Victor. Trying to find *you*. It was such a lonely place." For a moment, she sounded almost like a child. "Then I met Farrumohr. He taught me the secret of bringing the dead back using talismans. What the magi call Druj."

She resumed her restless pacing, silvery gown whispering against the stone floor. "When a mortal dies in the Sun Lands, one of the gates will open for a fraction of an instant to allow their passage to the Dominion. The chains permit five restless spirits to return before it closes again. I made the first set with my own hands, with iron mined from the mountains where the abbadax make their nests. And when I needed human Antimagi to wear the chains, Farrumohr agreed to show me the gate to Bactria if I swore to come back someday."

Victor looked somber. "What is this creature?"

"He is of the Dominion itself. Older than time. But he serves me now." Her foxlike features softened. "All I ever wanted was to make a new home. For us, all of us! You remember what it was like at the end. Daēvas being burned as witches." Her lip curled. "Something had to be done."

"Perhaps. But you didn't have to murder thousands," Victor said quietly. "It turned not only the humans against you, but your own kind as well."

"I thought you of all people would understand." She stared at him coldly. "But you ran away. You left me."

"Must we dredge up the past yet again?" Victor said wearily. "Perhaps if you tell me what it is you want—"

"What I want? Surely you know."

"I don't. I never have."

Neblis's hand curled into a claw. She reached for Victor, trembling, but seemed to think better of it. Instead, she stabbed one finger at the dark corner of the room. The serving girl flew off her feet, snared in bonds of air. She cried out as Neblis slammed her into the wall. Again and again, the girl's head whipping back and forth. Balthazar heard awful, wet cracking sounds. It all happened in a matter of seconds. Finally, Neblis let her hand fall; it still shook slightly. The girl's body slid to the floor. She landed in a sitting position, mouth ajar in an *O* of surprise. Then her head lolled to the side and Balthazar saw her neck was broken.

He bit down on his cheek until his tongue tasted of copper. *No choice.*

"You forgot me, Victor." Neblis's voice climbed to a higher pitch. "How could you forget me?"

Victor didn't reply. Balthazar got the impression it wasn't the first time they'd had this conversation. Neblis raised a hand again and the servant's body skidded along the floor until it reached the doorway opposite to Balthazar, leaving a wide smear of blood. Within moments, two other attendants scuttled over and dragged the girl away.

"Look what you made me do," she said dully. "An innocent child."

"Neblis..." Victor lowered his voice to a husky murmur. "Let us not wound each other further. We used to be friends."

"If you think to seduce me into removing your chains, you'll have to do better." She ran her fingers along his jaw, down the line of his throat to the powerful muscles of his chest. "Do you know how long I searched for you? Or have you forgotten that too?"

She leaned down until her face was only inches from Victor's. "Centuries. The dust of them lies on my heart still. I wandered from city to city, crossed mountains and deserts. And when I finally found you, *she* had stolen you away." She pressed a thumb to his mouth. "I thought seeing my face.... That you would remember. But you didn't." Her hand fell back to her side. "You didn't."

"Not that nonsense about some spell again," Victor snapped. "You're mad! How many times must I say it? There is nothing between us, and there never was—"

His head struck the pillar as she delivered a full-armed slap.

"Do you *never* wonder why you have no memories of anything before the war? Where were you born? Who were your parents? Say it, if you know!"

Victor gingerly tested his jaw. "You have an arm on you, woman," he muttered.

"Tell me what you used to call me, Victor, when we danced

beneath the moonlight." A tear slid down her cheek. "Tell me that and I'll let you go. I swear it."

He stared at her. "I would if I could, but I have never danced with you, Neblis."

Her face froze into a mask, like clay hardening in a kiln. She said in a dead voice, "That's *my* curse, Victor. To remember when you do not. How I wish it was the other way around."

She gestured to the brazier and a servant hurried forward, placing the flames just out of Victor's reach. Close enough to torment, to bind, but not to kill.

"Very soon, you will be bonded to me," Neblis whispered. "I will own you, Victor, body and soul. And Delilah will be the name you forget. This I swear."

Balthazar slipped away before she could catch him. His chest felt hollow, scraped clean like the mummified cadavers of the Egyptians. He knew he was a plaything to Neblis. But Victor... Did she truly love him?

And what did she mean about Victor forgetting her? What exactly had happened between them so long ago?

Balthazar's mind raced and he paid little attention to where he was going until he looked up and realized that instead of taking him to the gardens, his feet had sought the way to the dungeon. To the cell of the Prophet.

A shaft of light pierced the small grill set high in the door, illuminating the old man's face, peaceful in sleep. Balthazar watched his chest rise and fall.

I've been weak, he thought. Reluctant to do what must be done. Why?

Because he is a harmless old man. Because he was great once and has untold stores of mystical knowledge locked away in his brain. Because the magi made him suffer, and you hate the magi.

Because you like him.

Balthazar leaned his forehead against the cold iron. But what will I do if he persists in this folly of resistance? I am an Antimagus, sworn to serve. How will I keep him from Molon? Or Neblis herself?

Balthazar smelled her before he heard the soft footfalls behind him. That peculiar spicy-sweet scent that clung to her skin.

"What are you doing down here, Balthazar?" Neblis asked. Her eyes gathered the light from the crystal sconces, glowing catlike in the way of all daēvas. She showed no sign of having been ranting at Victor only minutes before. "I thought you'd be in your chambers." She twined a lock of his hair through her fingers and smiled. "I had half a mind to visit you there. I've missed the pleasure of your company."

"Restless, my lady," he said.

Neblis studied him. "You're angry."

Balthazar kept his features smooth. She couldn't know he'd been spying. The thought sent a spear of ice down his spine.

"No. Just a bit frustrated."

"Why?" She looked at the sleeping Prophet. "Is he being difficult?"

"No," Balthazar said hastily. "It's only that his mind is broken. But I'll dig out what he knows, don't worry."

"I wonder you haven't already, Balthazar. You're not usually so reticent. Do you have some tie to Zarathustra? Before the war?"

Balthazar shook his head. "No, my Queen. He was the High Magus and I was only a young novice. We never met."

She gave him a long, searching look. Balthazar hadn't lied, yet it wasn't the whole truth. He had a niggling feeling at the back of his mind the Prophet knew him better than he imagined.

"Do you drift away from me?" Neblis murmured. "What can I do to make you happy?"

Balthazar cleared his throat. *Can she see the doubt in my eyes?*

"A mere glimpse of your beauty makes me happy." He dropped to one knee and brushed her hand with his lips. "I live to serve."

"Do you?" She glanced again at the Prophet. "I wonder sometimes."

"Are you doubting my loyalty?" Balthazar would never raise his voice to his mistress, but he felt a surge of anger that she would treat him so blithely.

Neblis didn't answer right away. Then she let out a sigh. "No. Never that. Not you, Balthazar. We have been together too long and our ties run too deep."

She stood on her bare tiptoes and kissed him until he felt himself drowning in her, the sweet black waters closing over his head. In those moments, she could make him forget the things he had done for her, the bloody stains on his soul. In those moments, he would do anything she asked without hesitation. Balthazar was a man under a dark enchantment that was heaven and hell in equal measure.

"Come," Neblis said, pulling away. "There are matters we must attend to."

He steadied himself against the wall with one hand. His mouth burned where she'd kissed him. "What matters?" he managed.

"The Breaker, for one. She's in the Dominion."

Balthazar snapped to attention.

The Breaker.

She'd almost defeated him. And now she was coming *here*.

"Don't worry, Balthazar. I have things well in hand. But I must leave you for a short while to ensure that all goes smoothly. Come, we will consult with Farrumohr."

They made their way back to the upper levels. Neblis led him into the gardens to the glade where the demon lived. Since Balthazar had glimpsed it from his window, the pool had become a well again. Moss coated the ancient stones. A draft of frigid air from the opening raised goosebumps on Balthazar's arms. Molon waited for them. His eyes darkened when he saw Balthazar.

"Farrumohr has brought news," Neblis said. "The Breaker

travels with three daēvas. Victor's son. My errand boy, Lysandros."
Her voice grated. "And the whore Delilah. I hadn't expected her
but it makes no difference. The abbadax are hunting them as
we speak."

"You must be careful in how you deal with the girl," Balthazar
cautioned. "She shattered my necromancy like swatting a fly."

"Indeed." Neblis smirked. "I am counting on it, Balthazar.
And I've discovered the perfect bait for my trap. Farrumohr has
learned much about the girl. She has no secrets from me
anymore."

He frowned. "You've never explained—"

"Send me, mistress," Molon interrupted. He glanced at Balthazar from the corner of his eye. "Little girls don't frighten me."

Neblis looked annoyed. "No, you will remain here to watch
over Victor while Balthazar forges the cuffs. What I must do, I
will do alone. While I'm away, I expect you to obey him as you
would me."

Molon bowed his head, thin lips pressed together in
displeasure.

"Once I bring Victor to heel, we can use him to catch others
just as Xeros did. I will unite the Sun Lands, Moon Lands and
Dominion under one Queen." She adjusted the crown on her
head. "But first I must find my brother, Culach. We will have our
own army of daēvas this time."

"And what of Alexander?" Balthazar asked. "He marches on
Bactria with several thousand men, some of them former Immortals. I know he's young but his reputation as a general is
formidable." He didn't say it, but Alexander had managed to
achieve what Neblis and her terrifying Undead armies had not—
he had broken the power of the empire. "Don't underestimate the
Macydonians. Artaxeros did and look what it got him."

Neblis smiled. "Alexander is already here, Balthazar."

"*What?*"

She laughed. "Yes, my pets in the lake say he is camped on the shore. But he can never reach the House, not without a talisman of Traveling to get through the gate. Let him search for me. He will find only mud and eels."

"When will you call the legions back from the Plain?" Balthazar asked. "We need them here!"

"Patience, Balthazar. They will return when they finish the final task I have set them. And then Alexander will find himself caught in the jaws of *two* armies. If any of his daēvas survive, we will cuff them again." She sniffed. "They're accustomed to slavery. It will simply be a new master who commands them."

"You should let me deal with the old Prophet," Molon said in a wheedling tone. "When I am done with him—"

"Shut up, Molon," Balthazar snapped. "You would kill him and all his knowledge would be lost."

"What knowledge is that, Balthazar?" Molon asked innocently. "Has he told you anything useful at all? Or are you too busy praying together to the Holy Father—"

"Watch your tongue," Balthazar said coldly. "You go too far."

"Does he?" Neblis's obsidian eyes glittered. "The old man has been in my cells for three days with nothing to show for it. I'd expected him to break within hours. I thought that was a special talent of yours, Balthazar."

He drew a breath to give some excuse but Neblis had already turned away. "You have until I return. If he hasn't cooperated by then, Molon shall have his turn. Now, I wish to show you something." She waved a hand and servants brought forward the body of the girl she had killed in a fit of rage at Victor. Blood matted the child's hair. Once-bright brown eyes stared at nothing.

"Drop her in," Neblis said.

The servants hefted the corpse over the edge, their faces impassive. Neblis did not speak but watched the rim with a strange eagerness. A minute later, soft sounds came from the black mouth of the well. Much against his better judgment, Balthazar leaned over and peered down.

Every hair on his body stood up at the sight of the girl climbing out like a spider, pale hands finding crevices in the rough stone walls.

"Farrumohr can wear human flesh for a short time," Neblis said. "He told me it makes him happy, so I thought a reward was in order. The girl is fresh too." She frowned. "I'm not sure he cares, but it seems nicer."

Balthazar had glimpsed Farrumohr in his natural state only once. A creature of shadow and flame. And his voice.... The necromancer shuddered. Since that day, he had avoided looking into the well at all.

The dead girl clambered jerkily over the stone lip and Balthazar decided this was worse.

The corpse danced and capered like a marionette being manipulated by invisible hands. Brown eyes shone with an eerie, flickering light as though inner fires burned behind them. Neblis clapped her hands in delight as its jaw dropped open and wet, choking sounds emerged. Balthazar involuntarily stepped back.

He had seen newly summoned revenants claw their way out of the damp earth. He'd seen wights at the instant they possessed a human host. Blackness would roll across the eyes like a solar eclipse. In his long life, Balthazar had seen many things that haunted him still.

But when he realized that the sound was Farrumohr laughing, Balthazar discovered with some surprise that he could still feel horror. Even Molon looked faintly appalled. The yellow-haired necromancer kneaded his hands together, shuffling backwards to put space between himself and the gleeful demon.

"It's a rare treat for him to wear the flesh," Neblis confided in a low voice, still clapping time to Farrumohr's grotesque jig. "I told him that if he is *very* good, and serves me faithfully, I will find a way to bring him through to the Sun Lands. We've tried countless times, but the gates always reject him, poor creature.

Perhaps that nasty old man knows some way to unlock them, yes, Balthazar?"

He nodded absently. If Farrumohr ever escaped the Dominion.... Balthazar closed his eyes.

It would be a long, dark night indeed.

9

Several hours later, only four of them remained in the House-Behind-the-Veil. Neblis had departed the House alone. She knew the Dominion better than anyone except for Farrumohr. When Balthazar objected, she'd pushed him playfully back down onto his bed, stroking his belly until he grabbed her hand and forced her to be serious.

"I survived for years with no one to protect me, my darling," she'd told him. "The Shepherds will not catch *my* scent. I know how to avoid them. And when I return, I'll have an army at my back that will make all the world tremble."

Balthazar had watched her walk into the shadowy forest that lay across the river, just past the wards. She stepped like a dancer, barefoot and uncaring. When he turned back to the House, he saw a flash of yellow hair. Molon, spying from one of the high windows. He ducked out of sight as soon as he saw Balthazar.

That sick creature is up to something, but if he thinks to challenge my authority, he'll find himself in a cell next to the Prophet.

Still, Balthazar thought it wise to check on Victor. The daēva still lived, although his eyes looked half mad. If he died or escaped somehow.... Balthazar knew it was impossible, daēvas were powerless before fire, but Victor had managed to break out of Gorgon-e Gaz. He'd had help, of course. Guards turned traitor to the empire. But Balthazar resolved to keep a close eye on him anyway, especially with Molon roaming about with nothing to keep him occupied. Neblis would have both their heads if anything happened to her prisoner.

"I saw you in Karnopolis, you know," he said, squatting down before Victor. "On the day you rode out to meet Neblis's armies. Everyone thought the King was mad to open the gates. They outnumbered us a hundred to one. And there you were, the griffin pennant tied to your saddle, no armor. I thought it was suicide."

Victor dragged his gaze to meet Balthazar's. "I did too, necromancer." He laughed and a trickle of blood flowed from the corner of his mouth. "I did too."

"Why did you help them? Why did you let them leash you?" He toed the fire back a few inches. Victor sagged against his bonds.

"You wouldn't understand."

"How can you be sure? Perhaps I would."

Victor pinned him with his black-eyed gaze. "I did it for love, necromancer."

"For Delilah?"

Victor said nothing but a shadow crossed his face. A sorrow as vast and deep as the Cold Sea. He must believe Delilah was still bonded to the King. Balthazar realized Victor didn't know what had happened at Persepolae.

"Why did you come here?" he asked. "I don't suppose I need to say it was rather foolish of you."

Victor glowered. "You stole something from me, necromancer. I came to take it back."

"Ah. So you do remember me from the Salt Plain." Balthazar smiled. "I wasn't sure. A bloody, chaotic day." He grimaced. "The sandstorm the Water Dogs summoned was a nasty surprise. I was lucky to get out alive."

"The holy fire belonged to me! I was going to use it—" Victor trailed off.

"To break her cuffs?" Balthazar guessed. "To free her from bondage?"

Again, Victor did not reply, but the weight of failure lay heavy on his face.

Balthazar found he pitied him. "I'll tell you something," he said. "Delilah is already free." He pointed to Victor's cuff. "By the power of the girl who wears its match. She's the Breaker I asked you about."

"Nazafareen?" Victor asked in shock. "Do you speak truly?"

"I have no reason to lie." Balthazar stood. "As it happens, I understand you better than you think. And I wish your Delilah well, although I don't expect she'll have a happy end when Neblis finds her."

Victor laughed again, or tried to. Speckles of blood dotted the clammy stone floor. "If Neblis finds her, I'll rejoice, because it will be the last thing your Queen ever does."

"Perhaps. Or perhaps Neblis will bond you with the cuffs and she won't even need fire to bend you to her will. You'll be her plaything, as I am." Balthazar considered the brazier but left it where it was. Victor had suffered enough. "I'm going to visit with your old friend now. Don't try anything rash. The other Antimagi will be watching and they are not so lenient."

Victor tipped his head against the pillar again. This time, he wore a small, contented smile. "I won't run," he said. "I lack the strength anyway. But there's nothing Neblis can do to me now. My wife is free." Victor began to hum a little tune and Balthazar suppressed a smile himself. He felt oddly good. Better than he had in a long time.

As he took the familiar route to the dungeons, he thought of Victor and Delilah, and the siege of Karnopolis. How young he had been then. Just turned eighteen, a newly-minted magus. He'd lasted all of a month in this glorious new position before being charged with witchcraft.

In the empty keep, shadowed and silent, the past seemed much closer than the present.

"Balthazar!" The Prophet greeted him with a sunny smile as though they were old acquaintances meeting for a cup of wine.

Balthazar left the door open. If the upper levels of the House-Behind-the-Veil seemed dank, the cells were downright swampy, as though the walls themselves were weeping. This fetid atmosphere was one reason servants never lasted long. But the Prophet showed no signs of the coughing sickness—not yet, at least.

"How are they treating you?" Balthazar asked. "Have they brought you proper meals?"

"Oh yes, a delicious lamb stew. I haven't eaten so well in years." He clasped his hands on his lap and looked up expectantly, grey eyes bright. He didn't seem foggy at all today. "Now what can I do for you?"

"I have a surprise. One scholar to another." Balthazar had decided to offer the Prophet something of value before asking how to forge the cuffs. He felt comfortable in the old man's company and even trusted him, in a strange way. "I won't chain you if you'll promise to behave."

"If it lets me stretch my legs for a spell, I am content to go wherever you lead," the Prophet replied.

They walked to Balthazar's chambers in companionable silence. When Zarathustra saw the collection of scrolls and artifacts inside the airy room, he bounced on his toes like a child. "Very impressive, *very* impressive! Are these all devoted to alchemy?"

"If you mean magic, yes. Half of them have been banned by your brothers as heretical. The other half are so obscure, the magi don't even know of their existence. If they did, I'm sure they would ban those too."

Zarathustra fingered his long beard. "Yes, well...we didn't always see eye to eye about that. May I?" He picked up a circlet of a snake eating its own tail. It was cunningly worked in lifelike gold scales, with rubies for eyes that shone redly in the light of the sconces.

"An ouroboros," Balthazar said. "The Greek symbol of infinity."

"Power resides in this object," Zarathustra examined it closely. "A talisman?"

"Supposedly. I obtained it from a dealer in rare objects when I visited Thebes some years ago. He claimed it prolonged the life of the owner, but I haven't yet had occasion to test it."

Zarathustra handed the talisman to Balthazar, who slipped it into his pocket and walked to a large drafting table. "Do you have an interest in geography?"

"Very much so."

Balthazar selected several large scrolls and unrolled one on the table. "These are maps of the Dominion. I've been working on them for decades."

"Fascinating." The Prophet squinted at the scroll. "And yet I see there are still many blank spots."

Balthazar smiled. "I'm not sure the Dominion has an end to it. What you see is limited to the parts I've traveled through and reports from other Antimagi." He traced a finger along the yellowing parchment. "The names are all my own. I don't believe any other maps exist of the shadowlands. I call these mountains Jamadin's Spear, after the general whose army was lost in the Dominion. They border Neblis's realm." Balthazar touched a snaky blue line that wound its way to a large body of water at the edge of the map. "This river is an outlet of the lake that shelters the House-Behind-the-Veil. It leads to the Cold Sea. I think it's where the dead go on to the next plane. I've only glimpsed the shore from afar, but I hope to see it someday." He looked slightly abashed. "I even built a small raft, in case I ever have an opportunity to explore further. A foolish whimsy, I suppose."

"What of the Bridge of Chinvat, where souls are judged?"

Balthazar shook his head. "I've never come across it. Not all the dead obediently do as they are told. Some linger near the gates, hoping for a chance to return. Over time, they become increasingly malevolent. That's why the Dominion is a dangerous place. I only venture into it when Queen Neblis requires me to."

"Do you mean the hounds that chased us?"

"The Shepherds? Neblis says they herd the dead along to the Cold Sea. They don't like the living encroaching on their territory. Do you understand the concept of gates?"

"Like the pond we came through to get here?"

"Exactly. That was a Greater Gate. Anyone with a talisman of Traveling can use it. From what I've read, only twelve exist in our world. I don't think they can be destroyed." Balthazar moved a stack of scrolls from a wooden chair and dragged it over. "Please, sit down."

"I will, thank you. My old joints are not liking the dampness in this place." The Prophet settled himself. "Now, where are these gates?"

"I have seen three with my own eyes, magus. The one here in Bactria. Another outside Karnopolis that we passed through together. And a third where the city has grown around it. In Samarkand, I watched slaves drain a gate to the bedrock to build a manor house. A month later, it returned as a marble fountain. That is why I say they cannot be destroyed."

"They are part of the fabric of the world," Zarathustra said thoughtfully. "And you say there are a dozen of these Greater Gates?"

"I believe so. There is certainly one in Babylon, and likely Jerusalem. But they aren't the only way to enter the shadowlands. Other talismans can make *temporary* gates in any sort of pool. Wine, water, blood. They will close after minutes or hours, but they can be opened anywhere." Balthazar had used such a gate to escape his prison in Karnopolis. He'd paid the blood price to open it, but was reluctant to admit this to Zarathustra.

The Prophet tapped his spidery fingers on the map. "So the gate is always liquid? That's interesting."

"I think so too. Perhaps because it is the most permeable surface. And the area around a gate...it gives the impression of being underwater, on both sides. But once you go a few leagues in any direction, the effect diminishes and the true gloaming reveals itself. A mirror of our world in many ways, but without the sun, moon or stars."

"I noticed that when we went through."

Balthazar laid a palm on the map. "I offer you a fair deal. You can examine my maps to your heart's content and ask me anything you wish about the Dominion. If I know the answer, I promise to tell you. All I ask in return is for you to tell me what negatory magic is."

The Prophet looked at him with sharp eyes. "Negatory magic? Well, it uses fire to break talismans or throw up a shield against other magic. Those who can wield it are always a mix of human and daēva." He held up his bony wrist. "It is why Xeros put this cuff on me."

"*You're* a Breaker?"

"Why do you think I know something about them, eh, Balthazar?"

Balthazar digested this for a long moment. He had not expected it, but it made a kind of sense. "Do your powers work in the Dominion?"

"Yes. Not my elemental magic, of course. I'm weak in that anyway. But my negatory magic...very much so, I'm afraid."

"Why didn't you use it to escape me? My own powers were useless until we passed through the wards shielding the House, as was the cuff that binds you. As you say, neither elementary nor talismanic magic is effective in the shadowlands."

Zarathustra's shaggy white brows drew into a stern line. "Because it is much too dangerous to wield negatory magic here. I could feel the taint the moment we passed through the gate. The poison is even more potent." He sighed and gazed out the window. The view from the summit of the tower stretched for leagues, a panorama of dark woods and serpentine rivers. "I spent years trying to tame it and finally realized it was impossible. Negatory magic cannot be safely wielded by anyone, including myself. It's bad enough in our world but here.... I would rather be at the mercy of Neblis than risk touching it even for an instant."

"I would have tried, but we've always been different that way," Balthazar said idly, and then wondered how he knew this. "Could you use it right now if you wanted to?"

Zarathustra's long beard waggled as he shook his head. "It's out of reach again. The cuff blocks it."

"Because the cuff is a talisman." Balthazar tapped the map with one finger, staring unseeingly at the tiny world he had created. "And talismans only work inside the wards."

"Yes."

"Is this negatory magic truly so evil you would hand yourself over to Neblis before using it in self-defense?"

"Evil? Not necessarily. Unpredictable? Very much so. And mixed with the wild magic of the Dominion it becomes another beast entirely. I would not meddle with such things. Does that answer your question?"

"Partly." Balthazar walked to a cabinet and took out the stone urn he had stolen from Victor. "Do you recognize this?"

The Prophet's eyes widened. "The holy fire. So you told the truth."

"I always tell the truth," Balthazar said with a thin smile. "I could use this to break your cuff."

"If I divulge my secrets."

"Yes."

"Well, that is a kind offer." Zarathustra smiled back and held up his wrist. "But this was my own creation. I did not wish to be tempted to use the destructive magic. It's not a gift, Balthazar, but a curse."

Balthazar scowled and returned the urn to its shelf, locking the cabinet door with a small key.

"Does this mean I can't see more of your fine maps? They are well drawn. You have a cartographer's instincts wedded to an artist's keen eye, Balthazar. The mountains in particular are a wonder of realism!"

He waved a hand, irritated. "Go ahead. I don't suppose it matters."

Balthazar let him pore over the scrolls for several hours. When they returned to the cell, he called on one of the servants to fetch some luminous crystals and more vellum.

"I don't wish to leave you in darkness," he told Zarathustra stiffly. "We are not all uncivilized here."

"Don't fear, Balthazar, I carry the light of the Holy Father inside me," the old man replied serenely. "Faith is a beacon that cannot be extinguished."

"That may be so, but if it's in my power to ease your current predicament in some way, I don't mind doing it." He bit his lip. "I would like to see you moved to one of the drier chambers upstairs. It serves no one to have you fall ill from evil humors."

Balthazar stood at the sound of footsteps in the corridor, expecting the items he had requested. His face hardened at the sight of Molon's familiar sneer.

"I came to see how you progress with him," the younger Antimagus said. Angry splashes of color marked his pale cheeks. "Instead of an interrogation, I find you coddling the prisoner like an honored guest." He threw a fistful of parchment into the black water that pooled in the corner. Molon must have intercepted the servant on his way back to the dungeons. "Neblis will hear of this when she returns."

Balthazar stared at him until he looked away. "Do what you

will, but I order you in our Queen's name to leave now. Your presence is not required here."

"Oh, but I think it is." Molon lounged against the door of the cell, a vicious gleam in his eyes. "We shall spend some time together soon, *holy man*. You can count on it."

"Did you not hear me? Get out before I throw you out," Balthazar said coldly.

Molon kicked over one of the inkpots. It ran in little rivulets through the straw. He brought his foot back again to kick Zarathustra when Balthazar's fingers curled around his throat.

"Do not make threats you cannot keep," Balthazar hissed, pressing Molon against the cell wall. "I would gladly see you dead, and no one would mourn the loss."

Choking noises emerged from Molon's mouth and Zarathustra laid a restraining hand on Balthazar's shoulder. "He is a misguided man but not worth the sin of murder," he said in a soothing tone. "It's a little spilled ink, that's all."

Balthazar gave Molon a final shake. Then he threw him to the wet floor, where he lay red-faced and heaving for breath. Grime smeared his pale leathers in dark patches. Tall as he was, Molon looked like a stork with a broken wing, crumpled and pathetic. He stared daggers at Zarathustra.

"If I find you anywhere near the dungeons again—" Balthazar began.

Moving faster than he would have believed possible, Molon sprang for the cell door. Balthazar's fingertips brushed Molon's shoulder as the necromancer slid past him like an eel and dove into the corridor. The heavy iron door slammed shut. Balthazar heard the deep *thunk* of the key turning in the lock.

A whisper came through the small grill. "I'll return for you later, Balthazar. For both of you."

Something smashed, a sound like breaking glass, and absolute darkness descended.

✢ 10 ✢

MOLON

Since he was a small boy, Molon had dreamed of the creature named Farrumohr. Usually, the dreams came at night, but sometimes he would be in the middle of performing some task and he would hear that dry whispering in his ear. Later, he could never remember what the exact words were. Only that when he closed his eyes, he would see terrible things. Terrible, awful, wonderful things.

Sometimes—much more often, of late—he found himself standing next to the well with no recollection of how he got there. Down and down the blackness went, like a thousand midnights poured into the throat of the cistern. It frightened him to think he might sleepwalk to the edge and accidentally fall in. Molon wondered if the well had any bottom at all. Once he'd gathered the courage to drop a pebble into its inky maw. He'd waited and waited, but no splash ever came.

Were there even deeper levels of the underworld? Doorways like the gates, but leading to far stranger places?

The thought unsettled him.

Now he stood outside the cell door, one hand delicately resting on his bruised neck, the other clutching the key to the cell that Balthazar had left in the lock. Molon swallowed painfully. It had been careless of Balthazar to leave it there, he thought with a crooked grin. Very careless indeed.

He closed his eyes, knowing the voice would come, and it did. Telling him things. Showing him pictures so vivid Molon felt he was there. Queen Neblis standing over a kneeling Balthazar, her face a mask of rage. His screams as blood ran from his eyes. Behind them, a charred body chained to a pillar. It had been burned beyond recognition but Molon knew who it was right away. He recognized the chamber, and the gold cuff gleaming against scorched bone.

You will make this vision come to pass....

Molon nodded to himself. Victor would die and Balthazar would be blamed for his murder. And Molon would be rewarded. Farrumohr would see to that.

Molon had long ago forgotten his own family, or even the fact that Balthazar had stolen him from his bed one bitter winter's night. He hated Balthazar because the dark-haired Antimagus acted like he was better than the rest of them. He was handsome and smooth in his manners and Neblis favored him above the others. But with Balthazar gone, Molon could take his place as her consort. He thought of her red mouth and pointy teeth and found himself growing aroused.

First things first. He needed to dispose of the servants. Then there would be no eyes to see what transpired this night, no tongues to wag.

Only five remained in the House-Behind-the-Veil. Molon found them together in the kitchen, sitting quietly next to the cold ovens. Four seemed to welcome what he offered them, or at least they did not fight back. Only one tried to run. It was a brief pursuit.

Molon dragged the bodies outside and tossed them into the lake. The things lurking there unnerved him because he could only see them when they moved. A sudden flash of teeth in the gloom. He hoped they would remember him and the gift he had brought the next time he had to pass through their reedy domain.

Now it's time to pay a visit to Victor.

Molon watched him from the dark for a while. The chamber was large and if one stood at the edge, on the far side of the pillar, Victor could not turn his head enough to see. Oh, he knew someone had come! But the fire was too close and it blinded him, even his special daēva eyes.

"Who's there?" Victor called, twisting and straining against his chains. "I can hear you breathing. Balthazar?"

Molon did not reply. Let Victor wonder. He would find out soon enough.

Molon had always wanted to kill a daēva. They were fast and strong, though. Worse, they had magic. Real magic. Not just the unnatural vitality of the chains or the ability to command Undead. They could do things. Make things *happen*. Daēvas could hurt you.

But this daēva had been declawed and defanged. The House-Behind-the-Veil sat empty except for Balthazar, and he was helpless too. Molon could do as he wished and there was no one to stop him.

Finally, he came forward into the firelight. Victor watched him approach.

"What is it?" he demanded, studying Molon with black hawk eyes. He seemed amused at what he found. "Neblis must be desperate to have turned a boy into a necromancer. Run back to her skirts and tell her I'm hungry now."

"Neblis is gone," Molon said softly. "I'm the only one here."

"Then fetch me some food," Victor said in dismissal. Even naked and chained, bloodied and bruised, he gave off an aura of power Molon envied. "Water too, to wash it down with. Go on, boy!"

In reply, Molon drew a knife from his belt. He turned the

blade this way and that, admiring its edge in the firelight. "How fast do you heal? Say, if you were cut deeply?"

Victor laughed. "Find out, if you're curious. I've had worse done to me."

"Have you? You might not say that when I am finished."

Molon too had suffered pain in his long life, had taken it deep inside himself and turned it into flesh and bone and muscle and will. He knew its touch as intimately as an old lover. Knew all the different guises it wore. The ache-to-the-marrow of the chains. The sharp sting of iron and shrieking jolt of fire. The daēva seemed not to fear pain but he didn't embrace it like Molon did, whatever he claimed.

"Do what you will, necromancer," Victor said. "I no longer care."

Molon stood, silent and still. Then he stepped forward and plunged his knife to the hilt into Victor's stomach, just to the left of his navel. Victor clenched his teeth with a hiss. Molon left and came back with a scrap of moldy silk he found in one of the adjacent chambers. He pulled the knife out and pressed the cloth to Victor's wound. A lot of blood came out so he pressed down harder. The filthy cloth turned a deep red.

"Let's wait for you to heal and then we'll try it again," he said. "We have plenty of time together. There's no one here, you see. Neblis won't be back for days."

Victor's skin had gone grey and clammy. Molon thought he would faint. Instead, he spat in the necromancer's face.

Molon took the cloth from Victor's wound and used it to wipe the saliva from his cheek, leaving a thick smear of blood.

"Do you think your ears would grow back if I cut them off?" he asked in a conversational tone.

"Burn in the Pit," Victor growled.

"Well, that is certain," Molon said earnestly. "But I plan to live a long time before my judgment day comes around. And I also plan to keep you alive until you choose the flames. Until you decide to give yourself over to them because you can't tolerate my company for a single moment more. I could just burn you myself, but that wouldn't be nearly as entertaining."

"Neblis will have your head if you kill me." Victor grimaced, the muscles around the stab wound tightening. He shivered.

"Or perhaps I'll start with your fingers." Molon squinted. "You're already missing three. Is that your Druj curse, Victor?" He laughed. "Here. I'll show you some of my own scars if you like."

Molon had always been ashamed of his extreme thinness, the way his ribs poked against the skin like a plague victim in the final hours. But he found he didn't feel self-conscious with the daēva. They had a special bond now. He watched for Victor's reaction as he lifted the edge of his tunic.

Molon's torso looked like a map of some riparian land, with fine white lines branching out in all directions. He turned in a slow circle to show Victor how the shiny scar tissue covered him front to back, chest to thighs.

"I earned these learning to fight while wearing the chains. Every time my feet got tangled up, Antimagus Baradin would give me a good thrashing." He bit his lip, remembering. "It wasn't easy, especially with the collared stumbling around on the other end. He always said I was a clumsy ox. But after ten years or so, I finally mastered it." He looked at Victor, who stared back with complete disinterest.

"Get it over with, necromancer. Or are you trying to bore me to death?"

Dark blood suffused Molon's face. He let his tunic fall. "Done talking, daēva? All right. Let's get back to our game. My turn."

As he worked, Molon thought of his friend in the well and all the visions he'd been given.

Such terrible, awful, *wonderful* things.

PART TWO

What sweeter than this in the world!
  Friend met friend and the lover joined his Beloved.
  —Sufi poet Abu Sa'id Abul-Khayr

❦ 11 ❧

TIJAH

"**W**ake up, Cyrus." Tijah tossed another cup of icy water in his face.

The magus from Tel Khalujah spluttered and cracked open his eyelids. He'd been a commanding presence not so many years ago. But once-rugged features had grown thin and wasted. Tijah might not have recognized him except for his robes and his dark, predatory eyes. Those hadn't changed at all.

"Tijah? Holy Father, is it truly you?"

She said nothing. Cyrus tried to rise and realized she had tied him hand and foot. He didn't seem especially surprised at this development. His gaze landed on the children.

"Where's Myrri?" he asked.

"Why were you following us?"

He feigned confusion. "Following you?"

"Please don't say you were just passing by."

Cyrus sighed. "Why are you treating me this way? I've known you since you were a girl."

"Just answer the question."

He squirmed a bit. "All right. I saw you at Tel Khalujah."

"What were you doing there?"

"I had nowhere else to go. I've been living in the palace. They burned and defiled it, but some of the storerooms escaped the blaze. You've no idea...." He trailed off. "The Druj legions came in the night, only three days' gone. Once they'd breached the gates, it didn't take long for the city to fall."

She crossed her arms. "Where are the other Water Dogs? Zohra and Behrouz. Rasam. Gobryas."

"All dead. I laid them out for the scavengers myself."

Goddess. Tijah knew it was the Persian custom not to bury the dead until their bones had been picked clean by birds and animals, but the practice still disturbed her.

"And how did you manage to survive the attack? I saw no others."

"I hid in the wine cellars. There's a false panel where Satrap Jaagos kept his stash of rice liquor from Qin."

Tijah pulled out her scimitar and pressed the point to his neck. "Whenever you want to stop lying, I'm listening."

"Why would I lie to you?"

She pressed the point a little deeper. A drop of blood trickled into the collar of his robes.

He winced. "I'm sorry for what happened to Nazafareen and Darius. Truly. I'm not what you think I am."

"What do I think you are?"

"Loyal to Satrap Jaagos. To the empire."

Cyrus had a dry, cultured voice that perfectly matched his looks. He wasn't a man who was easily rattled. Tijah remembered his quiet authority. She'd always resented it, but she'd been afraid of him too. He'd been a powerful man in the satrap's household. Well, she was no longer a teenaged runaway, always looking over her shoulder, terrified her true identity would be discovered. And she had no fear of him now. Cyrus was just a pathetic old man in the tattered robes of a magus.

"The empire doesn't exist anymore," she pointed out.

"Of course it does. It just belongs to someone else. Jaagos, on the other hand...." He looked away. "I saw him die. Along with all his guards."

"And why should I let you live? You've been following us. That doesn't look very good."

A shadow crossed his face. "I'm going the same place you are. To Gorgon-e Gaz."

"You spied on us!"

"I'd crept out for water when I saw you passing. I hid on the other side of the wall. When I heard you talking, it seemed the Holy Father had sent me a sign." Again he trailed off.

Tijah snorted. "And yet you failed to announce yourself, instead lurking behind us like a wraith."

"I didn't recognize you! You look different with short hair." He tried to sit up, wriggling like an eel in a net, then fell back again, breathing hard. "Don't you even want to know why I was heading to Gorgon-e Gaz?"

"Not really."

The self-loathing in his voice caught her off guard. "Because I'm a sinner. Because I did something terrible and another paid the price for me. This is my chance to set it right."

Tijah studied him. The bitterness etched into every line of his face. She lifted the sword from his neck. "Go on."

"The details are no one's business but my own. But there is a daēva at Gorgon-e Gaz who does not belong there."

"None of them belong there," Anu spat. It was the first time she'd spoken.

"That may well be true. But my concern is for one only." He bared his teeth in a thin smile. "I know the layout of the prison. Every inch of it. Help me and I'll help you get inside."

"I'll sleep on it," Tijah said.

"There's no time to waste."

"You think I don't know that? I said I'll sleep on it!"

CYRUS HAD PLENTY OF FOOD IN HIS PACK AND THEY ATE BETTER than they had in days. Abid's kitten devoured scraps of dried meat until its tawny belly was round as a peach. Then it yawned and promptly fell asleep, a ragged ball of fur.

You're a tough little thing, aren't you? Tijah thought. Just like the kids.

As the sun set over the mountains, Anu kept glancing at Tijah, opening her mouth to speak and then closing it again.

"Spit it out," Tijah said finally. "What's bothering you?"

"Who's Myrri?"

"What?" Her face froze.

"He asked about someone named Myrri. I just wondered—"

"None of your bloody business."

"Sorry." Anu put on her sulky face and Tijah relented a little.

"I don't want to talk about that, but you can ask me anything else."

Anu thought. "You have a funny accent. Where do you come from?"

"A place called Al Miraj."

"What's it like there?"

Abid, who was making little spider web cracks in the ground, looked over. He loved a good story.

"No more than that," Tijah cautioned him. "You'll hurt yourself."

"I won't," he promised. "I can draw a lot of power before my bones start to ache. Watch this!" He rolled a dozen stones into a tottering pile.

"Al Miraj?" Anu prompted, shooting Abid her *shut up before I pound you* look.

"Right. Imagine the ocean, except it's made of golden sand instead of water. Dunes like waves, as far as the eye can see."

"Ohhh." Abid was entranced.

"We have camels but they're nasty, ill-tempered things. Kind of like Anu over there." Abid giggled and Anu stuck her tongue out. "The horses, now." Tijah smiled, remembering. "Our horses are the finest in the world, black as a moonless night and sleek as one of the old King's warships." She stretched her legs out, settling in. "All the men wear white robes and head coverings, and the women are kept inside. With veils and long dresses too, so you can only see their eyes."

"They made *you* wear a veil?" Anu could not fathom this.

"Well, I was much younger then. My father was a merchant, so we always had piles of silks and spices, pearls and ivory." She gestured airily. "My sisters and I used to lie about eating dates while slaves fanned us with roc feathers."

"You're teasing," Anu pronounced.

"Not at all. The best thing about camels is the milk. Sweetest you ever tasted. Oh, and we had daēvas, but in Al Miraj, they're called djinn."

"Djinn," Abid repeated. "Are they the same as us?"

The moon shone bright, rising in the wedge of sky between two peaks to the north. Abid crept over and snuggled into Tijah's lap. He hadn't done that for a while.

"They're the same." She glanced at Cyrus. They'd untied him to eat and do his business, then redid the knots. Tijah had checked each one herself. Now his eyes were shut, but something in his breathing made her think he was still awake and listening.

"Tell us a story," Abid said. "A story about the djinn!"

Ishan and Kalanna, Myrri signed. *It was always our favorite.*

"Hmmm. Let's see. I do know one."

"Tell it!"

She smiled and rested her chin on the top of his head. He didn't smell that bad, actually. Like hair and boy.

"Once upon a time, there was a djinn named Ishan. He was very handsome, with raven hair and the ability to speak with wild beasts. He shunned humans and kept to the forest, preferring the company of the boar and lion to that of men. But one day, he spied a beautiful woman bathing in the stream. It was Kalanna, the warrior-queen of Kush. Ishan was instantly smitten. But Kalanna didn't trust djinn. She had been raised to believe they were tricksome and wicked. So when he approached her, riding a great white stag, she seized her bow and loosed an arrow at him."

"Did she hit him?" Anu asked, eyed wide.

"Kalanna was famous for her skill as an archer. She had never before missed a target. And yet part of her was taken by Ishan too. Her heart wasn't in it and the arrow flew wide of its mark. Ishan fled into the forest, but he had not forgotten her." Tijah stroked the kitten, which lay curled up against Abid's chest. It purred happily at the attention. "He resolved to seek her out and win her over. So he disguised himself as a human and went to Kalanna's temple to make an offering. He shed his rough garb for fine silks, and brought a chest of jewels he'd gathered from the mountain streams. She didn't recognize him as the same djinn she had seen before. His beauty and charm proved irresistible, and soon they were to be wed."

"How could she not recognize him, just because he changed his clothes?" Abid demanded. "They never explain that in stories."

"Hush," Tijah said gently. "But his ruse was to be short-lived. On their wedding day, Kalanna's courtiers made a gift to her of six mating swans, white as snow and perfect in every respect. When the swans saw their friend Ishan, naturally they greeted him with loud trumpeting cries. And Ishan couldn't help himself. He greeted them back. It would have been rude to do otherwise."

"Very rude!" Anu laughed. "What happened next?"

"Kalanna was shocked at his deception, but she had fallen for Ishan with all her heart and soul. So she made him an offer. If he would let her bind him to the cuff, she would marry him. He could refuse her nothing. And so they were bonded and married and lived happily ever after."

A slightly disgruntled silence followed.

"There's an earlier version of that story," Cyrus said, opening his eyes. "From the time before the empire. Before Al Miraj was conquered and became another satrapy."

"I never heard any other version," Tijah said, frowning.

"Not many know of it. Not anymore. The beginning is the same. But the end? Kalanna doesn't bond the djinn. She gives up her kingdom and they ride off together, beyond the forest to the shifting sands of the Sayhad. They were never seen again, but legends told of an oasis with a beautiful marble palace and date trees heavy with fruit. No traveler would go near it because of the terrifying growls of wild beasts within."

"I like the second one better," Abid said decisively.

"Me too," Anu agreed with a tiny smile. "*Much* better."

࿓

THE NEXT MORNING, THEY ENTERED THE MOUNTAINS. TIJAH was forced to untie Cyrus or they never would have made the crossing, but she watched him like a hawk, and made sure Anu and Abid did too. When the first flakes of snow began to fall, the kids danced with excitement. They had never seen snow before.

"Just wait," Tijah said wearily. "You'll be so sick of it by the time we get to the other side, you'll be happy never to see a speck of it again."

They climbed steadily until night fell. The Khusk was an even more desolate place than the Great Salt Plain, Tijah reflected, dragging her feet up the steep, rocky slope. Her lungs couldn't seem to draw enough air, no matter how hard she tried. And the cold! With the sun gone, it sank deep into her bones until she thought her blood might freeze solid. She hunched into the thin jacket she'd taken from the village. *Oh, Mami Natu, make these asshole mountains end!*

"Your lips are turning blue," Cyrus observed when they reached the top of the ridge, with yet another waiting on the other side. "It's past time to stop. If the children stay back, I can make a fire for us. I have flint."

Tijah was so cold she'd stopped shivering. A lethargic numbness crept over her limbs. And still she hesitated, thinking of Myrri. She hated fire now. Hated it with a passion.

"Go ahead," Anu said matter-of-factly. "You'll probably die if you don't. Abid and I will be fine in the shelter of those rocks." She pointed to an overhang twenty paces off.

"Listen to the girl," Cyrus said.

Too tired and headachy to speak, Tijah managed a nod. A few minutes later, the magus had summoned a small blaze in a hollow of melted snow and she had to admit, the warmth felt glorious on her frozen fingers.

"Where are Nazafareen and Darius now?" he asked.

Tijah didn't see the harm in telling him. "With Alexander, I imagine. That's where they were headed. To Persepolae."

"And Ilyas? Tommas?"

"Both dead," Tijah said shortly.

Cyrus shook his head sadly. "We heard the news of what happened. That Darius was accused of treason. I never believed it. He was always a good lad."

"Really?" Tijah scratched her head. "I seem to remember you teaching us he was Druj."

Cyrus flushed. "Well, that's... It's simply doctrine."

She gave the fire a poke. "Right."

"And Myrri?"

Tijah paused. If she didn't tell him, he'd just keep pestering. "Also gone."

"I'm terribly sorry." He didn't ask how she'd died.

Tijah thought of how Myrri had kept her alive the last time she'd crossed the Char Khala. What had Nazafareen called it? Mountain sickness.

"Did you cross the whole plain alone?" Cyrus asked.

"Yes. It's all the same as Tel Khalujah."

"Holy Father." His hands fluttered to forehead, lips and heart, making the sign of the flame to ward off evil. "What are their numbers? The Druj, I mean."

"I don't know. Hundreds. Thousands. Does it matter?"

"You said they wiped out an entire regiment of the King's army."

"Yes." Tijah pushed away the image of the boy lying facedown in the water. He'd been beyond her help. She hoped whatever gods he prayed to had welcomed him home.

"Where was this?"

"A valley to the west. Where the Char Khala meets the Khusk Range."

Cyrus considered this. "Perhaps they were returning to Bactria. It could have been a chance encounter."

"It could have been. We have no idea what Neblis intends. Although I'll tell you one thing. She has your holy Prophet."

"What?"

"He didn't die in the war. The magi lied. They were keeping him prisoner."

"And how do you know this?" he demanded.

"I was there. We tried to rescue him, but one of her necromancers got in the way."

Cyrus rocked back, dumbstruck. "Alive?" he repeated. "How?"

"I don't know, but it's true. What do you think of that, Cyrus? The father of your faith, stuck in a dark little cell by his own flock."

"I...I can hardly fathom it."

"I met Alexander, you know. At his camp on the Hellespont."

"You *have* gotten around," Cyrus said faintly. "What was he like?"

She shrugged. "Seemed a decent sort. Better than the old King, that's for damn sure. He thinks all the daēvas should be free."

"Neblis will have to face the boy at some point," Cyrus observed. "You said he was marching on Bactria?"

"That's what the Immortal told us."

Cyrus cupped his hands to the blaze, the firelight softening his mournful features. "Then she will need to call her wolves home."

"It depends on how many wolves she has."

"Indeed. But if her army was much bigger than you've described, she would have marched straight for Persepolae and Karnopolis. The capitals of the empire. The seats of power that defeated her before. Instead, she harries defenseless villages. That implies weakness."

"Perhaps." Tijah was unconvinced. "But there are no Immortals to fight her this time."

"There are more than a hundred daēvas at Gorgon-e Gaz," Cyrus reminded her. "Veterans of the first war. The oldest and strongest of their kind. If they can be freed...."

"That's the plan." She crossed her arms. "Who are you going after? It must be your bonded. Nazafareen always thought he or she had been killed, but they're not dead, are they? Just locked up. Why?"

He turned away. "That's none of your concern."

"It is if we're traveling together. What did your daēva do?"

He stayed stubbornly silent.

"That bad, huh? Fine. Let's talk about the fortress then. Weaknesses?"

"None from the landward side. But from the sea...The daēvas who escaped broke it open, did they not? They can't have repaired it yet. I've seen maps of the prison in Jaagos's library. It's why I stayed behind at that city of death. It took me days of searching, but I found the scrolls in a cleverly concealed recess behind a statue of Zarathustra. I know where the Old Ones are kept. Where the guards sleep. All of it."

"You'd better be telling the truth." Tijah leaned forward so the flames lit her sharp cheekbones and slightly tilted eyes. She'd aspired to be a great beauty once. The sort of woman who made men stammer and stare. Now she just wanted to scare the shit out of them. "By the goddess Kavi and her nine flails, if you betray us, I'll make sure you *and* your daēva regret it with your dying breaths."

"Understood," Cyrus said dryly.

She gave him one last squinty look, this man who managed to survive the massacre at Tel Khalujah with hardly a scratch. "Good. Get some rest. I've got watch."

"I don't mind—"

"I said I've got it." Tijah half turned her back on him and stared into the frigid darkness. As tired as she was, she knew there was no danger of falling asleep.

She only made that kind of mistake once.

❦

COLD AND SNOW AND ICE AND WIND. THEY WERE THE ONLY things in the world, and it seemed there had never been a time when she'd been warm. If Cyrus wanted to kill her, he could have. She wouldn't have been able to stop him.

The kids would though. They seemed fine, laughing and scrambling up the trail like a pair of goats, cheeks pink and Anu's ratty hair flying in the wind.

I should have been born daēva, she thought dismally. *They're clearly a superior race.*

On the morning of the third day, they started the descent from the highest passes. When they reached the tree line, they made a little camp and Tijah curled up in her blanket and slept for a long time. She felt better when she woke. Cyrus sat cross-legged with his eyes closed, either praying or pretending to. Anu and Abid squabbled quietly over some game they'd invented with pebbles and pine cones while his kitten stalked a fluttering cabbage moth.

Tijah drank from a stream of icy snowmelt, listening to the birdsong, the first she had heard in days. Since before they found the Numerator.

It was a good omen, she decided. A sign there was still hope.

"Let's go," she called to the others. "It's not far now."

They broke camp and wound their way down the shoulder of the mountain. The sun came out, weak at first but growing warmer as the day wore on. It was like walking straight out of the deepest, darkest winter into early spring. Tijah's steps quickened. She could smell the Salenian Sea now, just beyond the last escarpment.

We haven't come too late, she told herself. *They will be alive and we will free them. Please, Goddess. Slayer of serpents and protector of the humble. Let me be your sword arm to deliver justice on these men.*

They topped a ridge and the horizon opened up wide before them. Cobalt water capped with white wavelets gleaming like beaten metal in the sun. A shingle of beach far below. An ancient stronghold, half thrusting into the water like the prow of a ship, half squatting on the sand.

Abid and Anu hurried up beside her. Cyrus too. He made a small noise in his throat.

Tijah sank to her knees. She buried her face in her hands.

The beach was black with Druj as far as the eye could see. They pressed against the walls in a seething mass. On the edge of hearing, the wights keened their voiceless insanity.

Not home to Bactria. This was where they'd been headed all along.

Tijah felt small hands on her hair, stroking, small arms twining around her neck. Abid, trying his best to comfort her. But all the tears she'd held inside for the people of the Salt Plain and Tel Khalujah and the Four-Legs Clan, the tears she still had for Myrri, burst out in a hot, choking torrent. She sobbed until her throat was raw. Until snot streaked her face like a two-year-old. She didn't care. It was over.

Nothing left. Nothing left but to die.

One step. Just one short step into open air and it would be done. No more hope. No more pain. Cyrus could take care of the kids. She wasn't fit to anyway.

You don't even have to look down. Just close your eyes and take one step....

Tijah heard a faint rumble, like distant thunder. The necromancers must be tearing the fortress down, stone by stone. They had arrived in time to witness the final destruction of Gorgon-e Gaz.

"Look," Abid said.

"No," she said, pushing him away. "I can't!"

"Look, Tijah." More insistent. "*Look*."

Wearily, she raised her face.

A crack had split the beach, just above the high tide line. Dry sand flowed into it like a waterfall, sweeping a knot of revenants inside before it closed up again.

She grabbed Abid by the shoulders. "Did you do that?"

He shook his head. "No, I swear!"

"Anu?

The girl gave Tijah her thin smile. "Not me."

It had been a small gesture. A drop in the bucket. The Druj closed ranks again as if it had never happened, like maggots squirming over a carcass. But what it meant....

"Dear goddess, they're alive," she whispered. "They're still alive in there."

Two dozen necromancers in their pale leathers rode up and down the beach, cloaks swirling. They commanded at least a thousand revenants, wights and liches. The last were nearly impossible to see because they blended into the background shadows, like veils of greyish mist. Only when they moved or emitted those unearthly screams did Tijah know they were there.

She was glad now for the thickness of the prison's curtain wall. The wights and revenants were packed so tightly together, the sheer weight of them might have toppled anything less than the mountain of stone that was Gorgon-e Gaz.

Her initial jubilation that at least some of the daēvas trapped inside were still alive deflated just looking at the nightmarish scene below. How could they possibly get through *that*?

Tijah remembered one of her father's slaves, Efemena, a wizened little woman with only three teeth but a warm smile. Efemena had served the Qindah family since she was a young girl, rising to head the household in all but name. Girls in Al Miraj were forbidden a proper education, but Efemena used to sneak bits of the empire's history into her bedtime stories. Where

Efemena herself had learned it, Tijah never knew. But the fact that she could read and write and do sums meant Efemena must have lived a privileged life before she was captured by slavers.

Efemena was already an old woman when Tijah was born. She had skin the rich brown of a carob cake, with woolly white hair she kept tucked beneath a head scarf. Tijah and her sister would snuggle in bed while Efemena told them epic tales of love and bravery and how the first djinn came to Al Miraj. How they were given as a gift to the satrap by King Xeros for his aid in the war with the Druj.

One spring day, they came across the mountains. Rank upon rank, in an endless flood, the smell of them borne ahead on the wind. Efemena's clever eyes bored into the girls. *No one knew why. A punishment for some wickedness, perhaps. No one knows the minds of the gods.*

All they knew is that the dead walked again.

"Tijah?"

She blinked and turned to Cyrus. He was staring down at the scene on the beach with a dazed look on his face, as if he couldn't quite make sense of what he was seeing.

"This is good," she said. "We got lucky."

"Lucky?"

"Yes. They're the only reason these daēvas are still alive. As long as Gorgon-e Gaz is besieged, the guards need them to keep the Druj at bay."

"I imagine so," Cyrus said faintly. "Holy Father. I saw them when they broke through the gates, but then I ran. We all ran. By the time I came out from the wine cellars, the Druj had gone. I didn't see them...all together like this." He looked at her. "What are we going to do? My plan won't do us much good now."

"I need to think." She pressed her hands into the small of her back. "We'll discuss it later." She turned away.

"Where are you going?"

Tijah raised an eyebrow. "Can't a woman get one minute alone?"

"Oh. By all means." Cyrus turned his back, embarrassed.

She walked until she was out of sight of the others. She did have the glimmerings of an idea, sparked by something that had happened in these mountains the first time she crossed with Ilyas. Before he went mad.

If Abid was truly so strong in earth.... Goddess, there were so *many* Druj. What she wouldn't give for Achaemenes and the others. She was loosening the button of her trousers when cold steel pressed into her neck. Tijah froze. She'd thought her years scouting as a Water Dog had honed her instincts to a fine edge. Made her impervious to being snuck up on by anyone or anything. Clearly, she'd just run into someone better. She heard the whisper of her scimitar as it was unsheathed from her back. A necromancer?

Goddess, don't let me die like this. Not with my pants about to fall around my ankles.

Male voices, whispering urgently back and forth. Tijah caught a word here and there—not enough to understand, but enough to give her hope.

"The King's tongue," she said. "Do you speak it?"

They ignored this. Tijah's arms were pulled behind her back and swiftly bound with rope. At least two men, maybe more. They pushed her ahead of them along a narrow, rugged path worn into the face of the mountain. Tijah placed each foot with exquisite care. With her hands tied, she'd never recover from a misstep. And the drop to the wave-battered rocks below looked to be at least five hundred feet. If they wanted to kill her, it would be a simple matter. One gentle push and a few endless seconds of rushing air.

It was one thing to contemplate meeting Innunu on your own terms, Tijah thought queasily, quite another to have someone do it for you.

"Where are we going?" she demanded.

Nothing. She paused to look over her shoulder and felt the knife press deeper. Not breaking the skin. A reminder.

"All right. Don't get feisty," she grumbled. "Just asking what you plan to do with me. Although I'll give you a friendly warning. The last men who took me prisoner ended up on the wrong end of my scimitar. It's very sharp, by the way. Take care you don't cut yourselves."

Stony silence greeted this remark, so she gave up talking and plodded along. They'd make a mistake at some point and she'd be ready when they did.

The path finally ended at a sheer rock wall. From a distance, it looked solid. But as they approached, she heard the sharp whistle of a falcon and a boulder blocking the entrance was rolled aside. Tijah stepped through into an open space, dry and sheltered from the wind. Black goatskin tents had been erected along the rough walls. Among them stood and squatted a dozen men with long mustaches and deeply lined faces from lives spent outside in the sun and wind. She could smell animals and the cold remains of cook fires.

Hands spun her around and she saw her captors for the first time. Two young men, around her age, maybe a little older. They wore layered tunics over broad trousers cinched at the ankles with embroidered bands—the same style of clothing she'd seen on the dead boy back at the gorge. Lightweight bows hung across their backs.

The first man had dark hair and striking light green eyes. He scowled at her, folding his arms across a broad chest. The second was skinnier. Honey-colored hair and a straightforward gaze to match. An attractive man, but with unfortunate ears that stuck out like jug handles.

Tijah stared at him. Goddess, he looked familiar. And yet she was certain she had never laid eyes on him before this moment.

"Jengis there thought you were a spy for the soldiers," he said in halting Aramaic, jerking a thumb towards his companion. "But even a half-blind idiot with a gut full of fermented sheep's milk could see you were a woman pretending to be a boy." Jengis scowled more deeply, a blush creeping up his smooth cheeks. "So why don't you tell us what you're doing in the Khusk Range when even the animals have fled."

As he spoke, the men gathered around, hands on the hilts of long knives strapped to their belts. There were a few women too, Tijah saw, although their bright, cheery shawls didn't match their grim expressions. If she had a choice, she'd probably take the men over that bunch.

Tijah was just opening her mouth to reply when a wind sprang up, lifting Jengis clean off his feet. The men fell back as Anu charged through the still-open entrance, head lowered like a bull. Tents flapped madly. Tijah dug her heels in, squinting against the dust. She saw Jengis slowly rotate until he hung upside down, those pretty eyes huge with terror.

"Put him down, Anu," she said. "These people aren't our enemies."

The ground started to shimmy and shake. "Abid!" she yelled. "Come here! Right now!"

"He's out there," Anu said, pointing to the goat path. The wind was already dying, and the tremors subsided.

"Gently—" Tijah winced as Anu dropped Jengis square on his ass. He bounced up, smacking the dust off, and pulled his belt knife.

"Demons!" he cried, as the other men nodded agreement. "She travels with demons!"

"We're not!" Anu spat as she untied Tijah's hands. Abid crept forward and stood at their side.

"We heard the men talking and followed you," he whispered. "Cyrus is waiting on the path. Anu ordered him to. I think he wanted to run away."

"They're daēvas," Tijah said to the men, holding her palms out. "Not demons. Children, like yours. Kept in slavery until my friends and I helped them to escape. Do you doubt the empire lies? I saw the army they sent for you. A Numerator admitted to me with his own dying breath that they came to massacre the Four-Legs Clan."

The crowd grew quiet at this.

"None of us mean you any harm," Tijah said. "We're just trying to help those daēvas down there. The ones in the fortress. That's all we want."

A tall man stepped forward. He began to speak rapidly in the musical tongue of the Clan. Some of the others nodded in agreement, but most remained impassive.

The jug-eared man's face grew darker with each word. "We are Four-Legs Clan," he said. "Descended from the line of Fereydun, the great hero who slew the dragon Zahha. Have we become so soft that we would run away to hide with the children?"

The group began to argue heatedly among themselves. And then a woman emerged from one of the farthest tents. She had the same honey-colored hair as Jug Ears but streaked with grey, and wore a shawl covered in tinkling silver coins. Hers was not bright like the other women's, but plain white. She slowly walked to the center of the circle, looking at each man until they fell silent again.

"Two days ago, the Numerators murdered my husband in cold blood," she said in Aramaic to the tall one who had stepped forward. "Your own brother. Have you forgotten already? Now the Druj come to our mountains. *Our* lands! If we do not fight them here, none of the clan will be safe." She pointed to Tijah. "And if this woman will help us, I say she is an ally."

"We owe the Druj a blood debt as well," Jug Ears said. "My sister Ashraf. It was six years ago, but I haven't forgotten her." He stared at the tall man, who looked away, pain and guilt etched on his face.

Tijah narrowed her gaze, the threads weaving together. "Your name is Kian."

He frowned. "Yes. How did you know?"

She smiled. "Because I know Nazafareen. Your other sister."

His face froze. "She lives?"

"Yes. She lives."

Smiles and more excited talk erupted at this. The tense atmosphere began to dissipate as the men sheathed their knives.

"Kian, see these children are fed," the woman said. "And find the one who hides outside. Tell him it's safe." She stuck her hands on her hips. "Jengis, stop gaping like a beached milkfish and give her back her sword. The only thing she injured was your pride. Perhaps it will teach you not to bully women until you know who their companions are." The woman turned to Tijah. "Come. We must talk alone."

Jengis grumbled a bit when he handed over the scimitar, but the others seemed resigned to doing what they were told. As the widow of one of the khans, she clearly had some authority and was not afraid to invoke it. Two of the women came forward, tentatively beckoning Anu and Abid to join them.

"It's all right," Tijah said, ruffling Abid's hair. "Thank you for coming to my rescue, but I don't think you need to worry. Go on. I'll find you shortly." She looked at Anu. "You're in charge of him. Try not to offend anyone too badly."

"I'll try," Anu said in a tone that implied nothing of the sort, particularly since she followed it up with the hand sign meaning *ratfuckers*.

Tijah snorted. What would Myrri make of this girl?

She'd like her, that's what.

"Come," the woman barked. "Idle chatter is for crows and simpletons. I don't think you're either, but only time will tell."

She started marching toward her tent, leaving Tijah no choice but to follow. Inside was a sleeping pallet covered with a wolf fur blanket and a pile of rainbow yarn, half-woven into a scarf. Thick rugs covered the stony ground.

"Sit," she commanded.

Tijah dropped to her knees as the woman took up a small loom and began working the shuttle back and forth. "My name is Samahe. You know my daughter. Now tell me, what sort of trouble has she gotten up to?"

Tijah cleared her throat. "Trouble?"

"Yes. We *are* talking about Nazafareen, are we not? Trouble follows that child like a lovesick ram after a fat ewe."

Tijah smiled. "Where to begin? We were Water dogs together at Tel Khalujah. Then she fell in love with her daēva and defied the King to protect him. Artaxeros threw her in the dungeons but she managed to escape. She's with the barbarian King now."

Samahe sniffed. "Why does that not surprise me? She always did think with her heart and not her brain. Nazafareen has more courage than half these men, but like a braying donkey, she doesn't know when to keep her mouth shut." This was said with fondness. "And her daēva?"

"They are still together. He loves her too."

"I wish them happiness then. I knew she would never marry into the Clan. None of these fools could handle her." Samahe sighed. "They are afraid and I cannot blame them. When the soldiers came, they said they wished to speak with the elders. That there was trouble in the north."

"So they said nothing about Nazafareen?"

"No. Why?" Samahe's eyes narrowed. "Has she something to do with it?"

Tijah didn't have the heart to tell this woman that her own daughter was indirectly responsible for the death of her husband.

"Not that I know of," Tijah replied, calmly meeting Samahe's gaze.

There was a long silence. "If she did, it's not the child's fault," Samahe said at last. "And I would ask you not to speak of it to anyone else. What's done is done. The Clan's blood is on the hands of the Numerators. My husband went out to meet them and they drew their swords and struck him down, and a dozen others too before we managed to flee. Our people and herds are with the Seven-Legs Clan now, across the mountains. A few of us stayed to lead the soldiers away on a false trail."

"And then the Druj found them," Tijah said.

"Yes. The lion came and devoured the hyena. But when it gets hungry again, we'll have its jaws at our throats."

"Do you think they will stay and fight?" Tijah asked, nodding toward the men outside the tent.

"In the end, yes. Nazafareen's uncle is not a bad man, but he fears for his wife and children and longs to return to them. He was forced to kill Ashraf with his own hand, you know. It was a mercy. My daughter was already gone even if her heart still beat, but he will live forever with the guilt. Ashraf was only seven." Her mouth twisted. "The others all lost family to the Numerators. They understand we must make a stand or there will be nothing left to defend. The Clans have lived in these mountains for untold generations. We carry the stone in our hearts and the streams in our blood. It seemed a lost cause before you came, but with daēvas.... Are you bonded?"

Tijah hesitated. "No. The two children are free. Nazafareen... she broke their cuffs. Not her daēva. She did it on her own."

Samahe nodded slowly, seeming unsurprised. "She has the blood. I always wondered if she would."

"The blood?"

Samahe stared at Tijah for a long moment, then nodded to herself as if she'd reached a decision. "I will tell you something I never told my daughter. Kian doesn't know either. But I am not Clan-born. They took me in as a child. My people are the Scythians. The warrior horsemen of the plains. And my mother...well, they thought her mad. She claimed to have been seduced by a demon."

Tijah blinked. "A daēva, you mean?"

"I don't know. Probably. But he got her with child. And then people started to whisper that she could do things. Make the wind blow and the clouds bring rain. My grandfather thought she was a witch. He treated her cruelly. I was quite young, but I remember some of it. She took her own life in the end. Rode her horse straight into the sea and never turned back. That is the way of the Scythians. Horse and rider would rather die together than live apart."

"Why did you never tell Nazafareen?"

"My adopted parents forbade me to speak of it. They raised me as their own. Told the Clan I came from distant relatives in the Char Khala. And keeping secrets is not one of my daughter's talents. She would have spilled the beans at the first opportunity and then tongues would wag. They would never accept her, or Kian, if they knew. Kin ties are everything."

"Why are you telling me this now?"

Samahe shrugged. "I could be dead tomorrow. If you ever see Nazafareen again, you can tell her the truth. That she has the daēva blood. My mother showed no sign of it until she was a teenager. I always wondered if it was a gift that came with a woman's first moon. As for myself, I would love to call lightning down on those monsters, but it seems to have skipped a generation." She smiled wryly. "So you were a Water Dog? You wear the cuff, and yet you are not bonded?"

"My daēva is dead," Tijah said, more harshly than she'd intended. "She died in a fire."

Samahe's brown eyes grew sad. "May the Holy Father shelter her. I'm sorry for your loss then. Let us avenge our dead together."

Tijah nodded. She understood vengeance. It was all she had left. And then Samahe surprised her by leaning forward and pulling her into a warm embrace. Her hair smelled of people and animals and some kind of sweet oil that made Tijah remember the frankincense trees growing outside her father's manor house.

She swept a hand across her eyes. She would always be Al Miraji. She would show her enemies no mercy. But right now, held in Samahe's strong arms, it felt like a small part of her had come home.

WHEN THEY RETURNED TO THE MAIN PART OF THE CAVERN, THE women were fussing over Abid's dimples and long eyelashes while Anu chewed her nails with her usual sour expression. Cyrus greeted Tijah warmly, although he seemed distant when she introduced him to Samahe and explained that he too knew Nazafareen. The magus looked pale, almost wasted. Tijah wondered if he was falling sick. The Four-Legs Clan and their herds thrived in the thin, cold air of the Khusk Range, but it could be deadly for those who weren't used to it, as she knew from bitter experience.

"It's nothing," he said when she asked him about it. Cyrus rubbed his hands together, putting on a strained smile. "I smell hot food. It seems the Holy Father will see to it we have full bellies tonight at least."

"Oh, does He cook?" Tijah muttered, earning a sharp look from the magus.

Moments later, bowls of steaming hot stew were handed out from an iron pot in the far corner, and both Tijah and Anu agreed it was the best thing they'd ever tasted.

When the meal was done, everyone gathered on the wide ledge outside. Altogether, two dozen of the clan—twenty men and four women—had remained behind in the Khusk. A pitiful army to send against the Druj. But as she looked at their faces, Tijah saw no fear. These were Nazafareen's people and she thought she understood her friend better knowing them. The granite streak of stubbornness that lay beneath Naz's irreverent exterior.

Darius is lucky she bonded him, she thought ruefully. *He's just as bull-headed in his own quiet way. Another woman might have given up trying to get a rise, but not Nazafareen. She'll happily poke you until you crack into a million pieces, but in the end, dear friend, that's exactly what you needed.*

A full moon rose over the sea, swollen and bright, painting the beach far below in shades of burnished silver. Tijah slid a whetstone along the edge of her scimitar, testing it with a finger until she drew a drop of blood.

"So," she said, looking down at the writhing shadows below. "What do you think about dropping this mountain on their heads?"

Everyone thought this was a fine idea, even Nazafareen's uncle.

"As you've already seen, Anu is strong in air," Tijah said, deliberately not looking at Jengis. "She can handle the liches. Right, Anu?"

The girl gave a firm nod.

"And little Abid here, his talent lies with earth. He can't draw too much of the power or it will hurt him, that's the price of it, but if he can find a weakness in the rock.... When I crossed these mountains a few months ago, necromancers used their power to trigger an avalanche. I say it's time we paid them back."

Abid studied the cliff face above. "I already looked," he said proudly. "There is a place where the ice has made it rotten. I think I can break it."

Tijah gave the Clan more or less the same speech she'd given the daēva children. A primer on how to kill Druj. Beheading worked for wights and revenants, but it was the necromancers that truly worried her. They didn't go down easily.

"What of the prisoners?" Kian asked. He exchanged looks with the other men. "We've always kept our herds far from

Gorgon-e Gaz and not only because the King's soldiers kill any who venture near. The creatures inside are dangerous, if you believe the stories. They fought for the Druj."

"Horseshit," Tijah said firmly. "They *saved* us from the Druj. King Xeros feared retaliation for bonding them into slavery, so he sent them here and used them as breeding stock. The children I travel with, their parents are inside."

"Even if that's true, what of the guards? What do we do with them?"

"That's trickier," Tijah said. "Cyrus can explain it better."

The magus stepped forward. "First, you must understand the bond. How it works. The human wearing the cuff controls the daēva's power. He or she cannot use it themselves, but they can open and close the flow, like a sluice gate."

Kian nodded.

"The bond cannot be altered, except in three ways." He held a finger up. "One, the cuffs can be given back to the holy fire that forged them. That will free the daēva forever. Two, the human may pass the bond to another by giving them the cuff. Three, the human dies."

"So we kill the guards?" Kian asked.

Cyrus shook his head. "No. Death only severs the bond to that particular person. If another does not take up the bond, the daēva's power will simply be trapped in the cuff. He or she would be unable to touch it."

"And we need them to help fight the Druj," Tijah said.

She had not told Cyrus there was a *fourth* way to break the bond: Nazafareen's magic. But since Nazafareen was not here, it hardly mattered.

"What do we do then?" Kian shared a look with his mother. "If we keep the guards alive, they will fight us. If we kill them, the daēvas will be useless."

"Daēvas are never useless," Cyrus said in a lecturing tone. "They are still stronger and faster than you will ever be. But I agree we need their power. That leaves only one option. We have to convince the guards it's in their interests to surrender. They will keep the bonds until we manage to break them permanently. But they will not hold the daēvas' power in check."

Kian laughed. "A small request. I'm sure they'll be happy to oblige."

"They will when I lay out the alternative," Tijah said with a grim smile of her own.

"Which is?"

"That I know a dozen ways to make a man beg for death without inflicting mortal wounds." Cyrus glowered at her. "Yes, yes. And that both Persepolae and Karnopolis have fallen, Alexander is the new King and he has outlawed the slavery of daēvas as well as men. They are all alone now, and if they hope for clemency, they'll do as they're told."

"Men are most likely to listen to reason when their own hides are about to be skinned," Samahe observed. "Loyalty is a funny thing. In times of war, it tends to get passed around like a bladder of cheap Ramian wine. Put it to them in the right way and those guards will be falling over themselves to swear fealty to the young barbarian."

"So we just need enough time to reach the fortress and liberate the reinforcements," Kian said thoughtfully.

"Exactly. We break through to the daēvas inside and *persuade* the guards to release their power," Tijah said. "There are more than a hundred daēva prisoners. More than enough to handle the Druj that are left."

"It could work," Nazafareen's uncle said. "If you're certain these daēvas can be trusted."

Tijah wasn't certain of anything, but she nodded in what she hoped was a confident way. "I met one of the daēvas who escaped some weeks ago. He despises Queen Neblis and is risking his life to see her defeated. A brave man, famous for his heroics during the war." All that was true, although if the other Old Ones were anything like Victor, getting them to obey orders would be like trying to teach a cat to belly dance.

"How do we get down there?" Cyrus asked. He was staring at the fortress with a strange, wistful expression.

"There's a road nearby leading down to the beach," Samahe said. "They use it to supply the fortress." She had a knife in her hand, and two more in her belt.

"May we speak for a moment?" Tijah asked her.

The two women stepped inside the cavern, leaving the others to work out the last details.

"I have a favor to ask," Tijah said. "I want you to stay with the children. If I die today, they will have no one to look after them."

"What about the magus?"

"I'm asking you," Tijah said. "I don't trust him. Not entirely. There's something he's hiding."

Samahe raised an eyebrow. "Everyone's hiding something, girl. The souls of men are like dark tents." She laughed. "Full of hidden obstacles and smelling of feet. Why should he be any different just because he's an emissary of the Holy Father?"

"He used to be bonded. He says his daēva is down there, but he won't tell me why."

Samahe sighed. "You care very much for these children, don't you?"

"They have no one else," Tijah said, dodging the question.

Nazarfareen's mother gave her a probing look and didn't seem to like what she found. "Don't let your grief make you do something stupid, girl. We've all lost people we love. Throwing your own life away won't bring her back. Men pretend they're the strong ones, but they're as brittle as late spring ice when it comes to grieving. A woman should have more sense." She made a noise of irritation. "Don't do anything stupid, girl," she said again.

Tijah stayed silent. She didn't trust herself to speak.

Samahe stared at her, hard. Then she seemed to relent. "Well, I suppose one old woman won't turn the tide of battle either way."

She led Tijah to her tent and retrieved the now finished scarf, wrapping it snugly around her shoulders. "For luck. If you intend to die with the Clan, at least you can look the part."

She kissed Tijah quickly on each cheek, pretending not to see the tears that glistened there.

⁂

"I'M STAYING WITH YOU," ANU SAID, PRODUCING HER MOST mulish look. They stood on the ledge apart from the others, as the men gathered the horses.

"Don't be an idiot. We need you up here, where you can see what's going on. I'll be fine."

Her scowl deepened. "You're going to go get killed, aren't you? Just like Achaemenes."

"We always knew it would come to this, Anu," Tijah said gently. "We have to fight. Your parents are inside, I'll find them —" She cut off as Anu hurled herself bodily at Tijah, wrapping skinny arms around her waist.

"I don't care about them anymore!" she wailed. "I don't even know them! You're the one I...want...." She broke down completely then, and Tijah felt her own throat tightening again. Mami Natu help us, she thought wearily. Don't let her see you cry too, that'll just make things worse.

"Samahe is staying with you and Abid—" she tried.

"But I don't *want* Samahe." The raw desolation in her voice cracked Tijah's heart right in half. She couldn't think of a single thing to say that wasn't a lie or false comfort, and Anu wasn't the type of child to tolerate that sort of nonsense. So she just held her, stroking her tangled, dirty hair, until the sobbing subsided.

"Be brave for me, Anu. You can." She tilted her tear-stained face up to the moonlight. "I think you're the bravest girl I ever met."

"Not as brave as you," she said, sniffling.

"Braver," Tijah said solemnly. "You never let them break you. And this won't break you either. No matter what happens."

Anu's lower lip trembled, but only for a moment. Then she set her jaw. "Kill the monsters, Tijah," she said. "All of them."

Tijah nodded, cupping Anu's cheeks the way her own mother used to when she had the night terrors. She wanted to tell her that when it was all over, she'd never leave her again. That they could stay together always. But Tijah never made promises she couldn't keep. "I will," she said.

⚜

ABID HUGGED HER FIERCELY. HE WAS EXCITED AT HAVING SUCH an important job, and seemed oblivious of Anu's black mood. Of course, she never looked exactly *happy*, so it was hard to tell. Tijah was just relieved she wouldn't have to face another tearful scene. Her heart felt like a bruise. Like something that might rupture at the slightest touch.

So she put on her Water Dog face and stepped up into the saddle, not looking at anyone, while Cyrus finished giving the Clan the final blessings.

I never promised, she reminded herself, knowing it was a lie. She hadn't said the words. But part of her had wanted to. And part of her wanted to keep that promise. The other part missed Myrri like a bottomless black hole in the world.

Grief is its own prison, she thought, looking down at the fortress, pale grey in the moonlight. *And I just want to be free*.

They rode single file through the mountains. The goat path led to a wider road, the same she'd taken to Gorgon-e Gaz when they were chasing after Victor. She hadn't thought of him in a long time. Now she wondered what had happened to his quest to steal the fire back from Neblis. Another piece of work, Victor was. As strong as his son and ten times as arrogant. Still, he'd come in handy right about now. So would Darius and Nazafareen.

But as her mother used to say, *If wishes were fishes, the Sayhad would be the Crimson Sea and we'd all be pirate queens.*

Higher and higher the moon rose. Tijah could hear the waves now, a rhythmic murmur. And above that, another sound. An overlapping cacophony of a thousand inhuman voices. She could almost make sense of it, catch what seemed like words here and there, but then it dissolved into a sea of pure chaos. The hair on the back of Tijah's neck stood up. She didn't need to understand what they were saying. The Undead's hunger for what lay inside the fortress was palpable.

Her horse sensed it too, whickering anxiously. Tijah soothed the creature with a hand on its trembling neck, hoping there were no sentries nearby. But why would the necromancers bother? They believed the mountains to be deserted of people, Tel Khalujah and the other satrapies burned. Alexander was the last remaining threat and he marched on Bactria.

The road wound down to the beach half a league from Gorgon-e Gaz. Abid was supposed to wait until they were safely off the cliff face before he triggered the landslide, but it wouldn't be long now. Tijah hummed with nervous energy. How she wished for Myrri's night vision! Then a flash of blue lightning rent the sky, briefly illuminating the beach. Another forked down, and another. At first she thought the daēvas inside had called it down somehow. But no thunder followed. And then she saw it was not striking the Druj but the fortress itself. Stone cracked as the necromancers wielded their dark magic.

"Holy Father," Cyrus murmured, reining up beside her. "I never thought I would see Gorgon-e Gaz defeated. Those walls are twenty feet thick. How much longer do you think they have before it falls?"

"I don't know. Hours. Minutes, maybe." She balled her fists in frustration. "Why don't the guards just let them use the power to fight back? There are over a hundred daēvas in there!"

"There can only be one reason. They are more afraid of their charges than they are of the Druj," Cyrus responded quietly. "They fear retaliation for years of ill-treatment."

"But they'll all die!"

A wind sprang up, coming from far out at sea. It drove tattered clouds across the moon, rising quickly to an ominous high-pitched whistle. The crashing of the waves grew louder.

"Opinions inside may be divided," Cyrus said in his dry voice. "Unless you think Anu could summon something like this?"

Tijah could hear the screams of the liches as they were torn apart in the gale. A scattering of raindrops hit her face.

"No," she said faintly. "Not Anu alone. I saw Tommas call a sandstorm once, but he did in concert with Darius and Myrri. So you think at least some of the daēva prisoners have slipped their leashes?"

"It would appear so," he agreed. "Their bonded guards must be cooperating. It's the only way."

"Well it's about damn time," she said. "And what's taking Abid so long?"

The rain quickly turned to a downpour. She could hear the men and women of the Four-Legs muttering to each other as the minutes slipped by. Tijah began to fear something had gone wrong. They'd agreed Abid would give them an hour to reach the beach. It had been at least twice that long. Finally, Jengis forced his horse through the knot of riders, reining up beside her.

"The daēvas have failed us!" he said angrily.

"Just wait," Tijah said. "Give him just a few more minutes—"

"We came to kill Druj! Are we to stand around all night, wringing our hands like old women?" he demanded disdainfully. And then he stood in his stirrups, swept an arrow from the quiver on his back, and let it fly.

Tijah followed its long arc down the beach, lit by flashes of lightning. Jengis gave her a triumphant grin as the arrow buried itself in the throat of a necromancer. He screamed, tumbling from his enormous stallion and dragging doll-eyed captives, linked by collars and chains to the Antimagus's wrist, to the sand behind him.

"Oh, you idiot," Tijah murmured under her breath.

For the Druj were turning in their direction now. She heard a collective growl of recognition as they spotted the small band of riders down the beach. Tijah felt the black, insectile eyes of the wights, empty of whatever had once made them human, yet alive with alien intelligence. One of the revenants raised its huge sword to the sky and bellowed. The Undead army swarmed down the beach.

So many of them. Too many. And yet that's how the dice have landed.

"Goddess Innunu protect me this day," she whispered. "Guide my sword truly against the enemies of the light. And if I fall, welcome me home to the Mother."

Tijah dug her heels in and the trembling horse leapt forward. She rode in the vanguard, the tip of the spear. Wind rushed in her ears, rain pelted her face. She could hear the wild war cries of the Clan behind, urging her on. And then out of the corner of her eye, she sensed a presence, heard the echo of ghostly hoofbeats. Tijah was afraid to turn her head lest it vanish like a half-remembered dream, but it brought a smile to her face.

We ride together, sister. One last time.

❧ 14 ❧

NAZAFAREEN

I dropped to my knees on the trampled grass. Darius was gone.

He could be dead and I wouldn't even know. The possibility brought a fresh spasm of misery. Too late I thought of the fire magic. My first instinct was still to reach for cold iron when danger threatened. Could I have wielded it against them somehow? But I hadn't sensed any talismans, or other magical devices. If I had, the huŏ mofa would have woken on its own.

What good was it if I couldn't even use it to save the man I loved? Fury swept through me in a crimson tide. I slashed at the grass with my sword until I could no longer lift my arms.

Delilah's shadow fell over me.

"Go away," I growled.

Seven dead abbadax curled on their sides, along with three of the horses. The last must have fled in terror across the prairie. I could smell the blood of the creatures, like some musky, exotic spice.

"That's what I intend," she said coolly. "But we must speak first."

I glanced up at Delilah's mournful face. She'd bound the gash in her arm with a strip of cloth. For a woman who'd lost both husband and son, she seemed surprisingly calm. Of course, that only made me angrier.

"What in the Pit does that mean?"

"Think, Nazafareen. Why did the abbadax take him?"

"To punish me," I muttered.

"No. It wanted Darius alive."

That got my attention. "You mean as another hostage?"

"Perhaps. Or...?"

I tried to tamp down the pain and rage. I couldn't help Darius this way. And I didn't want Delilah to think I was a child.

"So I would follow," I said slowly.

The wind sang in the grasses. We both gazed in the direction the abbadax had flown. Away from the mountains and Neblis's lair.

"Precisely," Delilah said.

"But why?" I slammed my sword into its scabbard, the fury bubbling up again. "Why? She already had us in the palm of her hand!"

Delilah frowned. "I don't know. But we walked into a trap. The nine she sent were only a distraction. The real danger lay above, but we were too foolish to look for it."

Her words had the ring of truth, but it still made no sense. I was tired of being in the dark. Tired of reacting to events I barely understood. "You have to tell me something," I said, no longer caring if I offended her. "Why is Neblis keeping Victor alive? What does she want with him?"

She regarded me without expression.

"He's at the heart of this, and I want to know why. I deserve to know!"

Her hand tightened around the staff. I glared back, fist clenching. At last she sighed and looked away. "Neblis thinks he wronged her."

That much was obvious. "And did he?"

"No!" Her blue eyes flashed, and how like her son she looked at that moment. "Victor never returned her feelings for him, that's all. Neblis is...disturbed. She convinced herself that he had loved her once and thrown her over for me."

"So she imagined it all," I said flatly.

"I'm telling you what I know for truth," Delilah said through gritted teeth. "She simply appeared one day. We were already married. I'd known Victor for many years. There were no secrets between us. We lived alone, deep in the forest—that is the way of our kind. Neblis walked out of the trees one day and tried to lay claim to him." Delilah shook her head at the memory. "Said she had been searching for him."

"How can you be so sure?"

"The look on his face when he first laid eyes on her.... A man cannot fake that. If she'd been an old lover, he couldn't have concealed a spark of recognition. Of guilt. But he smiled the way you would to greet a stranger. Polite. Welcoming. There was no artifice in it. And his confusion when she grew enraged at our union—again, I know Victor better than anyone. It was sincere."

"All right," I said grudgingly. "It does sound like she's mad or... I don't know. Perhaps she mistook him for another daēva?"

Delilah shrugged. "I cannot say. It was the last we saw of her for many years. But then she returned. It was shortly before Victor left to meet Zarathustra."

"Lysandros told me she took Bactria as a haven for the daēvas. She drove out the humans who lived there, but it was such a brutal purge, she turned the rest of you against her."

"Neblis claimed to have done it for all of us, but I do not think she meant to share it. She wanted Victor, that's all. When he went to Bactria bearing a message from the other daēvas, she refused to let him go. He finally managed to escape." Her face hardened. "But it hardly matters now. She is our enemy as surely as she is yours."

Something seemed off in her story, but it was clear Delilah

believed it. Maybe Neblis *was* mad. "So what do you propose?" I asked.

"I propose nothing," Delilah said, all icy and imperious again. "I am telling you I intend to go after Victor myself. To find the House-Behind-the-Veil and take him from her."

"So you love your husband more than your son," I said bitterly.

"I see no need to choose," Delilah snapped, although she already had. "You will go after Darius."

"Of course I will. But I'd stand a better chance of finding him if you came too."

The high grasses whispered to each other in the pocket of silence that descended.

"Darius is my only child," she said at last. "Victor and I...we tried to make a family. For many long years. I thought one of us was barren. After the war, at Gorgon-e Gaz, they brought us together. Only the one time. When my belly began to swell, it gave me something to live for even though I knew what was coming." Her mouth twisted. "Victor sired others. It was done against his will and I do not blame him for it. But Darius was *mine*. And they took him from me."

I said nothing. There was nothing I could possibly say.

"I tried to spare him the cuffs," she continued in a dead voice, "but the guards were too fast. So I watched as my perfect child was bonded. Watched his arm wither and die before my eyes. And that is how I knew him at Persepolae."

My cheeks burned. I expected her to tell me what a filthy thing our bond was. How Darius deserved to be free. Instead, she studied me for a long moment.

"You love Darius just as I love Victor. In this, we are the same. So I expect you to understand." Delilah abruptly turned away before she could see the surprise on my face. "Follow the river." She pointed off to the left. "That's the way the abbadax flew."

"How will we find each other again?"

She shook her head. "Just take my son through the nearest gate. Leave this place."

"But I have no talisman of Traveling." The full weight of this sank in and a fresh wave of despair washed over me. "We're trapped here. In the land of the dead."

"If you find Darius, with luck you will find Lysandros too. He can bring you both through."

It seemed a very thin thread on which to hang our hopes. "And you?"

Delilah gave me a mirthless smile. "The talisman Lysandros carries came from Neblis. She must have others."

I crouched down next to my poor horse. Her name had been Balius. She lay on her side, guts spilling through ragged claw marks in her belly. I touched her velvety muzzle and wished her spirit a safe passage to the next plane, then quickly unbuckled the saddlebags and discarded all but two days' worth of food and water.

Delilah took nothing but her staff.

"Farewell, Nazafareen," she said, cool as ever. "May the Nexus watch over us both, even in this gods-forsaken place."

"Good luck," I said, feeling a sharp pang of loneliness. Delilah and I were hardly friends, but she was the last of us. "I hope you find him."

She started running toward the mountains. I watched her until the grasses swallowed her up. Then I set off through the matted-down tunnel the abbadax had come through. Within a few minutes, I found the river. The current flowed swiftly, leaping and surging in the silvery half-light. It sounded loud in the desolate landscape, but I didn't mind because the alternative would have been absolute, crushing silence.

I felt like the last person on earth. The last *living creature* on earth. I walked and walked, keeping the mountains at my back. The dome of the sky was blank and grey. I scanned it for signs of the abbadax but saw none.

After an untold time, the tall grasses receded behind me and turned to rolling hills covered in purple heather. My mind wandered the way it will when you walk for hours with no particular destination. I thought about Tijah and Myrri, and that terrible night in the tunnels. *Where are you now, dear friend? Safe with Alexander, I hope. Forgive me for leaving you, but I had no choice. And Myrri.... Did you come this way, sister? Am I even now following in your footsteps?*

The mountains dwindled behind me. The ground grew barren and rocky. Great boulders shot with veins of yellow and pink quartz thrust from the earth. I scrambled over them using my hands as much as my feet. The exertion kept me from thinking too much. If Darius was alive, I would find him. I refused to consider any other possibility.

I kept to the riverbank. The abbadax had flown that way and it was the only thing in this place with any semblance of life. It had to lead *somewhere*. And the perfect stillness of the moors terrified me. They seemed the sort of place one could wander through forever and never encounter another living soul.

When I could walk no further, I sat down and ate some hard bread. Then I curled up and almost immediately fell asleep. I had meant only to rest for a bit, but my exhausted body didn't care if I was alone in a dangerous land with no one to watch over me. Once horizontal, it simply shut down. I don't think I dreamed. If I did, I had no memory of it.

I awoke some time later to the echo of my own name. It seemed to come from a great distance.

Nazafareen.

I rolled to a sitting position and looked around. The river lay on my left. I'd reached a narrow point where the course narrowed to frothy, rock-filled rapids. They made a steady roar that drowned out everything else. I must have imagined it. Still, it seemed to me the invisible watchers were back. I couldn't say why, only that I felt on edge.

I ate a handful of dates and went to the river's edge to wash up. As I cupped my hand to splash the cool water on my face, the voice came again, spidery fingers brushing the nape of my neck.

Nazafareen.

I leapt to my feet, scrubbing water from my eyes. There! A flash of pale skin and dark hair far downstream. It darted behind a mossy boulder. I snatched up the bag of food and ran in pursuit, trying not to trip headlong on the uneven ground. I leapt to the far side of the boulder. No one there.

Not Delilah. The person I glimpsed had been much smaller. The size of a child.

Specters sent to taunt me, I thought grimly, shouldering the leather sack. Or tricks of the twilight. The rest had done me good and I set out again at a brisk pace, avoiding the sandy banks where my footprints would stand out like a signal fire. I didn't think anyone was following, but I'd learned to hide my tracks as a Water Dog, even though I was usually the hunter and not the hunted.

The hours slipped away and the ground became softer, muddier. Stagnant pools appeared with dead trees poking from their depths like skeletons. The river widened and grew sluggish, joining other waterways until solid ground had all but disappeared. Despair lay heavy on my heart, but still I pressed on in the twilight. There was no river to follow anymore, and I wondered if my determination to follow it had ever mattered in the first place.

I knew nothing about the Dominion. What if the abbadax were not sent by Neblis after all? What if they were simply hunting for food or sport? They left no tracks to follow. If I'd only had the bond, I could find Darius anywhere. Of course, it was the thousandth time I'd thought this. How could I use the fire magic to my advantage? I didn't know.

The smell of rot thickened. Thick scum floated on the surface of the water.

Another flash of movement ahead. My imagination?

Not this time.

"Wait!" I cried out. A figure flitted through the dead trees, always keeping just ahead despite my best efforts to catch up. If it meant me harm, I reasoned, it could have easily crept up on me while I slept. And it knew my name.

I hopped from tuft to tuft, but even those were growing farther apart. I had no idea how far down I might sink if I accidentally fell into the black waters of the mire.

"Don't go that way," a high, clear voice said from behind me. "You'll be swallowed up in two steps."

I spun around, pulse beating wildly in my throat. Knowing, even before I saw her, who would be standing there. It had been six years, but I knew that voice as well as my own.

"Ashraf," I croaked.

My sister looked the same as I'd known her in life. Frozen in time at the age of seven, with impish features framed by long brown hair a shade darker than mine. To my vast relief, her eyes were not the hard black almonds of the wight that had taken her as we crossed the mountains. They were the bright blue of my memories.

She regarded me silently for a moment. She didn't seem a ghost at all, but flesh and blood. She wore a simple cotton dress with flowers embroidered at the hem. I remembered my mother sewing that dress for her a month before she died.

"You're not real," I whispered, nails digging into my palm. "Go away."

The apparition smiled. The gap in her teeth hadn't changed either. "Did you come back for me, Nazafareen? Is that why you're here?"

I stared at her, my heart an open wound. I must be going mad.

"I only wanted to warn you." She stepped forward and took my hand before I could pull it away, small fingers twining through my own like she used to do, and Holy Father, they felt warm. Solid.

I somehow found my voice, although it came out choked and strange. "Warn me of what?"

"She's looking for you."

No need to say *who*.

"I already know that." I heard the patronizing, older sister tone and bit back hysterical laughter. Here we were, falling into our old ways. Except this was the place of the dead and Ashraf.... I had last seen her plummeting into the depths of a howling blizzard after she tried to kill me. Twice.

Ashraf dropped my hand, hugging her thin body. "I saw her. The barefoot woman in silver. So quiet she is. I hid myself."

"Where?" I looked around the mire. "Close by?"

"I'm not sure." She paused. "Things move here. They *change*."

I stepped away from her, palm dropping to the hilt of my sword. "Why can I see you?" I demanded.

"Maybe I was meant to help," she said thoughtfully. "It's lonely here, Nazafareen. I miss mama."

The mention of our mother made my breath hitch in my throat. It seemed like not long ago we would all sit around the fire while my father told stories and she would knit her beautiful woolen shawls. She'd given me one when I became a Water Dog. It had been my prized possession, one of the only keepsakes to remind me of home during those long, lonely years as a novice.

"I haven't seen her or Kian in a long time," I confessed.

"I wish you'd brought my puppy," my sister said, lifting her pointy chin the way she always did just before she was about to cry, and something in me crumbled to dust. I took her in my arms, holding her tight. She even smelled right, a mix of goat and girl.

Ashraf loved our goats, treating them as pets no matter what Father said. She would kiss their faces—on the lips, if she could get away with it—and then chase Kian around threatening to kiss him too. Eventually he would let her catch him, and they would play wrestle among the tents. Kian always indulged Ashraf, while lording his two years' seniority over me, because she was the baby. The last time I remember them playing the goat-kissing game, I was thirteen and thought myself too old for such antics. I'd watched them scream and laugh with crossed arms and a haughty expression.

We were just getting ready to leave for the brutal trek across the Khusk Range. The Four-Legs Clan numbered four hundred and sixty-seven souls then, not counting the six babies who were due to be born after we reached the winter pastures. Father had just given Ashraf a puppy, hoping a proper pet might get her to lay off the goats. I was supposed to be watching her during the journey. Keeping her safe.

"I missed you," I whispered into her hair. "Every minute of every day. I'm so sorry." I started to cry then and didn't stop for a long time. All the tears I'd kept inside and forged into hatred for the Undead.

"I joined the Water Dogs for you," I said, when I could speak again. "To kill Druj."

"And did you?" she asked, her little arms wrapped tight around my waist.

"Yes."

"Lots?"

"Lots and lots. But never enough."

I found myself telling her everything. About Darius and Victor and Delilah. Then a thought occurred to me. "Do you know this place well?"

She nodded. "I've been here a long time."

Thinking of my little sister wandering alone in this dreary limbo brought a fresh wave of guilt.

"Aren't you supposed to...pass on? To somewhere better?"

She bit her lip. "Maybe," she admitted. "The Shepherds would catch me if they could, but I'm very good at hiding."

"Shepherds?"

"Ugly old things with big teeth." She growled ferociously. "I've seen them force the dead onto their black ships, even though some of those people don't want to go. I don't know what happens after. But they frighten me, Nazafareen. And they hate the living. You mustn't let them find you."

"What about the winged creatures called abbadax. Do you know of them?"

Her face darkened. "Yes. They mostly stay in the mountains."

"They took Darius. And another daēva named Lysandros. They flew in this direction. Did you see them?"

She nodded and my spirits lifted. "I heard their cries and ran beneath some trees."

"When was this?"

She looked confused and I understood time had ceased to have meaning for her the way it did for me.

"Try to think, Ashraf. I know you've been following me since the river. Was it then?"

She frowned. "Yes, I think a little while before." She smiled. "I didn't recognize you at first with your hair cut off and..." She gestured apologetically to my stump.

"It's all right. Would you help me find Darius?"

My sister nodded. "Of course. I will do what I can." She glanced around nervously. "Just watch out for the Shepherds."

"We shall be careful to avoid them," I said firmly. "And the first thing we should do is get out of this swamp. There's no cover here." I looked around at the still water and gnarled tree limbs. I still had that prickly feeling on the back of my neck.

Don't let this land lull you into thinking it's empty, Lysandros had said.

"I've seen monsters," Ashraf said solemnly, as if reading my thoughts.

"So have I," I said, squeezing her hand. "But we are Four-Legs

Clan. And I carry a sword now. If we find any monsters, I'll hack them to bits and feed them to the Shepherds."

Ashraf led us deeper into the mire, along hidden paths of gnarled roots and rotting tree trunks I never could have found on my own since they were submerged under two inches of black water. Yet she walked through the swamp as confidently as the satrap used to stride through his audience chamber at Tel Khalujah, and after a while, I relaxed and simply followed in her footsteps.

We talked quietly of home, of parents and cousins and aunts and uncles. She kept asking me questions I couldn't answer, mostly about how they were all doing now.

"I left a year after...."

How to finish that sentence, exactly? *After our uncle stabbed you in the neck? But you were already dead then, weren't you? At least, I sincerely hope you were. What does it feel like to be taken by a wight? Do you remember any of it?*

I cleared my throat. "I haven't been home in a long time," I said finally. "I told you that."

THE GROUND BEGAN TO GROW MORE SOLID, BUT THE MURK deepened. Bare branches gave way to feathery reeds. They bent and swayed although there was no breeze. I wiped clammy sweat from my brow. The air felt viscous as honey. Ashraf darted ahead, white legs flashing in the gloom.

"Wait!" I cried. "Stay with me!"

She ignored me as she always had. I cursed and ran to catch up, and just like that, the memory crashed over me. Ashraf chasing her puppy into the snowstorm as we climbed one of the high cols. Me dashing after her and finding only an icy ledge, the dog cowering in a crevice. Looking up to find my sister standing there, face cloaked in the shadow of her hood, snow drifting on her narrow shoulders as full dark fell.

She was only a child and yet she had terrified me worse than anything.

"Ashraf!" I yelled, not caring who or what heard me.

Then I saw that luminous glow ahead.

The gate stood at the center of a circle of stunted ash trees. It looked like a frozen waterfall, except that wasn't quite right. There was no ice, no hard edges. This gate was liquid but unmoving, as though time itself had stopped the flow of a churning river. A boot lay on its side a few paces away.

Darius's boot.

I threw myself at the gate, beating my fists against its glassy surface. Colors pulsed from somewhere deep inside, glacial blues and whites that seemed too bright in the eternal dusk of the gloaming. He was in there somehow. Trapped on the other side.

Ashraf had skidded to a stop before it. She looked uneasy.

"Where does it lead?" I demanded, seething with sudden fury. "Tell me!"

My sister turned to me. "We should go. Please. This is a bad place."

I kicked the gate. Despite the shallow liquid surface, it was like kicking a boulder. Impassable. But there was magic in it. Oh, yes. Something strong and subtle and old. Elemental, but with a degree of sophistication beyond anything I'd ever imagined.

"What's on the other side?" I snarled, rounding on my sister. She cowered away from me.

Ashraf's childish voice sank to a whisper. "I don't know."

I bent down and seized her frail arms. "I need to know how to get through that gate."

"You can't!" Ashraf wailed. "It's locked. I tried once. Only the lady in white knows how to open it."

"If there's a lock, there's a key," I hissed. "Where is it?"

Behind the gate, the shadows thickened, battering against the inside like moths drawn to a flame. Ashraf tugged at my arm. "We should *go*, Nazafareen."

"I'm not leaving him, do you understand me?" I grabbed her shoulders and snapped her head back. Once, twice. It shut her up, although she kept casting fearful glances at the gate.

"The key! Where is the key?"

Ashraf shrugged, mouth twisted in an angry pout. "I *told* you. Only the lady can pass through the gates."

I let go of her and moved closer, splaying my palm on the surface. It sank in about an inch before hitting that invisible barrier. The not-water lapped at my wrist. Frigid. Ethereal.

The boot.... I knew it as well as my own. The scuffed left toe. The places where he had patched the sole again and again. I'd offered to buy him a new pair but he hated breaking in new boots.

"What are you going to do, Nazafareen?"

I ignored her, letting the *feel* of the magic wash over me. Not a talisman. This was different. But I needed to be careful. I didn't want to shatter my bonds with Victor and Darius by accident.

Just thinking about using my power brought a wave of nausea, so bad that for a moment I wanted to die. The power of breaking burned like acid in my belly. I bent over and retched on the ground. The clearing darkened, the shadows pulsing in time with the gate.

Destroy it, the griffin whispered. *Go on, Nazafareen. It's what you're good at.*

Ashraf watched me, her face intent. Her eyes suddenly seemed older. Much older.

Something felt wrong but I didn't care. Darius was behind that door and I would get him out if it was the last thing I ever did. Just as he would do for me if he were the one standing here.

I probed warily at the ward. It was mostly water and earth, a complex knot I couldn't begin to unravel. But I didn't have to. I could slice through it. And if Neblis was waiting on the other side, she'd get more than she bargained for. Just the thought of her stoked my fury to a new pitch.

How convenient that Darius lost a boot just in front of the gate. Just think for a minute, Nazafareen.

The small voice sounded a lot like Tijah. And it made a certain sense. But something was rising in me now, clawing its way out, and if I tried to stop it, it would eat me alive.

I opened my mouth and the fire magic burst from my throat in a flood of sizzling blue light, rising and cresting like a wave as it rolled toward the gate. The magic of the Dominion, the very substance of the place, fed it like oil poured on fire. Tree limbs shuddered, groaning in deep sylvan voices, as the magic brushed past them. Dead leaves fluttered into the air, following a line as straight as the flight of an arrow.

I fell to my knees and still the power of the void streamed out and out, spreading in all directions now, an ocean of destruction. I felt as though I might vomit up every meal I'd ever eaten. The power charred and flayed me. It was a thing of the Dominion, its progeny come home at last. A scream tore from my throat.

The huŏ mofa struck the gate and the frozen water began to sluggishly flow again. Shapes swirled behind it like fish glimpsed at the bottom of a pond. The surface shimmered, fallen stars flickering in its depths. Ashraf clapped her hands. She ran toward the doorway. I wanted to stop her but I couldn't seem to draw a breath.

And then a new sound came, like the pealing of a giant bell. A bell the size of a house. I could feel it through the soles of my feet. Vibrating in my chest and skull and ribcage.

I clutched my head with my left hand, the stump of my right pressed against one ear. Gentle rain began to fall. I rolled to my back and watched heavy low clouds—the first I had ever seen in the Dominion—racing away from the gate in all directions. The tolling of the bell went on and on.

My head would crack in half if this continued. It would crack in half and my brains would leak out and then....

And then....

The thought trailed off, fading in perfect synchronicity with the ebbing of that monstrous bell. It still thrummed through the hills but it was just an echo now. I crouched in a tiny ball as the tide of noise receded. It seemed almost a physical thing, and I had the passing idea that maybe it was returning to the sea.

A *bell.*

Now what had made me think of that?

I stood in the middle of a circle of gnarled trees. A light rain was falling. My thoughts spun round and round, swarming like angry wasps.

Where had all the blood come from?

It soaked the front of my tunic. Still wet. Still warm. I knew it was blood from the organic, coppery smell, although the color seemed wrong. Too dark.

Mine? Or someone else's?

I started running my hands over my body to look for injuries and froze, staring in morbid fascination. *Oh.* My right arm ended in a smooth flap of skin. Severed at the wrist. A faint web of scar tissue traced the bottom of the stump. It looked burned, as though it had been cauterized. Two thick gold bracelets circled the forearm.

How could I have possibly forgotten *that*?

"You're dreaming." The words tumbled out awkward and raspy. I didn't recognize my own voice.

But everything was too vivid.

Including the sickness that doubled me over. I shuddered, waiting an eternity for it to pass. I felt hollowed out and yet filled with the residue of something unpleasant, like a film of scum floating on a pond.

Where was I? And how did I get here?

I started to get angry but that made me even sicker. So I sat down in the rain. I was alone. It would be night soon. I had only one hand. And that was the extent of it. Otherwise, my mind was a blank sheet of parchment. An empty husk. There was only this moment. This twilight place. The blood and the stump and the terrible ache in my stomach as though I'd eaten something rotten.

A noise made me turn. Slowly, not wanting to, but knowing I had to.

I thought about running but that's all it was: an idle thought. My legs did nothing. My stump of an arm lay cradled in my lap. If I'd had both hands, they might have been loosely clasped. Just watching and waiting to see what would happen next.

Through the trees, I saw a shimmering wall of water. Or not a wall. A *doorway*.

And something was coming through it.

❧ 16 ☙

A man.

He was very tall, with shoulder-length white-gold hair. Eyes like new spring grass after a rainstorm. And a scar winding along his jaw, ragged and deep.

He stepped out of that strange liquid doorway and walked toward me. His clothes weren't wet as they should have been, but the rain beaded on his hair and eyelashes. The way he moved. The way he looked down at me, imperious and savage. I knew he wasn't human, although exactly what he was.... I couldn't think of the word. He had the disciplined bearing of a soldier and wore elaborately carved wooden armor over bare skin. A twisted black sword hung at his waist.

You should have run when you had the chance, I thought distantly. *You really should have.*

The man regarded me with an expression devoid of emotion, the way you might look at an ant crawling towards your shoe. The next moment his hand lashed out and seized my throat, dragging me to my feet.

I battered at him, scratching and biting like a cat, but his grip only grew tighter. My toes lifted off the ground. I wanted to hurt him back but couldn't. The edges of my vision began to go dark.

And just before I fainted, I saw a young girl walking towards us, not from the doorway but out of the murk behind it. She had long brown hair and a gap-toothed grin. But as she crossed the rain-swept clearing, she began to change. With each step, she grew taller, older. By the time she reached us, she was a lovely woman with a high, elaborately worked gold crown. The spikes on top looked sharp enough to slice my finger right off if I tried to touch it.

"Culach," she said, and her voice was the buzzing of flies. "I feared I would never see you again."

His hand slackened and I sucked in a desperate breath, clutching his wrist and kicking at the damp grass. He stared at her for a long moment. The auburn hair, falling in soft waves down her back. The heart-shaped face and delicate neck.

"What have you done, Neblis?" he said, voice rough. "This is not right."

She smiled and from one eye blink to the next, her appearance transformed yet again. Red hair paled to match the soldier's. Onyx eyes brightened to emerald. Her nose lengthened, her mouth softened. The two became mirror images of each other, male and female. Beautiful and terrible.

"Is this more to your liking?" she asked coyly. "Is it my true face you missed? The other is only a trick I learned to amuse myself. Don't be angry with me, brother. I couldn't bear it." She held out her hands. "Not when we've finally found each other again."

He said nothing for a long moment, just drinking her in. Then he tossed me aside and swept her into his arms, crushing her to his chest as I scrambled away from them and tried to catch my breath. They murmured to each other. The woman cried a little and her twin wiped the tears away with his fingers. They seemed to forget anyone else was there and I thought I might crawl away unseen, but it was too late.

More soldiers were pouring through the doorway. They wore the same queer armor, like pale driftwood. Some carried black swords. Others wore bows across their backs. Hard, cold faces. Male and female both, all with that same white-gold hair like late winter sunlight on a field of fresh snow. They didn't make a sound. Just formed up, rank upon rank, preternaturally still, until they made a great circle around us.

"On your knees," the one called Culach hissed at me.

I had a sudden urge to attack, to claw at his eyes. From his almost amused expression, he guessed what I was thinking.

"Go ahead, little mortal—" he began, when the woman stepped forward. She must be a queen, with that crown and arrogant tilt to her chin. A hush descended. Even the wind seemed to hold its breath. For a long moment, she surveyed the multitude standing before her.

"Avas Valkirin," she cried. "Tribe of my heart and blood. I welcome you to the lands we have been so long denied. I welcome you to the Dominion!"

They saluted her, crossing their swords across their chests.

"Do not mourn the loss of your elemental magic. It is only temporary. There are other gates. Other worlds. A new empire shall rise in the Sun Lands and we will be its masters." She paused and her green eyes glittered with hatred. "But first we must rid the land of the vermin that infest it. They think daēvas are servants to do their bidding."

"You mean the Avas Danai!" one of the soldiers shouted, and some of the others laughed.

Neblis frowned. "True, it is our enemies who have suffered most. But these humans care not for tribes. They have designed a foul talisman to trap our power. And they would enslave you too in a heartbeat." She smiled, and how pretty she looked with the rain bringing a rosy glow to her cheeks. "Fortunately, I now have the means of both forging and breaking this talisman. In short order, the humans will find the tables have turned."

"Is this the one your servant spoke of?" Culach pressed the tip of his sword to my cheek. I froze, hardly daring to breathe. "She served her purpose, did she not? She opened the gate?"

"Yes, brother." Neblis gazed down at me with cold disdain. "And she's dangerous. More than you can imagine. It would be foolish to keep her."

A muscle grew taut in his jaw, stretching that vicious scar, and I knew I was about to die.

"Wait!" I screamed. "I don't know what I've done. What you think I've done. But won't you at least tell me my crime? I can't remember anything at all! Please." I babbled and begged until Culach delivered a sharp kick to my ribs.

"How does this creature speak our tongue?" he demanded, eyes narrowing.

Neblis frowned. "I don't know."

"You didn't teach her?"

"I met her less than a day ago. We conversed in the crude language of mortals."

They exchanged a puzzled look. "It doesn't matter," Culach growled. "Let us end this and march for Bactria."

He drew his sword back. Up close, it looked like a cross between wood and bone, with a swirling grain that blurred the eye. The hilt had no ornament but curved to fit Culach's hand like it had been made for him and him alone. The nausea began to rise in me again at the sight of the sword. Its needle-like point was an inch from my eye when Neblis pushed it aside.

"Wait a moment, brother." She examined me with bird-bright eyes. Her whole demeanor subtly changed. "I think she's telling the truth. I think she's lost, poor thing." She sank gracefully to the muddy ground. "What's your name?"

Poor thing? A moment ago she'd wanted me dead. I cast about for the answer.

What is your name?

I swallowed down the sickness roiling my belly.

Father help me, I don't know. I don't know!

The sky spun above us, a great wheel turning in the vastness of time. Rain stung my eyes. The army that had come through the doorway seemed to stretch to the edges of the earth, alabaster skin as smooth and unyielding as marble.

A large hand tilted my chin up, more gently this time. Culach. I glared at him, refusing to flinch away. Something stubborn in me didn't want to show them my fear.

"Speak it." The flatness had left his eyes, but he still terrified me. "Speak your name."

I shook my head, beyond words. Not only did I not know my own name, I remembered nothing before this clearing. Not a single cursed thing.

The woman cocked her head. "Have you truly forgotten, child?"

I nodded miserably. I must have been in some kind of accident. Taken an injury to my head. That would account for the blood.

"Please," I said. "Just tell me where we are." The light seemed wrong, neither day nor night, but nothing made sense anymore.

"She *does* speak our tongue," Neblis said, ignoring me. "And fluently. I don't think she's even aware of it. How fascinating."

Culach gave me a hard stare. "Perhaps she doesn't know who she is. Or perhaps she's just pretending."

He turned at a great flapping of wings. A pair of horse-sized creatures swooped down from the sky, alighting with harsh cries. Sharp talons clutched two men. Something about them reminded me of the soldiers, although neither was fair.

"I think we will know in a moment," Neblis said. Her voice sounded strangely eager.

The creatures dropped their prey to the ground and stepped back on clawed feet. The prisoners had been bound head to toe with thorny vines as thick as a ship's mooring rope. The first had black hair and violet eyes that stared vacantly into the rain. He'd been stripped and vicious bruises covered his body. When Culach saw him, his mouth spread in a slow grin.

"You didn't tell me *he* was here," Culach said to Neblis, fingering his scar. "What happened to his clothes?"

"Lysandros has a loose tongue," she said absently. "He needed to be taught a lesson."

"I'd be delighted to tutor him further—" Culach began.

Neblis laughed softly. "Your revenge can wait, brother."

"Why?" Culach demanded.

"Because we might need him. He knows the upstart boy-king I told you about. The one who at this moment besieges my house."

Culach's eyes narrowed. "Very well," he said. "What of the other?"

The second man had wavy brown hair. He was shorter but his shredded tunic exposed heavy muscles. He didn't even glance at Neblis or Culach. Blue eyes bored into me and me alone. Some powerful emotion churned inside him that I couldn't easily identify. Relief? Hatred? Surprise?

One of his arms was withered but it looked like an old injury. A severe burn, or perhaps he'd just been born that way. Blood trickled from a dozen small punctures where the thorns had pierced his skin. He lay on one side, arms pulled behind him, ankles tightly bound.

"Nazafareen!" he shouted. And again: "Nazafareen!"

My heart seized up. *Does he know me? Is that my name? Or is it some kind of trick?*

The winged beasts guarding him watched me with reptilian eyes. He began to struggle against his bonds. One of the creatures batted him with a taloned paw, lazy as a cat with a mousling. It left deep gouges across his cheek and still he fought harder. Horror filled me as the thing gave him another swat. His head struck a rock half-buried in the damp earth and he finally lay still, rain coursing down his bloody face.

Neblis took my elbow and drew me closer. I could feel the heat of the winged thing's breath as I looked down at the prisoner. He had a hawkish nose and dark brows that looked like they would be expressive when he was awake. Beard stubble roughened the clean line of his jaw. Even in his current state, he looked like a dangerous man.

They'd taken away his weapons and his boots but something remained around his wrist. A gold bracelet worked with a snarling griffin—the precise match of the one clamped around my own arm.

"What's his name?" I whispered.

His eyes flew open, chips of blue ice.

"Darius," he croaked. "My name is Darius. And you...."

He trailed off, eyes rolling back in his head. The beast leapt to its feet and let out a savage cry. It flapped it wings twice, then settled back down.

Darius.

It meant nothing. But I had no doubt now that the man knew me. The look on his face....

"This is Victor's son?" Culach asked, nudging him with a toe.

"Yes." Neblis turned to me, pale and expectant. "I might have to execute him for his crimes. What do you think of that?

"I...don't know," I stammered. "It depends on what he's done."

"You truly do not remember him?" She watched me closely. "Nor the cuff he wears?"

"I remember nothing at all," I admitted.

Neblis stared down at the man for a long moment. Her expression was strangely intense, as if she wrestled with some decision. For a moment, it softened to something like pity. She touched the curve of his mouth with one slender finger. He moaned.

"Nazafareen...."

Her features grew cold again. "Culach, would you leave us? I wish to speak to the girl alone."

He studied his sister with a scowl. "What do you play at, Neblis?"

She laid a hand on his arm. "Please, brother."

Culach nodded with some reluctance and went off to join a group of soldiers. They'd fanned out from the clearing, moving with swords drawn as if this were hostile territory. Neblis turned to me. "This man is your confederate. So is the other." Profound sorrow stole across her face. "They came here to kill me."

I shook my head in weak denial. But of course, she could be right.

"You must think me cruel treating them this way, but if I set these men free, they would try to kill us all." She rose gracefully to her feet. "I am not like them, child. I believe in showing mercy when it is possible. If you swore to serve me instead, I would be glad to spare your life."

"What would happen to them?" I looked at the prisoners.

"I haven't decided yet. But I *might* spare them as well. We shall see."

"Am I an assassin too?"

"I'm afraid so. That's why Culach attacked you. He was only trying to protect me."

I frowned. "I don't remember any of that."

She gave me a kindly pat on the hand. "You broke something, child. Something very old and full of complex magic. By destroying it, you destroyed a part of yourself. But you gained something as well. I think it gave you the ability to understand our tongue."

"But what did I break?"

"A spell. One designed for the express purpose of erasing memories." Neblis looked at the stump of my right wrist. "Poor girl. How they've used you. Shall I tell you how you lost your hand?"

I nodded, dreading the answer.

The Queen talked for a long time. She cried as she told me the things I'd done. Neblis spoke softly and without malice, but my cheeks burned with shame. What kind of person was I? *A killer and a thief*. As ugly and cruel as she was beautiful and kind.

I didn't want to believe her at first—it all seemed so unreal. But I could feel the darkness inside me. Biding its time. As much as it sickened me, I knew I was capable of violence. And I couldn't deny that I was covered in blood. I could see that with my own eyes.

"You murdered one of my guards in the forest," she said. "Near the gate. Stabbed him in the back."

The more she talked, the more I knew it in my bones to be true. How could *I* ever have been afraid of *her*? I wanted only to please her, to somehow atone for the wrongs I had done.

When she embraced me, the smell of her made my head spin.

"Hush now, daughter," she whispered in my ear. "All will be well. They made a monster of you, but I can still see the innocent child within. I will make sure those men never harm you again."

The rain eased and soldiers came and took the prisoners away. I was relieved not to have to look at them anymore, especially the one with blue eyes. I hated him now with a passion that nearly made me sick again.

He was the one who had chopped off my hand.

✣ 17 ✣

LYSANDROS

He lay in the rain, lips parted. It was cool and wet and tasted of magic.

The rain reminded him of home. Not Qin. His *true* home, where there was no fire to burn him, no sun to blind his eyes, just a huge yellow moon floating in the cobalt sky.

He remembered....

A day long ago, when he had been young and headstrong and thirsting for adventure. Victor, looking every inch the proud Avas Danai prince as he led his cousins to the gateway. Moonlight gleamed on white bonewood armor as they gathered before the still pool.

The Matrium of the seven houses waited for them there. Some of the women were as tall as Victor, others small and fine-boned. But they all wore the same expression of disapproval. Each held a handful of rich black earth.

"Do you come to stop me? Are you my jailers now?" Victor demanded. "We will return after we have discovered what lies beyond." He grinned. "We will seek out the Black Tower. The source of the Nexus! What if the ancient legends are true?"

Raisa stepped forward. Her hair was still dark and shiny as

onyx, her stern face unlined, although she was the oldest of the Seven. "You are free to go, Victor—against the urging of your family and clan. But we will not leave the gate to the Ael sa'Vrach open. It's far too dangerous."

Victor shared a look with Lysandros. *The Ael sa'Vrach. The in-between place.* Neither had believed it was more than a child's tale until Victor stumbled over the pool during a drunken quarter-moon swim. It lay far from both their houses, near the border with the Avas Valkirin.

"What are you saying, Raisa?"

"We made our decision. It shall be warded. Any who pass through it will be cursed to forget where they came from." Her face hardened. "The doorway will be sealed. There is no returning."

Victor's black eyes flashed. If only Raisa had told him privately, he might have reconsidered. But in front of all their houses? She should have known Victor would never back down from a threat. In such small, foolish decisions were all their fates sealed.

"If that is the price you demand, I will pay it," Victor said hoarsely. He surveyed the young daēvas who accompanied him. "Whoever wishes to remain behind can do so."

Anxious whispering broke the silence. A dozen or so moved to stand with the Seven, not meeting Victor's gaze. But others, Lysandros among them, stayed. The ones who loved Victor best.

"You are fools," Raisa said mildly. "But as you say, we are not your jailers. You have the right."

She held up a talisman of binding, hewn from the taproot of the summerleaf, and began to speak words Lysandros had never heard before. Raisa walked around and around the verge of the pool, weaving her magic into a steely web. The rest of the Matrium watched in silence. All Avas Danai, dark of hair and eye where the Avas Valkirin were fair. At last, she stepped aside.

"It is done. Whatever you find on the other side, you will not bring it back with you. The Moon Lands shall stay as they always have."

"How you fear change!" Victor said contemptuously. "Our tribe has become like salted earth. Nothing new grows here. What is life without risk?"

"So says the young wolf who has never known true hardship or loss. Go, Victor. Seek your fortune in the Ael sa'Vrach."

Her imperious gaze swept the daēvas who stood arrayed behind him. It lingered on Lysandros a few seconds longer than the others, for he was her son. But Raisa had already told him what she wished to say as Lysandros had strapped on his armor, and she was not a woman who repeated herself.

You didn't warn me, but perhaps you didn't yet know. The Matrium had convened afterward to discuss Victor's announcement. He had deliberately given them almost no time to react.

Raisa threw the handful of dirt at Victor's feet. One by one, the six other women came forward and repeated the gesture.

"Go, earth children," Raisa said softly, her voice now full of sorrow. "I hope your path is not a shadowed one."

"So be it. But there is no need to mourn us," Victor vowed. "We *will* come back someday, wards or no."

He waded into the pool. The water of the gate did not stir as it swallowed him up. Lysandros went second. He felt the sudden, terrible loss of his elemental magic. The rest was a fever dream until they had stumbled through a *second* gate into the world of men.

Now, centuries later, the Moon gate was open again. The spell shattered. But it was not his mother or the other elders waiting on the other side. It was their sworn enemies.

Lysandros's eyelids fluttered as wave upon wave of memories washed over him. Neblis and Victor. Lovers who had defied their parents' millennia-long feud to meet in secret trysts. And Lysandros had helped them.

Oh, Raisa. What have we done?

❧ 18 ❧

NAZAFAREEN

I shivered and pulled the heavy cloak tighter. We'd marched to a pass over the mountains. The view—dark pine forest dotted with lakes and serpentine rivers—stretched for hundreds of leagues in every direction. At the rim of the sky, I saw something grey and vast. Just a line, the very beginning of it.

"The Cold Sea," Neblis said. She stood next to me, silver hair streaming in the wind. The simple gown she wore left her arms bare, but she didn't seem bothered by the chill. "That's what Balthazar calls it at any rate. You'll meet him when we reach my house. It's where the talismans of Traveling come from."

The Cold Sea. It sounded like a lonely place. "What's on the other side?"

"Ah." She tilted her head. "Now that is the great mystery, for none who seek it ever return."

Even without memories to consult, I knew the sky here was wrong. It was never light and never dark, but always something halfway between. I felt too sick to eat even if there had been food. It was the backwash of the spell, Neblis said.

But once we had crossed the mountains, I could rest in her home. She had feather mattresses and soft, clean sheets and servants to care for me until I healed. It made me feel even worse that she was treating me so kindly.

"So you are a daēva?" The word came out awkwardly although she had told me about them. How they could work the elements and didn't age the way humans did. That there were two tribes, which had fought each other for ages. Avas Danai, which meant children of the earth, and Avas Valkirin, children of the air. "Am I one too?"

She smiled. "No, daughter, you're human. But only part human. You have our blood too, just like the Prophet Zarathustra. That's how you broke the spell."

"Who?"

"An old man who thought he could chain us to do his bidding." Neblis sighed. "I will tell you what humans have done to our people for more than two centuries now. Killed us, raped us, tortured us. Gave our children to the flames or left them to die of exposure." She gestured toward the blue-eyed daēva. "And they are collaborators. That cuff he wears? He used it to inflict pain on you, so you wouldn't run away. When you tried, he chopped your hand off."

I stared at the matching cuff around my own wrist. It made my skin crawl. "I want to take it off," I said. "Throw it away!"

Neblis thought for a moment. "No, it must be broken properly. I have the means to do so once we reach the House. You must be patient, daughter. But the other...." Her gaze lingered on the second cuff. It had a slight difference: the winged griffin held a sword in one paw.

"What does it mean?"

"It's the symbol of the Immortals. Our most dreaded enemies. The daēva who wears its match is named Victor. He is no danger to you, yet I wonder...." She reached out to touch it, fingertips poised a hair's breadth away, hesitating.

"You can have it." I pulled it loose from the stump and offered it to her.

Neblis stared at the cuff for a long moment. "It was made for a human to wear," she said softly. "I fear it might hurt, even with the magic suppressed." She turned away, expressionless. "Throw it away, I don't care."

I looked out over the ledge. A sheer drop to the valley floor. I brought my arm back and threw the cuff as far as I could into the void. Watched it glimmer as it fell.

When I turned back, the blue-eyed prisoner was staring at me. I glared until he looked away. I supposed he hated me for walking free while he was trussed up like a chicken.

Neblis studied me. "I don't blame you for any of it, sweetling. They manipulated you for your magic." She frowned slightly. "Do you think it might ease your burden to tell them to their faces that you will not be their puppet anymore?"

"I...if you think I should."

Neblis flashed pearly teeth. "It must be terribly difficult, losing your past. But this is a chance to become someone new. Perhaps that is the purpose behind what happened to you."

I glanced at her, afraid of being rude. "May I ask you something?"

"Of course, daughter."

"When I first saw you, you seemed to look like a child. You were walking across the clearing—and then you changed."

Neblis smiled. "A simple disguise. There are creatures in the Dominion that would kill me on sight, like those two." She looked over at the prisoners.

"But I thought elemental magic didn't work here." I had learned this earlier, when she explained about daēvas. "So how did you do it?"

Her emerald eyes darkened a shade. "I had help. There are other sorts of magic in the gloaming. Yours, for instance. I have a dear friend. His name is Farrumohr. He knows how to use the power of this place. He lets me change how I look." She grinned and her teeth seemed longer. Sharper. "Would you like to meet him?"

"I...."

No. No, I wouldn't. But the words didn't come.

And then Neblis laughed, patting me on the arm. She seemed herself again. "Perhaps now is not the time. But I think we should confront the prisoners. I must still decide what to do with them." She laid a cool palm to my forehead. "You're burning up, child! Are you feeling strong enough?"

I wasn't, but I couldn't refuse her. She led me to where the two men knelt on the cold ground amid a circle of Avas Valkirin. The blue-eyed one watched me approach with wariness. Something dark in me bubbled up, nasty and violent. This is what they had turned me into. My hands shook with fury as I thrust my stump in his face.

"If I asked her to, she would do the same to you," I snarled. "And I just might. But I am no longer your pawn."

He stared at me in confusion.

"You must speak the human tongue, child," Neblis whispered in my ear. "Do you remember it?"

I shook my head, but then I *did* remember. It was not as pleasing to the ear as the language I spoke with Neblis. The words sounded dull and heavy where hers was like a song. But I knew it.

"You took my hand but not my soul," I hissed. "They told me everything. Everything! I hope you burn. And *this*—" I held up the cuff. "This foul chain will soon be broken forever."

I thought he would spit at me, or curse me back, but his voice was surprisingly level. "I don't know what's happened to you, but it doesn't matter, Nazafareen. I still love you, as you loved me even when you believed I was Druj."

"Love you?" I laughed, and how ugly it sounded. "I despise you!"

He flinched at this, pretending to be hurt. "Look beneath your shirt," he whispered. "I gave you a gift before we parted."

Neblis darted forward, reaching into my tunic before I could move. She snatched something from around my neck. A gold chain, with an emblem hanging from it.

"You see, daughter?" she said triumphantly. "Ask him what this is."

"Tell me," I growled.

"The symbol of the Prophet," he replied, frowning. "But I only wore it because—"

"You mean the man who enslaved the daēvas?" I yanked the chain from Neblis's hand and ground it under my heel. "You have only proven your disloyalty."

"Nazafareen—"

"Don't speak my name!"

The nausea was coming again, hard and fast. I wanted to throttle him until his face turned purple and his tongue popped out. He shouted something about a *bond* but Neblis was pulling me away. I heard the other man curse her. The guards started beating them both.

"Rest here, child," she said, leading me to a pile of furs. "Culach will watch over you."

I curled into a ball, heart racing. The rage slowly ebbed away, replaced by exhaustion so deep and heavy it felt like death.

Nazafareen. Your name is Nazafareen.

The word echoed in my mind until it lost all meaning. I sunk into blackness, an infinite abyss. I wanted to stay there, but a voice like dead leaves skittering in the wind kept whispering in my ear. Louder and louder.

Wake up. Wake up. *Wake up!*

My eyes flew open. I was standing by an old stone well. White lichen covered the rim. The sky overhead was grey with thunderclouds, so dark I thought they would burst open any second. A huge stone house loomed to my left. It had no windows, only a blank façade topped with spires that seemed to twist in two directions at once.

Just glancing at it made my head spin. I leaned on the edge of the well to steady myself, but looking into its depths was even worse than looking at the house.

And then I heard something in the well. A stealthy scraping sound. I wanted to run but my legs had turned to marble. I saw a flash of pale skin.

A girl was crawling out of its depths like a creature from the bottom of the sea. The same girl I had seen in the clearing.

"Nazafareen," she cried, and her voice was so sweet but flames danced behind her eyes. "Help me, sister!"

She reached out a hand and I screamed in pain as her fingers closed around my stump, the skin blistering and peeling away. I tried to yank it free but she wouldn't let go.

"Breaker," she hissed. "*Breakerrrrr*...."

Her face changed to the blue-eyed daēva with his knife, sawing into me. I shrieked in pain and terror and threw myself into the well.

Falling, falling, falling into darkness.

✻ 19 ✻

LYSANDROS

W hispers in the twilight. Words in a tongue he had not heard spoken aloud in more than two hundred years.

Lysandros turned his head, wincing at the pain. Neblis crouched over Darius, her curtain of silver hair obscuring his face.

"Poor boy. Your true love has forgotten you. An awful feeling, is it not? A terrible feeling. To know you are nothing to her." She tangled her fingers in his chestnut hair. "To know I could cut this handsome head off and she wouldn't shed a tear. In fact, she would be glad. Poor, poor boy."

"You did this to Nazafareen," Lysandros growled. "How?"

"Not I," Neblis replied. "The stupid girl did it to herself. I led her to the gateway and laid my trap, but it was entirely her decision to slice through the wards. She found a nasty little surprise waiting and your own Avas Danai put it there."

"What do you mean?"

"I made her believe Darius was on the other side of the gate. I knew it was the one thing that might enrage her enough to throw everything she had at it. Farrumohr explained the nature of negatory magic. It's a simple equation. The stronger the emotion, the more power is unleashed."

Lysandros watched her pet Darius like a puppy. Even mad, she had an undeniable appeal. Victor had always liked beautiful women, and none was lovelier than Neblis.

"How is it you never forgot?" he asked." And how did you even pass through the gate? My mother locked it."

"I went through the day before you left." She dropped Darius's limp head and came over to Lysandros. "I intended to wait for Victor in the gloaming near the gate, but I lost my way." She looked into Lysandros's eyes. "So you remember now. It is broken for you at last." She tapped her teeth. "One wakes and one sleeps."

"Yes, I remember. Victor did love you, even if his parents couldn't abide the union."

"He loved me," Neblis said flatly. "And yet he left me behind. Abandoned me while he went off adventuring."

Lysandros shook his head. A wave of dizziness washed over him. "We didn't know what lay on the other side of the gate. He was only trying to protect you—"

"He tried to *leave me behind*." She took hold of herself with a visible effort. "And now his son will pay the same price I did. There's a certain glorious tragedy to it, don't you think, Lysandros? I wish I could say I planned it, but fate has torn these children apart, not I."

"You turned her against him," Lysandros said coldly.

"It wasn't hard. I've learned things from my friends in the Dominion. How to make a human love me, for one. Their wills are so weak." She sniffed dismissively. "This one resisted as best she could. She's stronger than most, I'll give her that. You know I'm actually coming to like the child! I never thought I'd say it about a mortal, but I might keep her for a while." She heaved a sigh. "Sadly, she's quite sick from the magic inside her. I doubt she'll live long. But I wonder what she could be induced to do to her lover before she dies?"

Lysandros yanked futilely against his bonds, the icy stone of the ledge searing his bare skin. "Darius has done you no wrong. He's not his father!"

"I *told* Victor," Neblis said, staring out at the valley below. "He wouldn't listen. He refused to believe. Again and again I told him. He *mocked* me." Then a new thought struck her. She pressed a hand to her mouth. "If you remember, perhaps Victor does too. He will realize his terrible mistake." She muttered to herself so rapidly Lysandros could barely follow. "I will tell him I'm sorry, of course he'll forgive me. I had no choice, I *had* to bind him with fire. He would have run otherwise, like he did before. But he must know. He must. He will love me again. He *will*."

She spun around and signaled to one of the abbadax. It crept over, hideous head bent low in submission. Neblis leaped onto its back.

"I must return to the House!" she shouted to someone he couldn't see. "Wait for me at the gate!"

The creature dove from the edge of the cliff, angling towards a lake that gleamed like a dusty jewel in the distance.

Victor was my friend, but he was also a bit of a shit, Lysandros reflected. So Neblis had tried to follow. Victor should have expected it. She'd been head over heels for him. He'd loved her too, but not in the same way. Not enough to stay. Only a moon before they left, Lysandros had nearly died helping Victor escape into the woods when Neblis's brother found them together. Victor had taken off running, naked ass flapping in the wind, while Lysandros was left to face her irate twin.

Boots scraped on rock. He tipped his head back. A pair of muscular calves stood over him. He might not have minded the sight except they belonged to the man who hated him more than anyone in the world. In *two* worlds.

"Lysandros." Culach crouched down a pace away, arms flexing

as he propped them lazily on his thighs. Lysandros had almost forgotten how huge he was. "I never thought to see you again."

"Culach!" Lysandros gave him a bloody grin. "What an unpleasant surprise."

"Still playing the fool? If I were in your boots, I wouldn't be laughing."

"I'm afraid I don't *have* any boots. You took them away." Lysandros wiggled his bare toes. "But that's the difference between us. You were always far too serious. And hot-tempered too."

"Only where my sister's honor is concerned," Culach growled. "Alas for you, she is gone. And my soldiers are tired of herding you along. You're slowing us down."

"Honestly, Culach, that scar I gave you...it's not so bad. With those green eyes, you might be *too* pretty without it—"

Culach laughed. "I'm afraid your silver tongue won't save you this time. Still, I don't care to lie to my sister when she asks if I killed you myself. She did ask me nicely not to." He smiled in a way that made Lysandros wither inside, though he maintained a bland expression. "Did you know that the abbadax breed in these mountains? They guard their eggs jealously. And when the eggs hatch, the fledglings emerge very hungry. *Starving*, in fact."

"How fascinating. I'm sure they're little bundles of joy."

"Not exactly. But you'll have a chance to meet some shortly. This ledge we stopped on? It's just above one of the nests." He cupped a hand to his ear. "Ah, listen! I think I hear the adorable creatures now."

Lysandros had held out hope that Culach was toying with him, but he did indeed hear something. A high-pitched squealing, like an iron nail being torn from wood.

"The *really* fascinating thing about abbadax is that the hatchlings come out fully formed and ready to kill their food. They must, because their parents abandon them. Only the most vicious survive."

"At least let the boy go," Lysandros pleaded. "He's done nothing!"

"He is Victor's son. And I'm not utterly without a heart. I wouldn't leave you to be eaten for supper *alone*."

Culach stood. "Ho!" he shouted to his troops. "We march for the gate!" He turned to Lysandros and winked. "Too bad you're Avas Danai. I always thought your violet eyes were pretty too." Culach laughed again to himself and walked away, elderwood sword swinging at his side.

About three minutes later, Lysandros heard a soft squeal, followed by a crisp snapping sound that he suspected was a beak. A grotesque head peered over the ledge. It was still molting, so stiff white down covered its head and throat. But the feathers that grew from its back gleamed along the edges with a metallic sheen. The thing clumsily tested its wings. Air battered his face.

He fervently hoped it might fall, but it clamped its toothy beak around a root and hauled itself up. The hatchling shook itself and peered at him with a bright yellow eye. It gave a cry. A second head appeared at the rim of the cliff, even larger than the first.

"Wake up, Darius!" Lysandros hissed.

Nothing.

He wriggled over until his icy feet brushed Darius's nose.

"Wake up, boy!" Lysandros cried again, poking him as hard as he dared. Darius had gotten the worst of the beating earlier.

"Stop it," Darius muttered. "Feels cold."

"Not as cold as you'll be when they peck your eyes out and squabble over the rest!" Lysandros exclaimed. "*Look*, damn you!"

Darius looked. His jaw worked but no sound came out.

"Yes," Lysandros said, struggling against his bonds. "As the wise men of Qin say, life is too precious to waste your time fearing death." He grinned bleakly. "Until it's imminent."

PART THREE

How shall a man escape from that which is written? How shall he flee from his destiny?
   —From the epic poem Shahnameh by Ferdowsi

✿ 20 ✿

BALTHAZAR

He exhausted himself pounding on the door and screaming impotent threats at Molon while the Prophet sat quietly in the darkness. Now he paced the tiny cell, fists clenched.

"He cannot keep us here," Balthazar growled. "When the servants come to bring you food...."

"Are there no magics you can work?" Zarathustra asked. "The necromancers were feared above even the Undead Druj during the war."

"If I had my chains, I could tear the cursed door off its hinges, but I left them in my chambers." He directed his words at the straw bedding where the Prophet huddled. "What if I removed your cuff? Would that release your power?"

"It has to be broken, like all the others. Only the fourth element can shatter a talisman. You know that."

Balthazar swore lustily. "And the holy fire is also in my chambers."

Silence descended for a long minute.

"What is Molon's intention, do you think?" the Prophet ventured.

"To kill us both. That much is obvious. And if he returns with his chains, he'll have the strength of ten men. I will be no match for him."

"Then we are in a quandary."

"Indeed." He slumped to the floor. "I can't believe I've been outwitted by Molon, of all people."

"Do not blame yourself." Zarathustra took on a lecturing tone. "A knife of the keenest steel requires the whetstone, and even the wisest man needs advice sometimes."

"And what would yours be?" Balthazar demanded impatiently.

"That you have made an enemy, but you did so in the service of friendship. If one would have a friend, then one must one also be willing to wage war for him." He reached out a hand in the darkness, fumbling for Balthazar's and holding him tight. The Prophet's voice was low and full of uncharacteristic emotion as he said, "We used to be friends, a long time ago. Perhaps we can again. It is your choice."

The magus's grip was strong, although his skin felt thin as old parchment.

We used to be friends...

Balthazar shook his head in denial, but a long-sealed vault in his mind was cracking open. Sitting in the pitch dark cell, with the old man's hand warm atop his own, Balthazar suddenly recalled drinking a cup of wine in Zarathustra's study when he was the High Magus of Karnopolis and Balthazar was just a novice. Dozens of candles flickered along the walls, but they were the only indulgence in the otherwise austerely decorated room. Despite his exalted titles, Zarathustra had never cared much for material comforts besides a decent flagon of Ramian red.

On that particular evening, they had spoken of magic and whether it was a sin or a virtue. Zarathustra believed it was neither, that the answer depended on the will of the person wielding it. Balthazar agreed. Where they differed was on the question of whether this even mattered. With Zarathustra's encouragement, Balthazar had grown bold in expressing his opinions. He'd taken the position that all knowledge was fair game. That it should be sought without moral limits.

"You have a keen mind," Zarathustra had told him, his long dark beard neatly combed and pointy felt cap of office tipped back rakishly on his head. "But I am somewhat anxious for your soul if you continue down this path. And I wonder if the Way of the Flame is your true calling."

Now Balthazar felt everything he believed sliding toward the abyss. Could it be true? What else had he forgotten?

"We knew each other," he said hoarsely. "When you named me as a former magus, it was no lucky guess."

"Yes, Balthazar. I knew you well. You came to the temple a full year before I was deposed."

"You were a...a mentor to me!"

The Prophet was silent for a long moment. "You had a blazing intelligence, a fierce curiosity and desire to learn. But you were misguided. I could see it even then. You had been wounded somehow, and you were afraid."

And as if that single memory was the keystone anchoring the fortress of denial Balthazar had built, acknowledging it caused the rest to collapse.

He remembered everything now. Every horrible detail.

He had been in Zarathustra's study when the King's men kicked the door open. Four soldiers had pinned Balthazar to the floor with their boots while the High Magus was beaten and cuffed. The next day, they brought Balthazar before the new High Magus, a fanatic who told him if he ever repeated what he'd witnessed to a single soul, he would be castrated and given to the brothels.

Balthazar had never spoken a word of it to anyone. He knew in his heart Zarathustra was dead. In his terror, he had obliterated the memory of that night from his mind. But how he'd hated the magi after that. A loathing so pure it had driven him headlong into the arms of their worst enemy.

Over the centuries since, Balthazar had done everything he could to destroy the man he'd once been as utterly as he'd destroyed the memory of the magi's betrayal. But something long dormant had stirred, first in Karnopolis when he'd helped the brothel boy, and later when he realized he could not let Molon have the Prophet.

He had used the chains on Zarathustra. Drained the man who had been like a father to him.

In the chill dungeons of the House-Behind-the-Veil, Balthazar laid his head in his hands and wept.

Zarathustra waited for a long time. Then he said gently, "It is not too late, Balthazar."

"Do not offer me false comfort," Balthazar replied dully. "There is no taking back what I have done. No making it right."

"Tell me all of it then, without holding back. I will weigh your sins."

Balthazar gave a bitter laugh. "It will make you sick to the depths of your soul, magus. Are you sure you wish to hear?"

"Little surprises me anymore, Balthazar. I am old and my time in this world is almost done. If I can ease your burden, I am glad to do it."

The cell door was thick, but not thick enough to block the sudden sound of a man screaming somewhere above. Balthazar closed his eyes.

"It's Victor," he said. "He is alone with Molon."

Zarathustra patted Balthazar's hand. The air stirred faintly as gnarled fingers made the sign of the flame, touching forehead, lips and heart. "Speak quickly, Balthazar. I fear the end is coming for all of us." His voice trembled. "Ah, Victor, my old friend. May yours be quick."

Balthazar drew a slow breath through his nose and began to speak. "My first murder was of my daēva, Davod. I forced him to the cistern behind the temple and tried to make him open a gate. When he could not, I killed him to pay the blood price. After they caught me, I killed again to escape the cells. I was already under Neblis's spell."

Even now, the thought of her made his heart race. She had always understood his deepest ambitions, or seemed to.

"Neblis promised she would find a way for me to learn elemental magic if I would help her take revenge on the empire. They had leashed her brothers and sisters, she said. Used them as slaves against her. She was so beautiful, so convincing. I wanted desperately to believe it was possible."

Balthazar stood and looked through the tiny grating. The screams outside had subsided. He didn't know what that meant.

"She said I would have eternal life if I wore the chains. At first, the Druj terrified me. But I quickly realized the chains protected me and the Undead would do my bidding."

"But you cannot wield elemental magic. She lied to you."

It was past time to face this truth. "Yes, she lied. She knew it was my heart's desire. That I would do anything to have it."

Balthazar talked and talked, dredging up deeds both unspeakably vile and shamefully petty. He spoke of the woman he had killed to gain passage through the lake when he had brought Neblis the holy fire, and the Numerator Araxa, whom he had induced to douse himself in Greek fire and set it alight. He recalled each innocent soul he had drained with his chains so that he might live for centuries and never age himself—including old Zarathustra himself. The Prophet listened without comment. This only made it worse.

In the pitch darkness, Balthazar saw the faces of those he had wronged—men and women, young and old—their eyes staring at him accusingly. So many....

"I murdered three magi, tortured them to death for information about where they were keeping you," Balthazar said, reaching the end of his confession. His throat was hoarse from talking. "I betrayed a Water Dog to mercenaries from Al Miraj. And I indirectly caused the death of her daēva. I don't know her name. She was one of those who came to rescue you. I let the Numerators burn the tunnels to flush them out. She was with Victor's son and the Breaker. I didn't intend for them to die, not in that way, but the flames came too close."

Zarathustra's laid a comforting hand on Balthazar's shoulder. "I've been alone for a very long time," he said at last. "Lost in the labyrinth of my own mind. You helped me find the way out."

"Not I—" Balthazar began.

"Yes. It is true you've strayed, Balthazar." The Prophet cleared his throat. "Rather far. But we correct error by doing right. That is what you must do now."

"Strayed! I suppose that's one way of putting it." Again, Balthazar gripped his head with his hands. "I'm afraid I no longer know how to do right, magus."

"Perhaps you'll remember. When it comes, the choice will be yours and yours alone. But that is not what we must face now."

Balthazar heard the clink of metal striking the floor. It could only be Zarathustra's cuff.

"I thought it could not be removed," he said, confused. "Or at least, that it made no difference."

"Can't you feel it?" Zarathustra's fingers brushed Balthazar's face, then fluttered to the chill walls. When he spoke, childlike wonder filled his voice. "The magic of the Dominion floods this place. The wards, Balthazar...they've broken!"

✣ 21 ✣

MOLON

He thought he heard the growl of a dog.

He'd been about to conclude his game. The sport had grown tiresome since Victor passed out. He'd proven harder to break than Molon anticipated, stubbornly refusing the release of the flames. Molon had tried waking him with slaps and cold water, but apparently even daēvas had their limits.

Or maybe he was already dead. Molon couldn't tell.

He'd fetched his chains, thinking he might collar the daēva at the last. Have a taste of his mind before he slit Victor's throat. Then he would go back down to the dungeons and see to Balthazar and the old man. He could burn Victor's body later. Make it appear the flames had devoured him. But the hand holding the knife paused in the flickering light of the brazier as he heard that low snarl.

It must be his imagination. Neblis didn't tolerate animals of any kind in the House, especially ones as dirty as dogs. Besides which, they were revered as holy by the magi. The so-called Water Dogs hunted daēvas for the empire. No, it was impossible.

And yet Molon felt unease creep over him as he turned to the dark archway.

"Is someone there?" he called.

The disturbing thought struck him that Victor had said almost the same thing.

Could he have forgotten one of the servants? They all looked the same, and they died so frequently it was difficult to keep track.

No one answered. But he thought he heard the click of nails on stone.

Molon rose to his feet, gory knife in hand. The chains trailed from one slender wrist. He'd moved the brazier seven or eight paces away because the heat of it was making him sweat in his close-fitting leathers. It cast a small circle of yellow light around the pillar, but everything beyond was obscured by shadow. He turned slowly, scanning for movement.

I am an Antimagus. Fear is nothing. Pain is nothing.

That had been his mantra, handed down by others who had undergone the training before him. But when Molon saw what padded out of the archway, his mouth ran dry.

Six Shepherds. Pink and black tongues lolled from shark jaws that could crush a man's skull. Behind them stood a painfully thin woman with long, tangled black hair. When she saw Victor, her face went from somber to terrifying. Vengeful. The beasts howled in unison, a chilling chorus.

Shepherds. *Inside* the House-Behind-the-Veil.

Impossible.

"This man is a foul creature," the woman spat, and was she actually speaking to the *hounds*? "If you truly hate the necromancers, you will give him what he deserves." Then: "Let me have the other. Please." Her voice broke. "He's my husband."

Six triangular heads swiveled in Molon's direction. Six pairs of muscular haunches bunched to spring. Yellow eyes gleamed in anticipation.

Molon turned to run. He made it two paces before the beasts hit him. One sank its teeth into his leg, dragging him to the ground. He felt hot breath on his face, the spray of saliva. And then they found his belly, tearing him open like a piece of rotten fruit, fighting over the scraps.

The woman ripped Victor's chains apart with her bare hands, wincing away from the flames. Then she lifted him in her arms and ran from the chamber.

Another daēva?

Molon saw this happen dimly, as though from a great distance. He lay on his back. One of the Shepherds leapt to his chest, placing its massive bear-paws on his shoulders. It grinned at him, dripping teeth inches from his face.

In a final, instinctive urge to live, Molon reached for his talismanic magic.

It wasn't there.

❧ 22 ❧

BALTHAZAR

"**O**f course, we could wait for Neblis to return,"
Zarathustra said calmly, as Balthazar struggled to
absorb what he'd just said about the wards. "I can't
imagine it will be long now. She must know it as well."

"But how could they shatter?" Balthazar himself felt no difference, but since he wasn't wearing his chains, he had no way to
judge. "The wards around the House have been in place for two
hundred years. Nothing has ever breached them."

"You said there is another with negatory magic?" Zarathustra
asked.

Balthazar nodded, then realized the Prophet couldn't see him
in the pitch darkness. "Yes, Neblis planned to use her to break
through to the Moon Lands. But she was only supposed to open
the single gateway!" He slammed his palm against the cell door in
frustration. "Something must have gone wrong. And we're still
trapped here. Negatory magic only works against other *magic*."
He laughed bitterly. "All that power, and it's useless against a plain
iron door. So we're back where we started."

"Do you truly not know?"

"Know what?"

The Prophet sounded amused. "This whole House is a talisman, Balthazar. One of the largest ever forged. It's how Neblis kept the Dominion at bay. There is magic imbued in the very stone around us."

"Then the time has come to use it," Balthazar said urgently.

Zarathustra sighed. "Yes, I suppose it has, if only for Victor's sake. I have not touched negatory power in...oh, let us just say a very long time. Since I was a young man and too stupid to know better. Stand away from me, over by the far wall, Balthazar. I'll try to release a small amount but I'm not sure what will happen. The Dominion amplifies it."

Balthazar obeyed. A few moments later, he heard a low vibration like a giant grindstone, setting his teeth on edge. Lines of cold blue fire raced around the edge of the cell door. Metal groaned and popped. The Prophet's mouth gaped open, eyes rolling back in his head. Balthazar leapt back as the door folded in on itself, compressing to a smaller and smaller knot of matter that finally winked out with a percussive bang.

Balthazar stumbled into the corridor, ears ringing. He blinked against the sudden light. Just behind him, the Prophet drew a ragged breath and Balthazar turned to lay a steadying hand on his arm.

"*Don't touch me, necromancer!*" Zarathustra hissed, baring his teeth. Grey eyes burned with fury. Shaking hands curled into claws as he reached for Balthazar's throat.

Balthazar recoiled, horrified. Without thought, his hand moving of its own accord, he did something that surprised even himself. He made the sign of the flame.

Zarathustra's eyes widened at the symbol of his faith, then closed. He bowed his head. When he looked up, the rage was gone, leaving sadness in its place.

"I'm sorry," he said. "I am not myself."

"There is nothing to forgive."

"I am tired, Balthazar. Very tired. But you must take me to

Victor before we leave this place. By the mercy of the Holy Father, we are not too late to save him."

Balthazar almost had second thoughts about his newfound salvation at the idea of facing the daēva unchained. Victor would not view him in a kind light. In fact, he would probably be inclined to exact some unpleasant revenge. But Zarathustra gave him a sharp look as if he knew exactly what Balthazar was thinking.

"I'll lead you there," Balthazar said with a small sigh. "It's not far. And I'll deal with Molon myself." His face hardened. "I should have done it years ago."

They hurried through the twisty, sloping corridors to the higher levels. Nothing moved in the chill halls. The House-Behind-the-Veil had never been a lively place, but now it felt like a tomb. The eyes of the ancient kings whose treasures Neblis had looted seemed to follow Balthazar as he splashed through icy puddles and traversed a series of wide galleries, sending echoes scurrying into the dim recesses. At last, they reached the stone chamber at the heart of the House.

Balthazar stopped abruptly in the archway, unwilling to lead the Prophet further. A lump of mauled flesh lay before the pillar, hardly recognizable as a man.

"I'm sorry, old friend," Zarathustra whispered, his voice broken. "I've failed you yet again." He made the sign of the flame. "May the Holy Father welcome you home."

Balthazar turned away from the gruesome sight. Another death to stain his soul. Then something struck him. He studied the body again. The old man had poor eyesight, but Balthazar could see a hank of yellow hair clinging to the skull.

"It's not Victor," he said in a low voice.

"Are you certain?" Zarathustra frowned. "Then who—"

Balthazar laid a quieting hand on his arm. Something moved in the shadows.

A flash of gold, molten in the dying firelight.

Balthazar's pulse raced. The glimmer resolved into a crown with points like shards of amberglass. That he still felt such intense desire shamed him to his core. It was almost as strong as the fear that dried his tongue to the roof of his mouth. Balthazar might be a different man than he had been an hour before, but not every string that bound his heart could be snipped so easily.

I will never be free of her, he thought numbly. Never.

Neblis strode to the pillar and knelt beside Molon's body. Her shoulders shook. Balthazar thought it was from grief. Then she stood and gave the corpse a savage kick with her bare foot. Her mouth opened wide, wider, and a scream erupted from it. It was a sound beyond anything Balthazar had heard before. Madness and sorrow and undiluted rage. Not for the death of Molon. For the loss of Victor.

Balthazar took a step back, his boot scraping softly on the stone. Neblis's head turned. She looked different. Hair like spun snow, eyes like quicksilver. She seemed more alien and more beautiful than ever. He felt a dreaminess creep over him, heady and seductive. The soft linens chafed unbearably against his skin. The honeyed scent of oleander, that deadliest of blooms, drifted across the chamber. He breathed it in, eyes slipping shut.

Balthazar's mistress had returned.

The urge to go to her bordered on compulsion. He was about to step out of the shadows when breath tickled his cheek. It smelled faintly of lamb stew.

"Perhaps we should run now," the Prophet whispered. He raised his hand and the flames in the brazier leapt to life. Neblis hissed like a cat, lips drawing back in a snarl, and Balthazar returned to himself enough to sweep the old man off his feet and barrel down the corridor in the opposite direction.

Her elemental magic wouldn't work, that was the only thing that might save them. The House-Behind-the-Veil was part of the Dominion again and subject to its laws. But she was still quick and strong. Twenty times stronger than Balthazar, maybe more. The wards shattering wouldn't alter that fact.

Balthazar careened around a corner, slipping on the slick, mossy stone and almost losing his feet. He had a talisman of Traveling in his pocket, he always kept it with him, so if they could just make it to the gate....

Behind them—very close behind—Neblis howled in wordless fury.

"Do something!" he yelled.

Zarathustra flung an arm back, bringing showers of stone and dust down in their wake. More empty rooms flashed past and then Balthazar was leaping through the small archway that led to the gardens. The cloying scent of night flowers filled his nose. A light rain was falling outside, the first Balthazar had seen in the Dominion. No weather ever touched this place. *Strange things were happening indeed*.

Just ahead of them, an abbadax crouched in the courtyard.

It screeched and spread its deadly wings, blocking his path. Raindrops glistened on its spine of knife-edged feathers. It raked the ground with a taloned paw, then began advancing toward Balthazar, armored tail lashing the delicate blossoms like a scythe through wheat.

He looked back just in time to see Neblis explode through the doorway. They were trapped. Visions of the Pit loomed in his mind's eye. Eternity spent atoning for his crimes....

Balthazar's head rang with a soundless vibration. The ground trembled beneath his feet. Thin cracks began to spiral up the tallest tower of the House-Behind-the-Veil. Neblis skidded to a halt, hands pressed to her ears. She shook her head like a dog with a flea. That strange cold fire leaked from the fissures, which widened as he stood there half-blinded and paralyzed with fear. Zarathustra growled something in his ear that barely sounded like human speech. His mild grey eyes burned with savage intensity.

Neblis fell to her hands and knees and crawled towards the

well, which lay only a few paces away. She moved like an insect. Like some many-jointed creature with chitin for bones. Balthazar had a sudden vision of the dead servant girl climbing out of its lightless depths, fingers caked with mud and eyes lit with demented merriment.

He had not prayed in a very long time, but he did so now.

Holy Father, I know I have no right to ask you for anything. But perhaps, in your infinite wisdom, you can keep the thing that lives in there from being home at this particular moment.

Zarathustra coughed. Black blood dripped from his nose.

"It is done," he whispered. "It is done."

The cracks reached the pinnacle and the tower began to topple—slowly, lazily, as though the air had turned to jelly. The abbadax reared up, massive head swinging in alarm. With a final piercing cry, it abandoned its mistress, taking off into the rain-swept forest.

Balthazar scrabbled backwards, the House looming above him like a malevolent stone giant. His heel caught on a loose paving stone and he fell hard, landing with the Prophet on top of him. Sharp gravel raked his back. Even as the tower plummeted to the ground a hundred paces below, the corkscrewed spire bent the eye, blurring Balthazar's vision.

His rooms were in that tower. He thought of the maps he had painstakingly drawn from memory, the vast collection of talismans and mystical scrolls he had amassed over the last two centuries.

Neblis reached a pale arm toward him, her palm open in a silent entreaty. She'd pulled herself up to the lip of the well. Her eyes locked on Balthazar, blue fire reflected in their depths. He remembered the first time he had seen her. He too had been lost in the Dominion. Neblis had found him and claimed him, tearing away the last shreds of his innocence. The man who had stumbled out of the gate in Karnopolis was not the boy who entered.

She was his lover and jailer. His Queen.

"Balthazar," Neblis whispered.

And then she was gone, buried beneath a thousand tons of her own magic.

A cloud of glittering dust rose from the rubble of the tower. White goosedown drifted through the air like snow flurries. The light flickered and died, leaving only the eternal twilight of the gloaming. Zarathustra lay unmoving in his arms.

Balthazar tipped his face to the rain. He tasted salt and knew it was his own tears, although he wasn't sure if he shed them for Neblis, the Prophet or himself.

I almost went to her. In the end, I almost went.

He feared the old man was dead until Zarathustra opened his grey eyes.

"You've done well, Balthazar," he said faintly. "I knew you would."

Balthazar sat up. He gently wiped the blood from Zarathustra's mouth with his own sleeve.

"What now?" he asked, feeling as lost and alone as he had the day his parents were taken away in the plague cart. He could see scraps of parchment in the rubble, wilting beneath the rain. All the knowledge he had meticulously collected for two centuries. The talismans whose use he had yet to decipher. Part of him wanted to drop the Prophet and start digging like a mole. To salvage what he could and run. That's what he would've done once, without hesitation.

Balthazar tore his gaze from the rubble. "Shall I bring you to our own world?" He patted his pocket. "I have a talisman to get through the gate. Alexander waits on the other side with his army. Or is the young conqueror not to your liking? Either way, we must decide quickly." He glanced around, peering into the dimness where the gardens gave way to the tall, swaying reeds that marked the boundary with the gate. "If the wards are truly broken, her pets in the lake will be loose as well. And they make the Shepherds look like playful puppies."

The Prophet gave a slight shake of his head. "Take me to the Cold Sea," he said. "I am ready."

"No!" The vehemence in Balthazar's voice surprised him, but he found he couldn't stomach the idea of losing his mentor so soon after finding him again. "I will not. Ask me anything else—anything!—and I'll do it gladly. But not this. You said you're part daēva. Whatever you have done to yourself, these injuries will heal with rest."

The Prophet smiled gently. "I told you, I am tired. It was never my wish to live so long."

"But...." Balthazar groped for words to convince him. "What of the world? War has come! You will be needed to help fight. Your powers—"

"You said it yourself: there is another. She's already taken my place. I felt the magic of Breaking in that rain, Balthazar. It's what destroyed the wards around the House. Neblis might think to use her, but I have faith the child is stronger than that." His eyes grew dim. "I've had enough of war. This one is for others to wage. My old bones are not up to the task."

"How can I bring you so far? It's not safe to travel through the shadowlands. You've seen what roams there yourself. We would be torn to shreds the moment we entered the forest."

"You said you had built a raft."

"That was years ago. I don't even know if it floats!"

"Then we shall test it. The current will carry us there. It is my last wish that you accompany me on this journey. To the shore only. Then you are free to do as you desire."

Balthazar bowed his head. "As you wish, magus."

He carried the Prophet through the gardens and propped him up against a willow that leaned crookedly over the river-bank. He had to search for some minutes before he found it. The gloaming played hide-and-seek like a mischievous child, and the place where you left something today might not be where you found it tomorrow. Finally, he pushed through a stand of spiky purple barberry bushes and there it sat. The raft was a flimsy-looking thing, made from rough-cut logs bound together with vines. Moss grew in the crevices of the planks like a mouthful of rotten teeth. He'd never really intended to use it, and hadn't even thought of it in ages before he mentioned it to Zarathustra.

He dragged it along the bank to where the old sage sat, humming a tune and watching the river leap and splash. Balthazar hoped that once the magus saw it, he would have second thoughts about setting out on this mad journey.

"You see? I have no boat-making skills. You'd be better off swimming!"

Zarathustra smiled. "Even the most humble of objects have their purpose. Let us give your fine raft the benefit of the doubt until proven otherwise."

Balthazar shook his head, but he helped the Prophet settle himself in the center. Then he waded out and pushed off. It wobbled severely as he climbed aboard and Balthazar was certain they would capsize. But then to his surprise, the little raft righted itself and the current seized them, sure and swift.

"I don't even know if the Cold Sea exists," he admitted as they sped along, the dark woods of the Dominion blurring past on either side. "It could be simply a dark fancy from too many years in the shadowlands."

"Why did you name it thus?" Zarathustra asked curiously. He lay with his head propped on one hand.

Balthazar thought for a moment. "I considered grander ones." He made a flourishing gesture. "The Sea of Oblivion! The Infernal Deep! Many others. But on those evenings when its winds would blow through the gardens of the House-Behind-the-Veil, like an icicle slicing through the spice of Neblis's flowers...I always thought of it as the Cold Sea." He shivered. "Even the wards couldn't keep that wind out."

"Well, I think you chose well. Simple is always best."

Balthazar gave him a sidelong glance. "Are you not afraid of what we might find there?"

"Perhaps a little," the Prophet admitted. "But I'm willing to face it. That is where true courage lies." His eyes grew sad. "We all have our sins. They are for the Holy Father to judge, not you or even I."

Their little raft drifted on, winding between sheer cliffs with only a ribbon of white sky above. The land gradually leveled out. Balthazar saw fields of poppies and dunes of bluish sand. Once, he saw a tall black tower in the distance and longed to investigate it, but the Prophet refused. Balthazar watched it dwindle behind them with disappointment.

Hours passed and still the river rushed inexorably forward, until he knew they were past the edges of his maps. Then the current grew sluggish. They entered a wide, marshy delta and he smelled freshened salt air. The sky widened, grew brighter, and it unfurled before him. A vast, still ocean, unmarred by a single ripple. When the water grew shallow enough, he leapt out and waded the raft to shore.

Balthazar helped the Prophet disembark. He seemed stronger and they walked together to the edge of the water. Soft black sand stretched along the beach. Balthazar saw not a single footprint or other sign that anything living had ever preceded them. It was like standing at the edge of the world.

"Now we wait," the Prophet said.

"For what?"

"For whatever comes."

Balthazar felt a vague sense of dread. The Prophet had said he would be free to turn his back on the Cold Sea and return to the living world, but how could he make such a promise? Who knew what sort of judgment would be handed down on these black shores? And Balthazar had little doubt he would be found wanting.

"How can you stand to look at me?" he demanded. "It's a cruel joke to pretend I am saved. Without the chains, I will quickly age and die, and when I do, I will suffer the torments of hell for a thousand lifetimes. What point is there in going on?"

The Prophet considered Balthazar's words. "I do not pretend to know the will of the Holy Father, but he has seen fit to let that ouroboros fall into your hands. A long life can be spent on good deeds, or evil ones. Most often it is both. That is the nature of human souls. But you are more fortunate than most, Balthazar. You have been given a second chance and the means to make it count for something."

The ouroboros. Balthazar had forgotten it. He slid a hand into his pocket and was glad to find it still there.

"I'm afraid," he admitted. "I've fallen very low, magus."

The Prophet smiled. "An old friend of mine used to say our greatest glory is not in never falling, but in rising again each time we do."

"Perhaps." Balthazar studied the line of the horizon, a darker grey against the steel waters of the sea. "I was there. When they took you away. And I never said anything."

"I remember."

"I thought you were dead. If I'd realized you were being held prisoner, I...." What would he have done? Balthazar honestly didn't know. "When the magi took me in, I had no one else. Nowhere else. I trusted them. And they betrayed us both." He turned to Zarathustra. "How can you forgive what they did to you?"

"They were afraid," the Prophet said quietly. "It was a great sin to chain the daēvas against their will. But instead of trying to make it right, Xeros chose to commit further sins to cover it up. And now we have come full circle. The right path is always waiting. One only has to seek it out. I will tell you a secret, Balthazar." The Prophet winked. "The cage is not locked."

Balthazar spun around as a harsh cry erupted behind them. He saw a black dot descending rapidly from the sky. The brief taste of freedom turned to ashes in his mouth.

His mistress wasn't dead after all. Somehow, Balthazar had known all along. She was too strong, too old. She could not be killed, not by him and certainly not by a tired old man.

And now he would pay the price for disobedience.

Beside him, the Prophet made the sign of the flame.

"It seems my passage to the next plane will be delayed, Balthazar," he said faintly.

"More likely sped up," Balthazar replied. He shaded his eyes with a hand as the dot resolved into an abbadax. Neblis's crown was gone. Her eyes blazed like pools of quicksilver. "And there's a good chance I'll be joining you."

❧ 23 ❧

TIJAH

She galloped toward the seething mass of Druj. The necromancers' faces were cloaked in shadow by the tumult of the storm but she could see them coming. A line of six. They carried staffs that whirled in blurring arcs. Behind them ran the revenants, eyes gleaming like silver mirrors with each fork of lightning.

Only seconds had passed since Jengis released his arrow, but it felt much longer. Tijah had experienced this in battle before, the peculiar stretching of time, the intense clarity, every detail etched in her mind. The smell of salt and rot. The hilt of her scimitar, warm against her palm, its reassuring weight an extension of her own arm. The delighted howling of the Druj at the sight of fresh meat.

One hundred paces. Seventy-five. Fifty.

The wind swept stinging spray into her eyes. Tijah blinked it away. Without conscious thought, she found herself signing with her free left hand.

Hold, sister. We meet them in the battle now.

How many seconds would she live before that horde engulfed her? Enough to kill as many as possible.

Tijah raised her sword as a thunderous crack rent the night far above. Her horse reared up and she fought to stay in the saddle. And then her mount was frantically backing away. Huge boulders rained down on the beach, a torrent of rock and ice sweeping away all in its path. She remembered the snow avalanche. The frightening rumble. This was a hundred times worse. Choking dust and sand filled the air. The rain helped tamp it down some but Tijah still wound the scarf Samahe had given her around her face like her old *qarha*, leaving only the eyes visible. It felt right somehow.

The worst of the slide passed right in front of her like a river, crashing into the storm-driven waves and sending jets of icy water high into the air. Abid had truly brought the mountain down on their heads.

If Tijah had ridden a few seconds longer, she would have been caught in it too.

Dumb luck, or the goddess is actually watching, she thought.

The war cries of the Clan turned to whoops of glee as they watched the Druj buried beneath a thousand tons of rock.

"Now!" Tijah yelled over the din. "Cut them down before the surprise wears off!"

She rode into the rubble, scimitar swinging left and right, slashing at the Druj that had somehow escaped the landslide. Some had taken terrible injuries but still lived. She cut their heads off as they flailed about. Others had been protected by the sheer press of bodies. She saw a grinning wight in the slender form of a teenage girl gut one of the Clan men with a spear, twisting it viciously as blood poured from his open mouth.

Kill the monsters, Tijah.

Goddess, she was trying. But there seemed no end to them, no matter how her arm ached from cutting and hacking. Tijah realized why with a sinking stomach. The Druj were starting to crawl out from under the rubble. Ordinary men would have suffocated or died from shattered bones. But these soldiers were already dead.

Tijah wheeled her mount around and spotted the two young Four-Legs men. The rain had slowed to a drizzle. "Jengis, Kian!"

They finished putting down a towering revenant and turned to her, weary and blood-soaked.

"We have to get inside Gorgon-e Gaz! Get to the daēvas and free them to fight! It's the only chance now."

Jengis and Kian nodded and the three of them started to cut a swath toward the fortress. A dozen of the Four-Legs Clan fought in little knots, scattered across the mound of shattered rock. The other half were missing. Tijah assumed they were dead. She hadn't seen Cyrus in what felt like hours.

The fortress itself had been half-buried beneath the landslide. She couldn't see a way to dig down to it, not that wouldn't take days. Only the wall facing the sea looked clear. But it had been ruptured by Victor and the others who escaped. They could slip inside through the crack, if it hadn't been repaired yet...

"Tijah?" It was Kian. His voice had an edge that made her turn in the saddle.

"What?"

"Look."

He pointed out to sea. At the wall of water rushing headlong for the beach. Just before it blotted out the moon, Tijah realized she couldn't hear the surf anymore because it had been sucked into the underbelly of the monstrous wave. Out and out the tide went, leaving bare sand for a quarter of a league at least. Tijah and Kian shared a horrified look. Then they began racing up the slope towards the fractured mountain, Jengis just behind.

The wave caught them a few heartbeats later. It slapped Tijah from her horse and spun her upside down. She curled into a ball as her back slammed against the rocks, squeezing her eyes and mouth closed in the grimace of the drowning. Utter darkness. Which way was up? No way to tell. Churning, tumbling, Tijah felt like the plaything of a giant sea serpent. And then her head broke the surface. Gorgon-e Gaz lay just ahead, its curtain wall thrusting out like a jetty into rough waters. She had been pulled out to sea.

She managed a single hoarse shout before her head went under again.

If wishes were fishes, I'd know how to swim, she thought, trying to keep calm, but the panic was setting in now, the vastness of the black ocean making her breath come in harsh, choking gasps. Tunic and trousers billowed out, tugging her down. She kicked and felt a boot come off. Her arms went numb. Gods, the sea was cold. The stone heap of Gorgon-e Gaz looked so close but it might as well have been a thousand leagues, for the current was drawing her out farther and farther with each second.

Tijah's head slipped under again.

And then she felt a force lifting her up and carrying her toward the beach. It deposited her, snorting and sputtering, on the sand. When she managed to look up, she saw Pegah. Blood trickled from the girl's nose. Tijah knew it came from working with water.

Pegah offered her a hand and Tijah took it. She felt slightly embarrassed at how much she'd disliked the kid. Pegah could have let her drown. There was no one to see it. Everything in the vicinity, living and Undead, had been battered on the rocks and swept out to sea.

"We have to help him," Pegah said, her voice intense, on the verge of breaking. She swayed on her feet and the blood thickened.

"Who?"

A moment later, Tijah saw them. Not everyone had been swept up by the wave. Atop the fortress, three necromancers stood in a ring around Achaemenes. One reached out a hand in a gesture perversely similar to Pegah's, as though offering help, and blue lightning arced from his fingertips. Achaemenes screamed. He fell to his knees.

Tijah reached for her scimitar and found an empty sheath. Then she remembered she'd had it in her hand. It must be at the bottom of the sea now.

Tijah yelled, "Hey, assholes!" Then she succumbed to a coughing fit.

Three heads swiveled toward her.

"Yeah, you!" She lowered her voice for Pegah. "Run. Right now. I've got this."

"But—"

"I said get the fuck out of here!" Tijah snarled.

Two of the necromancers started towards them. Pegah looked at Tijah, then at the Antimagi, her eyes shiny with fear. Half the human captives were dead, their flesh flaccid and pale as fungi. They must have drowned when the wave hit. Three were missing their clothes and Pegah flinched away from the disturbing sight of naked corpses. But the necromancers...They appeared untouched, dragging the bodies through the wet sand as if they weighed nothing at all. The captives who still lived were skin and bones, their eyes black hollows.

"Parvane and Anu are down the beach," Pegah said in a rush. "I'll go find them."

Tijah nodded as the girl dashed off. She watched the necromancers come with a loathing beyond anything she'd felt before. It was purer than her hatred for Ilyas and the King, or even the mercenaries who had tried to beat and rape her. Tijah still had a belt knife. She pulled it out and waited.

"Such a brave boy!" The first necromancer taunted as he drew close. "Are you daēva like the other?" He studied her, bloodless lips curled in a smile. "No, I think you're human."

"Not brave, just stupid," the other one chimed in. "I'll drain you dry, boy, until you're just a husk. And then I'll give what's left to the revenants. They've earned some sport."

"Funny," Tijah said. "I don't see any Druj left except for you two shitheads. I think my friends messed you up pretty badly. Almost as badly as I'm about to."

The first laughed. He had ruddy cheeks and thick blonde hair. A northerner. "With that?" He eyed her knife. "You could have a dozen armed men at your back and it still wouldn't make a difference. We are Antimagi. I wield power beyond anything you've ever dreamed of."

Tijah bared her teeth in a wintry smile. "You're just men who serve a powerful daēva. That's all. And once she's gone, you'll be nothing."

The blonde Antimagus looked at her for a moment, his face as lacking in human expression as his half-dead captives. Then he unhooked an axe from his belt. Moonlight caught the blade as he hefted it. "I'll only take your arms," he said. "Once you're collared, you'll hardly miss them."

Tijah held the knife lightly, balanced on the balls of her feet. Exhaustion dragged at her like a waterlogged cloak. She dug deep, looking for the unyielding deserts of Al Miraj, and found only more exhaustion. It had been a very long night.

Atop the fortress, Achaemenes fought the last necromancer. He was on his feet again, sword in hand. Iron rang on stone and a shower of blue sparks rained down into the darkness. If anything still lived inside Gorgon-e Gaz, there was no sign of it. Besides the two of them and the Antimagi, nothing stirred on the beach.

The Four-Legs Clan, all dead. The kids.... At least some of them had made it. They would finish things. She thought Achaemenes had a decent chance of winning, now that it was an even fight.

The yellow-haired necromancer swept his axe in a wide arc and Tijah belatedly leapt back, one knee buckling as she stumbled. It shocked her deeply to realize she'd almost been too late. Her reflexes had lagged—only by a second or two, but that could make all the difference. The necromancer pushed his advantage, forcing her back, while the other circled around to the side. Behind her, the Salenian Sea rolled in and out.

Her body was so tired. And yet her mind felt oddly clear. She remembered details of her mother's face she hadn't thought of in years. The ebony smoothness of her skin, except for the lines around her eyes, which derived not from laughter but from worry. Worry about her daughters and what might happen to them in a world where women were on a par with camels, and perhaps a notch or two lower than horses.

You'll always have Myrri, she had said once. *Protect each other as best you can.*

Tijah heard a sound to her left and ducked beneath a second whistling axe blade. The hafts were about as long as her arm. Too long to get inside their guard with her knife.

On the next pass, Tijah was too slow. The blade of the axe cut deep into her right bicep. She felt the tendon snap and her arm went instantly numb. The knife fell to the sand. She fumbled for it with her left and one of the necromancers kicked her in the face.

Tijah's ears rang, but she managed to get to her feet.

"Maybe we'll just take you in bits," the northerner said. "A piece at a time." He whirled his axe. "What do you think? Should I start with the hands or the feet?"

Tijah spat blood on his boots.

"Ears? Nose?" He turned to his companion. "What's your opinion, Vashi?"

"Just kill him and get it over with," Vashi snarled. "There could be others nearby."

Tijah held her face still. Over Vashi's shoulder, she saw Cyrus step out of the rubble.

Where have you been, magus? Why haven't I seen you in hours?

HE LEANED DOWN AND PICKED SOMETHING UP. THE SWORD OF

227

a revenant. It was nearly as long as Cyrus was tall. Made of iron and caked in old gore. His arms shook as he tried to raise it. His lips moved silently. A prayer?

The surf was a dull roar.

Tijah closed her eyes. When she opened them, both necromancers had closed in for the kill. They stood before her, eager but wary, as you would be of a cornered, wounded animal with sharp teeth. Behind them, Cyrus came forward, stepping over the dead and dying captives.

The yellow-haired Antimagus brought his axe back. His gaze rested on her neck. In that infinite moment before blade bit into flesh, Tijah thought not of Myrri, but of Tommas and Ilyas. How it was to watch them fight together. The fluid beauty. Two bodies, one mind. How they used to trick revenants into opening their guard. Despite everything, all the ugliness between them, they trusted each other.

The axe flashed down and Tijah didn't try to run, only twisted so it slid into her side instead. She'd hoped for a grazing blow, but the blade went deep. She screamed at the white-hot bolt of pain. The necromancers watched her writhe at their feet.

"I still say—" The northerner never finished his sentence because Cyrus's sword, the revenant's sword, whistled through the air, severing both their heads in a single swing.

Cyrus grunted. It was a sound of mingled surprise and satisfaction. The bodies twitched for a few moments, refusing to admit they were dead, until he stabbed them again in the heart and they fell still.

Dawn touched the eastern horizon, banishing the last remnants of the storm. Tijah watched the sky lighten to a pale yellow-rose as her blood pumped into the sand. A gull glided by overhead, scanning the sea for breakfast. And then Achaemenes was kneeling next to her. Dark brown hair fell into his eyes and he swept a hand across his forehead. She did not think he was a boy anymore. Not after today.

"No, no, no...." He kept repeating the single word, over and over again. Achaemenes tore a strip from his tunic and pressed it to her wound. Tijah gritted her teeth. Something inside her was torn beyond repair. She could feel it.

Goddess, just give me a clean death. No lingering. She only wished she could say goodbye to Anu.

"Go away," she whispered.

"You traded your life for mine," Achaemenes said, cradling her head in one hand. "Why?"

Tijah gave him a red smile.

Because if I hadn't, Pegah would have gotten herself killed trying to do it herself.

Because the goddess put me there for a reason. Because I'm so tired....

This was too much to explain, so Tijah didn't try.

"Go away," she whispered again.

The beach grew dim and she thought perhaps a whole day had passed and night was falling. But she could see the sun now, peeking above the horizon. Achaemenes shouted something and was answered by other voices. People were coming out of Gorgon-e Gaz. Cyrus ran toward them. A tall, sturdy woman with a long braid lifted him off his feet. Tijah thought they were both weeping.

Light touched her face, warm and golden.

What a lovely morning, she thought, and let go.

⚜ 24 ⚜

Tijah stood on the shore of her dream. There were no waves in this sea. Its surface stretched away like a cloudy sheet of glass. She could see Myrri in the boat, farther out now.

"I'm over here!" Tijah cried. "Come back!"

Myrri turned, her hands on the oars. She saw Tijah and gave that crooked smile, like she knew a good dirty joke and might tell it if she decided she liked you. Her hair was long again, tight curls brushing her shoulders. She wore a plain white tunic that left her arms bare. Myrri's skin glowed like burnished rosewood in the half-light.

Then her wicked grin faltered. Her hands fell from the oars. The boat spun in a lazy circle.

Tijah sensed someone behind her. She turned, ready to fight, but it was only Achaemenes.

"Go away," Tijah said, feeling like she had said this exact phrase to him before but fuzzy on exactly when that was.

"I'm sorry," he said, seizing her wrist.

Tijah tried to pull away. Achaemenes held her fast.

"It's what she would want," he said, looking at Myrri.

Tijah howled in fury. The boat was drifting away. Myrri stared out to sea, refusing to look over no matter how loudly Tijah screamed her name. Either she couldn't hear or didn't want to.

Pain shot up Tijah's arm to the shoulder. She looked down and saw a bracelet of thorns twined around her wrist. Blood oozed from a dozen tiny puncture marks.

Achaemenes whispered, "Stay with me."

That's when Tijah punched him in the face.

SHE WOKE IN DARKNESS. TIJAH TRIED TO SIT UP BUT A TERRIBLE pain in her side dragged her back down. She gingerly flexed the fingers of her right hand. They twitched weakly against the thick linen bandages swathing her torso. Her leg hurt too, a faint ache in the knee. Sweet goddess, her mouth was dry. Tijah blinked and caught a few fractured memories by the tail. Lightning forking down over a raging sea. The thunder of hooves on sand. Screaming. Death all around. The ocean rising up like a mountain, and then.... Antimagi.

Cyrus, like an avenging angel.

She felt a cool weight on her right wrist. That arm had also been wrapped in bandages, but something lurked beneath them. She probed until her fingertips brushed metal. From there, it took her about two seconds to put it together. The knee. The dream. The fact she wasn't properly dead.

Various other things, now that she'd come fully awake.

Like the deep, swirling pool of power at the corner of her eye. She couldn't touch it herself, but...

Tijah still wore Myrri's cuff. She couldn't bear to take it off, but she always kept it on her left arm, not her right.

Fury filled her and he must have felt it, must have been

waiting, because the tent flap pulled back and he stood there, silhouetted against the stars.

"You fucking bonded me," Tijah shouted. "Goddess curse you! You had no right. No right!"

"I had no choice," Achaemenes replied calmly. "You were dying."

"It was my fate! *Mine*."

"The children need you." He looked at her, looked away. "I need you. It doesn't have to be forever."

Tijah yanked the cuff off and flung it across the tent. It was a futile gesture that made her even angrier. Even without actually wearing it, he still lived in her mind. Had a nice little piece of property there, with a house and a garden and a comfortable chair to kick his feet up. She hated the masculine energy of him. The forced intimacy with a stranger.

"Oh, it won't be," Tijah snarled. "As soon as I can walk, I'll find Nazafareen, get her to break it. You can count on that."

Achaemenes shifted in the tent opening. He favored his left leg again. The bond had brought his infirmity back. Tijah could feel it, along with a host of other sensations, both mental and physical. Wariness of what she might do. Bone-deep exhaustion from lending her the strength to heal from wounds no human should have survived. There was a tightness around his eyes that hadn't been there before. He looked much older than his seventeen years.

"I'm sorry, I saw no other choice," he said again. "Cyrus agreed. He found a set of spare cuffs in the fortress."

Achaemenes took your pain into himself. Suffered for you. Is still suffering, although he hides it. You should be kinder to him.

That was Myrri, signing away with a disapproving look on her face. The new bond had not displaced her. In fact, she was mouthier than ever.

Tijah ignored her. She would not invite him inside her tent and she would not pretend to be pleased by this turn of events.

"I suppose you expect me to be grateful," she said in acid tones.

Did his lips curve in a smile, quickly suppressed? "No, I didn't imagine you would be. We haven't known each other long but...no."

She shook her head in wonder. "I'd have thought you'd had enough of being bonded. Letting a human hold your leash. Or are you afraid to be alone?"

He didn't answer this. Instead, he said quietly, "Why do you want to die? Is it because of your daēva?"

Rage surged. "Don't speak of her to me. Don't you dare!"

"I feel your grief like it's my own." His face softened. "I'm sorry, Tijah, so—"

"Get out!" She groped for the nearest hard object, found a water jug, and threw it at Achaemenes. He ducked. Pottery shattered outside. "Get. Out."

He held his palms up, backing away. "I'll return later. We can talk more after you've rested."

She felt from him...what exactly? Smugness was perhaps too strong a word, but something close. Relaxed confidence that she would have no choice but to accept their bond because she would never be rid of him, not awake nor asleep. Running away would do no good. He would always know where she was, just as she would always know where *he* was. If he was angry or happy or sad or thirsty, she would know this too.

Tijah growled in frustration. "Out!"

When he was gone, she fell back on her blankets, anger giving way to dazed despair. Nazafareen had spoken of *building walls* and *locking boxes* when she first bonded Darius. Ilyas had taught her the trick of it. Tijah had never even considered such a thing with Myrri, neither of them felt the need.

She did now.

Tijah wanted to weep. To scream until her lungs gave out.

Having Achaemenes in her head made her miss Myrri worse than ever. Like being kissed by the wrong person.

I will raise walls against you higher than the King's palace at Karnopolis, she vowed, rubbing her eyes. *And then I will hunt down Nazafareen and make her end this nightmare.*

☙❦❧

T<small>IJAH SLEPT FOR A TIME MORE AND SURFACED TO CHATTERING</small> voices in her tent. They were trying to be quiet and as a result, were even louder.

"Fetch some food, Abid, she'll be hungry when she wakes up."

"Will she live?"

"Of course she'll live, don't be stupid." That was Anu. "Achaemenes fixed her up."

"Is it true we're leaving today?"

"Yes, now go get a bowl of soup before I pinch you very hard."

"Pegah! Anu said she—"

And so on.

Tijah opened one eye, then the other. Daylight filtered through the cracks in the entrance. Anu sat cross-legged on the floor, along with Parvane and Bijan. Tijah realized she was extremely happy to see them and felt ashamed she hadn't asked about the children last night. She'd been too shocked and angry.

"Hello," she said, sounding like a raven risen from the grave.

Anu's face split in a grin. "Hello," she said. "You're up. It's been days."

"Couldn't sleep with all the racket," Tijah said, dredging up a smile. "Did I hear you send Abid somewhere? Does that mean we're all here?"

Anu nodded. And then they started talking over one another, telling Tijah three different stories at the same time, until Pegah came in and rode roughshod over everyone.

"We hid in a root cellar after we lost you," she said, toying with the ends of her hair. "Then Achaemenes got us out of the village and we made our own way to the mountains. We were only a few leagues away from Gorgon-e Gaz when he felt a huge discharge of power. I felt it too, we all did."

"That was me," Abid said, beaming. He had returned with the soup and was sitting with the other children. The kitten peeked out from inside his shirt. "Ow!" he exclaimed as it sank needle claws into his skin.

"We ran the rest of the way," Pegah said. "And we run really fast."

"The Druj were going to kill everyone," Bijan piped up. "We saw them from above!"

"So we joined together and called the sea," Parvane said. "That was Achaemenes's idea."

"It was a good one," Tijah admitted grudgingly. "Even if you did nearly drown me."

"We'd split up to look for survivors when I found you," Pegah said. "I'm sorry I didn't get back with help sooner." She looked down, a flush creeping up her cheeks as Anu scowled daggers at her. Some things hadn't changed, at least. "Thank the Holy Father for Cyrus."

"Where is he?" Tijah took a sip of the broth. She felt light-headed and ravenous.

"With his daēva. Shall I tell them you're awake?"

"In a moment. So you saved them? The daēvas inside?"

Pegah nodded. "Just after you fell. Abid broke through the rubble. The prisoners were in chains, hand and foot. The smell of the place...." She took a deep breath. "We wanted to kill the guards but the magus stopped it. He said we had to keep them alive until the cuffs are properly broken."

"And Cyrus was right. You know that."

"I suppose." Her voice was flat. Tijah wondered what the girl had seen when they liberated Gorgon-e Gaz. "Seventy-six daēvas survived. The magus says there are records. Of births and deaths, going back two hundred years." She shared a look with the other children. "He says he'll help us find out which ones are our parents."

"Can you take me to him? I must speak with Cyrus."

Pegah frowned. "Shouldn't I bring him here?"

"Carry me out to the beach, if you don't mind. I want some fresh air."

So the children wrapped Tijah in a blanket and Anu lifted her up with the power, as gentle as a feather on the breeze. The daylight hurt her eyes at first. When they adjusted, she saw more black tents pitched above the high tide line. Kian stood outside one of them, and Tijah called his name with a grin.

He waved back and she saw with another burst of relief that not all the Four-Legs Clan had perished in the fight. Six men stood stern-faced with arrows loosely nocked and pointed at a group of guards from Gorgon-e Gaz, who were easily identifiable by the King's griffin embroidered on their tunics. They sat in a circle, staring downcast at the ground. She counted perhaps three dozen. Far fewer than she had expected.

From a short distance away, in the shadow of the escarpment, a second group also watched the prisoners. Young faces and old eyes. Lean, predatory, graceful, with an animal magnetism it was hard to look away from. No visible weapons, but they didn't need any.

Achaemenes was speaking with a woman whose long braid brushed her thighs. Tijah thought it was the same one who had embraced Cyrus but her memory was fuzzy. She'd been dying, after all.

"Cassandane." Tijah turned her head. Samahe was standing next to the makeshift litter, shawl wrapped tightly around her shoulders. "She speaks for the daēvas, along with Mithre." She

QUEEN OF CHAOS

nodded at a black-haired man with broad shoulders and a vulpine
face.

"What happened?" Tijah asked. The man caught her eye and
held it until she looked away. Tijah suppressed a shiver.

"From what I've gathered, the guards kept waiting for reinforcements to arrive from Tel Khalujah," Samahe said dryly. "Of
course, they never came. Finally, ten of the daēvas were permitted
to use their power to summon a storm. But they drew too much.
Several died, and their bonded guards with them. One managed
to break through a wall before she succumbed to her wounds. Her
own guard lay dying and could not stop her using the power with
her final breath."

Tijah imagined the dire struggle going on in the prison as she
and the Clan fought to get inside.

"The daēvas on the other side were blocked from using their
own power by the cuffs, of course. But that is not their only
advantage, as you well know. They are very strong and fast. There
was a rebellion. Killings on both sides. Then your warrior-children
showed up and shattered the last chains. Anu threatened to toss
the surviving guards to the Druj if they didn't surrender."

"Good girl," Tijah said, and was rewarded with a small smile.
"So what are they like? The Old Ones?" Both Achaemenes and
the woman were staring at her now. Tijah's ears burned.

Samahe's face turned grim. "Some of them are sick from being
held for so long. Not just in their bodies but their minds. And the
ones who lost their guards cannot use the power. It's trapped in
the cuffs."

"How many of those?"

"About forty."

Tijah and Samahe studied what was left of the infamous
prison. Most of it had been buried in sand and rubble. The sea
washed over the ruins, creating tidal eddies that long-legged
seabirds now waded through, hunting for fish and other briny

morsels. Someday, anyone passing by would see only a few grey boulders, perhaps larger and squarer than the rest.

As far as Tijah was concerned, that day couldn't arrive soon enough.

"We must break the bonds," she said. "The guards can't be trusted. They could try to revolt. And even if they can't touch the power themselves, they can make the daēvas feel agony." She did not mention her own bond and Samahe did not ask, although her eyes strayed to the cuff for a moment. Clearly, she knew what had happened. Tijah supposed everyone did.

"Can it be transferred?" Samahe asked.

"Yes, but only to one who has the spark. One in a thousand. And we don't have nearly enough men, even if all of them had the gift."

Samahe nodded to herself. "That is what the magus said. So what do you propose?"

"We go to Bactria. Alexander marches on Neblis and Nazafareen will be with him. Like I told you, she has the ability. I saw her break the cuffs of the children. It's the only way."

"Bactria." The word seemed to leave a sour taste in Samahe's mouth. "Kian will go, if there's a chance of seeing his sister again. He is not married yet and has no greater ties. As for the others, I can't say. They may wish to return to the Clan."

"And you?"

Samahe shrugged. "Who do you think Nazafareen gets her stupidity from? Yes, I will go too. Although I wonder if we are not on a raft about to capsize in the spring floods, arguing over who gets to sit in the front."

Tijah laughed and goddess, it hurt. She'd survived, yes, but she was far from well. A wave of dizziness passed over her.

"I know a way through the Char Khala that will take only three days," Samahe said. "An old, secret way."

"Then we shall take it," Cyrus said, stepping up from behind her. He peered down at Tijah. "You look a bit better."

"So do you." She marveled at the change. He had not so much shed the years, but they no longer weighed him down. His face was still lined, his hair silver. And yet there was a light in his eyes, a vitality Tijah had never seen before.

"I am whole again," he said simply. "Would you like to meet her?"

Tijah raised an eyebrow and he signaled to Cassandane. She stomped over, muscles rippling. A sturdy woman. Frankly, she looked like she could break Cyrus in half with very little effort. They wore a set of matching cuffs. He must have taken his from her guard.

"You're the Water Dog," she said gruffly.

"Former Water Dog," Tijah corrected. "I renounced all that crap. Glad to meet you. We weren't sure we'd make it in time."

"We would have torn the Druj army to shreds if those idiots had let us, but they were too frightened." She turned her head and Tijah saw Cassandane's ear was missing. Not an injury, just gone. It had to be her infirmity.

"I know Victor. And his son. I think I can help you be free of those men forever."

Tijah explained what she had in mind and Cassandane said she would discuss it with the others. "Bactria, eh?" She gazed down the beach as if she could see the jagged peaks of the Char Khala. "I think they would march to the Pit itself if it would rid them of the cuffs."

⚜

ACHAEMENES CAME TO HER TENT THAT NIGHT. SHE KNEW HE was there before he asked permission to enter. They locked eyes without speaking for a long moment. He was the first to look away.

"I know you're still angry," he said. "But you have to let me help you. You can't travel across the mountains like this even if

Anu carries you on air the whole way, which we both know she can't."

Tijah scowled. "I'm fine."

"No, you're not." He squatted down so he could look her in the eyes. His bad knee didn't bend right, sticking out at an awkward angle. "When I bonded you, I was grievously wounded myself. I gave you all I could, but...it wasn't enough. Not to heal you properly. Now that I've rested, I can do more."

Tijah considered this. "You know how to heal with the power?"

"Some things, yes."

"How? I know the magi don't teach it. They want soldiers, not physicians."

"I taught myself."

Tijah gave a tight smile. "Thanks, but I'll pass."

"Then you can stay here," Achaemenes said mildly, rising to his feet. "Samahe and Cyrus agree we don't need any more burdens on this journey."

Tijah scowled. Was he bluffing? Or had her friends turned traitor?

"You'll slow everyone down," Achaemenes continued. "Most likely, you'll die. I suppose that's what you want, but it would be easier to just leave your body here for the gulls to dispose of instead of dragging it halfway across the Char Khala."

He made it to the door before she broke down. "Wait."

Achaemenes turned, his expression bland.

"How long would it take?" Not that this mattered, but she had to salvage her pride somehow. Pretend she was still weighing his offer.

"A minute or two."

"All right then." She tried to sit up and a wave of nausea made her swallow hard. Maybe it wasn't such a bad idea. She felt hot and achy. There could be evil humors in the wound. If she was being honest with herself, Tijah couldn't imagine getting up to pee, let alone climbing the high peaks of the Bactrian border.

Achaemenes limped closer. He'd traded his tattered blue tunic for the layered clothing of the Four-Legs men. It was probably that or one of the guards' uniforms, and who would want to wear the emblem of that rat-asshole Artaxeros II? Still, she couldn't resist a jab.

"Those pants look ridiculous," she observed. "They billow out like the sails on a trireme when you walk."

As usual, this failed to elicit the desired response. Achaemenes couldn't care less.

"I'll need to touch you," he said. "To take off the bandages."

Tijah nodded curtly. "Go ahead."

He pretended to look around. "Where's your scimitar?"

She refused to smile. "I lost it in the sea."

She didn't tell him that she had stolen it from her father. That she'd been born anew on that night when the sirocco winds blew and she and Myrri had slipped away into the howling darkness. How she'd hated and loved that blade in equal measure.

"We'll have to find you a new sword then. Now lift your tunic up. Please."

Tijah raised it just below her breasts. She winced. The bandages smelled bad.

Achaemenes pulled a knife from a sheath on his calf and slit the wad of linens up the side. Then he used the point to gingerly pry it away from her body. His face was impassive but she knew it had to be bad, because the smell got a lot worse. He lay his palm flat on her belly, covering her navel, and closed his eyes. She shuddered at the sensation. So different from Myrri....

"This might hurt," he said.

And it did. Blindingly. Tijah couldn't stop the tears from leaking down her cheeks but she didn't make a sound. When it was over, Achaemenes gently unwound the foul bandages and dampened a clean cloth in a basin. She was still breathing heavily as he wiped the gore from her belly, leaving unbroken skin beneath.

"Drink this," he murmured, holding a cup to her lips.

Tijah drank. She had never been so thirsty in her life, not even the morning she first woke up.

"The body is mostly water," he said. "Strange but true. Healing uses it up. It takes earth and air also, but mainly water. Be sure to take plenty of liquids for the next few days."

"How did you learn this?" she asked, eyes already sliding shut.

"I started with animals. A starling with a broken wing. A kitten born blind. In the nexus, all beings are the same. I was always careful not to do harm, but repairing the body is a subtle art. It took me years to master even a small part of it. You are healed enough to cross the mountains, I think, but we must wait to see how your body responds before I do more. Too much at once can be a fatal shock to the system." Achaemenes lay her back on the bed and tucked her in like a child. "Sleep, Tijah of Al Miraj."

She gave him a sharp look. "Are you reading my mind now? Stop that."

"That is beyond even my talents," he said wryly. "Anu told me where you come from."

Thank him, Tijah. What he just did for you has cost him. Again. Truly, you shame us both.

"Thank you," Tijah muttered.

Achaemenes stood, leaning on his left leg. "Don't die just yet." He smiled and it was a grim thing. "There will be plenty of time for that when we get to Bactria."

THE NEXT MORNING, THEY PLUNDERED WHAT WAS LEFT OF Gorgon-e Gaz, entering through a narrow crevice in the rubble. Tijah went inside with Anu and Pegah, and some of the former prisoners led by Mithre. Most had refused to enter it again—quite understandably, Tijah thought. The fortress was a dark, cold, cramped place. Her breath made a misty cloud as they moved down the stone corridors. She had slept for a very long time and felt almost like her old self again, although Achaemenes had been right about the water. She drank and drank and still her throat felt parched. As though a giant hand had wrung her out like a sponge.

"The kitchens are that way," Mithre said. He looked at a female daēva with reddish hair and skin like milk. "Nisha, take the children and bring out as much food as you can carry. Tijah, come with me."

His skin was brown like hers but he had curiously feline eyes the color of topaz. Mithre scared her a little the same way Victor had. They both reminded her of the dune snakes of the Sayhad. Sand-colored and retiring by nature, they wouldn't attack a human unless you accidentally stepped on one. Then you could count the number of seconds you had left on a single hand. Their venom was the deadliest in the known world.

They passed a series of tiny cells with bars as thick as Tijah's arm. She had never seen walls so thick. Clearly, keeping daēvas under lock and key was no simple matter, even severed from the power. Cyrus was somewhere in the warren of cells, looking for the records room.

"That was mine," Mithre said, casually nodding his head at one of the doors as if he was pointing out the bedroom of a fine manor house. "After Victor escaped, they threatened to put us all to the torch."

"Horse prick-loving bastards," Tijah muttered.

"Yes," Mithre agreed. "They never did, but they refused to give us food or water for a week." He led them around a corner, to a heavy oaken door. Mithre stared at it for a long moment. Then he flicked his wrist and the wood cracked in half down the center. He kicked in the two pieces with one blow. They landed on the stone floor with an earth-shaking thud. "I've been waiting two hundred years to do that," he said with a satisfied smile. "Welcome to the armory, Tijah."

She eyed the rows of gleaming swords and shields and grinned back. "I think the daёvas should have first pick, don't you?"

THEY BROKE CAMP THE NEXT MORNING. AS SAMAHE PREDICTED, most of the men chose to return to their families in the lands of the Seven-Legs Clan. Tijah didn't blame them. They had no reason to fight for Alexander. They'd suffered enough losses already. Kian stayed, and surprisingly, Jengis too.

Achaemenes kept his distance. Tijah was acutely aware of him nonetheless. She had tried building a wall around their bond, but it was more like a soap bubble—popping at the slightest touch.

On the first night in the mountains, she asked Cyrus if he would join her apart from the others for a small fire. It was cold in the mountains, colder than it should have been for late spring. But fire also sent a clear message to Achaemenes.

Stay the hell away.

"Did you find anything in Gorgon?" Tijah asked, holding her palms out to the crackling flames.

He nodded. "The Numerators would come every six months to inspect the prison. The guards were meticulous about recording births and deaths."

"I thought the daёvas lived practically forever."

"They do."

Children's laughter drifted over from the daёva camp. It sounded like Abid, or maybe Bijan.

"Anu and Achaemenes shared a mother," Cyrus continued. "She died at Gorgon a few years ago. A wasting illness, the scroll said."

Tijah raised an eyebrow. "I never saw Myrri sick a day in her life."

"Daēvas are generally not susceptible to normal sickness," Cyrus agreed. "I assume their mother chose to stop eating."

"Goddess. And their fathers?"

"The record for Achaemenes is missing. It was probably stored at the Hall of the Numerators in Karnopolis. One of the guards told me they were starting to transfer the records there. As for Anu, her father is one of the more damaged ones. He doesn't speak." Cyrus shook his head. "Poor child."

"What about the others?"

"I already shared with them what I found. They've been reunited with one or both of their parents."

"I'm glad."

"About Achaemenes." Cyrus gave Tijah a stern look she remembered well from his study at Tel Khalujah. "He only did what he had to. Frankly, I'm surprised he even offered. Not many would have. It was a great sacrifice on his part, Tijah."

"He still had no right."

The magus sighed. "I wanted to die too when they broke my bond with Cassandane," he said softly.

"What did she do?"

"Only what I asked her to. She killed a man."

Tijah sat up, curious. "Who?"

"A boy. The son of a very wealthy merchant from Persepolae. It's where I was born and raised. He raped my great-niece. It was his word against hers. Her father renounced her as a whore and she begged me to do something. Her life was ruined and this boy —he just went on as if nothing had happened. I'd been a magus for many years. I wanted to fight. To have a daēva. The invasion of the Druj, the war... The wounds were still fresh then. Every young man wanted to join the Immortals. They wouldn't take me because I wasn't physically strong enough, so I joined the priesthood instead."

"Sounds like the little shit had it coming."

Cyrus frowned at the curse, but then he nodded in agreement. "I'd hoped the Holy Father would punish him, but when he didn't, I took matters into my own hands."

"Can I ask you a personal question?"

"Go ahead."

"How old are you, Cyrus?"

"One hundred and fifty-seven years," he said. "Give or take."

Tijah gave a low whistle. "That's old."

"I suppose it is. Cassandane offered to help. We'd been together for decades at that point and would do anything for each other. She found the boy and threw him from a cliff."

"How were you caught?"

"Someone saw. A shepherd. At her trial, I begged them to spare her life. I confessed to everything. That it was I who had planned the murder. My family was well-connected, so instead of executing us, we were severed. Cassandane was sent to Gorgon-e Gaz. It's the only prison fit to hold a daēva. As for me, they let me keep the robes but they exiled me to Tel Khalujah. In Persepolae, it's considered an uncivilized backwater. The worst punishment they could think of. I was just glad to be near to Cassandane. Not a day went by that I didn't think of her, imagining ways I could break her free."

"You're lucky she forgave you."

"Yes, I am." Cyrus stood. "I would die before I gave her up again. And I'll spend the next ten lifetimes making it up to her."

"You're...in love?"

"Not as you imagine. Cassandane is my friend and companion." He paused. "But we share a soul."

"I understand," Tijah said. And she did, perfectly. "You never believed any of it, did you? The *doctrine* you pounded into Nazafareen and me. That all daēvas are wicked."

Shame filled his eyes. "I told you before. I'm a coward and a sinner. But the Holy Father has seen fit to grant me a second chance and I won't waste it." Then Cyrus gave her his familiar holier-than-thou look, which entailed a straightening of the back and peering down the nose. "You've been given a second chance too, Tijah. He works in mysterious ways sometimes but it's all for the best."

Tijah ostentatiously made the sign of the flame. "Well, I don't buy that shit," she said sweetly. "Think I'll stick with Innunu. At least when *she* fucks you up, she's honest about it."

Cyrus made disapproving noises at her heresy as Tijah slapped him on the shoulder and pushed up to her feet. "No offense intended, magus. I'm the first to admit I misjudged you. And I owe you one for those necromancers." She grinned. "I think you'll be a warrior magus yet."

She left him by the fire muttering about heathens. Somewhere in the darkness, not far, she could feel Achaemenes. Did the boy never sleep?

Better watch out, Myrri signed with an evil smile. *Cyrus may be an old man, but Cassandane? I wouldn't make her mad for all the gold in Nubia.*

৩১৩

THE CROSSING OF THE CHAR KHALA WASN'T AS BAD AS TIJAH had expected. Samahe's shortcut took them through sparsely wooded valleys between the high peaks and they avoided the worst of those jagged mountains. The four daēva children who'd found their parents stuck close to them, and the mothers and fathers lucky enough to be reunited were fiercely protective. Tijah hoped they would find some measure of healing from their ordeal.

Achaemenes was old enough to take care of himself. She'd seen Cyrus take both him and Anu aside when they'd camped one evening to explain what had happened to their mother. Grief had flared in the bond as Achaemenes digested the news of her death, but then it subsided. He had never known her, after all. And there was still a slim chance he might find the records for his father someday.

It was different for Anu. Tijah almost wished her father had died in the fighting.

"He won't even look at me," she confided to Tijah, as they washed their hands and faces in a stream. She frowned. "Or he looks, but he doesn't *see*."

"I'm sorry, Anu."

Tijah had asked Cyrus to point him out that morning. Anu's father was a slender man with a bushy, matted beard down to his chest. It was strange to see a daēva with such blank eyes. The others were caring for him as best they could but he wouldn't eat unless food was placed in his mouth. Then he'd chew and swallow with a perfectly placid expression, like a cow. When they wanted him to walk, someone would take his hand and he'd follow wherever they led.

Anu shrugged, pretending indifference. "I'd rather be with you and Achaemenes anyway." She said it casually, but Tijah felt the girl looking at her from the corner of her eye.

"You can stay with me, you know that," Tijah said. "But I don't plan to be bonded to Achaemenes very long. He can do what he wants to after we break the cuffs."

"What! Why?"

"Because...." Tijah sighed. "Just because, Anu."

"But I thought—"

"You thought wrong," Tijah snapped. She shook her hands dry. They tingled from the icy water.

When she looked up again, Anu signed at her to go fuck a herd of camels.

"Let it go," Tijah said warningly.

"But he likes you. I can tell. He watches you when you're not looking—"

"*Anu.*"

The girl scowled deeply.

In truth, Tijah had no idea where she would go after they found Alexander and Nazafareen. Certainly not Al Miraj. He father would sooner see her dead than unmarried.

"He's the only one who was ever kind to me," Anu muttered. "And he's my brother. Half-brother, anyway. I just want him to be happy."

Tijah pushed the girl's tangled hair from her eyes. "Trust me, he'll be happier as a free man. A free daēva. What have we fought for if not that?"

"I guess." Anu sounded unconvinced. "But I can stay with you?"

Tijah sighed. A kingfisher sped past them, its blue-grey crest tilted into the wind. "You can stay with me if you like, though I have little to offer."

Anu nodded to herself. "You can teach me to fight with a sword." She lunged forward, pretending to stab an enemy. "We'll be mercenaries, seeking gold and glory!"

"It's not a bad idea," Tijah said with a smile. "Come. Let's see if supper is ready."

There was plenty of game in the Bactrian forests, which had been empty of human habitation for two centuries. Each evening before sunset, Kian and Jengis would go out with their bows and bring back strings of rabbits and even a deer or two. The Old Ones ate sparingly but the rest of them feasted on roast meat and Tijah felt her strength returning, although her wounds still pained her after a long day's travel.

Mithre and Samahe had taken charge of the former guards from Gorgon-e Gaz. To Tijah's amusement, they actually seemed more afraid of the Four Legs woman. Goddess knows what she said to keep them in line, but they caused no trouble.

"They're lucky they hold the bonds," Cassandane observed. She sat shoulder to shoulder with Tijah on a fallen log, gnawing on rabbit bones. "Else they would be dead." She licked grease from her fingers. "I'm more fortunate than the others. I was only in Gorgon for twenty-seven years."

Tijah raised an eyebrow. "Sounds like a long time to me."

"Well, I won't pretend the years flew by, but we measure such things differently." Her broad face grew solemn as she watched Cyrus on the other side of the camp, deep in conversation with Achaemenes. The two of them had struck up an improbable friendship. Cyrus was fascinated by the daēva's ability to heal. The magus had studied medicine in Persepolae and was eager to trade knowledge about anatomy and the complex balance of water, air and earth that made up the body.

"He had black hair when last I saw him," Cassandane said ruefully. "But he's the same man inside."

"The mold of a man's character is usually cast long before he sprouts his first beard," Samahe said, joining them with a haunch of rabbit in her hand. She sat easily on the ground like a woman half her age. "Most of them change little except for the ears. For some reason, those continue to grow."

"Too bad the same isn't true for other parts," Cassandane said, and the women snorted with laughter. Tijah winced at the sharp pain in her side.

"What's wrong?" Cassandane asked.

"Nothing. It's nothing. My moon blood," Tijah lied.

The women nodded in sympathy.

"Well, I'm looking forward to meeting this Darius," Samahe declared. "I hope my daughter doesn't trample all over him like a Phrygian carpet."

"Oh, Darius wouldn't let himself be trampled, although he does indulge her temper." Tijah tossed a bone over her shoulder. "More than I would, that's for sure."

"You speak of Nazafareen?" Cassandane asked. "The one who breaks cuffs?"

"My willful daughter," Samahe agreed. "I imagine she'll be surprised to see me. It's been nearly seven years since I sent her off to the Water Dogs." The Four-Legs woman looked past them, into the darkening trees. "She took her sister's death harder than any of us, even myself, I think. To witness such a thing at a young age. It marked her. Leaving was the best thing she could have done." Samahe shook herself. "Well, I imagine we'll find her bossing this Alexander around like the lowest stable boy. He'll probably offer us half the empire to take her off his hands."

Tijah grinned. "It will be good to see her face again, and Darius too. We all grew close at Tel Khalujah." She held up her wrist. "And then she can rid me of this cursed cuff."

Cassandane chewed a morsel of meat with a thoughtful expression. "I think Cyrus and I are the only ones here who *don't* wish to break our cuffs. But he's never tried to control me and if I didn't bond him, he would soon grow old and die. That would make me sad. So I put up with his moods. He gets melancholy sometimes," she confided.

"All of us do," Samahe said, adjusting her shawl. "It is the human condition."

"Not like Cyrus—" Cassandane began.

They turned as one of the daēva scouts burst into the camp. He ran to Mithre, gesturing and pointing through the trees, but his body language was more excited than alarmed. A moment later, Mithre strode over to where the three women sat together.

"We've found the young King," he said. "Camped five leagues north of here. He has sentries in the woods but they didn't see Amadis. He thought it best to report back to me before making himself known."

"So the Immortal told the truth about Bactria," Tijah murmured. "Thank the goddess."

"We'll stay here tonight," Cassandane said. "Morning is soon enough to set out. We can cover the distance in a few hours."

"Morning!" Tijah wanted to find Nazafareen *right now*. "It's not full dark yet. Maybe I'll just go on ahead—"

"You'll stay here with the rest of us, girl," Samahe said in a tone that brooked no argument. "You can wait another day to be rid of that poor boy."

Poor boy? Did everyone think he had some sort of crush on her? Tijah's cheeks flamed and she muttered a foul curse, though not loud enough for Samahe to hear it.

Myrri nodded her approval with a crooked grin. *If you insist on breaking the bond tomorrow, sister, you'll have to live to see the sun rise.*

❧ 2 5 ❧

lexander's army camped on the shores of a dark, still lake. They found the young King staring pensively at the water, his childhood friend Hephaestion at his side. Both men wore iron breastplates and thigh-length leather skirts but no helmets. Hephaestion stood a full two hands taller than Alexander, but the Macydonian King's short stature in no way undermined his magnetism and aura of authority. He had a stocky build which, combined with his red-gold curls, made him quite easy to look at, Tijah thought.

They had met only briefly and she wasn't sure he would remember, but his mismatched eyes—one brown, one blue—lit up when he saw her approach with their emissary.

"It is the Water Dog who traveled with Victor," Alexander said warmly. "I had expected you to turn up at Persepolae. We won a great victory there, in large part thanks to your friend Nazafareen. Now who is this you bring me?" He surveyed the daēvas with open curiosity.

"Gorgon-e Gaz has been liberated," Tijah said, bending her knee. "This is Mithre and Cassandane. They speak for the Old Ones. The rest are waiting in the forest."

Alexander inclined his head respectfully and the daēvas returned the gesture.

"Samahe of the Four-Legs Clan of the Khusk Range," Tijah said, moving on to the next of their little group. "She is widow of the khan and mother to Nazafareen."

"Madam," Alexander said. "Your daughter did me a great service. Truly, I am in your debt."

Samahe looked surprised but nodded regally. "I would ask you to avenge my husband's honor, but the men who killed him are already dead. The Four-Legs Clan wants only to live as we always have, without outside interference."

"And you shall," Alexander said. "You have my word."

"This is Cyrus, the former magus of Tel Khalujah." Tijah concluded the introductions. "I'm sad to report the city was destroyed by Druj."

"I know." Alexander's face darkened. "I've been hunting them, but the main force has eluded me."

"They gathered at Gorgon-e Gaz to kill everyone inside its walls. It might have been all the legions combined, I'm not sure. Only that the force was many thousands strong."

"And how is it you're alive to tell me this? I understand from my scouts that there are more of you in the woods, but they say your number is less than a hundred."

"The Four-Legs Clan joined with free daēva children to break them out," Tijah said, glossing over her own role in the battle. "It was a close thing but we managed it." She looked around the sprawling camp. "Where are Nazafareen and Darius? I need to speak with them urgently."

Alexander sighed. "Gone. They went with Lysandros and Delilah to find Victor. Neblis has him. She threatened to kill him if Nazafareen did not go to Bactria."

"*What?*" Tijah's heart sank.

"They could be in Neblis's lair this very moment and we'd have no way to know," he growled, smacking a fist into his hand.

"This is the lake Lysandros told me to find. It has to be. There is no other like it anywhere nearby. He said she lives inside it, and yet I can find nothing! My strongest swimmers have dived to the bottom again and again. There is naught but mud. And so we sit here, *waiting*."

"I don't understand. Why didn't they march with you if you were both going to the same place?"

"Because they traveled behind the veil. Neblis gave Lysandros some kind of fey talisman. It is the same way he reached Persepolae."

"Behind the veil?" Samahe snapped. "Where is my daughter? Speak plainly!"

Tijah winced but Alexander took the rebuke in stride. "I have never been there myself so there is little more I can tell you. Lysandros believes it is the land of the dead. An in-between place."

"And she has gone haring off to fight this demon queen herself?" Samahe rolled her eyes. "I'd thought after raising that hellion for thirteen years I would have lost the capacity for surprise, but it seems Nazafareen has found new depths of idiocy to strive toward."

Tijah swore under her breath. "If you don't have Victor, you don't have the holy fire either, do you?"

He scowled. "No."

Tijah turned to Cassandane and Mithre. "I'm very sorry. We have no way to break the cuffs. Not until we find Nazafareen." She didn't mention her own, but the pitying look Cyrus gave her said he understood.

Stony daēva faces regarded her.

"You are welcome to what food and shelter we can offer," Alexander said. "But if I find no foe to engage in the next day, we will decamp and move east to join the rest of my army. I must secure the other satrapies."

"And leave my daughter in this limbo?" Samahe demanded.

"Madam," Alexander said with a weary sigh. "It is a hard decision, but Tijah says you have already disposed of the Druj legions I came to fight. Now I have an empire to consider. There are others to protect. The cities must be rebuilt and I cannot do it sitting here."

Samahe opened her mouth to argue. Tijah laid a hand on her arm. "Understood. They are in the hands of the goddess now."

Samahe sniffed but kept her peace.

"There is also the matter of the three dozen guards from Gorgon-e Gaz," Cyrus ventured. "They must be kept under close watch until the matter of the cuffs is resolved."

"It will be done," Hephaestion said. "As for the rest of you, the accommodations are rough, but we're willing to share." He turned to Cassandane and Mithre. "Would your people accept the tents of the freed Immortals? I assume it would be preferable to bunking with humans."

The daēvas shared a look and Mithre nodded stiffly. "We will wait here also, as there seems to be no other choice."

"Then it's settled," Alexander said, his gaze returning to the still lake. "And if Neblis has some trick up her sleeve, we are ready." He gestured to the eastern hillside, which had been stripped bare of trees. "I'm building new catapults. We will fight her with iron but if needs be, with fire."

⚜️

TIJAH STALKED OFF TO THE TENT SHE'D BEEN GIVEN. BEHIND the veil? Land of the dead? None of it made any sense. Who the fuck lived at the bottom of a lake, anyway? Whoever this Lysandros was, it sounded like he was a few spokes short of a wheel. She threw herself down on the thin bedroll.

I did my part, she thought sulkily. We took care of the Druj. Alexander can handle Queen Neblis. I just want to get rid of this cursed cuff and be on my way!

And what about your friends? Are you so fickle, sister?

Tijah sighed. *Of course not. I would help her if I could. But there's nothing for me to do!*

She felt him coming and sat up on her blankets.

"Tijah." Achaemenes loomed in the entrance. "I brought you something." He held up a dagger. It wasn't fancy, but the way the edge caught the light implied it was wickedly sharp. "One of the daēvas gave it to me."

Tijah knew his leg pained him. The hard mountain crossing and the cold had stiffened his bad knee. A dull ache that never went away. She sighed.

"Come in," she relented. And then grudgingly: "You can sit down if you want to."

"You're too generous," he murmured wryly.

He eased down onto the bedroll, letting his right leg rest straight in front. Tijah examined the knife more closely, testing its balance. It had a hilt of plain bronze. An infantryman's weapon but well-made.

"It'll do," Tijah said. She tucked the dagger into her belt.

That's all? You have nothing more to say to him?

"Thank you," she added.

Achaemenes gave a brief nod. She could smell his skin. He was always so gods-damned clean. In the mountains, he'd tried washing with melted snow, but she'd put a stop to it immediately after nearly jumping out of her skin when the icy water hit. Most shared sensations could be muted but not that one.

"We can't break the bond," she said. "Nazafareen is gone."

"I heard. I'm sorry."

"Right." She stared at the tent wall, willing him to take the hint and leave.

"I know you hate me," he said quietly. "I still wouldn't take back what I did."

"I don't *hate* you." Tijah groped for words. "It's just...."

"You don't need to explain."

"We barely know each other."

He nodded. "True. So why don't you ask me something. Anything."

She arched an eyebrow.

"Really, I won't be offended."

Tijah studied her boots. "Why are you so calm all the time? It's...unnatural."

Achaemenes laughed. "Am I?"

"Yes. It's not a thing you can hide." She picked at the beaten leather. "Not anymore."

He thought for a moment. "Part of me is in the Nexus always. The Oneness." He looked at her out of the corner of his eye. "There is no male and female. No *me and you*. Just us."

Myrri used to say the same, except she called it the Quiet Place. "I thought maybe it had to do with that nasty woman you were bonded to."

"Mina?"

"Yes, that one."

"She was no crueler than the others. Most amahs despise their charges. We are Druj and they are God-fearing women." He said this without malice. "May I ask you something now?"

"I guess so."

"Don't get angry."

The sounds of the camp filtered through the thin walls. Hammering and sawing. Iron striking iron. The shouts and laughter of men. Tijah missed the solitude of the Great Salt Plain.

"I can control myself too," she said. "Most of the time."

"What was her name?"

Tijah lifted her head and met his steady gaze. *Oh, what the hell.* "Myrri."

"Thank you for telling me."

"It means silent waters. She was mute."

"And yours?"

"Tijah means sword."

Achaemenes smiled. "I should have guessed."

"Well, I chose it myself. My real name is Zenobia Zumurrud bin Qindah," she blurted. She had never admitted this to anyone, not even Nazafareen. Tijah scowled as Achaemenes started to laugh.

"The first one suits you better," he said, fake coughing while she glared at him.

He didn't say anything else, so she added, "Myrri and I were bonded as children. It's the custom in Al Miraj."

His face grew grave again. "Why did you leave?"

"I don't want to talk about it." She moved to stand and winced.

"The wound still festers," Achaemenes said. "Let me see it."

"I'm fine."

He gave her a flat look. "Please."

Tijah lay back and Achaemenes placed his hands on her stomach. She braced for that terrible pain, but it never came. Instead, she felt a heat moving slowly through her body. Her skin tingled pleasantly. He watched her, not moving. A lock of hair fell across his face and without thinking, she reached up and brushed it aside.

What am I...?

Tijah meant to take her hand away, but her fingertips lingered on his shoulder. How had she never noticed the dimple in his chin before? And his hazel eyes, with those dark lashes? The heat built, suffusing her with an achy, feverish feeling. His hands slid down to her hipbones.

Achaemenes drew a ragged breath as Tijah laid one of her own hands on top of his. She shuddered slightly at the sensation. How curious that she had never felt this way when Myrri would brush her hair! She had felt something, yes, but it was a sisterly love. Sweet and comforting. But this...did Nazafareen feel the same when she touched Darius? A strange, looping echo of sensation? Oh, the possibilities!

And then her fingers brushed metal, the gold of his cuff, and the tangle of emotions in her head resolved into cold clarity. Not her desire. *His.*

He *tricked* me. Goddess! What a hideously embarrassing mistake.

She rolled away and the loss of him was like a bucket of ice water over her head. "I need some air," she muttered, stumbling blindly for the door.

He called her name, but Tijah didn't turn around.

DUSK WAS FALLING AS TIJAH WALKED THROUGH THE CAMP TO the far shore of the lake. She drew curious stares from the Macydonians as she passed. Her hair might be short, but even a desultory inspection revealed a woman's figure underneath the boy clothes. She'd expected leering glances and even a few crude proposals, but the soldiers in Alexander's army were a disciplined bunch. Cyrus had told her their King did not tolerate abuse of women—in fact, he despised it—and any who broke that rule would face severe punishment.

The shoreline grew rockier and the tents fewer until at last she found herself blessedly alone. Or at least, as alone as it was possible to get with Achaemenes lurking in the background.

Tijah picked up a stone and skipped it along the glassy surface. Five...no six. Not bad, considering she was out of practice. The way it seemed to *bounce* still felt like a kind of magic. Nazafareen had taught her how when they were novices together at Tel Khalujah. They would sneak down to the river by the daēva barracks and practice with the flattest, smoothest stones they could find. The best were the ones that fit perfectly in her palm. Whoever won the most skips got to make the other one do extra chores. When they grew older, the game changed so the loser had to sneak into the kitchens and steal a skin of the bitter, chalky wine they drank in the servants' quarters.

Oh, Nazafareen. Your mother is right. You're a goat-brained idiot.

Tijah whipped the stone back, flicking her wrist just so, and smiled as she managed ten bounces this time.

Darius is no better if he went along with it. And don't get me started on Victor, handing himself over to Neblis like a nice feastday lamb. Does no one have any sense other than me?

She threw the next stone too savagely and it plunked straight down into the inky depths.

Not that I have any either. Getting myself bonded! And to a randy teenager!

She hurled the last stone as far as she could, imagining it was the cuff. It plunked into the lake with a satisfying splash.

Silent laughter echoed in her mind. The soft, breathy sounds of hilarity that were all Myrri could manage. *Go ahead, blame him for all of it. None of that was you. Not even the tiniest bit. You're way too pure.*

Shut up, Tijah signed. *Shut up, shut up, shut up.*

Myrri wheezed louder.

He's a boy of seventeen. I'm twenty. Ever heard of cradle-robbing?

She gave her arms a brisk rub. A thin mist rose from the surface of the lake as the temperature dropped. Myrri was full of shit. She scowled. *Everyone* was full of shit. If only she knew how to swim, she'd dive into the lake first thing in the morning and find the door to Neblis's realm herself. Then she'd haul Nazafareen out by the scruff of her neck and make her fix this.

The mist grew thicker, sending tendrils questing along the shore. Tijah threw a final stone. It disappeared without a trace into the wall of advancing white.

She started walking back, following the edge of the mist. It gave off a terrible, bone-chilling cold. Dampness condensed on her lips and eyelashes, muting the sounds of the camp like a heavy blanket. Whatever Achaemenes had done to her—heat still flushed her face at the thought of what had almost happened—the pain in her side was gone. So perhaps he hadn't tricked her *entirely*.

Just like the time before, thirst burned her throat. She squatted down and reached through the mist to cup a handful of lake water. Not to drink, just to splash on her face. *I might be stupid but not enough to gulp down Neblis's personal moat.*

Suddenly, Tijah had the sensation of being watched. She looked around. Nothing moved and yet the spot between her shoulder blades crawled with unease.

Shouts erupted from across the lake, the sound strangely muffled by the curtain of fog. Tijah sprang to her feet. The mist began to churn like a bank of advancing thunderheads. A shapeless form emerged from its depths. It was nearly transparent, just a tattered grey veil. Almost like a lich, but without that dizzying darkness. Swirls of vapor coalesced into five attenuated lines. Fingers, she thought with languid, dreamlike horror. Reaching for her—

And then a shoulder knocked her aside. Iron met mist with a sharp *hiss*. Achaemenes swung his sword in a two-handed arc, slicing through the tendrils. They shrank away, dissolving back into the fogbank. He closed his eyes and Tijah felt perfect calm descend as her daēva sought the Nexus.

A wind rose, whistling in her ears. Achaemenes flung his arms wide, brown hair whipping around his face. But the wind hardly touched the wall of mist. His chest heaved and Tijah's own breath came quicker. Sympathetic magic, Cyrus called it. The price of elemental power.

Achaemenes fell to his knees, coughing violently. Tijah rushed over and slashed at a newly unfurling tendril with the dagger he'd given her. It retreated a short distance, smooth and featureless, but she knew what she'd seen.

The dice were rolling in her head again.

"What in the name of Innunu is it?" she demanded, throwing

an arm around his waist and hauling him to his feet. Achaemenes was tall even for a grown man, but she could still look him in the eye.

"Nothing I've ever heard of," he responded grimly. "But it resists being unknit with air." He offered her his sword. "Take it. I'll see what I can do with water."

Tijah slid the dagger back into her belt and gripped the hilt, stepping up to protect his weaker right side. She'd spent hours watching Tommas and Ilyas in the training yard at Tel Khalujah. Tommas had a bad leg too, but they were the deadliest pair she'd ever seen. The tension that crackled between them in daily life vanished when they fought together. It was the only time Ilyas let himself open to Tommas completely. One mind in two bodies.

Tijah was rarely the only one hanging about at the dusty edges of the yard. Tommas would often strip to the waist to spar, which tended to draw any woman between the ages of seven and seventy. And Ilyas...he might have been a complete fuckshit, but the man knew how to move. She had never seen a human as fast and cunning as Ilyas.

I would be dead ten times over without the tricks I learned watching you both. Perhaps they will keep us both alive—at least until we make it back to camp.

Tijah took a breath and dropped her defenses, meager as they were. She'd never managed to get rid of Achaemenes—that would be too much to hope for—but since leaving her tent, she'd kept him at arm's length. Now his awareness flooded her. Alert and unafraid. Not a hint of the lust that had swept her away earlier, thank the goddess. Achaemenes pulled a knife from a hidden sheath beneath his Clan vest. He didn't look at her, but a tiny smile played at the corner of his mouth.

"You were a Water Dog," he said.

She lunged forward, slashing at a questing feeler of fog. It shied back. "And you trained with the Immortals."

"So we both understand the basic principles of pairs fighting. That's good."

He'd tried to shave his beard, probably with the knife in his hand. A half-healed cut traced his jaw. Seventeen, with the eyes of a man twice as old. Perhaps he wasn't who she'd imagined.

"Duck, would you?" she asked mildly.

Achaemenes's brows drew together, but he got out of the way as she stabbed a ghostly shadow looming over his shoulder. The iron blade sizzled where it touched that grey vapor. Her heart lifted as the mist dispersed. But within moments, it began to thicken again.

Tijah shivered as power surged through the bond. She'd felt Myrri work it hundreds of times, but Goddess, it had been a long time. The aching sweetness pulsating just out of her reach. It flowed through her veins like molten ore, a raging river guided and shaped by her bonded daēva. Achaemenes drew deeper. A soft cry escaped her lips. And then he staggered back, sweeping a hand across his mouth as if he might be sick. The power winked out.

"That's not water," he gasped, pointing at the mist-cloaked lake. "I don't know what it is...something I've never seen before. Liquid darkness. It almost pulled me in."

The distant shouts turned to screams.

"We have to find the children," Tijah said, pulse still racing from the residue. "Stay close. Don't touch *any* element until we know what's happening."

They fought their way along the rocky shore and Tijah gave herself over to instinct. The backwash of power made her stronger, faster. Her feet pivoted to cover Achaemenes the instant before he moved. Her sword started a downstroke while he still occupied the space below. She knew that a second later, he would spin away, cutting the mist to ribbons with his knife. The iron slowed it down, but after a few seconds the amorphous blob oozed together again.

Achaemenes shielded his eyes as a ball of flame streaked over their heads, sputtering as it entered the lake. The mist glowed red, then faded to grey again.

"Alexander must be deploying the catapults," Tijah said, grinning. "It cannot stand against that."

Achaemenes steered her toward a patch of clear air. Sweat slicked his hair and she could sense his discomfort. "Let's just hope his aim is true. That came a bit close."

Darkness fell as they made their way around the lake. Tijah counted six more fireballs. Then they stopped.

A moment later, she burst through a lighter patch of fog. It had already crept to the middle of the camp. Men lay scattered between the tents, the mist coiling like liquid smoke among them. She could see now what lurked inside it. Spectral apparitions in roughly human form, all eyes and teeth. One of them bent low over a fallen Macydonian soldier, pressing its gaping mouth to his wrist. It seemed to grow more solid as it drank. Flesh and muscle swelled its cadaverous body. Thin red hair sprouted from its skull.

Tijah realized with horror that the blood was not only feeding the creature, but that it was starting to resemble its prey.

"Ghūl," she whispered, feet rooted to the spot.

Efemena had told her stories about them. How Innunu had thrown the ghūls into the underworld. In the folklore of Al Miraj, they preyed on unwary travelers in the dunes of the Sayhad. They looked like humans or animals—whatever they'd most recently devoured.

"Tijah." Achaemenes's face swam in front of her. "We have to keep searching. I don't think we can help these men."

A short distance away, Cyrus and Cassandane fought back to back, the magus wielding a short spear and his daēva carving a path with her sword through the formless creatures that surrounded them.

Tijah heard pounding hoofbeats and turned as Alexander rode

up on his massive black stallion, Bucephalus, the white star on its brow luminous against the grey mist.

"To me!" he cried. "Fall back to the forest!"

Bucephalus reared up as the young King raised his sword and charged toward a knot of besieged daēvas from Gorgon-e Gaz. The Old Ones were ferocious blurs of strength and speed but still no match for the things in the mist. Several of them had drawn too much power. The ones who'd died trying to channel earth sprawled in broken heaps, their limbs bent at unnatural angles. A few were unmarked except for blood running from nose and eyes. Tijah feared they had tried to use the fey water of the lake.

"Goddess, where are the children?" Tijah muttered, scanning the dark humps of the tents. Figures moved among them, some gauzy wisps and others all too solid. She couldn't tell if they were human or not.

"I don't know. We'll keep looking," Achaemenes said grimly. "At least those things fear iron."

They hurried past the makeshift stockade where the guards from Gorgon-e Gaz had been held. Tijah averted her eyes. All dead.

She whirled as Anu came flying out of the darkness. The girl pressed her face to Tijah's waist.

"They killed my father," she sobbed. "He didn't even fight back. Just sat there...." She dissolved into a fresh bout of tears.

"Where are the others?"

"I don't know, I don't know! Samahe took some of them into the woods!"

Achaemenes swept Anu into his arms and they ran for the tree line. Those who still lived were trying to do the same, but in the darkness and confusion, it was a panicked rout. Up ahead, Tijah saw a group of soldiers rolling barrels from near the catapults toward the area that had been cleared. People huddled there, shouting and urging them on.

"Go! Go!" It was Hephaestion, bloodied and horseless. "We'll make our stand in the woods!"

He strode back toward the ruined camp without waiting for her reply.

Moments later, they reached the trees. She turned in time to see Alexander's horse stumble over a pile of bodies, throwing him from the saddle. He crashed to the ground. Tijah heard a faint scream as the mist closed around him.

❧ 26 ❧

LYSANDROS

The fledgling crept closer, razored feathers flaring. Lysandros could see the pink of its throat flashing through the open beak, behind dozens of small, crooked and very sharp teeth. Its neck stretched like an overgrown and particularly ugly chicken as it flapped its wings twice and shrieked at them.

"I was not meant to die in such a humiliating fashion," Lysandros muttered, struggling against the tough vines that bound his arms behind his back. A second lead ran from his wrists to his feet, which were similarly trussed. The harder he fought, the more the vines seemed to tighten.

Lysandros was closer to the fledgling and thus likely to be eaten first, although the difference would probably amount to a matter of seconds.

"You're all piss and gristle anyhow," Darius mumbled into the icy rock. "I'm definitely the tastier one."

The fledgling lunged forward just as Lysandros gritted his teeth and tore one arm free, scraping off several wide strips of sun-gold skin in the process. He caught it by its serpentine neck and squeezed, blood coursing down his arm to the shoulder, snapping beak inches from his nose. Wings raked the ground, digging deep furrows in the ice. It didn't seem to have a jugular or any other recognizable anatomy. Just muscle and sinew. The thing might not even need to breathe at all.

"Oh, screw it," Lysandros muttered, yanking as hard as he could. The other arm broke loose, leaving a line of stinging gouges. He groped around and tore free a chunk of rock. The cold of it seared his palm as he smashed the pointy side into the fledgling's eye socket. Bone shattered and the eye dissolved with a gentle popping sound.

The fledgling did not take this well.

Lysandros threw himself awkwardly to the side, one hand cupping his testicles, as dagger-sharp feathers swept over him, so close they made a *whooshing* sound. The thing was half-blind and probably brain-damaged, but that only seemed to make it angrier.

From the corner of his eye, he saw Darius frantically sawing his bonds against a shard of ice. Pity he only had one good arm to fight with, although that was his own fault for choosing the bond.

"Some help?" Lysandros called. "Before it castrates me would be *perfect*."

Another wing-sweep. Another horribly close call.

He still had one hand locked around its throat, just barely holding it at bay, while the other continued to pound its head with the rock, to little effect. Clearly, the iron in their weapons during the last encounter with abbadax had been a greater advantage than he realized.

His feet were still tied, severely limiting his options. The fledgling's front legs twitched, seeking the soft organs of his belly, but it was the wings that scared him spitless. They swept up and down in deadly arcs. The angle wasn't quite right to slash him to shreds, but he couldn't hold it back forever. The thing weighed the same as a large pony.

Lysandros was just resigning himself to imminent disemboweling when the fledgling screeched, stiffened and went mercifully slack. Over its drooping head, he saw Darius, standing with one of the monster's own feathers in his hand, dripping blue blood.

"You have to stab them between the shoulder blades," Darius said, miming an up and down motion that struck Lysandros as vaguely obscene.

He shoved the creature away and used the rock to saw at the knots around his ankles, dark head bent low. "Quick thinking. And here I was, imagining you were just a lovesick sap who liked to play at swords."

"Hurry," Darius said quietly.

Lysandros didn't look up. "Don't tell me," he said. "I don't want to know."

"There are four more. And they look hungry."

"Didn't I just *say* not to tell me?" He worked harder on the knots, fingers bleeding.

The fledglings hissed and spat at each other as they advanced, but this sibling rivalry didn't seem to distract them from the meal that awaited.

If only I could touch the Nexus....

If only I hadn't listened to Victor....

If only I had some pants *on.*

Lysandros's hands were slippery with blood. He couldn't seem to get a grip on the vines. Thorns an inch long pierced his ankles. Darius bent down to help but Lysandros waved him away.

"There's no time! Just hold them off as best you can."

Darius kissed the cuff. Feathers of frost came away on his lips. "Goodbye, my love," he whispered. And something else. It might have been: *I'm sorry.*

Lysandros looked away, embarrassed, although part of him wished he had the courage to do the same.

Goodbye, son of Zeus...

The four fledglings flashed their needle teeth and skittered forward. Darius dropped to one knee, fingertips poised on the ledge, feet braced to meet them. No fear. Or so tightly contained, it didn't show.

A good man to die with, Lysandros had time to think, and then the first one's head caved in with a sick crunching sound. Steaming blue ichor sprayed across the rocks.

Lysandros craned his neck at the shadow looming over him.

"Put some clothes on, Lysandros," Delilah said crisply, leaning on her iron-capped staff. "I've seen enough horrors for one day."

"Mother!" Darius cried in warning.

She spun around as the second fledgling lunged. Her staff blurred, cracking it a dozen times. As it reeled on the edge, stunned, Delilah gave it a hard poke in the chest. The fledgling emitted a piercing cry and toppled backward into the void.

The two that remained didn't like the new odds. With sibilant hisses, they spread their wings and followed it over the edge. Delilah tossed Lysandros a knife. He sliced through the vines, sighing with relief.

Darius embraced his mother with a shaky laugh. "How did you find us?"

"I've brought Victor," she said, and Lysandros discovered to his profound amazement that Delilah actually knew how to smile. "I took him from Neblis's house. One of her necromancers...." She trailed off, grim again. "I tried to bring your father through the Bactrian gate but the lake was swarming with Undead spirits. So I started looking for another way. And then I saw movement on this ledge."

It was the devil's own luck we stopped here, Lysandros thought. The icy shelf of rock was visible for leagues in all directions, if you had the keen eyesight of a daēva.

"Come," Delilah urged, planting her staff on the ground and setting off. They followed her along the rugged path Culach and his soldiers had taken to a shallow crevice in the mountain that offered shelter from the wind. Victor leaned against the rock, shivering. He looked terrible.

"Thank the Gods! At least I'm not the only one who's naked," Lysandros exclaimed cheerfully, clapping him on the shoulder. Victor winced.

"Yes, but I look better," he replied with a ghastly smile.

Lysandros surveyed the half-healed slashes criss-crossing his stomach like a Go board.

"Usually," Victor amended.

"Let's be honest. We both look like shit."

Delilah stared at them until they fell silent. "I've come from the House-Behind-the-Veil," she said to Darius, who'd watched the exchange with amusement. "Nazafareen and I parted ways after you were taken. She went after you, and I went after your father. Along the way, I encountered creatures of the Dominion. They must have smelled the blood of the abbadax on me."

"Wait, let me guess. Fluffy little bunnies?" Lysandros quipped.

Delilah snorted. "They have the form of fearsome hounds. I thought they would attack, but they seemed more confused than anything else by my presence. I...I understood them when they communicated, although it was in a bestial language. They despise Neblis. They came to the House with me, hunting her."

Delilah went to Victor and put a slender arm around his shoulders. He leaned on her, head bowed, but Lysandros could see him sneaking a look. Lysandros felt certain Victor *did* remember about the Moon Lands now. About all of it. And he was wondering if Lysandros did too.

Lysandros didn't know Delilah well, but she'd been born in the Sun Lands, the daughter of two of Victor's companions. She wouldn't share their memories of the daēvas' original home.

"Can we have a word?" Lysandros said to Victor with an evil grin. "Privately?"

"Whatever you want to tell my husband—" Delilah began, stiffening like an angry cat.

"It's all right." Victor looked a shade greener. "If you wouldn't mind, darling."

Delilah arched an eyebrow but moved over to stand by Darius. They began speaking together quietly, Delilah fussing over his cuts and bruises while her son suffered the examination with a stoic expression.

"So." Lysandros rocked back on his heels, savoring the moment. "Anything you'd like to say?"

Victor studied him, black eyes impenetrable. "If you tell her—"

"That Neblis wasn't mad after all? That you seduced her and abandoned her?"

Victor looked away, but before he did, Lysandros glimpsed something he'd never seen in his face before. Shame.

"Raisa was right," Victor said in a hollow voice. "I am a fool."

Lysandros agreed, but somehow, Victor's misery wasn't as enjoyable as he'd hoped. He *had* loved Neblis. She was different then, full of laughter and mischief. The three of them would meet at the border of their two realms, a wild, untamed place of towering trees and secret, shimmering pools, and go swimming in the moonlight. Until Victor, show-off that he was, wanted to impress Neblis by diving to the bottom of the deepest pool. He'd urged her to throw her favorite necklace into the water, an exquisite choker of frozen dewdrops from the cloud-wreathed peaks where the Avas Valkirin made their home.

Victor had stripped and dived in headfirst—as he did all things. Long minutes passed. Lysandros began to worry. He was on the verge of jumping in himself when Victor emerged, Neblis's necklace gripped in one fist, gasping about a *portal*.

That still might have been the end of it. But Neblis couldn't resist telling Culach. Of course he'd followed her the next time she snuck off and discovered them all together. A perfect scandal erupted, and Victor got it into his head that he wanted to mount an expedition to the legendary shadowlands.

Lysandros sighed. "We were all fools."

Heavy, slate-colored clouds roiled the horizon on the far side of the mountains. Victor's eyes grew distant. "Ta'aeris," he whispered to himself.

Pretty sky daughter. It had been his nickname for Neblis.

"I suppose you'll say I deserved my punishment." His heavy shoulders sagged. "And perhaps I did."

Lysandros had been about to tell him what Neblis had done. How she was exacting her revenge through his son. But he suddenly didn't feel like twisting the knife any deeper. Victor could live with the knowledge that he'd destroyed his lover and it was enough.

"Well, now you've gone and ruined it for me," Lysandros said lightly. "Tell your wife whatever you choose. The truth or a barrel of lies, I don't care." He shrugged. "Delilah isn't stupid, so I'd advise the former. But it won't come from me."

Victor nodded. A gust of wind lifted his dark hair. They both shivered in the chill air. "Thank you. I will tell her...in my own time."

Lysandros glanced at Delilah, who was staring at them curiously. "I won't pretend I like her. She's a prickly woman. But I hope you treat this one better, Victor. She deserves it after the hell she's been through."

He spun on his heel and walked away before Victor could respond.

"What was that about?" Darius asked.

"Just a bit of unfinished business," Lysandros replied with a tight smile. "Now, these creatures of the Dominion. Where are they?"

"They followed after Culach, but for some reason they're afraid of Nazafareen," Delilah said. "They won't go near her."

At the mention of her name, Darius's face darkened. "I must go after her. Neblis did something to her...made her forget herself." He fell silent, blue eyes turning glacial. It wasn't anger, Lysandros thought, but pain.

"She broke the wards to the Moon Lands for *you*," he said

gently. "Neblis told me. But she was caught in the backwash of the spell. It wiped her mind clean. And then Neblis filled her with lies."

"Can it be reversed?" Darius asked anxiously.

Lysandros shook his head. "I've no idea."

"It doesn't matter," Darius muttered. "I have to find her."

"I'll go with you," Victor said, pushing unsteadily away from the wall.

"I doubt you could make it five steps unassisted, let alone run to the gate," Lysandros said. "And he'll need to run. Look."

He pointed to the pine-clad valley below. Culach had indeed made quick time. His soldiers were nearly at the lake. And Lysandros had the feeling he wouldn't wait for his sister, no matter what she'd said.

Delilah looked at Victor, then at Darius, her face a mask of indecision.

"Stay with him," Darius said gently. "He needs you."

She nodded in obvious relief. "There's something else. The hounds fear Nazafareen, but there is another they fear even more. A creature that calls itself Farrumohr. Their language is crude, but I think I understood the gist. He cannot be allowed to pass through the gate to Bactria. It would be...." She struggled for words. "A plague like none the world has ever seen."

"Where is this creature?" Darius asked. "What does it look like?"

"I don't know its form. But something has happened to weaken *all* the gates." Her long face grew almost fearful. "Did you feel the rain that swept through? They say the doors are wide open."

Darius nodded. "Then I won't need a talisman to follow them." He turned to Victor and took a deep breath. "I'm...I'm glad you're with us again."

Victor held out a hand. Darius clasped it. "Be safe," he said, grinning. "My Water Dog son."

Darius smiled back and turned to go.

"Aren't you forgetting someone?" Lysandros said airily. "I won't pretend I'm at my best, but I'm certainly in better shape than *him*." He jerked a thumb at Victor.

"You'll come with me?" Darius asked in surprise.

"Only if I get to kick Culach in the balls after we get there."

"Consider it done."

"You don't happen to have a spare pair of pants?" Lysandros asked Delilah. Then he cursed and started running, for Darius had already vanished down the steep path.

🕸 27 🕸

TIJAH

She sat through that endless night with Anu dozing in her arms, waiting for dawn.

The barrels had been full of Greek fire for the catapults. Under Hephaetion's direction, with the daēvas holding the line against the mist, the Macydonians had quickly dug a shallow circular trench. Once everyone was inside, Cyrus tossed a torch into the liquid. The mist could not cross the flames, but a light rain had started to fall and they wouldn't burn forever.

"How long do we have?" Tijah asked Cyrus.

He sat back to back with Cassandane, a brick propped against her boulder. The daēvas had retreated to the center of the circle, as far from the flaming barrier as they could get. The Macydonians formed a shield around them. There were pitifully few left.

"I've no idea. Just pray it lasts until daylight."

"And then what? Those things came before full dark. Who's to say the sun will stop them?"

He didn't answer. Cassandane had a far-off look in her eyes. "Do you think Victor lives?"

"No one knows," Tijah replied wearily.

"He agreed to pay the price. But Raisa was right. We never should have gone."

"What do you mean?" Cyrus asked, turning to his daēva. "Who is Raisa?"

She twined her long braid around her wrist. "I remember things. A place called the Moon Lands. We were Victor's companions." She shook her head, muddled. "There was a price for leaving, Raisa said. To forget the gate. To forget who *we were*. But something has changed. I'm starting to remember."

Fog pressed in on all sides of the circle. Their little patch of barren ground felt like an island floating in a sea of white.

"The Moon Lands?" Cyrus frowned. "I've never heard of such a place."

"It was beautiful," Cassandane said dreamily. "I don't know why we wanted to go...."

Tijah looked up as Samahe sank to the ground next to her.

"How's the girl?" she asked, looking at Anu.

"Sleeping." Tijah gave a tired smile. "Thank you. For looking after the others. They would have died if you hadn't kept your wits."

"Yes, well, even a fat old ewe will bite if you try to take her lambs away." She turned her sharp eyes on Tijah. "And you? How are you holding up?"

"Fine." She stroked Anu's tangled hair. "When I lost my daēva, I didn't want to feel anything ever again. But life has a way of interfering with our best plans."

Samahe laughed. "Indeed it does. And Achaemenes?"

"We fight well together," Tijah conceded. "He would have made a good Water Dog." Her cheeks reddened. "Not that I'm condoning what I was."

"I know what you mean, girl. Where is he?"

"Tending the wounded. He's a healer."

Samahe raised an eyebrow. "A man of many talents."

Tijah grunted. "He can be very annoying. Nothing ever ruffles his feathers."

"I see. Would you prefer a snorting bull like Nazafareen?"

"Definitely not."

"When I see my daughter again, I'll put a ring in her nose and give Darius the lead. Here, hand her over." Samahe helped Tijah settle the sleeping child in her own lap. "Why don't you check on your bonded?"

Tijah's legs had long ago gone numb from Anu's weight. They tingled painfully as she stood.

"I suppose I could use a little walk," she said.

The flames cast an orange light on the mist as she made her way past the still forms of injured men to the center of the circle. She nodded to Kian as she passed. He'd been one of the last to appear. She knew he'd been searching for Jengis.

Achaemenes knelt by Alexander. The King lay pale and still, but his chest rose and fell faintly. Hephaestion had carried him back moments before the fires were lit.

"I've done what I can for him," Achaemenes said, wiping bloody hands on a damp cloth. "He's young and his will to live is strong. There is still hope."

"You've given enough," Tijah said gently. His exhaustion was clear. "If you don't rest, you'll be useless tomorrow."

"I still don't understand," Achaemenes murmured. "If the mist was a trap set by Neblis, why didn't she spring it at once? Alexander has been camped here for the better part of a week."

"Who knows? But it must have a weakness."

"None of the elements work. Fire holds it at bay, but our fuel is almost gone. Iron is the only thing that seems to hurt it, and that only for a few moments." He lowered his voice. "I think we should have run when we had the chance."

She knuckled the small of her back and yawned. "Maybe so. But Innunu does not look kindly on those who run from battle.

I'd rather face the mist than the goddess's wrath when I climb the ninety-nine steps to the scales of judgment."

A chill dawn crept through the trees. The fires burned lower. As if sensing their imminent demise, the fog crept eagerly toward the outer edge of the circle. Thick clouds hung low over the lake, a dark ceiling pressing down.

"If only the sun would come out," Tijah said wistfully. "I would like to feel it on my face one last time."

Achaemenes nodded, only half-listening. He seemed to have given up. She looked around at the tired faces of the Macydonians. A palpable feeling of despair lay over the huddled group of men. But then Achaemenes turned to her, excitement shining in his eyes.

"I have an idea," he said.

He and Mithre gathered all the daēvas who could still touch the power, even the children. They stood in a line and joined hands. Some wore the tattered blue uniforms of the Immortals. Others were still clad in the rags they had taken from Gorgon-e Gaz. Parvane and Bijan stood with their mother, a dusky-skinned woman with a deformed back. Next to them, Abid clutched Achaemenes's trousers in his sooty fist. At the very end, Pegah and Anu twined their fingers together, though neither looked at the other and Anu's face might have been carved from stone.

Then Mithre began to sing. For a man who looked like a wolf in disguise, he had a surprisingly sweet tenor. Tijah couldn't understand the words, but his voice lifted her spirits. She thought of green growing things and trees so ancient their roots twined into the very bones of the earth. Of the restless movement of the ocean and the quiet, leisurely dreams of mountains. The hum of bees in summer and barking of foxes in winter. And in his song, all these things somehow seemed the same.

The soldiers raised their heads in wonder, listening. One by one, the other daēvas joined in, until their voices blended together in a tapestry of life and light and beauty. Tijah felt power course through the bond. A tear rolled down her cheek but she barely noticed.

A wind came, light at first but growing steadily stronger. The oppressive clouds drifted toward the west. A small patch of blue sky appeared. The fires sputtered.

And then a single ray of pure yellow sunlight lanced through. The fog boiled as it struck, sizzling like cold water on a black-smith's forge. A ragged cheer went up from the Macydonians. Inch by inch, the mist started to retreat. Tijah glimpsed darker shapes writhing within it. Sensed their hatred and fury. But they did not like the sun. As the tattered hole in the clouds grew larger, the fog rolled away like an ebbing tide into the woods and the ghūls went with it.

The last shreds spread out across the lake like a bolt of translucent silk. Then the mist sank back into the dark waters. Sunlight burnished the mirror-like surface.

The soldiers' cheers faltered when they saw the nightmarish scene in its wake. Alexander's mighty army had been decimated. Hundreds of men and horses sprawled on the ground where they had fallen.

The daēvas slumped against each other. Tijah caught Achaemenes's eye. He grinned broadly, then picked up Anu and kissed her on the forehead. Her giggle seemed to break the spell. The Macydonians leapt to their feet, clapping the daēvas on the back and thanking their barbarian gods for vanquishing Neblis's dark sorcery.

"I must go look for Jengis," Kian said. "It's possible...well, I won't believe him dead until I see his body with my own eyes."

"Kian." Samahe laid a gentle hand on his arm. "It's a grim task you set yourself. I know he was like kin—"

"I'll help him," Tijah said quickly. She understood all too well the pain of being denied a proper goodbye. Those unearthly voices still echoed in her ears, though the words were already lost.

"Mami Natu would like their song, I think. Give me a moment, Kian, and we'll see if any survived."

She went over to where the young King lay on Hephaestion's cloak. His color seemed better. Alexander opened his eyes as Tijah knelt beside him.

"The daēvas drove back the mist," she said. "Did you hear them?"

"I heard." He licked dry lips. "When I build my new capital, I shall raise a great monument to them," he whispered. "So that none will ever forget this day."

"And what would you call this great city?" Tijah asked with a smile.

"Why, Alexandria, of course!"

She laughed. "Of course. I'd like to see it someday."

Hephaestion leaned down to give Alexander some water. Tijah stood and wandered over to Kian and Samahe. The barrier still burned fitfully, but she supposed they could extinguish it with earth.

The last of the clouds drifted over the mountains and a clear morning broke over the valley. Sun-warmed pine needles scented the air. Tijah breathed it in. Even the faint ache in her knee—*his* ache—seemed tolerable for once.

"We must find the Seven-Legs Clan," Samahe said to Kian.

"But Nazafareen—"

"I don't know where she has gone, but she's beyond our reach. We must trust her daēva will watch over her. It's time our people returned to the Khusk. The pastures will be greening soon..."

She trailed off as a faint ripple rolled across the lake.

"Holy Father, what next?" Samahe muttered, pulling her shawl tighter. Tijah rubbed her eyes, hoping it was a trick of the light. Goddess, she'd never been more exhausted. But this was no illusion.

An army marched out of the still waters.

❦ 28 ❦

NAZAFAREEN

I woke to Culach grabbing me like a sack of onions and tossing me over his shoulder.

"Where's Neblis?" I demanded as the scenery sped past in a dizzying blur. His armor poked uncomfortably into my ribcage.

"Gone," he said. "We'll find her again, little mouse, don't worry."

"I'm not a mouse!"

He laughed. "You are to me."

"She says I'm part daēva," I mumbled. Hanging upside down was making my nose bleed again. I snuffled and coughed. Culach slowed and switched me to his arms.

"What's wrong with you?" he demanded, that awful winding scar inches from my face.

"I don't know."

"Do all humans have black blood?"

"I...no, I don't think so." I swiped the back of my hand across my nose and grimaced. It looked like an inkstain. Wisps of smoke rose from the sleeve of my tunic where the blood had touched it.

He blew out a breath and picked up the pace again. "Maybe Neblis can do something for you. But first we must find the gate."

Avas Valkirin soldiers loped along ahead of us and to each side. From their easy movements, I guessed they could run this way for leagues before they began to tire.

"I cannot abide this severing from the elements," Culach growled. "But my sister says they will return when we pass through to the Sun Lands." He glanced at me sideways. "She also says there is a fourth element there, as bizarre as it sounds. Something called fire."

"Have you truly never seen fire?" I asked, intrigued.

He shrugged. "That is like asking a fish if it's ever seen the moon. The word means nothing."

I hugged the stump to my body, staring at the griffin cuff. I didn't remember people or places, but I remembered fire. How it felt to work that molten current. Cracklingly alive, more akin to a force than an element. It could turn water to steam, earth to lava, air to raw, blistering flame. I knew because I didn't have to remember. It lived inside me.

Culach ran on without speaking. Every now and then, he looked over his shoulder as if sensing something behind us. But each time, he turned back with a shake of his head and continued on. Finally, we came out of the mountains and entered a thick forest. Despite their numbers, the Avas Valkirin made no sound. I closed my eyes for a while, listening to the wind sigh in the branches, Culach's breastplate smooth as polished ivory beneath my cheek.

When I opened them again, the trees had begun to thin. The landscape looked tended, with banks of deep crimson flowers and orderly gravel pathways. We passed the banks of a river and my breath died in my throat.

It was the windowless stone building of my dream. But one of the twisted towers had fallen down, half-burying the place where I'd stood. Something about the pattern of the rubble made the hair on my arms rise up. The well lay directly beneath the tower and yet its mouth yawned open. Chunks of rock formed a ragged circle as if they had been thrown *outward* with great force.

"I know this place," I whispered, rubbing my stump.

Culach held up a fist and the soldiers drew their weapons and fanned out.

"You can walk now," he said, depositing me roughly on my feet and stalking off. I trailed along behind as he entered an open doorway, reluctant to stay near the well. It was dim inside the building. I pressed against the wall of a long corridor as soldiers pushed past me.

"Search every room!" Culach called over his shoulder. "If my sister is here, I want her found!"

The stone felt wonderfully cool against my skin as I slid to the floor. This must be the house Neblis spoke of, but something had attacked it. Could the prisoners have escaped? I hadn't seen either of them since I'd fallen asleep. But surely Culach would have said something.

I leaned forward and coughed up a sizzling reddish black gob, then watched it eat into the stone between my feet with distant fascination. My mouth tasted of boiling copper. Tiny bolts of lightning danced in my fingers and toes.

The Avas Valkirin dashed up and down the corridor, stepping over me like I was part of the furnishings. Culach thundered commands in some far-off chamber. He sounded displeased.

I sensed a faint resonance of power all around, but it was already fading. In truth, I felt too strange to care much *what* was happening. It was hard to focus on anything for more than a few seconds. My belly was a glowing ember. If I sneezed—and this thought inspired a feeble laugh—would sparks fly out of my nose?

And then I felt it. Something in the rubble. I crawled to the doorway. The well yawned open in a silent scream. But that wasn't it...something else. Something that stirred the magic inside me. Like calling to like.

I crept forward on hands and knees. I could see the edge of an object, stone like the tower but of a darker grey. A container of some kind. With the tip of an eagle wing carved into its lid. The mirror image of the pendant I'd ground under my boot.

Open it. Thrust your stump inside.

I moved ahead a few more paces. But the well was so close now.... My limbs felt leaden. I didn't want to pass by it. Anything could be waiting inside.

And then a firm hand pulled me to my feet. Culach towered above, looking even grimmer than usual.

"Is Neblis here?" I asked, tearing my eyes from the urn.

"No. But there is a male body. Badly mauled." Culach stared at me like I should know who it was.

"Oh." I braced a hand on his arm as one of the soldiers jogged up. He wore his snowy hair in braids and carried a bow and quiver on his back.

"We found the gate," he said, voice tight with excitement. "It's not far."

"Lead me there," Culach ordered. "And bring the others."

He strode off and I forced myself to catch up, slipping through the ranks of the Avas Valkirin. The gloom thickened beyond the gardens. Tall, colorless reeds appeared, undulating like seaweed in an invisible current. The ground felt mushy underfoot. And then it began to rise. I saw a glow ahead.

Culach had paused before a rectangular doorway. The surface of it looked like a river flowing over hidden stones, swift and dappled in shades of black and silver.

"To battle!" he roared, drawing his sword. "We will bring a whirlwind down such as these Sunlanders have never seen!"

Culach stepped forward, and a shadow detached itself from the very edge of the gate where it faded into the murk. A shadow, yet solid somehow. I recoiled from it. Culach's green eyes went wide, but only for an instant. Then he squared his shoulders and passed through the doorway.

I looked at the soldiers to either side. Their faces shone with eagerness. One of them, a woman with short-cropped hair and eyebrows so pale they were almost invisible, reverently kissed her sword, then bared her teeth in a fierce grin.

No one saw the shadow but me.

❧ 29 ❧

TIJAH

Sunlight glinted on their silver-gold hair. They moved like the prowling dune cats of Al Miraj, coiled and deadly. A large man walked at their head. Tijah felt certain they were daēvas, but something about him troubled her. He seemed different from the others, although she couldn't say precisely how. A certain awkwardness, a stiffness in his limbs that looked *wrong*. He winced at the sudden light. Tijah could see he didn't like it.

Her breath caught in her throat. Next to him was Nazafareen.

She looked pale and worn. Purple shadows hollowed her eyes. She still wore the cuff around her stump, but Darius was nowhere to be seen.

"What is this?" Achaemenes breathed next to her. His shock echoed through the bond.

They didn't like the sun, but it didn't stop them coming. Too many to count. Tijah thought their small band of survivors must be outnumbered twenty to one.

For a long moment, the daēvas stood spread out in ranks on the shore, surveying the battlefield and the circle of flames.

"Friend or foe?" Cyrus muttered.

Cassandane hissed the words. "Avas Valkirin."

The ferocious expression on her face answered his question, though Tijah had no idea what the words meant.

"*Nazafareen!*"

It was Samahe. She leapt to her feet, running toward the edge of the circle. Strands of greying hair had pulled loose from her braid, but she looked young at that moment, a slightly plumper version of her daughter.

The tall daēva turned to Nazafareen and whispered something in her ear. Her face was impassive, icy almost. Tijah felt a twinge of fear.

"Samahe!" she cried.

Tijah heard the twang of a bowstring from somewhere in the daēva ranks. A black-fletched arrow arced over the dying flames and buried itself in Samahe's throat. She stumbled and fell to her knees. Kian made an animal sound of grief, dashing to his mother's side. He held her as her blood flowed into a spreading pool on the ground. Samahe gave a choking cough, hands clutching her neck. Then her head lolled back. The light fled from her eyes.

Nazafareen showed no reaction. None at all.

Tijah trembled with helpless fury. Grief gripped her chest in a cold vise. She would kill these creatures, every last one of them. And her dearest, oldest friend....

What have they done to her? Was she taken by a wight?

"I am Culach," the man said. He didn't shout but his voice carried in the perfect silence. "And you.... You are a pile of corpses."

Nazafareen raised her hand. For the first time, Tijah saw a glimmer of emotion. Pain. The flames winked out as if they'd never existed. Culach's army surged forward.

Tijah knew then that she didn't want to die anymore. She wanted to live. To get old and fat and rich. To see Alexandria through the curtains of a gold-enameled palanquin.

But it was too late.

Innunu's cold shadow fell over her.

You've used up more lives than a Numidian temple cat, Tijah, the death goddess whispered. *And I'm afraid...they've just run out.*

❦ 30 ❧

NAZAFAREEN

I tried to turn back but the press of bodies swept me forward, through the gate. Up the long slope we climbed, through a forest of grey reeds undulating like the arms of some deep-sea monster. The gloom gradually dissolved. Hot sunlight struck my face. The sudden change made me squeeze my eyes into blurry slits. I felt the faint tug of the other elements—earth, air, water—but those were pale reflections of the fire that called to me from somewhere up ahead.

I blinked hard, trying to make sense of what I saw. Bodies scattered everywhere, men and horses both. Hundreds of empty tents. And past them, a circle of weak flames. People stood inside it, staring at us. One of them called my name, an older woman. She ran forward and was felled by an arrow from the ranks of the Avas Valkirin.

Culach said something to them, but my head buzzed so loudly I couldn't make it out. Then he leaned toward me. Flames licked the void behind his eyes.

"Extinguish the barrier," he grated. "These are your enemies."

His breath reeked of the grave. I shook my head, sick with doubt. "I can't."

"*You can.* You are the Breaker. The fire worker. Take it into yourself."

He terrified me. I raised a hand and summoned the heat of the flames, drawing it like iron filings to a magnet. It fed the pyre already blazing in my belly. An almost pleasurable agony ignited every nerve. The beast lunged at its chain. It wanted to turn the trees to torches, to boil the waters of the lake into hissing steam. To mete out its wrath.

Our enemies. The cowards who enslaved the daēvas.

Faint curls of smoke rose from the blackened trench, but the fire shielding the people beyond it had vanished. It was inside me now. My skin felt as thin and dry as the shed scales of a snake. Culach grinned, his face a rictus of triumph. The soldiers raised their black swords. And then they turned at a disturbance in the lake.

The blue-eyed daēva. He slogged through the deep not-water, one arm raised over his head. Sunlight caught the cuff, making it blaze.

Even through the heat-haze of the power, I felt my own grow warmer. Something was coming back to life inside it, an animal sleepily crawling from its den after a long, hard winter. I felt the pain of his many cuts and bruises. The strange deadness of his left arm. But those sensations paled at the love that poured into me. A love so pure it made tears spring to my eyes. My rage withered before the force of it.

His name is Darius. And I am Nazafareen.

I remembered nothing else, save for one thing. We belonged to each other. Whatever Neblis said, this man would sooner die than harm me.

And if he loved me, perhaps I was not damned after all. Perhaps I could still choose.

He made it to the shallows before the soldiers seized him. Our eyes met just before they dragged him down. Darius knew. He smiled in the instant before a fist smashed into his teeth.

I took a step to run to him when Culach grabbed my arm. The thing lurking next to the gate looked out at me through the pane of his face. Old and cruel.

Culach raised his sword, then paused. His expression was perfectly blank, like whatever animated him no longer cared about putting on a mummery of life. "If I wore its flesh, would I have its magic too?" he muttered. "Its lovely killing magic?"

He pulled me closer, the small muscles in his face writhing like worms beneath the skin. Shadows gathered in the irises of his eyes, pooling into black pinpoints that seemed to suck the light from the sky. I tried to tear my gaze away, but he gripped my face in his huge hands.

"Look," he whispered, leaning forward.

Distant screams as the Avas Valkirin surged around us. My heart hammered in my chest, the ground tilted under my feet as I stared into those tunnels to some nightmarish otherworld. Like bottomless wells....

The shadow oozed across the surface of Culach's eyes and I knew with an icy conviction beyond terror that the thing was about to take me.

And what would happen to Darius when it did? Would he be taken too?

Fire still smoldered in me, an ocean of it, and I threw it all at the shadow in the very moment it struck. At the ancient magic that gave it form and substance. The air between us glowed red-hot. It coiled and thrashed, but oh, how strong it was! It didn't burn or break. It *pushed back*, snaking toward my eyes. I drew more and more, stretching for the furnace of the sun until my body felt light as ash, brittle as charred bone.

And finally the darkness tore loose like a leech, sinking into the depths of the lake. Caught in the riptide of power, the nearest line of Avas Valkirin soldiers went up in flames.

I collapsed on top of Culach's limp form, fingers clawing furrows in the mud of the shore. My skin had turned translucent.

I watched with that queer, remote sensation as lines of black tar crept through my veins, moving in the direction of my heart.

And then a beautiful dark-skinned woman was cupping my face. She wore a golden cuff on each wrist and they pressed like shards of ice against my cheeks. Curly hair floated around her head like a cloud.

"Goddess curse you, Darius, quit getting your ass kicked, she's fucking dying here!" the woman hollered.

The howling of dogs filled the air. She let go of me, my head tumbled to the side, and I saw grey shapes darting among the Avas Valkirin, nipping and snarling.

He's coming for you. Can you feel him? Closer now. So close...

And then strong arms lifted me up. Blue eyes looked anxiously into mine.

"What do I do, Tijah?" he pleaded. "Tell me!"

She gazed down at me, brow creased. "I...I don't know. Mami Natu, look at her arms."

"Let me see." A man shouldered her aside. The raven-haired prisoner. He blanched when he saw me. "Huǒ mofa," he muttered. "It's the fire. How do we put out the blaze?"

"Lysandros, please." Darius sounded broken.

"I know, I'm thinking! Maybe.... We have to get her through the Moon gate," Lysandros said decisively. "And fast. You'd better run, boy, like you've never—"

Darius charged back into the lake, dodging the snarling dogs and screaming soldiers. I dimly saw tall reeds and then the gardens of Neblis's house. He ran and ran, his breath keeping time with my stuttering heartbeat. Trees and rocks and ice. And at last, a glowing rectangle of blue-green light.

We passed through. The first and last thing I saw was a moon, huge and bright in the starry sky.

✦ 31 ✦

BALTHAZAR

He stood, sheltering Zarathustra behind him, as the abbadax swooped down to the sand ten paces away. Neblis slid from its back, nimbly avoiding the razor-sharp feathers. Streaks of dried blood stained her gown but he could see no injury.

"Balthazar." She studied him with quicksilver eyes. "I am at a loss."

"My Queen." He felt his knee bending and forced it straight again.

"You were my most loyal Antimagus. My *beautiful boy*."

For an instant, her features melted into a vision of his sister Artunis, with long dark hair and a laughing mouth. He blinked and it was gone. *I'm going mad....*

Neblis pinned him with an unblinking stare, a mountain leopard sizing up a rabbit. "But you left me for dead. Let that old liar work his foul magic against me."

"You cannot have him," Balthazar heard himself say.

Neblis looked at the Prophet. Something flickered in the depths of her eyes. "Cannot? You would command me now, Balthazar?"

When he failed to reply, she shook her head sadly. "I plucked you from that prison they locked you up in, gave you everything you asked for, and this is my payment. To return and discover that Victor has gone. That you let him *escape*." Her teeth ground the word to dust. "Your other betrayals pale in comparison, but we shall get to those as well."

"You used me," he said, but the accusation rang hollow. Balthazar knew full well he had allowed himself to be used.

"I loved you!" Tears shone in her eyes. "And may the elders banish me, I still do. Please. This filthy, conniving old charlatan has poisoned you against me. I need you, Balthazar. Our plans may have altered, but they are not ruined. Culach marches on the Sun Lands. When we take what is rightfully ours, you will have power beyond your wildest imaginings!" Her voice lowered to a silky caress. "You will wear the cuffs of ten daēvas, my love. The elements will be yours to command, as I always promised. You're destined for greatness, Balthazar. It's why I chose you, why I set you above the others."

A sudden image seized his mind. He stood in the blackened ruins of Karnopolis, the city of his birth, the city that had spurned him and starved him and named him witch, arms thrust wide. Calling to earth, to air, to water. Raw power thrummed in his veins as he built the greatest capital the world had ever known, a monument to his dark Queen.

Balthazar's heart raced. Yes, he would use the power to build... to create things of such beauty one would weep to behold them. A new age would come. An age of magic and wondrous deeds. And Balthazar would stand at the center of it. The dark prince at his mistress's feet.

Neblis bared her pointy teeth in a grin. And the visions gave way to a memory, distant but still clear as his own reflection. A daēva named Davod. *His* daēva. The sound of the blade as it cut his throat. The metallic smell of his blood.

I am a thief, Balthazar realized. *Of lives, of children, of power rightfully belonging to others. And in the end, it has left me more helpless and debased than ever.*

"Nothing would bring me greater joy, my Queen," Balthazar said, and her smile widened. "But I think you would require the services of an Antimagus for such a thing." He inclined his head. "And I am just a man."

A long moment passed. Coldness descended on her features like night falling over a snowy field. "As you wish, Balthazar. I had hoped you would make a different choice." The abbadax flexed its wings. "I'm afraid I have little use for men, and less for old fools." Her gaze turned to the sea. "At least you have chosen an appropriate place to meet your end."

"It is never too late to seek the light—" Zarathustra began.

"Do not preach to me!" she seethed, striding towards him. "You! Who enslaved us! Death is too good for *you*, magus. No, I will keep you alive, collared, as my own personal Breaker." She laughed. "Oh, you will live a long time yet. I carry no talismans. Your magic cannot touch me. You are *weak*."

Balthazar tried to block her path but she moved too fast. Neblis seized Zarathustra by his robes and flung him aside. She rounded on Balthazar. The rage she had held in check bubbled to the surface like poisonous vapors from a cauldron. "But *you* will not leave this place."

An inhumanly strong hand gripped his throat, lifting him from the ground. The mouth he had once kissed so passionately pinched into a vicious slash. An instant later, icy water engulfed his head. He thrashed in the shallows, the surface only inches above. Balthazar discovered that the Cold Sea was no gateway. Not a facsimile of water but the very thing itself.

You are a pilgrim, Balthazar. And this is your final journey.

A heavy lethargy began to overtake him. His struggles grew fainter.

I strayed from the path and it has led me here, to this fathomless twilight. To the bottom of the Cold Sea, where all the rivers and streams that ever were come to join their eternal mother. What a fool I was to imagine that redemption was possible. And yet...in the end it was my choice and mine alone, as Zarathustra said it would be.

I will die remembering magic. And that too is my choice.

Snowflakes spun above him, weaving and dancing in patterns as intricate as the finest lace. He stood on the riverbank, a boy of nine, and the daēva with the bird's nest hair spoke to the wind and the water, and they listened. His heart full nearly to breaking with the beauty of it, and the sorrow that he could not speak to them too.

What a grand show it had been to a dirty little urchin of the pleasure district! Sunlight gilding each crystal with fire as the daēva knit them into the shapes of animals and constellations, a dizzying display just for him. He had begged for more and then more, his empty belly forgotten.

"Teach me!" Balthazar had cried. "Teach me to do magic!"

The daēva laughed, and then he had gone, leaving Balthazar with snow melting in his cupped hands. He was still standing there like a boy bewitched when Artunis found him. She had asked him if he'd gone swimming, and he'd told her no, and she'd asked why his hair was all damp then. He'd made some excuse. The snow was his secret. The only thing he had left to keep.

I should have told you, he thought. My sweet Artunis.

Balthazar opened his mouth to let the sea rush in and claim him. And then the hand pinning him down was torn away. He rolled to his back, gasping. Spots danced before his eyes, his own breath harsh in his ears. But as he returned to full consciousness, he heard another sound, like a saw eating through wood planks. Rhythmic and close. Balthazar pushed up to hands and knees.

A dozen Shepherds stood in the water up to their chests, red tongues lolling as they panted. On the shore, five more savaged the body of the abbadax. Balthazar's gut tightened. All things considered, he preferred to drown.

"No!" Neblis whispered. She crouched on the sand, hair wild. "You cannot take me!"

The great hounds slowly tightened their circle. Balthazar's skin tingled as the nearest one brushed past him, the hair along its back stiffening as it gathered itself to spring. Neblis shrieked. One of them snagged her gown in its teeth, dragging her toward a black-sailed ship that waited at anchor down the beach. The others closed in, not tearing her to shreds as he expected but herding her away.

"Help me!" she cried to Balthazar, eyes wide with terror. "Please! I'm sorry I hurt you." Her voice broke. "Don't let them.... *Balthazar!*"

He looked away, unable to watch. Even after she had tried to drown him, he couldn't be glad to see her in the custody of the Shepherds. Neither would he do anything to stop it. *I'm a coward to the last.*

Balthazar's heart lurched as he saw the last dog pad toward the still form of Zarathustra. It had tawny brown fur that darkened to midnight black around the eyes and forehead. Each paw print in the sand was twice the size of Balthazar's own boots and he was not a small man. He struggled to his feet, shivering violently. A wind had sprung up. It plastered the wet tunic to his body as he splashed forward.

"Magus!" he screamed.

The Shepherd lowered its massive jaws toward Zarathustra's face...and gave his cheek an affectionate lick.

Balthazar goggled as the Prophet's eyes cracked open and he patted the dog on the head, gently fending off its sloppy overtures. "Yes, yes," he murmured. "I'm awake now." He accepted Balthazar's proffered hand and stood.

The Shepherd's yellow eyes locked on Balthazar. Its lip curled in a snarl.

"It's all right," Zarathustra said soothingly. "There's no need for that. It is not this one's time."

The snarl evolved into a low whine. A strand of saliva dangled from one jagged tooth. Balthazar took a step back.

"He will swear to leave and never enter the Dominion again." Zarathustra gave Balthazar a pointed look. "Won't he?"

Balthazar nodded fervently. "You...speak to them?"

"To a degree."

"But they're savage killers!"

"Only of Antimagi," Zarathustra said. "They are creatures of the Dominion, yes, but they are not evil. They serve a purpose. One can't have the dead wandering about lost after they come through the gates. The Shepherds guide them beyond, willingly and...unwillingly."

They both looked down the beach. Neblis's faint cries of outrage could still be heard as the Shepherds forced her onto the ship.

"What will happen to her?" Balthazar wondered.

The dog at his feet made a strange whimpering noise. The Prophet frowned, head cocked as though he were listening.

"It says they can smell a taint in her. A darkness. I think that maybe Neblis was not so wicked when she first came to the Dominion. But something found her. Something very, very old." The Prophet looked troubled. "She cannot be let loose, and yet it is not entirely her fault that she has come to such a lamentable pass." The Shepherd tipped its furry muzzle back and bayed at the sky. "His brothers and sisters will keep her safe. And safe from harming others."

"Farrumohr," Balthazar said, grimacing at the name. "He's some kind of demon, native to this place. He would whisper in her ear."

The Shepherd snapped at the air. Balthazar took this to mean that Farrumohr was not a creature they looked favorably upon.

"I must leave you now, old friend." Zarathustra glanced to the left, away from Neblis, and Balthazar saw to his astonishment that a second boat had appeared, beached on the sand.

"But where will you go?" He gestured to the grey expanse. "What lies on the other side?"

The Prophet shrugged. "What is life—or death—without a little mystery? I will discover the answer to that question when I get there." He pursed his lips musingly. "Perhaps there will even be goats. I *am* fond of the creatures."

Balthazar suppressed a grin. "The Holy Father keep you then."

"He always has." The Prophet gave a playful smile. "Be good, Balthazar."

"I will try." He opened his mouth. Closed it again. A thousand words choked his throat. He finally settled for two. "Thank you."

"Don't forget your promise," the old man said, clambering into the boat. The last Shepherd crouched at the bow, its snout pointed into the wind. "You must never return here. Not until you come through a gate the proper way. Dead."

Balthazar laughed. "I'll keep my promise, if *you* promise to put in a good word for me on the other side. I might need it."

He waded into the sea and gave the boat a shove, aiding it toward deeper waters.

The Prophet turned and gave a final absent-minded wave. He sat erect on the wooden bench, one gnarled hand braced on the gunwale. A breeze lifted his long grey beard. He did not look back again.

❦

BALTHAZAR STOOD ON THE SHORE AND WATCHED THE TWO SHIPS sail away. He watched until their black masts slipped below the horizon and their long frothy wakes subsided, leaving the Cold Sea as placid as a pond again. He was chilled to the bone and soaking wet and glad to be alive.

I am a man, but not just a man. I will always be something more. That is one thing I cannot change.

Balthazar touched the talisman of Traveling in his pocket, traced its crooked spirals with a fingertip.

I'm free to be anyone. To go anywhere. I am a pilgrim.

A smile lit his darkly handsome face.

And perhaps there's magic in that as well.

PART FOUR

I sent my Soul through the Invisible,
Some letter of that After-life to spell:
And by and by my Soul return'd to me,
And answer'd: 'I Myself am Heav'n and Hell
—The Rubáiyát of Omar Khayyám

❧ 32 ❧

LYSANDROS

The urn sat between them on a bench in the gardens. It was stoppered, but the blue fire within—the fourth element—still burned. Even the Dominion couldn't extinguish it.

One of the Macydonian soldiers had found the urn tipped on its side in the rubble. The heavy stone lid was engraved with a faravahar, eagle wings spread wide. Such a small thing, Lysandros thought when he first saw it, to be the source of so much pain and misery.

"I don't wish you to go," Alexander said morosely. The young king lay on a litter, wrapped in heavy blankets. He had insisted on seeing Neblis's infamous House-Behind-the-Veil for himself before departing for the eastern satrapies.

"Nor do I," Lysandros agreed. "And yet I must."

Alexander sighed. "Then I will safeguard the holy fire until you return."

Lysandros nodded, grateful that Alexander had ceded the point so easily. It had been two days since the mist rose from the lake. Two days since Culach's armies were driven back. He suspected Nazafareen had done something to help break them, but it had all happened so fast. By the time he'd reached the gate, the Shepherds were nipping at his heels. They'd raced through together in a general melee. He'd seen Culach fall, and one of his Avas Valkirin rush forward to claim the body. Whether Neblis's twin was dead or alive, Lysandros had no idea.

That morning, a messenger had reached them from Karnopolis. The city was now under the watchful eye of a contingent of Alexander's soldiers who'd marched from the ruins of Persepolae, but some of the magi had managed to flee with their charges during the chaos. Dozens of cuffed daēva children remained unaccounted for.

Lysandros himself had been the only daēva to escape forced conscription into the Immortals two centuries before, living in comfortable exile in Qin while his cousins were enslaved. It nagged at his conscience still.

"I have to find them," he said quietly. "You understand, don't you?"

Alexander gave a wan smile. "You are an honorable man, Lysandros. I would not love you otherwise."

The King had chosen a dozen mounted men to carry a proclamation that would be read in every city and village across the empire. It declared the daēvas to be free creatures and warned that any who tried to subjugate them would find themselves in irons. But both knew the words would be worth nothing until the cuffs were broken.

Lysandros knelt beside the litter. "Bond me," he whispered. "For you, I would accept it."

Alexander's mismatched eyes widened a fraction in surprise. Then he raised a hand to Lysandros's cheek. "I would never ask that."

"But—"

"The gods have blessed me, Lysandros. Never fear, I will live to a ripe old age." His cocky grin softened. "And I couldn't bear to see you maimed. You're perfect as you are."

Raven hair brushed copper. The heady scent of Neblis's gardens surrounded them as they kissed, long and deep.

"Come back to me," Alexander whispered. "Promise it."

Lysandros bowed his head and stood. "I swear." He gave the urn a last glance. "Now go build an empire to last a thousand years."

He felt his lover's eyes on his back as the gate enveloped him.

✢ 33 ✢

TIJAH

She stood at the bow of the *Amestris,* the Salenian Sea parting like sheets of silk on either side of the ship's prow. A light breeze filled the square sails as barefoot crewmen moved around the deck, following the bellowed orders of Captain Barsine. The *Amestris* belonged to Kayyan Zayhar, Alexander's smuggler friend. The young King was still stitching together the pieces of his new empire, but her false nameplate—the *Photina*—had been removed and the ship proudly flew Alexander's sunburst banner now.

"The water is darker than the port of Karnopolis," Anu observed. "Colder too."

Tijah slipped an arm around the girl. She had finally been persuaded to wash and comb her hair. It hung in pretty amber waves down her slender back.

"Do you remember the sign for water?" she asked.

Anu promptly held out three fingers, turning them sideways and bending the knuckles so they looked like wavy lines.

Tijah nodded approvingly. "Ship?"

The girl cupped her hand and lay it on the palm of the other, rocking it gently from side to side.

"Very good. How about poxy-stricken horse thief?"

Anu giggled and made a complex sign.

"No, you have to hook the little finger," Tijah corrected. "Otherwise it means poxy-stricken *magus*."

On the starboard side, Cyrus glanced over with a look of long-suffering reproach. Cassandane leaned easily against the rail next to him. Tijah still wasn't entirely sure why they had offered to come, although she suspected Cyrus was driven by guilt for all he'd done. He needed a new cause.

Neblis had vanished. So had the Prophet. Kian invited Tijah and Anu to come with him when he left to find the Four-Legs Clan, but no matter how she tried, Tijah couldn't picture herself herding goats. And she had other business to attend to.

He'd taken the loss of both mother and sister hard so she'd felt doubly guilty for refusing. At least he had Jengis to accompany him. They'd found the young man unconscious under one of the catapults.

"Will the Avas Valkirin try to invade again?" Anu asked.

"Not with the Shepherds watching the gates to the Moon Lands," Cassandane remarked over her broad shoulder.

Lysandros said the beasts had harried Culach's army all the way through the Dominion to the gate, though it had hardly been necessary. After seeing the effects of fire, the daēvas seemed to have lost any desire to conquer and only wanted to go home.

"Maybe we will cross paths with Lysandros someday," Anu said wistfully. She had taken one look at the black-haired, violet-eyed man and developed a childish crush. "He is hunting daēvas and we are hunting gates."

"Not just gates," Tijah said absently, watching the frothy water race by ten paces below. "The restless dead too."

An untold number of them had broken through before the Shepherds came. The things in the mist had not been sent—they'd surged through on their own when the wards failed. Lysandros believed there'd been an especially large number of ghūls gathered at the gate in Bactria because Neblis *fed* them. No one knew yet what had happened at the eleven other gates. The only certainty was that Nazafareen had damaged or destroyed every single ward in the Dominion.

The boundaries weaken, Lysandros had said. *The gates are unquiet.*

That same night, as Alexander readied what was left of his men to march south, Myrri had come to her one last time.

They sat facing each other in the little boat. It spun in lazy circles in the middle of that glassy ocean.

Monsters walk the earth, Tijah, Myrri signed. *Druj with no masters.*

She left it there, but the look on her face added, *And what are you going to do about it, sister?*

Tijah scowled, suspecting where this was going. *I will hunt them.* She held up the cuff. *As soon as I break this with Zarathustra's fire.*

Myrri shook her head. *It is a task that will take more than one lifetime, sister. We both know that. So now you must choose.* She leaned forward and lightly kissed Tijah's lips. *Go. I cannot linger anymore, else I will turn into one of those who have forgotten themselves and exist only to return.*

But—

Myrri's face hardened. *Go, or I will throw you overboard myself.*

It's not fair! Tijah howled. And then she was spluttering as frigid water closed over her head. She woke in her tent, gasping for air.

Innunu, guide me. I don't know if I can do this again. Not even to save the world.

And then the question that lay at the heart of it. That she had refused to contemplate but could no longer ignore.

What if he dies?

They cannot ask this of me. It's too much!

Tijah had argued with herself until dawn. And then, with a heavy heart, she had made her choice.

Now she sensed a presence behind her. An ache in her leg that never went away. She kept her eyes fixed on the horizon.

"I hear Babylon is the greatest city on earth," he said. "Greater even than Nineveh before it was razed to the ground."

Tijah half turned. "More than a thousand years old," she replied. "It's hard to imagine."

Achaemenes could've gone to the Moon Lands with the others. Instead, he had chosen to stay with his sister. And with Tijah.

"Do you truly think we'll find a gate there?" He held a dull grey stone in his fist. A talisman of locking that had been Lysandros's final gift from his people. It drew on earth magic and could not be used in the Dominion—only on the living side of the gates.

"The scrolls say so. But we still only know of five. The others...they could be anywhere."

"Not anywhere. The necromancer believed they're all in great cities. We'll find them."

Alexander and Lysandros had managed to piece together some of Balthazar's treatises on the gates. The one in Bactria had been just outside the capital that Neblis destroyed. The necromancer's theory—expounded on at yawn-inducing length—was that the gates were centers of power. They attracted human settlements like wasps to nectar. Lysandros had promised the talisman would glow with the cold fire of the moon when it drew near to a gate. And that was all they had to go on.

Five known Greater Gates. Seven unknown.

And what had already come through?

Myrri was right. Their task would take lifetimes to complete —if they were lucky. All the former Immortals and Old Ones except for Lysandros and Cassandane had returned to the Moon Lands, taking their children with them. Anu had thrown a truly spectacular tantrum when they tried to make her go too. Finally, Mithre had relented.

She's a fierce little thing, he'd said to Tijah with a wolfish grin. *Are you sure you want this one?*

Yes, Tijah said. *I'm sure.*

And she was—more so than about anything else.

A tug on her arm made Tijah look down. Anu's face glowed with excitement.

"Porpoises!" she cried.

They swam alongside, diving and resurfacing on either side of the prow, grey backs shining in the sunlight. Tijah remembered standing with Nazafareen on the deck of this same ship after they'd fled the village of Karon Komai. Nazafareen had been bonded to Victor then and made him horribly seasick —Darius too.

Tijah smiled to herself. She'd been awed by the vastness of the plain of water around them. The way the deep currents dragged the *Amestris* along like a toy ship tied to a string.

The world is wide, Nazafareen, she'd said. *Wider than I ever imagined.*

Nazafareen had pulled her close. Her head just reached Tijah's shoulder. *I hope you get to see all of it someday.*

The porpoises seemed to grin at them. Anu laughed in delight.

How I miss you, nomad girl, Tijah thought sadly. *I will see the world for both of us. At least I'll have plenty of time to do it.*

An ocean of time.

❦ 34 ❦

NAZAFAREEN

D im light brushed my eyelids like the wings of a moth.
I opened them and saw a dome of silver leaves above. A dense canopy woven together so tightly only a glimmer passed through it. And yet the branches grew as straight and true as the beams of a roof.

You're dreaming again, Nazafareen.

It reassured me to think of my name. It was still one of the only things I remembered.

I rolled to my side on a bed of thick, spongy moss. The bloodstained tunic was gone, replaced by a shirt and trousers of some soft material that had a pleasant *alive* smell, like newly mown hay.

What an odd room! A dream, but much more pleasant than the last one. Smooth-barked trees made up the walls, crowded so closely together they left no room for lower branches, only the leafy crowns that enclosed the roof. Every fifth tree curved midway up to create oval windows. The one above me framed an enormous moon riding high in the dark sky.

I felt a pang of loss and realized I could no longer feel the blue-eyed daēva through the cuff. He was gone.

But so was that terrible magic, like a hungry rat living in my belly.

"I hear you speak our tongue now."

I jumped up, peering into the shadows. "Who's there?"

"Do you remember me?"

A tall, dark-haired man leaned against an arch in the trees at the far end of the room. He had a powerful build and wore clothing in a similar cut to mine.

"No," I said defensively. "Should I?"

"My name is Victor. I am Darius's father."

I took a step back, the carpet of leaves crackling beneath my bare feet. "What is this place?"

"You are in the lands of the Avas Danai."

He must have seen the fear on my face for he laughed softly. "No one will harm you here. The Matrium are a bit cranky about what you did to the gates, but they'll come around." He smirked like a cat that just got into the clotted cream. "They're already halfway to forgiving me for my long absence."

"The Matrium?"

"All in time, girl. How do you feel?"

I thought about this for a moment. "Empty."

"Do you need food?"

My stomach rumbled in reply. "That too, but mainly in other ways." I scrubbed a hand across my face, embarrassed at how my voice cracked. "It's gone. It's finally gone."

"There is no fire here. Only three elements. Can you feel those?"

Earth. Air. Water. They made up everything around me, but when I called to them, they answered in whispers—not a howling shriek like fire. "A little bit."

"I think I'd better tell my son you're awake. He's refused to leave your side for the last two days. Delilah finally hauled him off to get his wounds cleaned." Victor slipped away into a dim hall beyond.

I sat back down on the moss, unaccountably nervous.

You don't even know him. How can you have such feelings for him?

And yet I did.

I stared at the doorway, chewing my ragged nails, until I heard soft footsteps. Then I pretended to be admiring the moon.

"Nazafareen."

He came to me warily. Watching for some sign. He looked different somehow. Even with my weak ability, I could sense earth magic wrapping around him like a cloak.

"Hello again," I said awkwardly, switching to human speech. I hadn't forgotten how I'd treated him before.

"So...." His gaze slid to the moon. We both stared at it like fools for a long moment.

"Victor says you're feeling better," he said at last. "Do you....?"

"No." I shook my head. "Not a thing. Nothing before...*her*."

"Ah." A flash of disappointment crossed his features.

And then I noticed. Smooth, unblemished skin where it had once been grey and withered. "Your arm!" I exclaimed. "It's...it's better."

He smiled, and there was a bittersweet note in it. "Yes. Our bond is truly gone here. The fire that held it together dissolved when we passed through the gate."

Moonlight shone on his dark hair as he slid his cuff off and dropped it on the moss.

"May I?" he asked, sounding tentative. "I've never been able to touch it before."

I held out my stump. He looked at the cuff for a long time. Then his fingers closed around the snarling griffin. My breath caught. He worked it loose and dropped it next to the first one.

"You can never leave the Moon Lands, Nazafareen," Darius said. "I'm so sorry. Victor says you'll die if you try. Your fire magic is too strong."

"It doesn't matter." I shrugged. "I don't remember anywhere else. I wouldn't know where to go."

A shadow crossed his face. "You say that now, but I don't think you understand. You'll never see the sun again. This is a land of eternal night."

"But you have the moon." I pointed through the window. "And stars. Not like that other place. It almost seems a nightmare now. Hard to remember anything clearly." I rubbed the smooth skin of my stump, not wishing to speak of the well, or the thing I'd seen inside Culach. "Will...are you staying too?"

"Nothing could drag me away," he said seriously.

A weight lifted from my chest. "I'm glad," I said.

No sun, yet the air held the fading warmth of a late summer evening in the mountains. I knew this for truth without knowing *how* I knew.

"You told me once that you wanted to live in a little house of your own." Darius smiled. "You wanted goats too, but I'm afraid we don't have those. I was going to teach you to read. But perhaps you can teach me my parents' tongue."

I nodded. He stood so close. The smell of him, clean and masculine.... What had happened on the lakeshore still echoed in my bones. I didn't know him at all.

And yet I did. In some deep place where such things are never truly lost.

"Perhaps...." I took a breath, feeling brazen and not caring a whit. "Perhaps you could help me remember...things. If you tried very hard."

A slow smile tugged at the corners of his mouth. "A wise suggestion, Nazafareen. If we try very, very hard, even without the bond, I might be able to elicit a spark of recognition—"

My hand twined in his silky hair. I aimed for his lips but we both turned our heads the same way and my crooked nose bumped into his beaky one. He laughed softly, and his breath filled my mouth.

"I don't need the bond to make you feel me," he murmured.

And Darius was right. He didn't.

EPILOGUE

The Dominion slept again.

Many of her children had left, but more would come. Unhappy souls who couldn't bear to cross the Cold Sea. Who hungered to wear the flesh again. When they stayed too long, they changed. Became *other*. Not living nor dead, but creations of the Dominion's own dark magic. A magic deeper and older even than the Nexus itself.

The Shepherds were her children too, keeping the balance between light and dark. Even now they paced before the gates, snapping at the air. Shades flitted among them, weak and form-less. Too weak to pass. But they would grow stronger in time. And there was nothing but time here, years stretching to millennia in the feeble beat of a heart.

The Dominion slept, shrouded in her mantle of eternal twilight, and the oldest of her children, the one who sometimes called himself Farrumohr and sometimes other names that would curdle a human tongue to speak, huddled at the bottom of his well.

He hurt.

Oh, how he hurt.

The Breaking magic had been turned on *him*, and the web he had so painstakingly woven for centuries lay in tatters. His form was nearly as wispy as the pathetic creatures that battered like flies at the gates. Never had he been hurt so.

The taste of the warm, living body Farrumohr had briefly inhabited filled him with a terrible longing. He could not remember who he himself had been, if indeed he had ever walked beneath the sun. Human? Daēva? Another race entirely? But he thought perhaps he had, untold ages ago. And one thing Farrumohr knew with certainty: he wished to do so again.

So close, this one was. So close....

But now he was hurt. Very badly hurt.

The flames of his eyes burned low and he too slept. A peaceful silence descended on the Dominion's rivers and streams, her shadowy forests. In the ice-clad high passes, the abbadax sat on their nests with heads drowsily tucked under wings. Vines crept through the archways of the House-Behind-the-Veil, draping the broken talisman in tiny white flowers. The tides of the Cold Sea rose and fell.

And Farrumohr dreamed.

Of terrible, awful, wonderful things.

NOTE TO THE READER

I hope you've enjoyed the Fourth Element Trilogy! And I'm happy to announce that the adventures of Nazafareen and Darius, Victor and Delilah, Culach and others continue with five more books in a new series titled the Fourth Talisman. Read on for the first three chapters of *Nocturne*!

I encourage you to sign up for my newsletter at katrossbook-s.com so you don't miss new releases or special offers. And if you have a moment to leave a review, they're a huge boost for authors and help us to keep writing books at affordable prices.

Cheers, Kat

P.S. If you're missing Tijah and Achaemenes, you can also follow their quest to close the Greater Gates and hunt down ghūls in *The Thirteenth Gate*. As we know, daēvas live an extremely long time—as do their human bonded. In researching my historical mystery, *The Daemoniac*, I fell hard for the late Victorian era. Its eccentricities and excesses; its unique blend of science and super-stition. And I got a crazy urge to bring some of the Fourth Element characters forward in time and discover who they had become two thousand years later. Thus was born the idea for the Dominion Mysteries.

The Daemoniac is something of a prequel, but it all comes together in the next book, *The Thirteenth Gate,* where you will find daēvas with cane-swords and gothic castles and grimoires and all sorts of fun things. You'll probably figure out the former identities of the Lady Vivienne Cumberland and her personal secretary, Alec Lawrence, pretty quickly. Ditto her ward Anne.

Cyrus and Cassandane make appearances, along with Balthazar (whom I've grown oddly fond of). There will be magic and mystery and nods to the Sherlock Holmes canon, of which I'm a huge fan. So if you like genre mash-ups, this might be the new series for you.

Now...on to Nocturne!

CHAPTER ONE

LACUNA

Nazafareen raised the hood of her cloak, tucking errant strands of light brown hair behind her ears. Cool air crept through the crack in the door, redolent of pine and spruce. She waited for six long heartbeats. Nothing stirred in the night. She knew Darius would be occupied in his workshop. Sentries patrolled the Valkirin border farther out, but with care she could avoid them. They weren't looking for anyone leaving.

She slipped into the shadows of the trees. Artemis the Huntress Moon rode at the farthest point of her long elliptical orbit, so distant she looked like another star in the inky heavens. Selene hid behind the mountains to the north. Only cool white Hecate peeked through the leafy canopy above, but she was the smallest of Nocturne's three moons and cast the faintest glimmer of light.

Nazafareen couldn't see in the dark like the daēvas, who had been born to eternal night. She was a child of the sun—even if it was lost to her now. So she made her way with caution, soft rabbit-skin boots silent on the carpet of pine needles. The light of the lumen crystal in her window faded to a pinprick, then vanished altogether. She felt small and alone in the dark wood—

but also blessedly free. Nazafareen had only left the Dessarian compound twice in her time among the daēvas, both occasions unsanctioned. They would never let her roam on her own. Her very presence there was a closely guarded secret.

Once clear of the last line of houses, she relaxed a little. The forest was sparse and open, with little undergrowth to snag her feet. She passed stands of pale bonewood—the daēvas made armor from that—and spreading oaks, skirted shallow pools full of whistling frogs that fell silent at an alien presence. She took the same path she had last time, following a resonance almost too faint to detect, like a snatch of music on the wind.

She climbed a rise. The forest thinned to open meadow and she got her first sight of Hecate, three-quarters full, floating above the distant mountains like a silver coin. Despite chafing at her confinement, Nazafareen had come to love the way the deep twilight softened the edges of things like a velvet cloak. The brightness of the stars and subtle coloring of the moons.

The great forest of the Danai had never known the touch of summer or winter, spring or autumn, but the passage of the seasons could be tracked by the travels of Artemis the Huntress. Her orbit took a full year to complete but when she returned, her light supposedly made it almost as bright as true day—solar day. The tides would surge, covering the land for leagues. Nazafareen hoped to see that. Darius had told her what an *ocean* was, but she still found it hard to imagine so much water.

She crossed the meadow and descended into a thickly wooded valley. Finally, she saw a greenish flicker through the trees ahead. Her steps slowed, the hair on her arms lifting.

She had reached another sort of border.

The gate to the Dominion waited ten paces ahead. It looked like a rectangular doorway with no frame—just a glowing hole in the night. The surface had the shimmery quality of running water.

Nazafareen stepped closer. And closer still.

Two months before, Darius had carried her through the gate

CHAPTER ONE

in his arms, nearly dead from her own fey power. Breaker, they called her. A mortal with daēva blood and the ability to shatter magic. She had drawn too much of it.

A lake. A green-eyed man with a scar and an evil sickness inside him. The crowns of trees burning like torches.

She dimly remembered a battle. Her bond with Darius flaring to life and being snuffed out again when they passed through the gate to Nocturne. It was why the daēvas were hiding her. Because that green-eyed man was a Valkirin, the clan that lived in the mountains, and if he ever discovered she still lived....

Nazafareen stared at the gate in queasy fascination. Her own world—her past—lay on the other side, but she had no memory of it. Darius said she'd broken a ward that contained a spell of forgetfulness. The backwash had wiped her own mind clean.

I want to know who I was. Who I am. I have the right.

She sighed, absently rubbing the stump of her missing right hand. It had been a stupid impulse to come here. Fleeing through the gate wouldn't restore what was lost. Magic had erased her past and only magic could restore it.

Darius seemed to think her condition was irreversible, but Nazafareen refused to accept that. Someone, somewhere, knew something and she intended to find them. Except that the daēvas wouldn't let her leave. And part of her didn't want to go. Not without Darius.

She stood before the gate as Hecate set. The lunar night was nearly over. Soon Selene would appear, her bright yellow face heralding the dawn of the lunar day. It was time to return before they found her gone. She started back through the trees, the scant light growing dimmer by the moment. True night was coming, the brief period where none of the three moons was visible. The length of it varied from day to day. The daēvas called it the lacuna and it might last anywhere from a few seconds to an hour or more.

Nazafareen scanned the sky. A thin veil of clouds had swept in.

323

So much for starlight, she thought. *Let's hope it's a short one tonight.* She pulled her cloak tighter and retraced her steps through the valley, moving as quickly as she dared.

Nazafareen paused at a soft sound behind her, like a breeze rustling the leaves—except that there was no wind. She wished she'd brought the lumen crystal. There were animals in these woods. Mostly small game, but Darius's father Victor had seen wolves near the mountains. Her hand dropped to her belt knife.

One of the frog pools shimmered just ahead. Hecate sank beneath the rim of the sky. The forest seemed to take a last, lingering breath of anticipation. She glimpsed an owl gliding from branch to branch in the canopy. And then the lacuna descended, as dark as the bottom of the sea.

She'd always been safe at home with her lumen crystal when true night fell. Sometimes Darius came by and they played a board game with little wooden animals. The pieces had curving horns and barbed tails and different magical powers. All were cunningly carved to the smallest detail. Nazafareen usually won, though she often cheated when he wasn't looking. A petty victory, but sweet nonetheless.

She glanced up, hoping the clouds would pass. *Just a little starlight to guide me...*

The dry rustling came again, behind her and low to the ground. Moving fast.

Before she could blink, thick coils of scaled muscle wrapped her in an iron grip. Nazafareen grunted, scrabbling for the knife. Her fingers brushed the hilt too late. It slithered higher, pinning her arms. She fought to draw breath against a crushing weight on her chest. The knife slipped from her grasp as she tumbled down a muddy bank. Cold water closed over her head.

Darius had warned her about the forest. She got the feeling he knew about her occasional wanderings. He hadn't said so directly, or even asked her to stop. Perhaps he knew she needed to get away from time to time. That she'd go mad if she didn't.

There are snakes, he said. *By the way*.

Of course, he'd neglected to mention how bloody big they were.

Down they sank to the silty bottom. Nazafareen swallowed her panic and sought the Nexus, that place of nothing and everything where elemental magic could be touched. It wasn't easy with the life being squeezed out of her, but she knew it was her last hope.

She reached for earth and focused on the snake's slender articulated spine. Darius would be able to snap it in an instant. She tried to do the same, bubbles of air slipping through her lips—the last air she might ever taste—but earth was the heaviest element to wield and she'd always been terrible with it. Once, as a lesson, he'd set her to moving grains of sand from one anthill to another. The ants had accomplished the same task much faster.

A glint in the corner of her eye.

Frail moonlight lancing through the water, touching...something.

Her belt knife?

Blood pounding in her temples, she reached for water—and felt it stir feebly in response.

Come, she urged. *Come!*

A weak current lifted the knife, drifting it toward her open hand. As soon as the hilt touched her palm, Nazafareen stabbed at the cold reptilian flesh, driving the blade deep. For an awful moment, the snake clenched tighter. She twisted the knife. And then the coils binding her loosened just enough to pull her arm free. A second later, she plunged the blade into the snake's flat black eye. It sank away into the depths.

Nazafareen dragged herself from the pond and lay on the bank, chest heaving. After long minutes, the frogs resumed their peeping song. She laughed softly, though it hurt. The Valkirins didn't need to come after her. She was doing a fine job getting killed all on her own. If the lacuna had lasted a few seconds longer.... She rolled to her side, wincing. Then she stood and walked back to House Dessarian.

Selene had risen in the west when the first outbuildings came into view. The walls were live white birch, their boles and branches weaving together like clasped fingers to form a leafy roof. Every sixth tree grew crookedly away from its neighbor halfway up the trunk, creating an oval window. The dwellings of House Dessarian were not laid out in orderly rows, the way she heard mortals built their cities. These were haphazard, most barely within shouting distance of each other. Most of the daēvas still slept and no one saw her slinking through the shadows like a wet cat.

Finally, she reached the house they'd given her, smaller than the others but cozy enough.

She opened the door—and found Darius sitting at her kitchen table.

Daēvas looked much like mortals, if a touch...feral. There weren't any obvious differences. It was more the way they moved. Lithe and graceful at rest, blurringly quick when they chose. They were stronger and healed faster. They could wield earth, air and water. But they had a weakness, a fatal one.

Fire.

Which was why the fourth element was banned in Nocturne. Why the daēvas made their home on the dark side of the world.

Nazafareen masked her surprise at finding him there. Darius kept his wavy brown hair short, a holdover from his time as a soldier. As always, she found the intensity of his bright blue gaze disconcerting. He raised an eyebrow at her sodden cloak.

"Where have you been?" he asked in a level tone.

"I felt like a swim," she said, daring him to contradict her.

"Fully dressed?"

"It was a little cool out for my taste."

Darius barked a laugh. "You're an awful liar." His expression grew serious. "It's not safe, Nazafareen. You know that. At least take me with you next time."

She hung her cloak on a peg and sat down across from him.

"I'm sorry, Darius, but I feel a prisoner here. I know that's my own fault. The Danai were kind to take me in. But I...I wanted to see the gate."

He leaned forward, eyes narrowing. "You went all the way to the gate? Are you mad?"

"Just to see it. That's all."

Darius exhaled. "To see it. Why?"

"I don't know." She felt suddenly angry—not at him. At everything. "Curiosity. I don't wish to talk about it."

Darius looked away.

Now you've hurt him.

"What's that?" Nazafareen asked in a softer tone, pointing to a cloth-wrapped bundle on the table.

"A gift. It's why I came."

"May I see it?"

"Of course."

She felt him watching her as she struggled to undo the twine with one hand. Darius knew her too well to offer his help. Finally, she remembered her knife, holding the bundle in place with her stump and slicing it open. The cloth fell away.

"Oh." She looked up at him in delight. "Darius, it's beautiful."

He smiled. "It's called an astrolabe. I made it from yew."

Nazafareen turned the wooden sphere over in her hands. Three moons, each of a different size and distance, spun around it on circles attached to a polar axis.

"I'll show you how to move them to correspond with the heavens," he said with a warm smile. "Then you can track the return of Artemis."

Nazafareen smiled back. There was something stern and unyielding in him that only seemed to soften when they were alone together. She fiddled with the astrolabe for a moment, sliding the moons around and around. It was a clever thing, and cunningly made. His skill with wood amazed her considering the short time they'd been there.

"Thank you," she said solemnly. "It's a wonderful gift. But I have nothing for you."

His gaze held her. "Let me teach you. I enjoy it."

"We've tried—"

"It takes time. And you're stubborn."

"Me?" Nazafareen laughed. "You make a boulder seem pliable." She thought of the snake. "But perhaps it wouldn't hurt."

In truth, she desperately wished she could use elemental power like the daēvas. The Danai—Darius's clan—were especially strong in earth. They nurtured the only forests in the world. The master craftsmen of House Dessarian and the six other houses made furniture and weapons and other items for trade, commanding premium prices for their products.

"Then let us begin with a simple talisman. Extinguish the lumen crystal and then light it again."

They spent the next few hours practicing with air, which Nazafareen found the easiest element to work with. She'd grown more adept at finding the Nexus and could feel the torrents of power swirling around her. The difficulty lay in making them do what she wanted. She could manage the lumen crystal, but trying to move objects—even small ones like their game pieces—left her swearing through gritted teeth. Darius was patient as always, though the man could be *relentless* in his own quiet way. When she finally upended the entire board, not using the power, he laughed and slid his chair back.

"You're tired," he said, rising. "And I have work to do." He paused at the door. "But I want you to promise me you won't return to the gate alone."

Nazafareen stared at him. She wanted to trust him. But the secrets he kept had become a chasm between them that grew wider by the day, even if he refused to see it. All her frustrations boiled over.

"Then tell me everything." She held up her stump. "Tell me how I lost this."

He flinched away from her gaze. "I already have. We were soldiers—"

"Yes, yes. I know the story by heart. Your words hardly vary when you tell it. But it rings false. What was the purpose of the bond? Who forged the cuffs and why? How did you come to be born in my world when your kin are here?"

For a moment, he looked as though he might speak. His eyes searched hers, but then a door seemed to close.

"It doesn't matter," he said with quiet desperation. "Truly it doesn't, Nazafareen."

She folded her arms. "You may think you're protecting me, but the not knowing is worse. Did I do something wrong? Was I some kind of monster?"

"No." He turned away. "Not you."

CHAPTER TWO

FARAVAHAR

Darius strode into the darkness, hand instinctively dropping to his hip. No sword hung there anymore, yet in moments of anger, he found himself reaching for it just the same.

I am no longer the satrap's dog, sent out with a pat on the head to hunt and kill, he thought savagely. *Those days are over.*

If only she would let it go. Darius would be happy to trade places with her. To not remember the horrors of the empire. If he'd cared to analyze his own reluctance—which he didn't—he might have found a tangled thread of self-loathing at the heart of it. But Darius had learned from an early age to lock his feelings away and try to forget them. It was how he'd survived.

So he went straight to his workroom and picked up a chisel instead, delicately chipping away at a piece of ash he was carving into a figurine. Bonewood swords and bows were the most popular items they traded with the Marakai, but Darius refused to make weapons.

Nazafareen misunderstood. He hadn't lied to her, not precisely. He'd told her they'd served as soldiers to a crumbling empire, what was called a bonded pair. How they had fought the undead Druj together, and even worse things. How Nazafareen had given her hand to save him—though he'd been vague about the details. And how Neblis, the daēva queen who controlled the Druj armies, had summoned her brother Culach through the gate that linked their two worlds. Nazafareen used her power to defeat Culach's invasion but she'd paid a high price, losing her memories and nearly her life.

It was all true.

But her instincts were also correct. Darius had not told her everything.

He paused, the piece of ash in his hand forgotten, and glanced at a small lacquered box in the corner where he kept his cuff. Pure gold and engraved with the image of a snarling griffin, the cuff was a talisman that required fire to work. Once, when Nazafareen wore its match around her wrist, the cuffs had contained their bond. He missed it desperately.

If he told her the truth—all of it—she would see the bond as an evil thing, and he couldn't bear that. So he had...glossed over certain things. And sworn his father Victor and mother Delilah to secrecy about it.

Darius felt himself grow calmer as he shaped the piece of wood, using both tools and trickles of earth power. Working wood was the place where he lost himself, where he escaped from the simmering tension with Nazafareen. He loved her, perhaps too much.

She thinks I love her for who she used to be, but in truth she was the same in all the ways that matter. If only she wasn't so stubborn...

A heavy tread on the stairs announced the arrival of his father.

"I'm heading out to the border," Victor said by way of greeting. "I thought you might come."

"I'm busy," Darius replied, briefly glancing up and returning to his work.

He'd said no repeatedly, but Victor wouldn't stop asking. He was a large man, taller than Darius with broad shoulders and black hair. Victor still wore a sword, though the other Danai carried bows. He'd bought one for Darius from the Marakai traders. Darius didn't want it. He'd given it to Nazafareen instead; even one-handed, she was deadly with a blade. Victor hadn't been offended. Instead, he'd taken to sparring with her. The two were much alike in some ways.

"We could use someone with your skill, both as a tracker and fighter," Victor persisted. He glanced out the window. "Galen is coming."

Every day since they'd come to Nocturne, Victor led a patrol to the northern reaches of the forest, where the River Arnor marked the end of the Danai lands and the foothills of the Valkirin mountains began their sharp rise from the earth. Val Moraine, the ancestral seat of their enemies, lay a mere twenty leagues beyond the river. So far, the border had been quiet.

"It's a chance to get to know your brother," Victor said.

"Half-brother," Darius replied. He and Galen had different mothers. Victor didn't see it, but Darius got the impression Galen didn't like him very much. "And I've told you before. I don't wish to be a soldier anymore, not even for you."

His father sighed. "We're doing this to protect Nazafareen."

"Are you?" Darius lay down the chisel and picked up a rasp. "I wonder sometimes."

Victor scowled, his dark brows drawing together. "What does that mean?"

"Never mind."

"Say it."

Darius looked up. "All right. You have a grudge against Culach and his entire holdfast."

His father's dark eyes flashed. "Am I the only one who understands they're still a threat? We should finish them now, while they're weakened. But Tethys won't listen. She's afraid of starting a war."

"And you aren't?" Darius shook his head. "Haven't you had enough of fighting?"

"And what about Nazafareen? Will she hide here forever? That's no life."

The words came too close to what Darius had been thinking himself. He could tell she was nearing a breaking point. Neither of them truly fit in here. The Danai tolerated her for Victor's sake, but she was a mortal—and she had enemies.

"You're right. Which is why I think we should leave."

"And go where?"

Darius had considered the matter carefully. Even if they went to a distant Danai settlement, she could still be found.

"The Isles of the Marakai."

Victor frowned. "Have you discussed this with her?"

"Not yet. I'll ask Tethys first. See if she can make arrangements the next time they come to trade."

"Running away," Victor said with flat disapproval.

"Call it what you will. At least she'll be safe." He gave Victor a long look. "Don't tell her until I talk to Tethys."

Victor shook his head. "You keep too many secrets. It will poison you both."

Darius glanced out the window to where Galen waited with a group of young daēvas. They worshipped Victor. He was a charismatic man, handsome in a brutal way, the hardships he'd suffered writ across his face. Victor was a near legend at House Dessarian. He'd vanished through the gate to the shadowlands more than two hundred years before and his sudden return—with a new wife and son, and mortal girl with strange powers—had caused quite a stir.

Not everyone was glad to see him. Victor had recruited friends for his misadventure, most of whom hadn't come back. But the younger daēvas—the ones who didn't know better—were quite taken with him. Some had even started to wear swords in imitation of their returned hero. Darius knew Victor hadn't told them the whole truth either.

"I'll tell her about the Marakai tomorrow," he said.

"You should tell her all of it." Victor studied him. "If she loves you, it won't change anything."

When Darius didn't respond, he turned and headed back down the stairs, to Galen and the other Danai sentries. Darius watched out the window as they vanished like mist into the woods.

He returned to the figurine was carving. A bearded man with spreading eagle wings. It was one of the queer aspects of this world that it mirrored the one he had come from in many ways. The faravahar was the symbol of the Prophet, whom the mortals revered in Samarkand—just as they had in the empire. This piece would be shipped off through the Marakai to the Persian cities of Solis, where such religious trinkets were sold on the streets.

Darius used to wear one around his own neck. He'd given it to Nazafareen when they'd ridden into the Dominion to find Victor. He still believed in the Way of the Flame—good thoughts, good words, good deeds—even if he hated the magi. Dark thoughts crowded in again.

Darius picked up the chisel again.

CHAPTER THREE

BREAKER

Nazafareen changed out of her wet clothes, pulling on a fresh tunic and trousers. She was still angry but more than that, she felt restless, unmoored. She despised sitting around doing nothing. Victor refused to let her join his patrols lest she be seen. She couldn't learn to shape wood with only one hand. And her only real power was both useless and dangerous. Like the cuffs, the breaking magic drew on fire. Using too much had set a blaze in her own body, an inferno that was only extinguished when she passed through the gate to Nocturne.

But she might have other talents she didn't know about. It all came back to that. If nothing else, restoring her memory would make her feel whole again. Then she could decide where she belonged—Nocturne, or back in her own world.

Nazafareen stared at the scattered playing pieces on the table. She was tired of being told what to do. Tired of waiting for others to move her about as they saw fit. If Darius wouldn't tell her the truth, she'd find someone who would. Not Victor—he made excuses every time she sought him out. And Delilah, Darius's mother, had never liked her.

But Tethys...she might know things.

Nazafareen had met the matriarch of House Dessarian only once, when Tethys came to inspect this mortal woman Victor's son had dragged back with him. She'd uttered a few terse words of welcome, clearly insincere, and then taken her leave in a swirl of green silks. Nazafareen recalled her as tall and whip-thin, with an ability to loom that rivaled Victor's.

Tethys had never come again, but Nazafareen knew where she lived. So she gathered her courage and made her way through the woods to a glen where a ring of junipers poked like spears from the earth. The path led to a narrow gap in the trees. Nazafareen followed it through and paused, inhaling the mingled perfume of a hundred different plants. This must be Tethys's night garden, though it seemed too simple a word for what she'd created. Nazafareen's fingers brushed a tangle of vines with velvety, half-open buds—then yanked back as a hidden thorn pricked her thumb. She sucked on it and tasted blood. *Better to look than touch, perhaps.* All the flowers were dark, bruised colors: eggplant purple, wine red, violet blue. Fireflies flashed on and off in the undergrowth like tiny yellow lanterns.

Nazafareen drew a steadying breath, awed by the fairytale quality of the place. At first glance, the garden seemed to have been left to run riot, but closer inspection revealed a master's hand at work. A subtle order to the chaos. Nazafareen knew all the plants and trees in the Danai lands fed on moonlight. Exactly how was a jealously guarded secret.

She found Tethys kneeling on a patch of newly-turned earth, planting seedlings with glossy heart-shaped leaves. Tethys had the same dark hair and bird-of-prey nose as Victor and looked only a decade older, although her true age was hundreds of years beyond a mortal lifespan.

"I'm sorry to disturb you," Nazafareen said, feeling like an interloper. "I hoped we could speak."

Tethys looked up at her, then patted the dirt with strong, calloused hands. "You think I don't know where you go?" Her voice was dusty and hard as a dry riverbed. "The gate you shattered is warded again. Someone approached it earlier and I'd reckon that someone was you, child."

Nazafareen was twenty years old, but she supposed Tethys would see her as a child still. The daēvas measured such things differently. *So Tethys knows. Well, of course she does.*

"I'm sorry. I meant no harm."

Tethys moved on to the next seedling, handling it as gently as a newborn infant. "Had you stepped through, you could never return."

"I wasn't planning on leaving. I only wanted to see it. And I never meant to shatter your wards in the first place." Nazafareen considered, then added ruefully, "Or maybe I did. That's the problem. I can't remember."

Tethys sighed. "Come, help me. I cannot speak with you like this. I'll get a crick in my neck."

Nazafareen knelt on the ground next to her. Tethys held up a seedling.

"This is feverbane. The seeds are useful for spicing wine or curing evil humors in the blood. Take it."

Nazafareen accepted the seedling with a reverent hand. She poked a hole in the dirt with her finger, then covered the roots and pressed the mound firmly around the fragile plant. Tethys nodded in approval.

"I would ask you some questions, if you're willing."

Tethys gave her a sidelong glance. "And if I'm not?"

"I'll ask them anyway."

The Danai woman smiled, a faint twitch of her thin lips. "Go on, then."

"I know you helped make the ward I broke. Were my memories erased? Or simply sealed away?" She hesitated, fearing the answer. "Could they be restored?"

Tethys picked up another plant and eased it from the pot. "Such a thing has never happened before. But I examined you quite thoroughly before you woke, when Darius first brought you here."

"Yes, he did tell me that. He said I couldn't be cured."

"And that is the truth."

Nazafareen's heart fell.

"Not by me, at least," Tethys added.

"By who then?"

Tethys gave her a hard look. "Are you sure you wish to know? Some people might see it as a gift. A chance to start life anew without the burden of regret."

Nazafareen shook her head. "If I have regrets, they are mine. And how can I learn from them if I don't know what they are? No. I wish to learn the truth." She hesitated. "Has Darius spoken of me?"

"If you're asking whether I'm privy to the secrets he keeps, the answer is no. Darius doesn't confide in me. He may be my grandson, but we hardly know each other."

"Then who can help me?"

Tethys considered her question for a long moment. "The Marakai are the strongest healers among us. Water is the essence of healing and that is their gift. They can accomplish wonders, but we are speaking of physical wounds. Your injury is to the mind."

"The Marakai. You mean the sea daēvas?"

Tethys nodded.

"But they might know a way?"

"They might. Who can say?"

"I think I must go ask them then."

"We send a delegation to the shore of the White Sea twice a year, to trade. I suppose you could go along next time."

Nazafareen tamped down her impatience. "And when will that be?"

"Three more waxings of Selene," Tethys said placidly.

"So long?"

Tethys looked at her strangely. "Long to you perhaps." Her tone sharpened. "Do you have complaints about your treatment here? Are we such poor company?"

"Not at all," Nazafareen said hastily. "And I thank you for the offer. I suppose I'll have to wait then."

They planted the last of the seedlings. Tethys rose to her feet, brushing earth from her hands. She turned to Nazafareen.

"There is something else?" she asked with touch of asperity.

"What do you know about breaking magic?"

"In Tjanjin, they call it huo mofa. It is a rare ability, and dangerous to the user. But I suppose you know that already."

"But where does it come from? Is there a way to use it safely?"

Tethys eyed her with pity. "I don't know the first. As to the second...better not to touch it at all, don't you think?" She looked pointedly at the path into the woods. "You'd best run along now, child. You oughtn't be wandering alone anyway."

Nazafareen suppressed a sigh and made her farewells.

That's what they all said.

She hurried along the dark path, lost in thought. Would Darius go with her to the Marakai? Would he support her in this? If not, she would go anyway.

She threw open her front door and groped for the peg. Moonlight spilled in a broad shaft through the window. She smelled something, queer and cold, like the air just before it snows. That rarely happened in the Danai forest, their magic kept it from freezing despite the lack of sun, but sometimes a storm blew in from the Valkirin range that was too strong even for the daēvas to divert. Then she heard a soft creak from one of her chairs. So Darius had returned. Well, she would ask him now. No point in putting it off. And if he said yes, perhaps they could leave right away.

Nazafareen reached for air and lit the lumen crystal —and froze.

A man sat at her table, but it wasn't Darius. He had long silver hair and a foxlike face. White leathers trimmed with fur covered him from head to foot. A long sword inlaid with jewels rode at his hip. He held her astrolabe in slender, pale fingers.

"Hello, mortal," he said.

Nazafareen opened her mouth to reply and found she couldn't draw breath. Something squeezed her lungs in a cold vise. He stood and walked over to her, frowning. He moved with the prowling grace of a daēva, but not a Danai. Not with those icy looks.

They've found me.

"So young," he murmured, studying her face with luminous green eyes. A shadow of unease flickered across his features. Then his gaze fell to her stump and hardened. "You're the Breaker who burned my clan."

Nazafareen heard the rasp of a sword leaving the scabbard. Black motes danced before her eyes. He had her pinned as neatly as the snake.

How strong he was! She dimly sensed he was using air to hold her, to gag her, simple air, and yet it felt hard as marble. Frantic, she eyed her own sword. It leaned against the wall near the door. She strained and it toppled over, then began to slide ever so slowly across the floor.

The Valkirin watched it with an amused expression.

"You cannot harm me now, can you?" He raised his own blade. Again, she saw a shadow of regret cross his face, quickly stifled. "I vow to make it swift. Swifter than the death you gave my cousins."

The door to the room burst open with an explosive crash, nearly tearing free of its hinges from the violence of the blow. Darius rushed inside. His wintry gaze fell on the Valkirin. Earth magic surged in a roaring, bone-jarring tide. The ground convulsed beneath Nazafareen's feet, clods of dirt scattering outward. The web of air snaring her fell away. She coughed, left hand clutching her throat. The Valkirin vaulted through the window. Darius followed.

Nazafareen grabbed her sword and staggered out the door. The two daēvas streaked through the woods, the assassin's white leathers bright in the darkness. She heard rumbles up ahead and dashed past a jagged crevice where the earth crumbled away into a deep sinkhole, the white tips of tree roots erupting like huge worms.

At last she caught up with them. The Valkirin was trapped on an island of solid ground no more than ten paces wide. Darius stood on the other side of the crevasse. A trickle of blood ran from his nose, the price of throwing all that earth around. His face could have been carved from granite.

"You won't leave these lands," he said with tightly controlled fury. "Sheathe the blade."

The Valkirin lowered his sword slightly but didn't put it away.

"Let me kill her," he pleaded. "It's for the best. For your people and mine. She's a danger to us all!"

"Who sent you?" Darius growled. "Was it Culach?"

The assassin gritted his teeth as fingers snapped like kindling. He switched the sword to his right hand.

Nazafareen ran toward Darius. She heard shouts as the other daēvas caught wind of the attack. Dark shapes pelted through the trees.

"I carry a message from Val Moraine," the Valkirin announced in a ringing tone. "The Avas Danai are harboring a mass murderer. If you don't hand her over—"

Darius crossed the gap between them in one graceful bound.

"And I have an answer," he said.

Nazafareen tossed him her sword and he seized the spinning hilt just in time to parry a blow from the assassin's own blade. There was no cautious circling. No testing of defenses. Instead, they hammered at each other, one blade of bonewood, the other

343

of iron. The assassin was good, but Darius was better. Inch by inch, he pushed the Valkirin toward the yawning pit at his back.

Then the assassin turned to Nazafareen. The ground gave way beneath his heels as he drew a huge breath and blasted it at her. She cried out in surprise as the wave of air lifted her off her feet and threw her backwards.

"Nazafareen!" Darius cried.

She hit the ground just in time to see the assassin aim a vicious kick at Darius's knee. He raised his sword, smashing the hilt into Darius's skull. Nazafareen heard it fracture with a sharp crack. The Valkirin brought his sword back again, this time for a killing stroke—when a black-fletched arrow punched through his chest.

Nazafareen spun and saw Galen three paces behind her, bow in hand, his eyes wide.

The assassin fell back, the glaze of death falling across his foxlike features. Blood bubbled around the arrow in his chest. Somehow he summoned the strength to speak—to her.

"You die," he gasped, staring at her with loathing. "Or they all die."

The words sent ripples through the crowd of daēvas. Victor leapt across the ragged crevice, face a thunderhead, and thrust his sword into the Valkirin's heart.

Nazafareen ran to the edge, but it was too wide and deep for her to cross. Darius lay sprawled in the dirt. Blood matted his hair, a black stain in the moonlight. She felt a stab of sheer terror until she saw his chest rise and fall.

"Don't touch him!" Tethys hurried over. "He cannot be moved, not until I give what healing I can."

Tethys sprang lightly across the gap and knelt beside Darius. Her eyes grew distant. Nazafareen felt complex threads of power weaving around both of them.

"What's happened here?"

Nazafareen turned and saw Delilah, Darius's mother, striding up. She looked nothing like her son except for the intense blue eyes. She'd always been thin to the point of emaciated, but Nazafareen suspected she was stronger than she looked. Delilah never came to see her. It was obvious she had no love of mortals.

"I found the Valkirin in my house," Nazafareen said. "He was about to kill me when Darius came. Darius chased him and they... they fought."

Delilah gave her a long look. "Are you hurt?"

"No, I'm fine."

Victor drew his wife aside. They spoke in low voices. Delilah's inscrutable gaze rested on Nazafareen.

Well, if his mother didn't hate me before, she certainly does now.

When Tethys signaled it was safe to move him, two Danai brought a litter and gently maneuvered Darius back to solid ground. All Nazafareen's earlier anger dissolved into stinging tears that she angrily scrubbed away with a sleeve. She trailed along behind as they carried him to Galen's house, which was the closest. Tethys sat at Darius's bedside and cupped his face, murmuring to herself. Darius stirred feebly, his eyelids fluttering. His face relaxed into sleep.

"He will need a great deal of rest," Tethys said, looking drawn and exhausted herself. "I cannot say when he will wake."

Nazafareen felt her heart unclench a little. Darius would live.

Victor ran a hand through his dark hair. "This provocation cannot go unanswered, Tethys. They violated our borders and nearly killed my son. I warned you this was coming. We should have acted long ago."

Tethys drew herself up. "You were gone for more than two hundred years, Victor," she said evenly. "Things have changed."

"Have they?" he sneered. "They seem exactly the same to me. The Valkirins at our throats and House Dessarian doing nothing to put them down."

"How dare you?" Tethys hissed. "You left me your...*mess* to deal with, which I did. But you have no right to second-guess how I run this house."

"Peace, mother, I'm sorry if I gave offense," Victor said, although he still managed to sound arrogant. "But you heard what he said. If we don't surrender Nazafareen, they'll come in force. The survival of our house is at stake." His temper sounded close to catastrophically snapping. "We know who's behind this. Let me handle it."

Tethys gave a humorless laugh. "I know how you handle things, Victor. Like a rampaging bull."

"And what would you do?"

Tethys's predatory gaze fell on Nazafareen. "Go back to your house, girl," she said sharply. "This is Danai business."

Nazafareen steeled herself for battle.

I won't be treated like a child, not even by this ancient, powerful woman. Let her see this rabbit has teeth.

"It concerns me," Nazafareen said levelly. "I have the right to know what you intend to do."

Tethys opened her mouth to reply when Victor stepped up and laid a hand on her arm.

"She's right," he said softly. "There's little use in keeping secrets now." He raised an eyebrow. "Unless you intend to throw her to the wolves?"

Tethys pursed her thin lips. "Give me more credit than that," she snapped. "Very well. She can stay. But she'll keep quiet."

Nazafareen knew better than to argue the point. She sat down on the floor at the foot of the bed and tried to make herself small, which wasn't difficult.

"As I was saying," Tethys continued, "you seem to have forgotten the fact that they have Mina. We have Ellard. The whole purpose of the hostage arrangement is to keep the peace. It's worked so far."

"Worked?" He laughed mirthlessly. "They just sent an assassin to kill Nazafareen in her own home. Would you call that a breach of the peace?"

Nazafareen covered a smile. Tethys was right—Victor snorted and bellowed and didn't care who he trampled beneath his hooves —but she liked that he was standing up for her.

"It's more complicated than you know, Victor," Tethys said quietly.

"What haven't you told me?"

"Over the last two years, some of us have gone missing. Vanished into thin air."

A frown came over Victor's darkly handsome face.

"How many?"

"Four. Two from House Dessarian, a brother and sister, and one each from House Martinec and House Kaland. They'd gone to assess the far southern groves. It should have been no more than a week's journey. When they didn't return after two, scouts went looking. Not a trace was found." She glanced down at Darius, tucking the blanket around his shoulders with a gentle hand. "And before you start hurling accusations, five Valkirins have vanished too—each one traveling alone. We blamed each other until it became clear we've both suffered losses."

Victor let out a slow breath. The floor creaked under his bulk as he paced the room.

"How could you keep this from me?"

"Because I didn't trust you not to go rushing off again," Tethys said calmly. "If something is indeed hunting daēvas, the clans need to stick together. Or at least not start a war."

"I agree," Delilah said.

It was the first time she'd spoken.

"You don't know the Valkirins—" Victor growled.

Delilah cut him off. "I'm not suggesting we do nothing. But your mother is right. Action taken in anger and haste would be a mistake."

Tethys gave Delilah a nod of approval. "You'd do well to listen to your wife, Victor. She seems to have a modicum of sense. Do I trust the Valkirins? Of course not. They're underhanded and ruthless. Violence is in their blood. But Val Moraine may have acted alone in this. Halldóra of Val Tourmaline is the most reasonable of the bunch. I'll send a bird to her tonight. And then we must convene the Matrium. The other Houses should know of this. It concerns us all."

"Then do it quickly," Victor advised. "Once Culach learns the attempt failed, he'll send more to finish the job." He glanced at Nazafareen. "The Valkirin was waiting for you?"

She nodded.

Victor scrubbed a hand across his jaw. "How did he know which house to go to? And how did he discover you were here in the first place?"

Everyone fell silent. Nazafareen avoided their eyes. Tethys already knew—well, she supposed the others deserved to hear it too.

"I was in the forest yesterday," Nazafareen admitted, shame making her cheeks burn. "I know I shouldn't have gone out alone."

"You shouldn't have gone at all," Delilah muttered, casting her a baleful look.

"I don't disagree," Tethys said dryly. "But the girl isn't to blame. If the Valkirin scout had seen her, he would have killed her on the spot. He'd be halfway back to the mountains before we found the body. He took a great risk coming into the heart of the settlement, and paid the price for it." Her gaze narrowed. "No, it makes no sense. They found out some other way."

"You mean someone told them?" Victor demanded.

"I don't know." Tethys sighed. "We've kept her presence a secret from the other Danai Houses and few here know the full story of what she did. But secrets have a way of slipping out."

"What about Ellard? He's the obvious suspect."

Nazafareen had seen him once, walking with Galen in the

forest. Both moons were full and his silver hair had stood out like a beacon in the darkness. Heart racing, she'd run to Darius's house. Then she learned that Ellard lived here. He'd been swapped as a hostage for Galen's mother long ago and raised at House Dessarian.

"Ellard is bound by wards," Tethys said. "Strong ones. I did it when he first came. If he took any action against us—in word or deed—I would know about it."

"And he wouldn't anyway," Galen put in quickly. "I'm with him all the time. I know him. It's not Ellard, I promise you."

"It's possible a spy slipped past your sentries, Victor," Tethys said. "This assassin seemed to have no trouble."

Victor grunted. "I intend to find out who was on duty tonight. We'll get to the bottom of this."

"What about the body?" Delilah asked.

"There are herbs to preserve the flesh against decay, for a time at least," Tethys said. "I'll see he's attended to."

"We'll keep the corpse as a bargaining chip," Victor said decisively. "They're fussy about their fallen. I heard they have catacombs deep in the mountains dating back a thousand years. A city of the dead. They'll want him back."

Nazafareen wondered if the Danai returned their own dead to the earth. No one had died since she'd been there so she couldn't say what their rites were. But it didn't surprise her that the Valkirins preferred the cold embrace of stone. They had an icy look about them, with their silver hair and white skin. She imagined rows of pale warriors laid out in the darkness of the earth's bones.

"Ellard says his name was Petur," Galen put in. "That he's from Val Moraine."

"Of course he is." Victor sounded irritated. "Who else could be behind this but Culach?"

The way he spoke the name—like a curse—revealed a bitter

hatred that had been carefully tended for years, centuries even. She wondered at its original source.

Culach.

She remembered him from the Dominion. He'd been large and frightening, but he'd carried her when she fell sick. She hadn't been afraid of him then. The fear had come later, after he passed through the gate. He had...changed. Flames burned in his eyes.

The thing inside him had wanted to take Nazafareen too, but she'd driven it back to whatever lightless depths it had come from. The memory raised gooseflesh on her arms.

She'd thought Culach might be dead, but it seemed dead things had a way of coming back—no matter how deeply you dug the hole.

Now available for purchase on Amazon!

NOCTURNE

Nocturne, a wilderness of eternal night.
Solis, a wasteland of endless day.

Nazafareen is a Breaker, a mortal who has the rare ability to shatter spell magic—although her power carries a high price. With the memories of her former self erased and nowhere else to turn, she comes to Nocturne hoping to start a new life under the triple moons of the darklands.

But when an assassin forces Nazafareen to flee to the sunlit mortal city of Delphi, she finds herself embroiled in a deeper mystery whose origins lie far in the past. Why was the continent sundered into light and dark a thousand years before? And what really happened to the elegant but ruthless creatures who nearly reduced the world to ashes? The new Oracle might know, but she's outlawed magic and executes anyone caught practicing it. Nazafareen must hide her powers and find a way out of the city—before it's too late.

As the net slowly tightens, something ancient and vengeful begins to stir in the arid death zone called the Kiln. A dashing daeva named Darius is pursuing Nazafareen, but so are a multitude of enemies. War is brewing again. Can she stay alive long enough to stop it?

ALSO BY KAT ROSS

The Fourth Talisman Series

Nocturne

Solis

Monstrum

Nemesis

Inferno

The Fourth Element Trilogy

The Midnight Sea

Blood of the Prophet

Queen of Chaos

The Dominion Mysteries

The Daemoniac

The Thirteenth Gate

Some Fine Day

ACKNOWLEDGMENTS

To Jessica Therrien, Christa Yelich-Koth and Laura Pilli, who read early drafts and were instrumental in fine-tuning both the story and the writing. To my mom, Deirdre, for her mad copy-editing skillz and most of all, for making me love books. And to my son, Nick: you are the bravest person I know.

Thanks to everyone at Acorn Publishing for your wise advice on bookish things and constant encouragement. To Robert Altbauer for making such a beautiful map at such short notice.

And a huge shout-out to all the lovely bloggers and fans who have been so kind and supportive. Writing can be lonely, and the friends I've found through these books makes all the difference.

ABOUT THE AUTHOR

Kat Ross worked as a journalist at the United Nations for ten years before happily falling back into what she likes best: making stuff up. She's the author of the dystopian thriller Some Fine Day, the Fourth Element Trilogy, the Dominion Mysteries and the Fourth Talisman series. She loves myths, monsters and doomsday scenarios.

www.katrossbooks.com
kat@katrossbooks.com

GLOSSARY

Abbadax. Winged creatures of the Dominion. They serve Queen Neblis.

Al Miraj. The southernmost satrapy of the empire, it is surrounded by the Sayyhad desert. Daēvas are called *djinn* there. Al Mirajis worship their own gods and very few follow the Way of the Flame.

Amah. The nursemaids assigned by the magi to bond daēvas until they are old enough to be sent to the Immortals or the Water Dogs.

Avas Danai. Children of the Earth. The daēva clan of Victor and Lysandros.

Avas Valkirin. Children of the Air. The daēva clan of Neblis and her brother, Culach.

Bactria. The land to the north of the Char Khala range. Once a satrapy of the empire, now the realm of Queen Neblis. It is a wilderness, with all the people who once lived there having fled or been enslaved.

Barbican. The stronghold in the middle of the Great Salt Plain where the daēva cuffs are forged.

Breaker. See *negatory magic*.

Cuffs. Gold bracelets that create a magical bond between a human and a daēva that allows the former to control the daēva's power. In some cases, the wearers will also experience each other's emotions. The cuffs are generally worn for life.

Daēva. Creatures considered *Druj*, or impure, by the magi. Their origins remain a mystery, but they have the ability to work elemental magic. Most daēvas have a particular affinity for earth, air or water and are strongest in one element. However, they cannot work fire, and will die merely from coming into close proximity with an open flame. Daēvas live for thousands of years and heal from wounds that would kill or cripple a human.

Dominion, also called the gloaming, shadowlands or veil. The land of the dead. Can be traversed using a talisman to open gates, but is a dangerous place for the living.

Druj. Literally means *impure souls*. Includes Revenants, wights, liches and other Undead. Daēvas are also considered Druj by the magi.

Elemental magic. The direct manipulation of earth, air or water. Fire is the fourth element, but has unstable properties that cannot be worked by daēvas.

Faravahar. The symbol of the Prophet. Its form is an eagle with outstretched wings.

Four-Legs Clan. Nomadic herders of the Khusk Range.

Fourth Element. See *Holy Fire*.

Gate. A passage into the Dominion. There are twelve Greater Gates in the Sun Lands. Temporary gates can also be opened with a talisman.

Ghūl. Restless dead who manage to return to the living side of the gates. Ghūls assume the form of their last meal, whether human or animal. Their natural state, prior to feeding on blood, is ghostly and cadaverous.

Gorgon-e Gaz. The prison on the shore of the Salenian Sea where the oldest daēvas are held. It is also where daēvas are bred. The bloodlines of all daēvas in the empire can be traced back to Gorgon-e Gaz.

Hands of the Father. The order of the Numerators that hunts daēvas. Their sigil is an eye with a flame.

Holy Fire. Said by the magi to have been a gift to the Prophet directly from the Holy Father. Also known as the fourth element, it can both forge and break daēva cuffs.

Immortals. The elite division of the King's army. There are always precisely 10,000 Immortals, half of them human and half daēva. They fight in bonded pairs. If an Immortal dies in battle, the cuff is designed to be torn off so the fallen soldier can be bonded by another.

Infirmity. Also called the *Druj Curse*, it is the physical disability caused to daēvas by the bonding process.

Karnopolis. The winter capital of the empire, seat of the magi.

Lich. A thing of shadow whose touch brings death, it can only be unknit using the power.

Macydon. The kingdom across the Middle Sea that invades the empire. Led by King Alexander.

Magi. The priests who follow the Way of the Flame. In the old days, some of them bonded daēvas to help fight the Druj, but this tradition has waned over time.

Matrium. The seven female heads of the most powerful Avas Danai houses.

Moon Lands. The daēva world, reached by gates in the Dominion.

Necromancers. Also called Antimagi. They are the lieutenants of Queen Neblis. Necromancers draw their power from talismanic chains attached to human slaves, and which are imbued with the power of the Dominion. When a slave is killed, five Druj Undead are born. Many necromancers are former magi who now serve Queen Neblis.

Negatory magic. A rare talent that involves the working of all four elements. Those who can wield it are known as Alchemists or Breakers. Negatory magic trumps both elemental and talismanic magic. The price of negatory magic is rage and emotional turmoil. It derives from the Breaker's own temperament and is separate from the Nexus, which is the source of all elemental magic.

Numerators. A powerful order in the bureaucracy of the empire, they collect taxes and hunt down illegal daēvas.

Persepolae. The summer capital of the empire.

Purified. The order of magi that guards the holy fire at the Barbican.

Qarha. A protective face scarf worn by Water Dogs.

Revenant. Said to be the corpses of an ancient warrior race come back to life, they stand close to eight feet tall and fight with iron swords. Must be beheaded.

Satrap. A provincial governor of the empire. Satraps are permitted a small number of daēvas to keep the peace.

Shepherds. Hounds of the Dominion, they herd the dead to their final destination at the inner sea of the shadowlands. Extremely hostile to anything living, and to necromancers in particular.

Sun Lands. The human world.

Talismanic magic. The use of elemental magic to imbue power in a material object, word or phrase. Generally, the object will perform a single function, i.e. the shells that open gates in the Dominion, the daēva cuffs and the necromancer chains.

Tel Khalujah. The satrapy where Nazafareen served as a Water Dog.

Water Dogs. The force that keeps order in the more distant satrapies and hunts down Undead along the borders. Human Water Dogs wear scarlet tunics, while their daēva bonded wear blue.

Way of the Flame. The official religion of the empire. Preaches *good thoughts, good words and good deeds*. Embodied by the magi, who view the world as locked in an eternal struggle between good and evil. Fire is considered the holiest element, followed by water.

Wight. A Druj Undead with the ability to take over a human body and mimic the host to a certain degree. Must be beheaded.

Zarathustra. Also called the Prophet. The founder of the Way of the Flame and creator of the first daēva cuffs. Considered a saint.

Manufactured by Amazon.ca
Bolton, ON